THE SILVER SERPENT

Scott Mariani is the author of the worldwide-acclaimed action-adventure thriller series featuring ex-SAS hero Ben Hope, which has sold millions of copies in Scott's native UK alone. His books have been described as 'James Bond meets Jason Bourne, with a historical twist'. The first Ben Hope book, *The Alchemist's Secret*, spent six straight weeks at #1 on Amazon's Kindle chart, and all the others have been *Sunday Times* bestsellers.

Scott was born in Scotland, studied in Oxford and now lives and writes in a remote setting in rural west Wales. You can find out more about Scott and his work on his official website: www.scottmariani.com

By the same author:

To find out more visit **www.scottmariani.com**

SCOTT MARIANI

THE **SILVER SERPENT**

Harper
North

HarperNorth
Windmill Green,
Mount Street,
Manchester, M2 3NX

A division of
HarperCollins*Publishers*
1 London Bridge Street
London SE1 9GF

www.harpercollins.co.uk

HarperCollins*Publishers*
1st Floor, Watermarque Building, Ringsend Road
Dublin 4, Ireland

First published by HarperNorth in 2022

1 3 5 7 9 10 8 6 4 2

MIX
Paper from
responsible sources
FSC™ C007454

www.fsc.org

This book is produced from independently certified FSC™ paper
to ensure responsible forest management.

For more information visit: www.harpercollins.co.uk/green

THE SILVER SERPENT

PROLOGUE

Deep in the Northern Territory, hours from anywhere, Kip Malloy stepped out of the air-conditioned comfort of the ute and a wave of parched hot air hit him as though someone had opened the furnace door. The month of March was coming into autumn, but out here in the bush it was still blisteringly hot, even for a hardened local like Kip, who'd been born and raised in these parts and had never left the Territory in all his sixty-two years.

He'd been driving for hours, and turned off the highway a long way back. The road to Mad Mick's homestead was little more than a rocky trail though the wilderness, danger-ously easy to lose your way on for the last fifty clicks or so. But Kip had been coming here since he was a boy and knew it better than anyone alive, now that the old man was dead.

Pulling in through the dilapidated gates and heading up the long, dusty track, like always Kip couldn't avoid that feeling of awe at the sheer scale of his late uncle's spread. Australian outbackers were pretty used to long distances and big, wide-open spaces. Kip's own land, far to the north of here, ranged across several hundred acres of the Northern

Territory coastal wetland areas, too big an area for one man to patrol in a day or even two. But it was dwarfed by the size of Mad Mick's place, stretching from the southern edges of the coastal wetlands over the arid empty grasslands, across canyons and steppes all the way to the northern fringes of the outback desert regions, what folks called the Red Centre.

Several generations of Malloys had striven hard to make whatever agricultural use of their land they could, though even the best of it was only good for grazing cattle, too arid to support cropping. Once upon a time Mick's grandfather, Kip's great-granddaddy the legendary Shelby Malloy, had proudly farmed more than ten thousand head of prime Hereford stock over nearly half a million acres. But Mick, on inheriting the vast spread from his father in 1964, while still only twenty-four years of age, had other ideas and staunchly refused to farm an inch of it. He'd sold off the entire herd and spent years tearing down the hundreds of miles of fencing his forebears had laboured over generations to erect, intent on letting the land revert back to wilderness. He'd never married, seldom ventured beyond his borders, let alone anywhere near what some people termed civilisation, and as the decades rolled by his increasingly eccentric ways had earned him the nickname by which he was now universally known.

For the next half a century and more, 'Mad' Mick Malloy had lived the life of a solitary wanderer, roaming his enormous territory, sometimes on horseback, mostly on foot, communing with the wild side of nature, often disappearing for weeks on end into the bush equipped with only a tent, an ancient rifle and the barest minimum of kit. It had been on one of those long rambles, while camping out at a remote place called Horseshoe Ridge, that he'd encountered the deadly taipan snake that finally had put an end to his long, colourful life. Had Mick been carrying any antivenom along with the sat phone he'd used to call in the flying emergency medics, he might have been saved. In the event, it was too late.

Mick's younger brother Keith had been killed in 1970 when his light aircraft came down in a river gorge, leaving a wife and a ten-year-old son. Growing up without a father, young Kip had been extremely close to his uncle, and as he'd got older he'd been a frequent visitor to the homestead. When Kip's mother passed away from cancer just twelve years later, Mick was the only family left to him. And now that Mick was gone too, it seemed as though an era had come to a close. As his sole remaining relative, Kip had been informed by the deceased's solicitor, a lawyer based in Alice Springs named Rex Muldoon, that he had inherited everything: 'everything' being the few pennies the old man had to his name, a run-down old house with a few outbuildings, a derelict Holden Wagon, and some five hundred thousand acres of land.

Kip had been left wondering what the hell he was to do with this unexpected inheritance. With a thriving business of his own to run, he was too busy to look after a bloody great spread hours and hours away to the south. Yet at the same time, the idea of a stranger taking it over had seemed plain wrong. For weeks, he'd wrestled with the problem of what to do.

Then, on his first visit to the homestead after his uncle's death, Kip had made the discovery that changed everything.

3

Back again now, he walked inside the empty house. The place was just as he had left it. Stepping into the hallway he could feel the old man's presence so vividly that it would have come as no surprise if he'd suddenly appeared from a doorway, the crusty white-bearded face burned deep mahogany by a life spent under the fierce sun, wearing that battered old leather broad-brimmed hat of his and grumbling out some sour greeting to his beloved and only nephew.

But only the ghost of Mad Mick inhabited the homestead now. Kip wandered from room to silent, empty room, noticing with sadness how the dust was already layering the surfaces. Dust was a fact of life out here, like the flies and the spiders. The air was stifling, even hotter than outside, and Kip's shirt was sticking to him within a minute. Along a dim passage was the small, cluttered office where he had made his sensational find among a stack of his uncle's papers.

Mick hadn't been a great one for neat filing and his personal documents had been in a predictably chaotic mess. And there, carefully secreted away in an old cigar box at the bottom of a drawer stuffed with unpaid bills and vehicle registration paperwork, had been the pair of items whose discovery startled Kip almost out of his wits.

For as long as he could remember, going back half a century to the days of his childhood, he'd been enthralled by his uncle's flamboyant tales of what he believed lay hidden somewhere beneath his land. Mick Malloy's relentless, decades-long quest to locate it had in no small part helped to earn him the reputation of being as nutty as a fruitcake, a few stubbies short of a six pack, ripe for the funny farm, a dipstick, a dingaling, or any of the other uncomplimentary epithets that the locals had labelled him with for spending his life chasing after a myth.

Kip had always been perfectly certain that his uncle wasn't crazy, and strongly defended his good name against such accusations – in fact he'd got into more than a couple of fistfights over it as a younger man, when guys in bars teased him about being Mad Mick's nephew. Eccentric, for sure. A difficult and bloody-minded sod with little in the way of social graces and no scruples whatsoever about saying what was on his mind, however offensive. Without a doubt. But mad? Not an effing chance, mate. Kip had come up hard, never been slow to respond with his fists and would blacken the eye of any bastard who dared use that name in his presence.

And now here had been the proof that the old sod might have been right all along.

The first item inside the cigar box Kip had found hidden in his uncle's office was a metal nugget about the size of a galah's egg. It was raw and lumpy and didn't look like much, but Kip knew that it was solid silver, because that was what his uncle had been searching for all those years.

The second item in the box was a hand-drawn map. It was crude and rough, with nothing on it to indicate its significance, but taken together with the silver nugget there was no doubt in Kip's mind that it marked the location of the rich subterranean deposit, uncle Mick's long-sought-after mother lode. So the crafty fox had actually found it! All those stories had been true. All the years of searching had been vindicated, all the naysayers proved wrong.

How long had Mick known the truth? Not so very long, Kip reckoned. The map wasn't old. He could tell that for a fact, seeing as it had been sketched on the back of a nasty letter from the Australian Taxation Office, dated just a couple of months back. There was still some fresh dirt encrusted in the rough surfaces of the silver nugget, and the cigar box in which Mick had concealed the items still smelled faintly of tobacco. The evidence all seemed to point to a recent discovery.

As stunned as he was by the revelation, what astonished Kip even more was that the old man had never breathed a word about his find. He'd been down here twice to see him during those last few weeks before he died, checking on his health, making sure he was looking after himself properly. How could Mick have kept something like this from his own nephew, after having confided in him all these years? Kip had felt a sense of hurt at being excluded, at first. But then on reflection, he thought he knew the answer. The reason why the old man had been so secretive could be summed up in just two words.

Wiley Cooper.

Now that Kip understood why his uncle had made the choices he had, his own mind had soon been made up and he'd known what needed to be done. He'd entrusted the silver nugget to the special care of someone best placed to keep it securely hidden. Someone his uncle would have trusted too. Kip regretted that he hadn't let his wife, Lynne, in on the secret. He'd never lied to her before now and hated doing it, but he reasoned that she had enough concerns to deal with already and he didn't want to worry her – that was how he justified it to himself, anyway.

Sad how one lie tended to lead to another, for all his good intentions. Poor Lynne didn't even know Kip had returned here today. He'd fed her a fictitious cover story about driving out to Yulla Yulla to see a man about a horse, and he felt rotten for having deceived her. The truth was, he didn't even know himself exactly why he'd felt impelled to return here today. Perhaps he just needed to say goodbye to the place and all its memories, before that chapter of his life closed completely and forever.

Kip took his time, lingering from room to room. After a while, thinking he was letting maudlin sentimentality get the better of him, that his uncle would have poured scorn all over him for being pathetic and unmanly, he decided he should go. He probably shouldn't have come here.

That was when they turned up.

Hearing the crunch of tyres outside in the dirt yard, Kip went to a window and peered through the dusty pane. Who could this be? Visitors were not expected at the homestead. Half a dozen brawny men in a crew-cab four-wheel-drive truck, even less so.

The dust cloud thrown up by the crew-cab drifted away like smoke on the wind. Kip watched as its doors opened and all six men stepped out into the searing bright sunlight. They couldn't have failed to notice his own ute parked in front of the house, and they looked as surprised as he was that someone else was out here at the remote homestead. After exchanging a few words that he couldn't make out, two of them ambled over to check his Toyota. He'd left it with the doors unlocked, the windows wound down to stay cool in the sun, and the key in the ignition. He was already bridling at the appearance of the strangers, but when they opened his driver's door and started poking around inside his vehicle, he knew something was wrong.

Then when they pulled out the registration documents he kept in the glove compartment, verified the vehicle owner's identity and plucked the key from his ignition with a lot of hostile and cautious glances towards the house, he knew something was very wrong indeed.

The man who'd taken his key hurried back to give it to one of his pals, a tall burly character in a denim shirt and a broad-brimmed hat, whose dominant body language made Kip think he must be the boss man of the group. The boss man said something else Kip couldn't catch. He looked thoughtful. The rest were still looking sullenly over at the house. Then the boss man motioned to them, and three of the men reached into the back of their truck and came out with scoped hunting rifles. The boss man grabbed a weapon for himself and worked the bolt. *Snick-snack.* Loaded and locked.

Now Kip was getting alarmed. Many folks in rural Australia routinely carried firearms for hunting or protection against wild critters. He himself owned various rifles, but they were all back at the farm. As his tension quickly began to escalate and he realised these men meant business, it occurred to him that his uncle's trusty old bolt-action Weatherby .30-06 was still in the bedroom wardrobe where Mick stored it when not in use.

Moving quickly away from the window, he hurried into the bedroom and retrieved the weapon. This was the same rifle Mick had taught him to shoot with as a boy, and he could still hit what he aimed at. It was always kept loaded. He worked the bolt and chambered a round from the magazine. His heart was thudding as he walked back out of the bedroom with the aught-six clutched in his fists. He'd never seen these men before, but he had a pretty fair idea who they were, and who they worked for. Which meant he could guess what this was about. And that made his blood boil.

Looks like good news travels fast, he thought angrily as he strode towards the front hallway. But how had the bastards found out the secret?

He told himself to stay calm. The guns were probably just for show, for intimidation. There was no real reason to suppose they were going to start shooting. But if they did, they'd be damned sorry. Kip hadn't backed down from a fight in his entire life and he wasn't about to start now.

By the time he'd reached the front door and marched out to confront the men, they'd scattered and spread out. Four of them, he couldn't see at all. One was just visible behind the corner of an outbuilding, about forty yards from the house. The boss man with the hat was hunkered down low behind their truck with his rifle resting across the bonnet, watching the house through his scope. As Kip emerged into the sunlight he saw the gun barrel twitch his way.

Another man might have flinched and ducked for cover, but Kip stood his ground and immediately brought the wooden stock of the Weatherby up to his shoulder. Iron sights. The old man always said that if your target was big enough to see with the naked eye, you didn't need a scope.

Kip fixed his aim on the brim of the boss man's hat and held it there. He yelled, 'Whatever it is you mongrels want, you're not welcome here. So I suggest you turn around and bugger off right now!'

'Drop the gun, Malloy, if you know what's good for you!' the boss man roared in reply, still aiming back at Kip.

'You've got five seconds to do as I say, mate, or this is liable to get ugly.'

'Relax, we just want to talk!'

'Yeah?' Kip shouted. 'Well, I'm not interested in hearing it!' His finger slipped inside the trigger guard. The old man had the trigger set so light you only had to caress it to touch off a round.

'Come on, Malloy. We're not looking for trouble.'

'Then put the gun down.'

'You put yours down first.'

A sharp, cracking report came from behind the corner of the outbuilding. Whether or not it had been intended to hit him, the high-velocity round shattered a window of the house behind Kip. He didn't flinch, but stood his ground and fired back at where the shot had come from, the rifle recoiling hard against his shoulder. The shooter quickly ducked back out of sight around the edge of the wall as Kip's bullet tore out a fist-sized chunk of masonry and howled away into the far distance. He stayed planted and worked the Weatherby's smooth bolt to eject the empty round and chamber another. Swinging the muzzle across towards the truck he fired again, this time deliberately blowing out the truck's left headlamp. That was all the warning shots they were going to get.

'Hold your fire!' the boss man yelled from behind the truck. 'Hold your fire!'

'You drongos want a war, you'll get one,' Kip promised them. His third round was chambered and this next bullet would be in earnest.

'It was an accident! Pete didn't mean to shoot!'

'Then tell the bloody fool to put that gun down before he does something else he'll regret,' Kip shouted back. 'Three seconds left, boys. Or someone's going to get hurt.'

'No need for that, Malloy. Like I said, we just want to talk!'

'Two seconds,' Kip said.

'Don't be stupid, Malloy! Put the gun down and come with us. He wants to work this out!'

'He can go to hell. One second.' Everything about Kip's steely expression, his body language and his tone of voice made it absolutely clear that he meant it.

But that one second never came. Because in the next instant something hard and heavy struck him a blow to the back of the head. His vision exploded into a dazzling white starburst and then faded instantly to black.

Chapter 1

Switzerland

Ben Hope was on the road when he got the call, winding his way through the tight twists and switchbacks of the Grimsel Pass, climbing to over seven thousand feet with the rugged green valleys and blue reservoir lakes spread out below him like a picture postcard.

More than just the most breathtaking views anywhere in the Swiss Alps, for a man of a sporting disposition the remote thirty-eight-kilometre pass offered some of the most exciting and challenging driving to be had anywhere in the world, and Ben was someone who found it hard to turn away from a challenge. The throaty roar of the twin-turbo engine all but drowned out the jazz blaring from his speakers – Courtney Pine with Zoe Rahman had been his soundtrack for the last hour – as he accelerated hard out of one switchback and sped into the next with all the fierce concentration and aplomb of a racing driver. The windows were wound down and the cool mountain wind was whipping at his hair.

Yes, he had to admit that life was pretty good for him at this moment, partly because he'd given himself a couple of weeks' holiday and intended to enjoy his time off to the hilt. For the last two days he had been making his way across France from his home in Normandy, into Switzerland. It was a drive he could have made in a matter of hours in his high-performance BMW Alpina, but he'd been taking his time, staying in nice little out-of-the-way guesthouses and enjoying the local food and wine. He'd navigated the even twistier and stunningly magnificent stretch of road from Santa Maria through the high Stelvio Pass; and of course while he was in the area he'd had to check out the world's smallest whisky bar, located in the small Alpine village of Müstair: 280 varieties crammed into little over eight square metres of space, and his only regret was that he hadn't had time to sample them all.

The joys of being your own boss. And Ben also felt good, because the real purpose of this pleasure-trip through Switzerland was to pay a long-anticipated visit to one of his only two remaining relatives, someone he hadn't seen in a long while and was looking forward to catching up with again. Right now on this perfect, sunny early afternoon he was less than two hours' drive away from Zermatt, where his younger sister Ruth had recently built herself a beautiful new ten-bedroom home in the countryside.

By all accounts, Ruth's life was on the up, too. On top of being the youngest female executive director of a Fortune Global 500 company, the Swiss-based Steiner Industries business empire she'd taken over from her adoptive tycoon father Maximilian, she had a new man in her life and it sounded as though they were serious about a future together. Ben was extremely happy for her, and he looked forward with pleasure to making his possible future brother-in-law's acquaintance later that afternoon.

It hadn't always been this way. Like the dramatic peaks and plummeting troughs of the mountain road he was travelling at this moment, there had been many ups and downs on Ruth's bigger journey through the years, and it had been the same way for Ben, too. There'd been a time, a long, long time in fact, when he'd thought she was lost to him forever. Of all the incidents that had marked and shaped the course of his life, her abduction from a Moroccan street market as a child and the many painful years of searching for her had been the thing that had changed him most, not just because of the agony he'd suffered, or the way that her disappearance had led directly to the deaths of both of their parents. More than that, the traumatic event had ultimately set Ben on the path to becoming a kidnap and ransom or 'K&R' specialist, rescuing the victims of the most evil, cruel industry in the world that preyed on innocent people and profited from tearing them away from their loved ones. A career at which he'd excelled and one he'd been especially qualified to pursue, thanks to his prior years with 22 SAS, the British Army's most elite Special Forces regiment. He'd saved a lot of people and put a stop to the nefarious activities of many a kidnapper.

That was all in the past now. Or was it? As well as catching up with his sister, Ben was also planning on using this break to do some serious thinking about his own future. It had been a few years since he'd officially quit his dangerous job tracking down kidnappers, moved from his then home in

Ireland to a sleepy corner of Normandy and set up a tactical training establishment with his old friend Jeff Dekker.

He and Jeff had first got to know one another back during their days in Special Forces, though Jeff had been with the Special Boat Service, the SAS's naval counterpart. Their training facility, known simply as Le Val, had over the years become the go-to place for private security, specialist police or military units wanting to sharpen up their skills in VIP close protection, hostage rescue, raid and counterterrorism operations. Ben and Jeff had poured everything they had into their school, aided by their business partner the redoubtable Tuesday Fletcher, and their efforts had paid off handsomely. They were all deeply proud of Le Val's reputation as the best in the business, and their achievement in building it from the ground up.

But Ben was a restless man, who'd always had an aversion to settling down in one place for too long. There were times when he worried that he'd become too set in his ways, stuck in a rut and getting stale. He had a recurring dream in which he'd become prematurely old and grey, trapped inside a cage from which he yearned to break free. Outside the cage was a white sandy beach leading to a vast blue ocean dotted with beautiful, enticing forested islands that nobody had ever explored. And on the shore was a jetty with a motor boat moored up, just waiting for him to jump into it and take off.

You didn't have to be Sigmund Freud to work out the symbolism.

Lately that dream had been troubling him more often, and his self-questioning nature had caused him to wonder if perhaps, just perhaps, it might be time that he changed direction again. Maybe he'd done all there was for him to do at Le Val; maybe he needed a fresh challenge to sink his teeth into, new horizons to explore.

But what could he do? He'd been self-employed ever since leaving the army, and his was a particular skillset not well suited to normal civilian life. He lacked the qualities that his sister Ruth possessed in such abundance. He'd be terrified at the prospect of having to go into an office each day, wearing a suit and tie, chained to a desk when he wasn't dragging his heels in and out of brain-numbing corporate meetings. That was assuming anyone in that world would even have employed him. So what other options did he have? Get back into K&R?

Ben wasn't especially good at expressing his innermost emotions and anxieties to people, but he planned on talking to Ruth about these feelings. She was someone he could confide in, and she had a lot of wisdom. Maybe she'd tell him that these self-doubts were just a phase he was going through, and that he should hold on to a good thing and not make any rash decisions.

All these things were turning over in Ben's mind when his phone went. He eased his foot off the gas and pulled into the side of the straight stretch of road he was on to take the call. The caller ID told him it was Tuesday phoning. Which was a little out of the ordinary, because the guys wouldn't generally contact him unless something was up at Le Val that they couldn't handle on their own.

Tuesday Fletcher was one of the cheeriest, most laid-back and imperturbable people Ben had ever known. The situation had to be pretty damn dire to wipe that megawatt grin off his face. But the moment Ben heard his voice on the line, he knew this had to be bad news. Ben tensed, anticipating the worst.

'It's Jeff,' Tuesday said. 'Something's happened.'

Ben's mind was instantly filled with anxiety. Jeff was a qualified pilot and kept an old Cessna Skyhawk at a flying club near Le Val, which he liked to take out for a spin now and then. Had there been a crash?

He was momentarily too stunned to speak. Before he could say anything, though, Tuesday had already dispelled his worst fears.

'He got a call from Australia.'

Which came as a relief, but didn't sound too good either. Jeff's mother, Lynne Dekker, had emigrated Down Under some years ago and remarried, to a local guy named Kip Malloy. Jeff had confided to Ben that his mum had some health issues. Ben was relieved to hear Jeff was okay, but worried that Lynne must have died.

But in the next moment it turned out that Ben was off track there, too.

'Kip's gone missing,' Tuesday said.

Ben reached for his cigarettes. Tuesday's news was shocking, though on reflection maybe not completely unexpected, given what Kip did for a living. He was a farmer, but not the kind of farmer who raises crops or herds sheep. He was the owner of a considerable spread in the coastal regions of Australia's Northern Territory, where he bred saltwater crocodiles for the meat and leather trade. Ben had come across his fair share of crocs in Africa and alligators

17

in the American Deep South. Those were nasty enough, but he happened to know that their Antipodean cousins were far and away the most dangerous reptiles in the world. These throwbacks to the age of the dinosaurs could grow to outlandish sizes and had jaws that could snap a sturdy canoe in half with a single bite. Just why anyone would want to have anything to do with the creatures, Ben had no idea. And Kip's place had over a thousand of them.

A vision came into his mind of poor Kip getting dragged into a river or tipped out of his boat and torn to pieces. You'd disappear after that, all right, because there wouldn't be much left to find.

He said, 'Missing, or gobbled up by one of those things?'

'That was my first thought too,' Tuesday replied. 'But that's not what happened. He didn't go missing on the farm. Apparently he'd gone off to a local town to see some guy about buying a horse, and he never came back.'

Ben shook a Gauloise from the cigarette pack and took out his lighter. 'When did this happen?'

'Six days ago. Lynne started to worry when he didn't come home that night, and called the police. They've searched all over the place and drawn a total blank. His car's vanished, too. Not a trace of him to be found anywhere. And the guy he was meant to have gone to see says he didn't know anything about it and never saw him. Neither have any of the residents of the town. Kip's well known there, and you'd think someone would have seen him and talked to him. But it looks as if he never reached the place. Or went somewhere else. Nobody knows. It's a mystery. Lynne's going to pieces.'

Ben asked, 'How's Jeff taking it?'

'Not well,' Tuesday said. 'He's been climbing the walls and chewing holes in the carpet ever since he got the news. And in case you're wondering why I'm phoning you about this and not him, he doesn't know I'm calling. I told him he should, but he said no. I asked him why not, and he said, "Because Ben would want to offer to help, and I don't want him to." So again I asked why not, and he said, "Because Ben would deal with a situation like this on his own, and that's what I'm going to do."'

That sounded like Jeff, all right. Ben's old friend was independent-minded to a fault and capable of being extremely stubborn.

'Let me talk to him,' Ben said.

'He's on the other phone right now, speaking to travel agents and getting nowhere fast. He's determined to jump on the next plane to Australia, but he's going nuts because they're all booked up, even from Heathrow, and the soonest he can get a flight is three days from now.'

Ben put the cigarette to his lips and thumbed the wheel of his lighter. At the same time, the wheels inside his head were turning, too. Times. Distances. Margins. Options. Connections. Pieces moving around his three-dimensional mental globe of the world like chessmen laying out their strategy on a board. He'd fallen silent, deep in thought.

It could work.

'Hello? Ben? Are you there?' Tuesday said.

'I'm here. I'm thinking.'

'Thinking what?'

'Thinking that there might be a way to get there a lot

faster,' Ben said. 'Hold on a minute. I'll call you back.'

Ben ended the call and immediately punched in another number.

'It's me,' he said when Ruth answered on the first ring, as if she'd been standing right by the phone expecting him to call. She sounded cheery and upbeat.

'Hello, me. What time are you getting here? Don't forget I have restaurant reservations for eight o'clock this evening.'

Ben took a breath and came right out with it. 'I'm sorry, Ruth. Change of plan. I hate to do this to you, but I'm not going to be able to make it after all.'

Her tone changed to one of dismay. 'But I've been so looking forward to seeing you. And I really wanted you to meet Lukas.'

'Me too.'

'Let me guess. Something's come up, correct?'

'You might say that.'

'Can't be helped, I suppose,' Ruth said, irritation creeping into her voice. 'What is it this time? Let me guess. I know. Someone's threatened to shoot the US President and only you can stop it from happening?'

Ben wasn't sure that he would actually make much effort to stop that from happening. 'Not exactly.'

'Then what? It'd better be good, whatever it is.'

'Jeff's father-in-law. He's gone missing.'

'The Australian crocodile guy?'

'That's him.'

'Missing how?'

'Missing, as in, he's disappeared and nobody knows where he's gone.'

'I can help with that one. It's a no-brainer. He'll be inside the belly of one of those scaly green monsters of his.' Ruth didn't sound entirely sympathetic.

'Apparently not,' Ben said. 'It happened somewhere else.'

'Where? What?'

'Can't say. Nobody knows. That's the whole point of being missing, isn't it?'

'All right, I get it. And I'm sorry if I seem uncaring. It's terrible, it really is. I hope the poor man's all right and that they find him soon. Have they called the police?'

'First thing they did.'

'Then surely the police will help?'

'Just like they helped so much when you went missing that time, Ruth,' Ben said. The moment the words were out of his mouth, he regretted being so direct.

'You sound like you're taking this very personally, big brother.'

'Jeff's my friend.'

'I know he is. But what can you do? Australia's a long way away.'

'Yes, it is,' Ben said. 'And that's also what I'm calling about. I need a small favour, Ruth.'

She grumped. 'That'd be a first, you asking for a *small* favour.'

'Maybe not that small,' he admitted.

Five minutes later, he was back on the phone to Tuesday at Le Val.

'Tell Jeff to get his Cessna ready to be at Le Bourget airport in Paris by eleven o'clock this evening, to hitch a ride on a

Steiner Industries business jet that just so happens to be going his way.'

'Just so happens? Tuesday said, sounding amazed.

'With a quick pit stop in Dubai for refuelling, barring delays and weather permitting, he should be able to make the trip in less than a day. It's only about nine thousand miles.'

'Just a hop and a skip,' Tuesday said. 'I'll let him know.'

'Tell him there's just one condition,' Ben said.

'Which is what?'

'Which is that I'm coming too.'

Chapter 2

The plan worked out just the way Ben had anticipated, though it had meant a mad scramble for both him and Jeff separately to reach the private jet terminal at Le Bourget in time for their RV with the Steiner Industries Bombardier Global 7500 jet. When Ben screeched up to the terminal with only minutes to spare, Jeff had only just landed, and the jet's crew, headed by their chief pilot Pierre, were impatient to get going.

The privileges of private air travel meant there was the minimum of hassle involved. Ruth had been busily pulling strings and taken care of everything from her end; for all intents and purposes Ben and Jeff were executive associates of the company, employed to scout contacts for a new Steiner Industries corporate venture. That vague language was enough to sneak them under the cordon of red tape, and provided them with a fast-tracked business visa that allowed free movement within Australia for thirty days. Ben had called on favours from his sister before; this was a big, expensive one, but she'd come through brilliantly for him.

That had been the easy part. Persuading Jeff to accept his help had been another matter. Still, they were here now. Jeff's initial proud reluctance to accept anyone's help had softened over the course of his trip to Paris, and as they met on the tarmac he gripped Ben's hand with emotion. 'I don't know what to say. I owe you one, buddy.'

'Let's find Kip first,' Ben said.

The Bombardier Global was one of the longest-range private aircraft in the world, capable of flying more than seven thousand nautical miles nonstop. It also had a passenger cabin six feet longer than a Gulfstream's, and they would have been wallowing in luxury if not for the pressing anxiety of the moment. They landed in Dubai with fuel to spare, topped up their tanks as quickly and smoothly as these things could be done, and set off again on the second leg of their journey. Nineteen hours after their departure from Paris, the jet touched down on the runway at Darwin International Airport, Northern Territory.

It was two a.m. local time and the scorching early-autumn daytime temperature had dropped to a chill, the tarmac slicked to a black mirror by a downpour of heavy rain. Ben and Jeff were no strangers to long-distance travel, but the jetlag was a killer and their body clocks were all screwed up. The journey was far from over, however. This was a big, big country and they were still more than six hundred miles from their destination. For the next leg, independently of Steiner Industries, they'd chartered a twin-engined Beechcraft Baron to transport them southeast across the Northern Territory to the remote town of Borroloola, whose airstrip was unsuitable for landing anything much larger than a light turboprop aircraft. Borroloola was situated on the McArthur River, just sixty or so kilometres upstream from Kip Malloy's spread at Hobart's Creek near the Gulf of Carpentaria.

But as the Bombardier Global finished refuelling and flight checks for its return journey, there was as yet no sign of their charter plane. 'Looks like we've been left in the lurch, damn it,' grumbled a frustrated Jeff.

Ben glanced up at the ink-black sky and the pounding rain that formed haloes around the floodlamps of the taxiway. He doubted whether any light aircraft pilot in their right mind would want to take off in this, with visibility down to near zero. There was nothing for it but to wait.

The private terminal had a small waiting area where they spent the next few hours. Jeff, exhausted with jetlag but too nervy to settle, alternately dozed for short periods in a chair and resumed his restless pacing, constantly glancing through the window for any sign of their plane. Ben sat quietly defying the no-smoking signs and listening to the steady drum of the rain on the roof. On and on it went, not easing until the first blood-red glimmers of dawn were breaking in the east. Shortly afterwards they saw the lights of their charter aircraft coming in to land.

'The guy certainly took his bloody time,' Jeff muttered irritably, snatching up his kit bag. As the Beechcraft Baron taxied around towards the terminal they stepped outside into the fresh dawn light. The side hatch swung open and a figure emerged, and it was apparent that the guy wasn't a guy after all. Their lady pilot was a petite blonde of about thirty or thirty-five, dressed in shorts and flip-flops, a red baseball cap and a rumpled old paratrooper jacket a size too large for her. She jumped down and came striding confidently up to them with a beaming smile and an extended hand. Her eyes were the most startling blue, so bright they could have been lit from behind.

'Abbie Logan. Which one of you is Mr Dekker?'

'What time do you call this?' Jeff said brusquely.

Her smile widened and she shook her head. 'Sorry to keep you waiting, mate, but I've got rules about flying blind through a bloody rainstorm. Even for two handsome gents like yourselves. Now, if you're ready, let's see if we can make up a bit for lost time, eh?'

Soon the city of Darwin was far behind them and they were heading into open country with the blossoming crimsons, golds and purples of the sunrise spanning a vast disc from one end of the horizon to the other. Jeff was glum and taciturn and hunched in a seat towards the tail, while Ben moved up front to sit with the pilot, watching the scenery roll by below. Abbie Logan looked completely at ease at the controls, wearing her headset over the red baseball cap. She'd rolled up her jacket sleeves and her arms were tanned and strong. 'Didn't catch your name,' she said to him over the thrum of the twin props that filled the cabin.

'I'm Ben.'

'Pleased to meet you, Ben. First visit to the Territory?'

'First time in Australia,' he replied.

Her cheeks dimpled into another smile that contrasted whitely against the tan of her face. 'Yeah? Welcome Down Under. You and your grumpy mate here on business?'

'You might say that.'

'Only you don't look like the regular business types. Travelling kind of light.'

Ben glanced back at Jeff and saw that he'd dozed off again. 'I'm sorry if he came over a bit rude before. He's just a little uptight.'

'Hey, no worries,' she replied with a cheerful shrug, and went on flying.

The rising sun was soon a burning orange ball on their port quarter as they maintained their steady course south-east. Abbie flicked out a pair of teardrop aviator sunglasses and donned them against the glare, hiding those vivid blue eyes. 'Going to be a scorcher, I reckon,' she declared. Ben was inclined to agree. It was a long way from the cool springtime temperatures of Switzerland and Normandy. Come to that, it was hard to imagine a world more different to either. Abbie had levelled the plane at a low cruising altitude of five thousand feet and the landscape that rolled by beneath them was an endless, virtually flat wilderness that seemed to stretch for a million miles in every direction, punctuated here and there by great river gorges, spectacular rock formations and escarpments, wetlands and patches of tropical forest.

'We're over Kakadu National Park,' she explained. 'Two hundred thousand square kilometres of it. Some of the Aboriginal peoples have been here for at least sixty-five thousand years.' As she spoke she eased back on the stick and let the plane gain altitude to soar over a huge striated rock formation. Dropping down the other side of the rocks they skimmed over a vast lake where clouds of mist drifted like smoke on the water. Disturbed by the roar of the low-flying plane, a large flock of egrets erupted from the lake's surface and took to the air, a rippling, pulsing white wave of thousands of beating wings.

'That's Anbangbang Billabong,' Abbie told him. Then pointing at another towering escarpment to their port side she said, 'And that's Nourlangie Rock, but the Aboriginal people call it Burrungkuy. See those caves down there? They've got some of the oldest cave art in the world. Painted by Neanderthals, they reckon. Though I know a few modern-day Neanderthals who couldn't paint a picture to save their bloody lives.'

'Amazing scenery.'

She flashed a grin at him. 'Pretty awesome, isn't it? Looks like Paradise. But believe me, mate, you wouldn't want to be stuck out here alone. Plenty of tourists go missing, if they're daft enough to go wandering off into the woop-woop without the right kit. Now and then some poor bugger gets taken by a croc. Last one, all they ever found was a bit of his leg with the shoe still on it.'

That brought Kip Malloy back to Ben's mind. Dangerous country it might be for the unwary traveller, but even a seasoned outbacker like him could be unlucky. 'I take it you're from these parts yourself?' he asked Abbie.

'Born and bred,' she replied proudly. 'Never been out of the Territory.'

'Not even once?'

Abbie shook her head. 'This is the only world I know. Can't say I've ever been tempted to see more of it. Why should I, when I've got everything I want, right here?' She looked at him. 'What about you, Ben? Where do you call home?'

'I've moved around a lot. These days I live in France.'

'But you're a Pom, right?'

'Half Irish,' he replied. 'I lived there for a long time, too.'

She smiled. 'That's better. Nothing against Poms, mind you. Not really.'

'You don't sound so sure.'

'My people were from Limerick, going back a while. My great-great-great-great-great-granddad was transported to a penal colony for his part fighting the British in the 1798 Irish Rebellion. Just one of the forty thousand folks from the old country who were stuck on ships and brought over here to be worked half to death in their concentration camps. Thanks to the good old British empire, about a third of non-Indigenous Australians can trace their roots back to Ireland.'

Ben said, 'Then it looks as if I'm going to fit right in here.'

'Planning on staying long?'

'As long as necessary.'

'What is it you do?'

'Right now I'm in education,' Ben said.

'Teacher?'

'More like a trainer,' he said. He glanced back again at Jeff, who was still fast asleep with his head lolling on his shoulder. 'After that, I don't know what I'm going to do, or where I'll go.'

'Could always move out here,' Abbie said with a smile.

He chuckled. 'I'll certainly think about it.'

The morning wore on. By the time the sun was halfway up in the sky it was already searing hot. There was a sheen of perspiration on Abbie's face. The aircraft's pressurised cabin meant you couldn't simply crack open a window, the way you could in Jeff's prehistoric Cessna back home. She reached out a tanned, toned arm and turned up the air conditioning full blast. 'Told you it was going to be a scorcher, didn't I? Still, got a nice tailwind happening and I should be able to get you into Borroloola in about another hour or so.'

'So how long have you been flying?' he asked her.

She looked at him over the top of her sunglasses. 'Hope you're not going to give me that "what's a pretty girl like you doing in a job like this" crap.'

'Not in a thousand years. I've known quite a few female pilots.'

'My dad taught me to fly before I was sixteen. He used to say, "Life's problems all seem pretty small when you're looking at them from high up."'

'Wise words,' Ben said.

'I love it up here. Room to breathe. I'll fly anything, go anywhere. No runway, no problem. We also operate an old chopper, for when the landing gets a little tight. That'll set you down in places where there aren't even any places.'

Ben smiled. Abbie Logan was someone with a passion for her job. He asked, 'Is this a regular route for you?'

She shrugged. 'I used to fly the mail plane over that way. Drop-off was twice a week. So I know the area pretty well, yeah.'

'That's the only way they get their mail around here?'

'It's a big country, mate. The Northern Territory has 1.35 million square kilometres. Reckon that's about six times the size of the UK. With a population of just 245,000 next to your sixty-odd million. I can't believe those poor sods even have room to breathe.'

30

'So all these remote communities must be pretty close-knit,' Ben said. 'I'm guessing everyone must know each other.'

He was thinking of what Tuesday had told him, about the strangeness of nobody having seen Kip Malloy when he supposedly visited the nearby town the day he disappeared. What she was telling him seemed to tally with that. Which lent more weight to the idea that maybe Kip hadn't actually gone there.

That in turn threw up more ideas. Such as the one that had come into Ben's mind even as he was driving back from Switzerland: why would Kip Malloy have lied to Jeff's mother about where he was going when he disappeared? Had he been leading some kind of double life? Beyond what little Jeff had been able to tell him, Ben knew comparatively little about the missing man, far less than the extensive background dossier he'd have compiled about one of his kidnap cases back in the day. And that meant anything was possible – but for the moment at least, he hadn't any intention of expressing these troubling thoughts to Jeff.

'For sure, most folks around here know one another,' Abbie replied, bringing him back to the present moment. 'That's if they're not actually related to one another,' she added with a laugh. 'We don't see a lot of new faces.'

'Can't be easy keeping secrets in these small communities,' Ben said.

'Dunno about that, mate,' she replied. 'I mean, everyone's got a secret, haven't they?'

31

Chapter 3

Abbie's flight time estimate proved to be right on the money. Just a little over an hour later, they came in to land on the bumpy, loose-surfaced runway at Borroloola airport. Jeff was awake by then and watched with a keen pilot's eye as Abbie buzzed in low and expertly set the plane down.

'Here we are, boys,' she announced, taxiing to a halt next to a cluster of buildings and a small refuelling station. 'Welcome to the official capital city of Nowhereland.'

Jeff had been here before, on a previous visit to his mother's new home, but for Ben this was a new experience. Stepping out of the aircraft transported him back to his memories of any number of Special Forces deployments in the hottest, dustiest and remotest theatres of operations across the world. If it hadn't been for the pair of kangaroos he could see hopping across the beaten-earth runway, he might have been on some remote plain of Afghanistan or even somewhere in the barren wilderness of east Africa. As far as the eye could see and probably much further than that, the endless reaches of open, empty, scrubby grassland extended for 360 degrees all around them, dotted here and there by patches of parched, crooked trees. After the cool pressurised cabin of the aircraft the air felt like dragon's breath.

'Well, nice meeting you, mate,' Abbie said as Ben collected his one piece of luggage from the plane, the old green canvas haversack that had accompanied him on many adventures around the world. 'You need me again, you got my number. Enjoy your stay.' Then she was off again, taxiing away towards the runway to fly to her next job. Ben watched the plane take off and climb into the pale, cloudless sky, shrinking until it became a tiny white dot over the emptiness.

He caught himself wondering if he'd ever see Abbie Logan again. Her smile seemed to linger in his mind. He shook his head to clear his thoughts. There were more pressing matters to focus on.

When the plane was finally gone, he and Jeff were alone again and feeling like the last two humans alive on a deserted planet. The silence was absolute. 'Terry should be with us soon,' Jeff said, looking at his watch. He shielded his eyes with his hand to scan a lonely, distant stretch of road. Terry Napier was one of Kip's employees, who was due to drive them the sixty kilometres north to the remote farm at Hobart's Creek.

They didn't have to wait for very long. Far off in the distance Ben spotted a dust cloud tracking roughly south-west towards them. It took a good ten minutes to reach them; at last the dirt-streaked pickup truck rolled up. Terry Napier was a big, rough-featured man in his forties, with a face the colour and texture of saddle leather and a nose that had been broken more than once in his life. A broad-brimmed hat shaded his eyes from the sun and that, together with his bandy-legged gait as he got out of the pickup to meet them, gave him the look of a cowboy. He stuck out a rough, square hand. 'G'day, Jeff. How was your trip?' He glanced at Ben but didn't acknowledge his presence.

'We got here as fast as we could,' Jeff replied. 'What's the latest? Anything new?'

Napier shook his head. 'Wish I could say there was, mate. Nothing.'

Jeff puffed his cheeks. 'Christ. How's my mum?'

'She'll be glad you're here. Lynne's a strong woman but at a time like this she needs all the support she can get, I reckon.'

'This is my friend and business partner, Ben Hope,' Jeff said. 'He's come to help us find Kip.'

Napier gave a sort of grunt and thrust the big hand Ben's way. It felt as dry and tough as a catcher's glove, with a grip that could throttle a saltwater crocodile. 'Best be on our way, then,' he muttered. 'Lynne'll string me up by the bollocks if I don't bring you home quick.'

They loaded their stuff in the back of the pickup and got on board, Jeff riding up front and Ben in the rear of the crew-cab. 'Bad business,' Napier kept muttering as they set off along the dusty road. 'Bloody bad business, and that's a fact.'

'Any idea what happened to him, Terry?' Jeff asked.

'Dunno, Jeff. Not a clue.' Napier glanced back at Ben in the rear-view mirror. 'So your cobber here lives with you in frogland, eh?'

'We work together,' Ben said.

34

Napier gave another grunt. 'Never been there myself. Tried a bottle of their froggy wine one time. Didn't rate it much. So this your first trip to Oz?'

'I'll try anything once,' Ben said.

'Thought you'd come and help us out with our problems, did you?'

Ben couldn't say he was feeling too much love emanating from Terry Napier. Maybe he just had that effect on some people. He replied, 'Finding people is what I used to do.'

'Ex-copper, are you?' Napier asked, his eyes meeting Ben's in the rear-view mirror with an icy stare.

'Not in this life,' Ben said.

'Ben and I go back a long time, Terry,' Jeff said.

Napier obviously had some awareness of Jeff's military past. Making the connection he said to Ben, 'So you're another soldier boy.'

There was a lot Ben could have said in reply, but rather than be bothered making the effort, he just shrugged.

Napier was still watching Ben, his eyes flicking back and forth between the mirror and the empty road ahead. He said loudly, 'I'm sure we all appreciate you coming all this way out here to the back of beyond to give us simple locals a helping hand. But the fact is, if anyone can find Kip it's someone who knows this land inside out. That's if he can be found. Nobody's got bugger all idea where he's gone and this is a—'

'A big country,' Ben finished for him. 'So people keep telling me.'

'You know this place like the back of your hand, Terry,' Jeff said. 'What would you say the odds are?'

Napier seemed to enjoy being asked for his opinion, even though he wasn't slow to offer it anyway. 'You ask me, mate, if Kip was coming home he'd be there by now. I reckon he's a goner.'

'You don't seem too upset about that,' Ben said.

Napier fired another cold look back at him in the mirror. 'I've known Kip for fifteen years and been his farm foreman for the last eleven. He's one of the best mates I ever had. Don't see the point in going around blubbing like a sheila about it, that's all.'

In sixty kilometres the only other vehicle they saw was a heavily laden camper van with canoes and mountain bikes strapped to its roof. From the dry scrubland around Borroloola the terrain had gradually morphed into subtropical forest and lush coastal wetlands, the greenery intercut with countless winding waterways, some of them little more than swamps, others fast-flowing rivers. Where the road passed close to the water's edge, what Ben had taken for a brownish-green log lying among the riverside rushes suddenly burst into movement and slithered rapidly down the muddy shore. The big croc disappeared below the surface leaving only a few ripples.

Napier turned off the main track onto a rougher, narrower trail through the trees. Breaks in the foliage offered glimpses of a high mesh security fence, not much unlike the one that bounded the perimeter at Le Val. It ran for a couple of kilometres before Napier took a two-way radio from a holder on his dashboard and said into it, 'Terry. Incoming. Over.' A voice crackled back at him, 'Gotcha, Terry.' Soon afterwards, they pulled up at a tall double gate where a couple of guys in shorts, T-shirts and baseball caps ran over from a nearby hut to let them through. From there, the track wound on for some distance further, past more wire-fenced enclosures and various clusters of buildings. More men were at work here and there, driving around in ATVs, mending fences, attending to their general duties. Ben asked Napier, 'How many people work for Kip?'

'Think it's about twenty, no?' said Jeff.

'Twenty-three,' Napier said. 'We just took on another couple of lads last month. Business has been on the up and up. With Kip gone, though, I don't know.'

Now they were arriving at the main house. Kip and Lynne's home was a large single-storey farmhouse with a hip roof and deep wraparound veranda supported by colonial-style wooden columns. But it wasn't the attractive traditional rural architecture that caught Ben's eye as they pulled up by the farmhouse; rather, it was the Holden Commodore patrol car parked outside, emblazoned with a kangaroo topped with a crown and bearing the legend NORTHERN TERRITORY POLICE.

The sudden and unexpected appearance of the police could signify various things. It might mean very good news. Alternatively, very bad. Jeff asked anxiously, 'What's this about?'

'No idea, mate,' muttered Napier. 'But I reckon we'll soon find out.'

The three of them got out of the pickup and walked across to the house. Jeff was first up the front steps and pulled open the fly screen door. Lynne Dekker, now Lynne Malloy, was standing in the hallway talking with the two police officers when she saw her son walk in, and gave a gasp. She'd had Jeff young and wasn't much over sixty, but she looked frail and aged. The fraught expression on her face told Ben that whatever developments the police had come to report, they weren't positive.

She broke away from them and flew into her son's arms. 'Oh, Jeff! It's so good to see you.'

Jeff hugged her. 'Mum, what's happening? Why are the police here?'

The two officers hovered in the background, looking fidgety. One was a sergeant, fat and grey and more than twice the age of his skinny constable, wearing a broad hat like a forest ranger's. Their faces were morose.

Definitely not good news.

Lynne wiped a tear from her eye. She was trying to stay strong, but clearly shaken to the core.

She said, 'They've found Kip's ute.'

Chapter 4

The Toyota Land Cruiser had been discovered by a group of young backpackers, who just by chance happened to stumble on the overturned wreck at the bottom of a deep, rocky gorge in the middle of nowhere. To their relief, there wasn't a corpse inside. The open driver's door made it look as if the vehicle's occupant or occupants had abandoned it on foot. Doing their civic duty, the kids hurried off to the nearest spot they could get mobile reception and called the police.

Sergeant Wenzel described how, on arrival at the remote location, his constables had investigated the abandoned vehicle more closely and verified that it did indeed belong to their missing person. For reasons as yet unclear, the scene of the accident was some seventy kilometres from Yulla Yulla, where Kip was thought to have gone that day and in whose surrounding area the search had been focused until now. The nearest road was a winding dirt track near the top of the gorge. A trail of disturbed rocks marked where Kip's Land Cruiser had come off the road and gone down the steep slope, rolling at least once before it hit the bottom. The crash had made the horn jam on; it was estimated that it could have taken up to about twenty-four hours for the electrical draw to completely drain the battery, whereupon the dashboard clock had frozen in time. Their best guesstimate was that the accident had taken place on the same afternoon Kip had disappeared.

'What was he doing there?' Jeff asked Sergeant Wenzel, who shrugged and replied, 'It's deep in the bush. There are a few tracks but we've no way to know where he might've been heading. But there is one other thing, as I was just about to tell Mrs Malloy before you showed up . . . '

'What other thing?'

'You've found something?' Lynne Malloy said, her drawn face suddenly brightening with hope. 'Something that could tell us where he's gone?'

The sergeant's stony expression didn't change. 'Not exactly. But we did find an item inside the vehicle that could potentially shed some light on the cause of the incident.'

'What item?' Jeff said impatiently. Hanging back by the front doorway where he could listen in from a discreet distance, Ben could tell that Wenzel was reluctant to spill the beans.

And now the policeman came out with it. 'The officers at the scene recovered a bottle of grog. It was lying open in the driver's footwell, uncapped, most of its contents gone. The whole inside of the vehicle was reeking of stale booze.'

'What kind of grog?' Lynne said. The hope was dashed from her face, along with all its colour, and the muscles in her cheeks and mouth were tauter than a bowstring.

'Bundy,' said the younger constable, speaking for the first time.

'What the hell is bundy?' Jeff asked. He looked ready to ram his arm down the cops' throats and physically yank the information out of them.

'Bundaberg rum,' Sergeant Wenzel explained for the benefit of a non-local. To Lynne he said, 'From what we can tell, it looks like he must've been driving around with the bottle between his knees when it happened.'

Now Lynne's pallid face was beginning to redden. 'Hold on a minute. Are you suggesting that Kip was boozing at the wheel? That what you're trying to say? That he was driving drunk and that's why he crashed the car?'

Wenzel gave a sigh. 'I'm sorry, Mrs Malloy, but that's our best guess right now. He's got to have been drinking. Why else would anyone be at the wheel of a moving vehicle with an open bottle to hand?'

Jeff's mind was churning so fast, his eyes were darting from side to side. 'You said the car had rolled when it came down the slope. How do you know the cap didn't come off the bottle then? It could have been shaken loose in the accident.'

'It's a screw-top,' the younger cop said, mimicking the act of unscrewing the cap. 'Wouldn't come open unless you meant it to.'

'What a fine story this is, officers,' Lynne Malloy said hotly, and glowered in disgust at the both of them. 'There's just one little problem with it. My husband wouldn't behave that way.'

'That's not what Jimmy Conroy says,' Wenzel replied. 'He's told me in the past that he'd had to chuck Kip out of his pub more than once. Said he could get out of control when he was all boozed up on the hard stuff.'

'You're talking ancient history,' Lynne shot back. 'Kip hasn't set foot in Jimmy Conroy's dingy pub, or any other pub for that matter, in more than twenty years. He made a vow long ago to leave his hard-drinking days behind him, and hasn't touched a single drop of spirits in all that time. Nothing more than a couple of beers now and then. With all due respect, officer, I think I'd know if my own husband had a drink problem.'

The sergeant and his colleague exchanged glances. 'I've got to be frank, Mrs Malloy,' Wenzel said. 'You've only been married to the man for what, four, five years? In my experience that's not long enough to be sure a bloke's on the wagon for good.'

'Whoa, you're out of line there, pal,' Jeff cut in sharply. 'If she says he wasn't drinking at the wheel, then he wasn't drinking at the wheel, okay?'

'Look, folks, I understand that nobody likes to hear this kind of thing,' Wenzel said, spreading his hands in a conciliatory kind of gesture. 'I don't much like it either. But like I say, based on the evidence, if someone else has a better explanation for what happened, then I'd like to hear it.'

Ben had remained quiet so far, but at this point he felt he had to say something to move this discussion along before it became confrontational. 'Sergeant, whatever might or might not have happened to cause the crash, what's your best guess as to where Kip went from there?'

As though seeing him for the first time, the cops both turned a cold gaze in Ben's direction. Wenzel asked, 'And you are?'

'This is Ben Hope,' Jeff said, repeating what he'd told

Terry Napier earlier. 'He's here to help us find Kip. He's got a lot of expertise in that department.'

The sergeant didn't seem impressed. The deep frown lines etched into his face deepened. He folded his thick arms across his chest, where they rested comfortably on the jutting slab of his belly. 'Expertise, eh? Law officer, are you, Mr Hope?'

'Thanks for that one, Jeff,' Ben thought to himself, annoyed at being landed in it once again. Out loud he said, 'I'm just a friend of the family, volunteering whatever services I can offer to try and bring Kip back safely.'

'Well, that's fair enough. But I'd remind you that finding missing people is the police's job.'

'And I'm sure you're right on the ball in this case, sergeant,' Ben replied politely. 'Would I be right in saying that your theory is, Kip managed to leave the scene of the accident on foot and went off searching for help?'

The sergeant considered a moment, as though deciding whether to share that information, then replied, 'Well, I can only go by what's there. There's no sign of blood inside the car, or anything to suggest he might've been injured. It's pretty common for drunks to walk away from crashes without a scratch on them. Seen it before.'

Lynne had been swelling like a volcano ready to pop, and now she erupted. 'MY HUSBAND IS NOT A DRUNK! You bloody fools, how can I possibly make this any clearer to you?'

So much for steering the discussion away from getting confrontational.

Jeff laid a hand on her arm. 'Mum, he's only trying to do his job, okay?'

43

'But as to where he might've gone,' continued the sergeant, 'who can say? I reckon he couldn't have got far on foot.'

'Not with a gutful of bundy inside him, that's for sure,' the young cop added, sotto voce.

Wenzel turned and shot him a severe look. 'That's enough of that, Tommy. What I mean is, it's pretty harsh terrain in those parts, even by Territory standards. Few years back, we had a missing persons case just a couple hundred kilometres to the east of there, and one of our officers died of dehydration during the search. Pete Blakey. Good bloke, sadly missed. So all I'm saying is, for a fella to survive out there more than a couple of days, in this hot weather we're having . . .'

'Kip was born and bred in the outback,' Lynne said. 'He's tough.'

'Tough as they come. I know that, Mrs Malloy. Anyhow, we're doing all we can to find him. Got an air patrol on its way down from Darwin to cover the whole area better than I can do on the ground. Hoping they'll find some sign of him. That's your husband's best chance right now.'

'If they don't find any sign of him?' she asked in a tremulous voice.

'Let's cross that bridge when we come to it, eh?'

'Unless . . . I mean, just because he wasn't found, it wouldn't have to mean . . . that is, someone could have picked him up.'

'If the dingoes hadn't got him first,' the younger cop offered helpfully.

'Tommy, I said that's enough of that talk,' the sergeant snapped at him. Tommy shrugged. 'Just saying, Sarge.'

Wenzel glanced at his watch. 'Anyhow, we should be on

our way. As soon as we know more, I'll keep you informed.'

Jeff nodded. 'Appreciate what you're doing, sergeant.'

'Oh, Mrs Malloy, I almost forgot,' Wenzel said as Lynne was showing them out. 'Your husband's ute is in the police pound in Minyerri, but I see no reason why we need to keep it there any longer. What do you want us to do with it? Reckon you'll be wanting the insurance to take a look.'

'I don't give a damn about the insurance,' she replied stiffly. 'Right now it's all I have left of my husband. That car's his pride and joy.'

'Thing is,' Wenzel said, 'it's pretty much a write-off. It'll have to be trailered here. Got to say, though, I don't really have the manpower to spare—'

'Don't worry about it, Sergeant,' Jeff said, standing behind his mother's shoulder. 'We'll come over and collect it in the morning, okay?'

'Fair dinkum.' Wenzel plucked a folded paper from his uniform breast pocket and handed it over. 'That's the release form. You just have to sign it and show it to the duty officer when you pick 'er up.'

They watched from the entrance as the cops got back into their patrol car and drove away. It was only when they were gone that emotion got the better of Lynne Malloy. Jeff tenderly helped her back inside, sat her down in the cool shade of the living room and offered to bring her a drink of something. She waved it away, tears flooding down her face, her expression pinched with distress and anger. 'That's the best they can do? To tell me my Kip was driving drunk – like this is all his fault? I don't accept it. No way! They don't know what they're doing. They don't have a clue!'

45

Ben hovered self-consciously by the door, feeling as though he was intruding on this personal family scene.

'Mum, you remember my friend Ben,' Jeff said, pointing over at him.

She sniffed, collecting herself. 'Of course. We met once before.' That had been at Le Val, the one time Ben had been introduced to her and Kip. 'Pardon me for being so rude in not welcoming you before.'

'Not at all, Mrs Malloy.'

'Please, you can call me Lynne. And thank you so, so very much for coming. You have no idea what it means.'

'It's the least I could do,' Ben said.

Jeff knelt on the floor in front of his mother's chair and clasped both her hands in his, looking at her with infinite tenderness in his eyes and all the reassurance he could muster. Ben felt strangely moved, watching his friend try to comfort his mother. Ben's own mother had passed away many years earlier, and her end hadn't been a happy one; for much of his life he'd been without that kind of relationship.

Jeff said, 'Mum, Ben has done a lot of this kind of thing before. He knows what he's doing. Now at least we have a rough idea where Kip might have gone. We'll bring him home, okay? We'll find him. I promise.'

Lynne nodded, and melted sobbing into her son's arms. Jeff held her tight, a look of pure agony in his eyes. He cast a glance at Ben, and Ben made a small smile and nodded consolingly. What was he supposed to say?

'Yes, we'll find him.'

But finding him alive – that was another matter.

46

Chapter 5

One of the many things that Ben had learned about his old friend over the years was that Jeff Dekker was no cook. Regardless, nothing could deter Jeff's absolute insistence on doing all he could to look after his mother, and that included taking the reins in the kitchen that evening. As a result, the three of them sat down to a dinner of flavourless beef steaks grilled to the consistency of shoe leather, served up with a side salad of cold baked beans.

But the fact was that anything tastier would have been wasted on the occasion, and the miserable meal was the perfect accompaniment to the disconsolate mood that hung like a cloud over the dinner table. Hardly a word was spoken, while Lynne Malloy could barely eat a bite and sat haggardly toying with her food, now and then letting out a deep sigh. Jeff valiantly offered a few encouraging sentiments to try to kickstart some kind of conversation, but soon gave up and went back to glumly chewing on his tough steak, with a face like a mastiff gnawing on a lump of knotty wood. The only consolation was the fridge full of chilled beer to which Lynne insisted they help themselves. As the unhappy meal dragged on, empty bottles began to accumulate in the middle of the table.

By ten p.m. Lynne had had enough, and announced she was going to take two sleeping pills and go to bed. 'Well, here we are,' Jeff said when she was gone. 'What now?'

The discovery of Kip's abandoned vehicle had changed everything. Ben didn't like to say it, but he said it anyway. 'If the airborne patrol finds him, there may not be much for us to do. Might be worth getting ready for the worst, Jeff. In which case your mother's going to need all the support you can give her. I'll stick around a few days and then go back to Le Val. You hang on here as long as it takes.'

Jeff stared sullenly at the remains of his steak. 'Well, shit. That's a cheery prospect.'

'Sorry I can't offer anything more positive right now.'

Jeff gave a bitter laugh. 'All this way, and now we're here there's bugger all we can do but wait for something to happen. I can't stand this frustration.'

For Ben, the reality was that most missing persons searches were no different: the endless waiting and the nail-biting were all part of the game. There wasn't always an explosive finale, still less a happy outcome. You could only do what you could do. He stepped back over to the fridge to get them another cold one, but Jeff declined. 'I'm done. Think I'll hit the sack, too.'

Left on his own, Ben walked out onto the veranda, smoked a cigarette and slowly drank his beer while leaning on the railing and listening to the nocturnal chorus all around him: the incessant chirp and buzz of insects, the raucous cry of some night bird, the croak of frogs. He felt weary and

48

disheartened and a very long way from home. Crushing out his cigarette he returned inside to wash and tidy away the dishes.

He'd been allocated a small but comfortable guest bedroom at the back of the house, but it was too hot to sleep and in any case he'd have been too restless and uneasy. Thinking he might be able to walk it off, he headed back outside and wandered away from the house, exploring the grounds. There were dim lights shining here and there from the small wooden cabins in which most of the workers lived. He could hear the sound of a guitar softly strumming. Further on, past outbuildings and equipment sheds and a large chicken enclosure, he came to an area where the trees grew more thickly and the air seemed cooler. The constant hum of insects, the lap of water nearby; looking up at the stars, all different down here on the far side of the world.

Walking on, he found himself at a break in the trees from where, beyond a four-foot steel mesh fence, he could see a broad expanse of lake, tranquil and deep, shining silvery under the moonlight. From somewhere out there came a violent slooshing rush of moving water and a guttural roaring of a kind Ben hadn't heard since his visit to the alligator-infested bayou of Louisiana. It sounded as if something had just been predated upon by one of Kip's numerous reptilian friends. It was a jungle out there, all right.

He stepped closer to the mesh fence, lit another cigarette and stood there for a while, watching the trickle of his smoke catch the moonlight and pondering the strange beauty of the night, so serene and tranquil and yet seeming to harbour so many untold secrets and hidden dangers.

'I wouldn't get too close to that water, mate,' said a voice behind him.

Ben turned, startled. A trained SAS trooper of his experience had situational awareness so instilled in him that he could instinctively feel the presence of another person even a distance away. For Ben that ability was like a sixth sense, or he'd thought it was. He'd had no idea he wasn't alone, and yet there he was, standing right close by as though he'd been there the whole time: the short, squat, dark figure of a man with a great mop of white hair and a beaming smile that glittered by the glow of the moon. His eyebrows were almost as bushy as the great snowy beard that grew halfway down his barrel chest.

'Heard you and your buddy was here to find Malloy,' the apparition said.

'News travels fast,' Ben said, recovering from his surprise and wondering who on earth the man was.

'You help me friend, that makes you me friend too, I reckon. Sammy's the name. Sammy Mudrooroo.'

'Ben Hope,' Ben said, and he and the Aboriginal man shook hands. The man's grip was dry and powerful. 'You work here, Sammy?'

Sammy Mudrooroo replied, 'Yeah, on and off. Been coming here a long time, mate. Kip, he treats me pretty good. You gonna find'm for us.'

'I'm certainly going to try,' Ben said.

Sammy shook his head. 'Nah, mate. Not try. You're gonna find'm.'

Ben's new friend sounded utterly confident about that. Ben almost replied, 'I wish I could be so sure.' The words were still unformed in his mouth when Sammy Mudrooroo startled him a second time by replying exactly as if Ben had spoken his thoughts aloud. 'Course you are,' he said with a chuckle, and the moonlight glinted in his eyes. 'That's what you come for, ain't it? You're the bloke who goes finds people.'

Ben said, 'Am I?'

'What they say.'

'Who says?'

'They.' Sammy smiled again, and prodded at Ben with a stubby finger. 'You the one, mate. You the one.'

'Someone been talking about me?' Ben wondered if the gossip had come from Terry Napier. He had the impression that Napier was someone who enjoyed shooting his mouth off to anyone who would listen.

'You gonna find Malloy for us,' Sammy said with that same enigmatic smile. 'And you gonna protect it. You don't let them have it. No chance of that happening, mate. Not now that you're here.'

Ben frowned, baffled. 'Protect what? Not let who have what?'

'S'what Mick would've wanted,' was all the answer that came back. Now Ben was beginning to wonder whether this Sammy Mudrooroo might be raving, or drunk. What the hell was he talking about?

'They said he was mad,' Sammy said. 'No, mate. He weren't mad. He knew the secret. Follow his trail, if you want to know it too.'

'Secret? Trail? I'm sorry, friend, but I really don't understand.'

Sammy leaned towards Ben and gripped his arm with an iron hand. He shook it three times and then let it go. 'You go seek the silver serpent, mate,' he added mysteriously. 'Then you'll find out the truth, I reckon.'

Ben was too bewildered to reply. Sammy Mudrooroo made a fork with his fingers and pointed them back at his own eyes, then tapped his head. 'Sammy sees everything, mate. Hear everything, too. Always watching. You remember that.' And with an enigmatic wink and a last moonlit gleam of a smile, Sammy turned and walked off towards the shadows. A rustle of coarse foliage, and he was gone.

'Hold on. Wait!' Ben chased him into the spot where he'd disappeared, but there was nothing but empty bushes. He seemed to have melted into the night as though he'd never been there at all, as if Ben had dreamed him.

Ben blinked. It was surreal. He found himself wondering if maybe he'd had one too many beers that night. No, his wits were sharp and his memory was too vivid to have imagined it. He spent several more minutes hunting around for Sammy Mudrooroo. Finding no trace of him anywhere, he gave up and returned to the house.

Strange.

But things were soon to get stranger.

Chapter 6

The experience stayed with Ben through much of the night, until he eventually drifted off to sleep sometime before dawn. And it was still hovering in his head, like the weird fragments of a dream, when he joined Jeff for breakfast in the morning.

Jeff had more concrete matters on his mind. 'I've been trying to raise Sergeant Wenzel on the sat phone, to find out if there's been any news. No luck so far.'

'They'd let us know if they found anything,' Ben said.

'You reckon? Not like you to trust the cops.'

'I'm not sure we have any other choice at this juncture.'

Jeff's attempt at brewing coffee was more successful than his cooking. They were into their third cup when Lynne appeared, shaky and exhausted despite having slept for nearly nine hours. Hearing the news, or the lack of it, she looked ready to crumble into pieces. But she wasn't her son's mother for nothing, and bravery and stoicism ran deep in the Dekker blood. She composed herself and sat with them at the table, determined to go on with her day as best she could. There was a little zip-up pouch at her elbow. Opening it, she took out a small amber pill bottle, shook out a couple of green and white capsules and knocked them back with a gulp of coffee.

'What's that for?' Jeff asked.

'Don't worry about it,' she replied nonchalantly. 'Hey, what are you doing? Give those back.'

Grabbing the bottle and examining the label Jeff said, 'These are heart pills, Mum. Since when did you need to take heart pills, for God's sake?'

'It's nothing, all right?' she said more defensively. 'Just get a little dizzy sometimes. Stress causes it. Christ knows I've got enough of that lately.' Pointing at Ben's pack of cigarettes on the table, she asked, 'Do you think I could have one of those?'

Ben wasn't sure if the cigarettes made for a great combination with the pills, but he wasn't about to refuse. He replied, 'Be my guest,' and slid them across to her, along with his battered, trusty old Zippo lighter.

Jeff stared at her. 'Mum!'

'Oh, get off my case, Jeff, will you?'

'Are you nuts? You don't even smoke.'

'I used to, when you were little. Everyone did, back in those days. Now's as good a time as any to take it up again.' Lynne lit up like an old hand and puffed away. 'Christ, that tastes good. Kip would blow his stack if he ever saw me smoking, though. His mother died of lung cancer and as far as he's concerned tobacco's on a par with crack cocaine. Wouldn't have it in the house. The farm hands are afraid to even think about lighting up a ciggie, if he's around. They probably reckon he'd thrash them with his belt, and they might not be far wrong.'

Seeing his opportunity, Ben said, 'Speaking of the farm hands, does a man called Sammy Mudrooroo work for you?'

Lynne blew more smoke. 'Sammy? He's been here for ever. He and Kip go way back. Can't really tell you much about him. No idea how old he must be. Seventy, maybe. Why do you ask about him?'

'I met him last night. Interesting character.'

'You might say that. Sammy sort of comes and goes as he pleases. It's not really an employer–employee relationship he and Kip have.'

'He said something odd to me. About a silver serpent.'

'I don't know what that means,' Lynne said with a shrug. 'Sammy has his own ways of expressing himself. Doesn't always make a lot of sense. Not to me, anyhow.'

'He also mentioned someone called Mick.'

'Mad Mick?' she replied. 'That's the only Mick I know. He was Kip's uncle.'

'Was?'

'He passed away not so long ago. Think he was eighty-two. I never met him.'

'Sammy mentioned that some people thought he was crazy.'

'Oh, Kip wouldn't hear him called "Mad Mick". Neither would Sammy, for that matter. Kip told me that Mick and Sammy virtually grew up together. But he had quite a repu- tation around the area for being . . . well, a little colourful, let's say. Kip loved him like a father, though. He was really upset when he passed away.'

'I'm sorry to hear it,' Ben said. 'What happened to him?'

'He was bitten by a snake. Owned a huge great big stretch

of land a long way south of here. Spent half his life going walkabout all around it, even when he got old. Kip always used to worry about him . . .' She went suddenly silent, heaved a gasp, and in the next instant the tears started welling up again. 'Oh God. I'm talking about Kip as if he was gone, too.'

Jeff clasped her hand. 'No, Mum. You mustn't think that way.'

After breakfast it was agreed that, since there wasn't much else they could do, they should set off early to collect Kip's Toyota from the police pound in Minyerri. Ben and Jeff stepped out into the volcanic heat and soon found Terry Napier and another of the hands, a young guy with a lean, ratlike face and narrow-set eyes called Finn Mulkey, in the farm workshop where they were fixing a broken light bar on the roof of one of the all-terrain buggies they used to patrol the enclosure. Napier and Mulkey were sharing a joke and it was clear that they were good pals. Jeff asked if they could borrow a suitable truck and trailer. Wiping the sweat out of his eyes, Napier replied that they could use the Mitsubishi Shogun and pointed over to where it was parked.

'You sure it's up to the job?' Jeff asked, dubiously eyeing the aged, battered workhorse of a thing.

'No worries. Might not look like much but she's tip-top.'

'Hot enough for you, fellas?' Mulkey said, grinning at the two Brits as they set about hitching up the trailer.

'I've been in hotter places,' Ben said.

Mulkey seemed taken aback. 'Yeah? Like where?'

'Oh, you know, a couple of deserts, the odd jungle here and there.'

'This won't go on for long,' Napier said, squinting one-eyed up at the sun. 'Big rain's coming. Then you watch all this dried-up shit turn to mud and the river comes up eight foot like a bloody tidal surge, carrying whole bloody trees with it.' He grunted. 'As long as the floods don't wash away the north end of the croc fence again, we'll be all right, eh Finn?'

'Fucking right, mate.'

Ben asked matter-of-factly, 'Either of you seen Sammy Mudrooroo this morning?'

'Him?' Napier said with a derisive snort. 'That one comes and goes as he pleases. You'll probably find him in the nearest bar, or propped against a tree somewhere, sloshed on Jack Daniel's.'

'Or getting off his head sniffing bloody petrol, like they all do,' Mulkey added, grinning in amusement.

'Bloody idiots,' Napier went on. 'Why Kip ever gave a bloke like that a job, beats me. But that's Kip for you. Always was a soft touch when it comes to the abbos. Bunch of good-for-nothings, the lot of them, if you want my opinion.'

Ben looked Napier in the eye and said, 'I didn't ask for your opinion, Terry. I just asked you if you'd seen him.'

'Not me, mate,' Mulkey said, shying away from the tension between the two older men.

Ben asked, 'Does he live here on the farm?'

Napier replied acerbically, 'He's got a cabin Kip built for him, but he'd rather be out there in the bush living rough like a bloody savage. What do you want to talk to him for, anyway?'

'It's not important,' Ben said.

Napier gave him a look and muttered something about 'What'd you bloody ask me for, then', but Ben wasn't going to get sucked into an argument with this guy.

By now the trailer was all set up, and it was time to go. With the sat nav programmed for Minyerri, Ben took the wheel for the outgoing trip and they headed off along the dusty, near-empty roads for the four-hour trek. The distances involved made any kind of travel across the region a time-consuming business. Most of the day would now be given up for the sake of recovering a car, and Ben could only hope that by the time they returned to the farm there would be some positive news waiting for them.

The temperature rose steadily as the morning wore on, and by the time they reached Minyerri sometime after midday the blue sky had been burned white by the fierce glare. The Shogun's air-con gave up the ghost halfway through the trip, prompting Jeff to curse Terry Napier and crank open all the windows, which only invited in a lot of hot unbreathable air and great swarms of bloodthirsty insects. 'These sodding flies love me to bits,' he complained bitterly, swatting another. 'Why'd I seem to taste so much better than you?'

'You're just a sweet guy,' Ben said. He couldn't help but wonder if Napier had fobbed them off with a malfunctioning vehicle on purpose.

They drove on in silence for a while. Jeff was deep in thought, frowning to himself. 'What I can't understand,' he said, 'is why Kip would've lied to Mum about where he was going that day. He's a straight-up guy. Dishonesty isn't in his DNA.'

'I don't know him as well as you do,' Ben said. 'But men have been known to lie to their wives.'

Jeff glanced at him, sensing what he was thinking. 'Another woman? No way. I don't believe it. Not Kip.'

'Whatever you say, Jeff. Then there has to be another reason. We just need to work out what.'

'Unless they find him.'

Ben nodded. 'Yep. Unless they find him.'

'What are his chances, Ben?'

'Your guess is as good as mine.'

'This is fucked up,' Jeff said. 'We're doing nothing here.'

Chapter 7

They hadn't expected Minyerri to be much in the way of a thriving metropolis, but even so Ben was struck by the impression of poverty and misery that the tiny township emanated. It wasn't the dusty roads made of ochre-coloured dirt, and it wasn't the forlorn clusters of faded, worn old houses that lined them like gravestones. Most of the place's couple of hundred inhabitants seemed to live in improvised dwellings that made parts of the Third World Ben had spent time in look positively upbeat. Children dressed in dirty rags, kicking a deflated football around in their garbage-strewn playing area. A wizened old man sleeping on a tattered foam bed next to his makeshift tent, clutching a bottle and surrounded by flies, while feral dogs scavenged about for scraps nearby.

'Jesus, what a shit pit,' Jeff muttered as they drove by the depressing, dismal scene. 'Tell you what, if this is what western 'civilisation' has done for these people, they'd be a lot better off without it.' Ben was thinking about the ancient cave paintings of Burrungkuy that Abbie Logan had told him about, and the nature of human progress. Sixty-five thousand years on, maybe those extinct Neanderthals were having the last laugh.

Along with its single schoolhouse, the police station appeared to be one of Minyerri's better buildings, but not by much. As Ben and Jeff walked in, the place gave off the same languid, despondent atmosphere as the rest of the town. An Aboriginal family sat in a small seating area by a grimed window, waiting to be seen. The mother was nursing a tiny brown infant on her knee. The father had a swollen eye and a bleeding cut on his forehead but seemed patient and resigned. A couple of officers wandered by without giving them a glance. At the other end of the room, a duty officer sat alone at a desk next to a clattering fan that seemed to be doing nothing but stir warm air around and excite the insects.

If Ben and Jeff had been eagerly anticipating an update in the missing persons search, they'd have been disappointed. It soon turned out that Sergeant Wenzel wasn't around; nobody at the station was too sure where he'd gone, and it seemed he was out of radio range. 'You'll be contacted if we hear anything,' the duty officer informed them.

'Yeah, sure. Anyhow, this is what we came for.' Jeff gave him the release form that Wenzel had provided. The duty officer spent a long moment poring over every word of the single page as though it were the 1688 Bill of Rights, then turned to a computer screen, tapping the occasional key and muttering under his breath. At last he unglued himself from his chair, peeled his damp shirt away from his back, mumbled something about 'Come this way' and led them around the rear of the building to a wire-mesh-enclosed concrete yard containing what there was of a police fleet, along with various other impounded or crash-damaged cars and trucks. Some had been there so long, the weeds were growing up through the wheel arches.

'That's the one,' the officer said, and flapped the release form in the direction of a dirty, badly dented silver Toyota Land Cruiser parked outside a large storage shed awaiting collection. 'You fellas all right loading 'er up yourselves?'

'Yeah, we're all right,' Jeff replied. Happy to get out of the sun, the duty officer shuffled back inside to whatever highly pressing crime-fighting duties required his attention.

Ben backed the trailer into the yard and they got to work, using the Mitsubishi's electric winch to roll Kip's dead Land Cruiser aboard. The 4x4 looked exactly like a vehicle that had rolled and slid down a long, rocky slope and come to a sudden halt at the bottom. Sharp stones had ripped gashes in the bodywork, the front end was crumpled like an accordion, and the windscreen was an opaque mass of fissures.

When Ben climbed into the cab to release the handbrake he noticed that Wenzel had been right about the interior smelling like a brewery. Even the pizza-oven temperature inside the vehicle hadn't cooked off the lingering stink of stale rum. He wondered what other clues might shed any light on Kip's mysterious movements prior to the accident. Once the Land Cruiser was rolled up onto the trailer, Jeff got busy securing it into place with heavy-duty straps while Ben clambered back into the cab to have a nose around.

Everything seemed to be perfectly normal and unsuspicious. Kip kept his vehicle documents in a faux-leather folder in the glove compartment. A real drunk might have another small bottle stashed in there too, but there was nothing. The cops had been able to partially recharge the dead battery in order to get a time reading from the dashboard clock. Ben was pretty sure they'd already have checked the onboard sat nav in case it revealed any information about Kip's recent travels, but he tried anyway and soon came to the same conclusion the police would have: the sat nav had never been used, no destination details entered into its memory. Kip obviously wasn't into fiddling with his onboard gadgets. 'That would have been too damn easy,' he said to himself.

'I'm all finished here,' Jeff called from below. 'You ready to head back?'

Ben was about to reply, 'Yeah, let's get out of here' when he spotted a peculiar dark stain on the underside of his forearm where it had been touching against the interior door sill. At first he thought it must be a dead fly squashed against his skin, and he went to flick it away with revulsion. But touching it, he found it sticky, like tar. He sniffed his fingertips.

The driver's door suddenly swung open and there was Jeff, cut off at the waist by the raised trailer and looking up at him expectantly. 'I said, you coming?'

'Smell that,' Ben said, and held his finger under Jeff's nose.

'Yugh. What the hell is it?'

'It's all over the inside of the door trim.' Ben pointed out the little spots and spatters of the same sticky dark-brown substance stuck to the sill beneath the window. Jeff prodded at one of them with his own finger, sniffed at it again and said, 'Smells like—'

63

'Tobacco,' Ben said. 'That's what it is. The kind you chew instead of smoke.'

Peering out of the open driver's door, he noticed more of the little dark flecks stuck to the bodywork. They'd have been easy to miss, among all the road dirt. The mental image that came to him was easy to picture. He'd never tried chewing tobacco, but it was popular among people like hunters and stalkers who used it to get their nicotine fix without creating a telltale smell that could scare off wild prey. When you chewed it, the tobacco released juices which after a while mixed with saliva to create an excess that needed to be spat out in the form of black gunk. That was probably the nastiest part of the habit, as far as he was concerned. Along with the dark juice, you'd be spitting out little masticated lumps of the stuff. Driving a car, you'd wind down your window to save getting it all over yourself and the interior. But if you were moving at speed, the airflow might blow some of the spat-out gunk down onto the door sill. That was what Ben decided had happened here.

It seemed a simple enough conclusion to draw, but in light of the facts, Ben knew he was faced with another anomaly.

'Your mum seemed very clear on two things,' he said to Jeff. 'One, according to her there's absolutely no way that Kip was drinking at the wheel, or that he'd even touch a drop of the hard stuff any more these days. Two, because of what happened to his mother he's so dead set against tobacco he won't tolerate anyone smoking around him.'

'She knows Kip better than anyone,' Jeff replied. 'If that's what she said, you can take it as cast-iron.'

'I don't doubt it. But then, where did this come from?' Ben dabbed at another of the sticky stains with his finger and held it up like a court exhibit.

'You think it could have been the cops?' Jeff asked, frowning.

Ben wiped his finger clean and shook his head. 'I can't believe that they'd be that sloppy.'

'Then maybe someone else used the car. Like one of the farm hands.'

'Even if they did,' Ben said, 'you think they'd risk leaving a mess like this, knowing Kip was liable to thrash them with his belt? Wouldn't they clean it up afterwards? You heard what your mum said, that this car was his pride and joy.'

'Then if nobody else used the vehicle, maybe Kip's got a secret habit nobody else knows about,' Jeff said.

Maybe more than one, Ben thought. Or maybe there was another explanation. He fell silent for a few moments, reflecting. The spilled booze and the tobacco debris weren't the only little mysteries that were puzzling him. His thoughts ran back to his encounter with Sammy Mudrooroo, and the strange things he'd said. The dots didn't want to join up, and they wouldn't until there were more of them. Working it out, piece by piece. Ben was on familiar ground with that process, but it perplexed him no less.

Jeff was a warrior, not a detective, and his patience for figuring out apparently insignificant clues was limited. 'I don't know what the answer is, mate,' he grumbled. 'But I do know that we won't be home until after dark if we don't get a bloody move on. You want me to drive?'

They didn't talk about it any more. After another long,

dusty trek it was late afternoon as they neared Hobart's Creek. For endless kilometres Jeff's phone had been out of range of any signal, but as they drew closer to the croc farm a message pinged into his inbox. It was a text from his mother, to say there had been some news.

It wasn't the result that any of them had been hoping for: Sergeant Wenzel had been in touch earlier in the day to report that the air search of a large area of empty wilderness surrounding the crash site had come back with no trace of Kip, either dead or alive.

Lynne had taken the update like a body blow. By the time Ben and Jeff returned to find her standing out on the veranda, she was well into her third or fourth stiff rum and coke. Her eyes were pink and her voice was hoarse, but true to form she was fighting like hell to stay positive. Jeff was worried about this latest stress bringing on another one of her dizzy spells, but she brushed off his concerns. 'They might not have found him yet, but at least they haven't found a body,' she kept repeating, with a determined set to her jaw. 'I'm going to believe in that. I'm still convinced my Kip is out there somewhere, making his way back to me.' She turned to Ben. 'The police have given this their best shot. It's up to us now, isn't it?'

Ben said nothing.

'Can you find him, Ben?' Her voice cracked as she spoke. Her eyes were filled with such pain that it hurt to look at them.

'I told you I'd find him, Lynne. One way or another, I give you my word that I will bring your husband back to you.'

Chapter 8

It was one thing to promise a grieving woman that he would bring her missing husband home. It was another thing to deliver on that promise.

Ben had operated in some of the wildest and most inhospitable places on Earth. But he'd never before felt so overwhelmed by the sheer mind-boggling vastness of the wide-open empty country around him. Welcome to Planet Outback. Needles in haystacks and drops in oceans seemed like the most paltry metaphors to describe the challenge of finding a single man in the midst of this seeming infinity. For all his expertise, he felt as overpowered by the odds as an astronomer charged with locating the tiniest asteroid travelling through the furthest reaches of outer space, out there on the fringes of some nameless galaxy a hundred billion light years in the distance. He resisted the nagging thought that maybe he shouldn't have come here; that it was a lost cause; that he'd lost his touch – but it wouldn't go away.

As the sun began to dip in the western sky, a blood red orb flattening itself egg-shaped into the gold and purple haze, he left the house and set off across the farm grounds. This time he had a particular purpose in mind. Following the directions of one of the hands, he found Sammy Mudrooroo's hut a few minutes' walk from the house, nestled on its own in an avenue of thick foliage near the western perimeter of the Hobart's Creek compound. Sammy's accommodation was a small, basic wooden cabin with a single window and a flue pipe chimney sticking up from the corrugated roof like the smokestack of Stephenson's Rocket. Ben hopped up the three weathered wooden steps to the front door, knocked, waited for a response, knocked again. When there was still no response he gently pushed against the door and found it unlocked.

He stepped inside. 'Anybody there? Sammy?'

The cabin consisted of just two rooms, a living space and a tiny bedroom, and so it didn't take more than a glance to tell that nobody was at home. The narrow bunk was stripped bare of any sheets, and gave the impression of not having been used for a while. The wood-fired cooking stove in the living area was clean and ash free. The shelves were empty; so was the simple plywood wardrobe. A fine sprinkling of the ubiquitous Northern Territory dust layered every horizontal surface, not a single imprint or finger mark anywhere to be seen. If Sammy Mudrooroo ever used the place at all, he didn't leave many traces behind.

Ben was disappointed at not finding him there, but not too surprised after what he'd been told about Sammy's tendency to come and go as he pleased. Partly because it felt wrong to snoop through a man's house without due cause, and partly because there was obviously nothing here to find, he didn't stay long. As he closed the door behind him he was still mulling over Sammy's enigmatic words to him the night before. *Go seek the silver serpent. Then you'll find out the truth.* And *follow Mick's trail, if you want to know the secret too.*

Sammy had his own way of expressing himself, all right. But what if his words had made more sense than they appeared to, at face value? What was the secret that Kip's uncle had apparently been holding onto?

Ben wondered if their meeting in the darkness had been just coincidence, or whether Sammy deliberately sought him out to talk to him. If so, then what, if any, was the underlying message he'd been trying to convey? The more Ben tried to work it out, the more baffling it all seemed.

He was heading slowly back in the general direction of the farmhouse when, from the other side of a stand of trees, the sounds of ferocious splashing and guttural roaring caught his ear. He followed the sound, brushed through some low-hanging branches and spotted the familiar figure of Terry Napier, this side of a five-foot steel mesh fence. Ben had been so deep in thought that he'd lost his bearings; he now realised that this was the very same spot close to the water's edge where last night's encounter with Sammy Mudrooroo had taken place.

Napier was standing with his back to Ben, too busy with what he was doing to notice he had company. He was wearing a thick plastic apron like a slaughterman's, and a pair of heavy gauntlets that came up to the elbow and made his hands look absurdly oversized. Close by was the open tailgate of an ATV, its load bed piled high with slabs and chunks of raw meat and chicken carcasses.

To the other side of the fence was an astonishing sight. Where the night before its surface had reflected the moonlight as smooth and clear as a mirror, now the water close to shore was worked up into a churning, boiling, thrashing turmoil of white foam and spray.

As Ben walked closer, he could see the reason why, and it was like nothing he'd ever seen before. The lake was alive with crocodiles. Dozens, scores, maybe even hundreds of them, too many to count as their great armoured tails lashed the water into white foam and their scissoring jaws surged up from the surface to vie greedily for the hunks of meat and poultry carcasses that Napier was grabbing with both gauntleted hands from the back of the ATV and lobbing in a high arc over the fence. The air was filled with the snapping crunch of teeth and the grunts and roars of the violent feeding frenzy.

Ben was just a few steps away when Napier turned and saw him approaching. 'All right, mate?' he called over the raucous din. His face was red and shiny with perspiration.

'Feeding time at the zoo?' Ben said.

'They're more settled this time of the evening, when it's cooled down a bit. Makes 'em easier to handle,' Napier said as he grabbed another pair of dead chickens by the feet and tossed one, then the other, over the fence where they were instantly engulfed in a couple of snaps. A swarming mass of crocodiles, some of them more than six metres long, had crawled up out of the water on their stumpy, clawed legs to gather at the foot of the fence. Ben could smell their rancid breath as their jaws opened wide, bristling with uneven conical teeth as big as pine cones. The damn things looked like dinosaurs, up close. The fearsome 'gators of the Louisiana bayou were harmless little newts by comparison. He wondered how many animal carcasses it must take to keep a thousand of the monster reptiles fed for a year. Enough to keep the local meat trade happy, that was for sure.

'Out for a bit of a wander, are you, mate?' Napier asked. There was an unpleasant undertone to his words, but Ben ignored it.

'Just trying to get my thoughts together. You heard the latest?'

Napier shrugged. 'Yeah, it's a shit deal, all right. Poor old Kip, eh? Still, nothing we can do. Just keep praying he'll be all right. In the meantime, got to keep the place running. Can't let this lot go hungry. You want to have a go?'

'That's all right, Terry. I think I'll stay back here out of the way, thanks.'

Napier gave a lopsided grin, showing teeth like those of the crocs. 'Smart man. It's a risky business. You get too close or throw too slow, you stand to lose more than just a finger or two. Like the poor sod at the croc farm down the coast who got his arm bit off at the elbow a couple of years back. These buggers might look slow and clumsy but they can move like greased bloody lightning when they want to. See that great big bastard over there?' He pointed with a thick leather-clad finger.

'I see him,' Ben said, gazing across a calmer stretch of water towards something that looked like a giant military amphibious vehicle lurking just beneath the surface, moving very slowly and implacably watching the shore with a yellow, slit-pupilled eye.

'Watch this.' Napier yanked a large chunk of meat from the flatbed. It looked to Ben like a hind quarter of mutton, but he was no butcher. Napier rocked back on his heels with a grunting backswing and launched the joint powerfully into the air. It sailed over the teeming, scaly mass of reptiles on the bank and splashed down with expert precision right in front of the enormous creature he'd pointed out.

A split second later, the surface of the water erupted in a violent blast like a depth charge exploding. A pair of monstrous jaws rose up out of the foam, clamped down on the prize with a snapping crunch like the sound of an iron mantrap and dragged it down into the murk, leaving nothing behind but a storm of bubbles. Ben had the impression that the living body of any human unfortunate enough to find themselves in the water would have disappeared just as quickly and completely, with no time even to scream for help.

'That's Flowerpot,' Napier said with a satisfied leer. 'Meanest croc that ever swam, seven and a half metres from nose to tail, if he's an inch. He's been here since Kip started up this place thirty years ago. They reckon he's well over twice that age, but don't be fooled. He'll still come straight at you over the top of this fence faster than you can say "whingeing Pom", if you don't watch yourself.'

'I'll be sure to make a note of it,' Ben said.

'You do that, mate.' Napier's leer was gone and there was that icy gleam in his eye that Ben had first noticed on the drive from the airstrip.

Ben maintained eye contact until Napier broke it first and looked away. Then he stepped closer to the fence and leaned nonchalantly with his back against it, as though the man-eating monsters the other side of the wire mesh didn't exist. He drew a Gauloise from his pack, took his time lighting it, blew a puff of smoke towards Napier and said, 'So tell me, Terry. You've known Kip for a good while. Fifteen years, correct?'

'That's right,' Napier replied, slightly thrown by the unexpected question. 'Like I told you.'

Ben nodded. There was a muted roar behind him and something butted against the fence, but he ignored it and casually flicked ash from his cigarette. 'Almost as long as I was in Special Forces.' He didn't normally reveal that part of his past to people, but he was willing to make an exception in Terry Napier's case.

Napier said nothing.

Ben said, 'In my experience, when you've worked closely alongside a bloke for that length of time you get to know him pretty well.'

'I reckon I know old Kip as well as anyone, yeah,' Napier answered suspiciously, astute enough to know there were more questions coming.

'Like his habits, his little ways,' Ben said. 'And any secrets he might have. The kinds of secrets he might confide in a close friend, but not tell his wife.'

Napier narrowed his eyes. 'You mean like a bit-on-the-side kind of secret? Because if that's what you're getting at, then I can tell you—'

'It's not,' Ben said. 'But what about those other little vices and weaknesses a man might not want his other half to know about? Like whether he enjoys a sneaky hit of the hard stuff now and then, when nobody's any the wiser?'

Napier said, 'Can't say I've ever seen him at the booze. Then again, who can say?'

'What about other habits, like tobacco?'

'Kip, a smoker?'

'There's other ways to indulge, or so I'm told.'

Napier looked about to say something, then shrugged and shook his head. 'Again, I can't say.'

'You don't sound too sure. Considering that Kip's well known to take a hard line against tobacco use on the farm, by all accounts.'

'Yeah, yeah, I suppose he does,' Napier said. Ben thought his response sounded a little hesitant, a little strained and unnatural, as though he knew perfectly well that Kip disliked those things, but was holding back from saying too much.

'What're you asking me all this for anyway, mate?' Napier demanded, plainly uncomfortable with the line of questioning. 'I've got a job to be getting on with.'

'Feeding crocs is your job, asking questions is mine,' Ben said. 'I have just a couple more, if you'll bear with me.'

'Go on then,' Napier said resentfully.

'What about his uncle? How well did you know him?'

'That nutty old fart? Wouldn't have wasted the time of day on him, mate. Everybody knows he wasn't the full quid.'

'Kip and he were very close, though. Lynne said he was quite cut up when the old man died.'

Napier gave another shrug. 'Yeah, reckon it hit him pretty hard. Then again, it's an ill wind, like the saying goes. He stood to do not too badly out of it.'

That piqued Ben's curiosity. 'How so? Money-wise? His uncle left him a packet?'

Napier shook his head. 'Nah, mate, I don't reckon the crazy bugger had two dollars left to rub together, by the end. Not after spending the last fifty years squandering everything generations of Malloys before him had built up.'

'Then what?'

Napier opened his mouth to reply, but then checked himself as if, again, he was afraid of saying the wrong thing. A change came over his expression, anxiety furrowing his brow. Ben found the change interesting. Thinking back to what Lynne had told him, he remembered her mention of the large acreage that Kip was set to inherit after his uncle's death. He said, 'Not money, but land. Is that how Kip stood to do well out of it, Terry?'

'I dunno much about it,' Napier said, glancing away. 'Old Kip's not a big talker.'

But you do know more than you're letting on, Ben thought. He sensed he was gaining traction here, and decided to press a little harder. His next question seemed strange, even to him, and it might be a long shot, but he asked it anyway.

'Did Kip ever say anything to you about a silver serpent?'

A long shot, maybe, but nonetheless it seemed to have a dramatic effect. Napier's body language stiffened noticeably and some of the colour drained from his cheeks. He looked at Ben with a frown and replied, 'A what?'

'You heard me. A silver serpent.'

To which Napier could have replied, 'What the hell's that supposed to mean?' As anyone would naturally tend to do, when confronted with such an odd question out of the blue. But instead his cheeks flushed redder than before, and he looked away again, no longer the cocksure tough guy out to intimidate the Pommie stranger, but a man apparently very eager for this conversation to end. 'Nah,' he said, speaking more softly now. 'Nah, he never said anything about that. Like I told you, Kip's not much of a talker.'

'I see,' Ben said, looking at him closely. 'It's just that you said you knew him as well as anyone. I thought maybe it might ring a bell, but I can see I was wrong.'

The crocs were beginning to lose interest now that their mealtime seemed to be over, and retreating back to the water. Just then, the crunch of approaching footsteps made Ben and Napier look around; it was Napier's assistant Finn Mulkey, walking towards them carrying a bucket and a shovel. Napier's uncomfortable expression slackened visibly with relief at the sight of his colleague, and his face slowly cracked into a grin. 'Here, Finn, gotta tell you what the Limey bloke said when he saw this lot' – waving at the departing crocs. 'Said, "I think I'll stay back here out of the way, thanks."'

Mulkey thought this was pretty amusing, too. 'S'matter, mate? Don't you want to get a little kiss from a crocodile?' He made a loud smacking sound.

'Anyway, mate,' Napier said, addressing Ben with renewed confidence, 'there's not a lot more I can tell you. I'd best be getting on with things.'

'Of course. Thanks for your help, Terry. I'm sorry I took up so much of your time.'

Ben walked away without a backward look at either Napier, Mulkey or their beloved reptiles, and returned straight to the house. By the time he got there, the half-formed plan of action in his mind had taken shape and his next move was clear to him.

Jeff was sitting with his mother at the kitchen table, over mugs of coffee. Lynne looked as if she'd been crying again. There was a box of tissues in front of her. She plucked one and quickly used it to wipe her eyes as Ben walked into the room. Jeff looked morose. He'd aged five years in the last two days.

'There you are,' Jeff said, brightening. 'Wondered where you'd got to.'

'Just figuring things out. Walking helps.'

'You look like you've got something on your mind,' Jeff said.

'I do.'

Ben sat at the table opposite them. 'Tell me again about Mad Mick's land,' he said to Lynne.

Her initial blank look quickly became one of puzzlement. 'Not much to tell. Kip said that once upon a time it was one of the biggest farms in the Territory. Maybe *the* biggest, with thousands of head of cattle. Mick seems to have spent a lot of his life working to return it to wilderness, and now it's basically worthless, except as grazing land. But even if Kip had ideas about restoring it to what it used to be, he's not a cattle farmer, and we've got no use for a huge big spread like that. Half a million acres is about the size of Nottinghamshire, my home county. And it's literally right out in the middle of nowhere. Two thousand square kilometres of empty bushland, full of snakes and spiders and precious little else.'

'Did Kip think about selling it?'

'That's what I told him he should do, but he wouldn't hear of it. Said it was too precious to let go of, and that's not what his uncle would have wanted. He was really adamant about that, but at the same time I could tell it was eating him up. He doesn't normally get stressed out about things, but this business with his uncle's land really got to him and he'd not been himself lately. Reserved, preoccupied, quite irritable sometimes when I tried to raise the subject. We didn't exactly argue. He just closed up and refused to discuss it any further. End of conversation. It wasn't like him at all. But then, I suppose grief can have a funny effect on people. He was really cut up about his uncle.'

Ben asked, 'Do you know where the land is?'

'I've never been. But I could show you where it is on a map. Takes about three, four hours to drive there. Why do you ask?'

'I'd like to go and take a look at it,' Ben said.

Chapter 9

Lynne Malloy said, 'I don't understand. Why the sudden interest in Mick's land? Is there something you're not telling me?'

Jeff was looking keenly at Ben. After all these years of close comradeship they were strongly attuned to each other's ways and Jeff could tell that his friend was onto something. 'Ben's bound to have his reasons for asking, Mum. Trust him.'

'I want to,' Lynne said helplessly. 'But frankly I don't see how this can help. Kip is out there somewhere in that wilderness. We need to be searching for him, not gallivanting off to some dead old man's disused cattle ranch. It's in a totally different direction from where Kip went.'

The raw agony coming from her was palpable. 'Lynne, there's no point covering the same ground the police have already covered,' Ben explained gently. 'If they couldn't find anything over that whole region using air surveillance, we have no realistic chance of getting luckier by ranging around on foot or by car. Most of the terrain will be inaccessible to a motor vehicle anyway. And there's no way to tell where

79

he could have gone after the Land Cruiser went off the road. We literally wouldn't know where to start.' He realised that those words sounded to her like an admission of total failure, and he hated having to say them.

Lynne cast a disbelieving look at Jeff, then back at Ben. 'So you're not even going to look for him,' she said in a flat tone. 'He's out there, maybe lost, maybe suffering, maybe desperately in need of help, and you're not even going to look for him.'

'We need to understand what happened here,' Ben said. 'I believe there's more to the story.'

'His car crashed. What more to it could there be?'

'I don't know enough yet to say what. But if my suspicions are right, we might be able to learn information that will give us a much better chance of finding him than just going off on a blind search.' He could see she wasn't buying it. 'Please, Lynne. I know this is very hard for you. I'm asking you to trust me.'

Jeff was visibly bursting to know what was in Ben's mind, but he would bite back his curiosity until they were alone and could speak more freely.

Lynne fell silent for a long moment. Then she made a hissing sigh and raised her arms in a gesture of resignation. 'All right. What choice do I have? I'm going to have to trust you. I just hope you're right.'

'So do I,' Ben might have replied to her, if he'd been completely honest. Instead he said, 'Show me the map.'

Lynne got up from the table and went over to a pine dresser whose shelves were crammed with books, manuals, catalogues and assorted household files. 'He's got a collection of them, covering the whole of the Northern Territory. Let's see . . .' she said, running her finger along the row. 'I think this is the one you need.' She fished out a folded ordnance survey map, brought it back over to the table and spread it out over the surface. The map was old and grubby around the edges, and it had been folded and unfolded so many times that the creases were worn thin. The map's scale was 1:50,000, like the ones Ben had used for advanced land navigation with the SAS. The scale meant that one centimetre on the map equated to five hundred metres on the ground. It was a quality item, full of topographical detail with mountains, valleys and the smallest road, down to a track. Lynne pointed at a faded X that someone had marked years ago with a felt pen. 'That's the position of Mick's place,' she said. 'Nearest town's a place called Kurrawarra, some distance to the east. He's been going to see his uncle since he was a kid, and he knows the way so well he doesn't need a map any more.'

'Good old Kip,' Jeff said, smiling. 'Last man on the planet who still has paper maps.'

Lynne smiled too, despite herself. 'He can't stand GPS, calls it a load of newfangled bullshit. He prides himself on being able to navigate the way our ancestors did, using a compass, the sun and the stars.'

'Same as we were taught in the military,' Jeff said.

'He's got a spare compass in the drawer here, if it's any use to you,' Lynne said, returning to the dresser and rummaging for it. She handed it to Ben. It was the proper deal, with a rotating bezel showing angles of degree and a declination scale to adjust for the difference between true north and magnetic north and a built-in ruler marked with orientation lines. It had been a while since Ben had done it the old-fashioned way, but laying the compass flat on the paper it didn't take him long to work out his bearing, in case the GPS signal out there in the bush proved to be less than reliable. If Mick's estate was the size of Nottinghamshire, about half a million acres or two thousand square kilometres, then it wouldn't do to lose their way. Overreliance on modern technology could be a dangerous mistake.

'Mind if we borrow this map?' Ben asked.

'Not like I've any use for it,' Lynne said.

'Now it's just a question of how we're going to get there,' Jeff said. 'I have to say I don't much fancy another ride in that Mitsubishi pizza oven Terry Napier fobbed us off with. My arse is still blistered from the seat.'

'You could take my little Honda,' Lynne offered. 'But I'm not sure it'd make the journey. I only ever use it for shopping trips to McLennan. That's the nearest small town, forty-odd kilometres away.'

'The roads are going to be pretty rough out there, Mum,' Jeff said. 'We don't want to mess up your nice car, any more than we want to get stranded.'

She reflected for a moment. 'Or else you could use Kip's truck.'

Ben and Jeff exchanged glances, both having the same worrying thought. Was the stress of the situation affecting her memory?

'Mum,' Jeff said gently, 'I hate to remind you, but Kip's truck is a basket case, remember? We brought it back from Minyerri. It's not going anywhere.'

Lynne shook her head. 'No, no, not the Land Cruiser. I was talking about the Mean Machine.'

Ben and Jeff looked at one another again. Jeff said, 'The Mean Machine?'

'That's what he calls it, anyway,' she replied. 'I call it his Tonka toy. He built it himself, years ago. Used to be his main runaround, before he decided he was getting too old for a young man's car and treated himself to something more modern and comfortable.'

'Too old? Christ, I wish I had half his energy,' said Jeff, who had seen Kip jump a stallion bareback over a tall fence and grapple a five-foot baby crocodile with his bare hands.

'He hasn't used the Mean Machine in a while, but as far as I know it's still serviceable. You boys would be more than welcome to borrow it.'

The light was beginning to fade as they stepped back outside, and the night chorus of birds and frogs had begun. Lynne led the boys around the back of the house through the falling dusk to a prefabricated metal outbuilding that Ben had previously assumed must be a workshop or equipment store. It looked something like the hangar in which Jeff kept his Cessna back home, with no windows and a roller shutter door. Lynne pressed a button and the door clattered up. She flipped on a light switch and the dark interior of the building was lit bright by overhead neons. Around the metal walls, shelving units were heavy with spare auto parts, tool boxes and all the toys of the enthusiastic home mechanic, everything neatly organised and immaculate. The centre space was dominated by a hulking shape covered in a tarpaulin.

'There it is,' Lynne said, pointing. 'Kip's other pride and joy.'

Jeff stepped up to it, grabbed a corner of the tarp and pulled it away. 'Wow,' he breathed.

The Mean Machine was probably the most purposeful, rugged and spartan off-roader that Ben had seen since he'd last ridden in an SAS desert assault vehicle, back in the day. Its dull matt-black bodywork, once belonging to a Land Rover but heavily modified, stood tall enough on its massive knobbly tyres to ford a medium-sized river, with an exhaust snorkel that would let it drive in all but the deepest water. Massive bull bars and underbody bash plates and bristling light bars ensured that the monster could scramble over the most punishing, rocky terrain, ram its way through the densest bush or illuminate the darkest wilderness like daylight. That, with the spare wheels and jerrycans strapped to the back, would enable it to range over a vast area.

Ben clambered up inside the cab, encased within the solid steel roll cage, and settled into the rally-style bucket seat with its three-point harness. Everything was stripped to the most utilitarian basics, while Kip had crammed the interior with anything that could conceivably be needed out there in the wilds. There was a long-range radio fixed to the dash, a collection of camping and survival gear stashed in the back, first-aid kit, a fire extinguisher; and behind the front seats was a steel rack on which rested a scoped hunting rifle and a well-used Remington pump-action shotgun.

The key was in the ignition. Ben gave it a twist, and the inside of the garage instantly filled with the throaty rumble of the Mean Machine's V8 turbo-diesel power plant. A volt meter on the dash showed a good battery charge and the fuel gauge was reading full.

'Seems to work,' he said.

'Is it okay?' Lynne asked anxiously, standing at a distance with her arms folded.

'Oh, I think this'll do the job just fine,' Jeff replied.

'Then it's all yours,' she said. 'I can only pray it helps us to get Kip back. Because if I've lost him for ever, I don't think I can go on.'

'We'll be out of here before dawn,' Ben said.

Chapter 10

They set off as the very first glimmers of the rising sun were beginning to bleed through the lower edges of darkness. Ben nestled deep into the body-hugging driver's seat and pushed hard along the empty roads with the entire battery of lights flooding the way ahead with strong white brilliance. The Mean Machine wasn't just as rugged as a tank; it surged ahead like a spirited horse at the slightest touch of the accelerator, reeling in the horizon with startling performance as they munched up the miles southwards towards Mad Mick's land.

'So tell me what's on your mind, buddy,' Jeff said, now they were able to speak in complete privacy away from the house. Though they had to do so in raised voices to be heard over the noise of the engine.

'Remember I told you I'd run into Sammy Mudrooroo?'

'I remember. He said some weird stuff to you. Some bollocks about a silver snake?'

'I'm not sure it was bollocks,' Ben said. 'It sounded like it meant something.' He repeated what Sammy had told him. 'Look for the silver serpent. Then you'll find what you're looking for. I'm paraphrasing, but that was the essence of it.'

'All right,' Jeff said. 'Does sounds like it means something. What, though?'

'That's what I can't figure out,' Ben said. 'After what your mum told us about what happened to Mick, I thought maybe the silver serpent was some reference to the snake that killed him. But that doesn't make sense.'

'You're damn right it doesn't.' Jeff sighed. 'I don't know, mate. Silver serpent? I mean, give me a break. Silver serpent,' he repeated in a gruff, disparaging tone. 'Kip's disappeared and all this guy wants to talk about is a sodding reptile.'

'I wouldn't take it literally,' Ben said. 'I don't think he was talking about an actual snake. I think it has some other meaning. As if he was trying to give me a clue to follow. But without being too specific or revealing too much.'

'Still sounds like a load of mystical mumbo-jumbo to me. Are you sure this Sammy guy wasn't pissed, or tripping on something?'

'Now you're beginning to sound like Terry Napier.'

'Just saying. Got to be realistic, Ben. You know as well as I do, they've got big problems with drugs and alcohol in poor communities.'

'No,' Ben said. 'The man sounded perfectly sober and lucid to me. He knew what he was saying. Let's not get hung up on the stuff that sounds weird or crazy. Why would Sammy think that looking for a silver serpent would give us a lead on what we're looking for? Namely, help us find Kip?'

Jeff spread his hands. 'You tell me.'

'I know it sounds strange,' Ben admitted. 'But the more I think about it, the more I'm sure that Sammy had a deliberate reason for telling me these things. He's well aware of the reason why you and I are here in Australia. And I think he wants to help.'

'Help by talking in riddles?'

'There's more,' Ben said. 'Sammy talked about a secret.'

'What kind of secret?' Jeff asked, pulling a face.

'A secret that Mick knew. And which we could learn too, if we followed Mick's trail.'

Jeff's expression was half lit by the greenish glow of the instrument panels, the worried frown he wore all the time these days etched deeper than ever across his brow. 'Ah. I get it now. So that's the reason why we're heading off to the uncle's place? To follow his trail?'

'Perhaps there's something there for us to find.'

'Perhaps,' Jeff said. 'Then again, perhaps not. Meanwhile Mum's going slowly nuts back home. And here we are, travelling all this way south and leaving her totally alone there, based on the say-so of some complete stranger we don't even know if we can trust.'

In all the years they'd been friends, all they'd been through together, even during moments of life-threatening crisis, there had very rarely been any disagreement between them. But this time felt different. Jeff was so personally drawn into this situation that he was becoming edgy and defensive. Ben could feel his mounting resistance, hear it in his tone of voice, and sensed that Jeff was privately angry with him for leading them on what he considered to be a wild goose chase. Jeff might like to joke around at times, but he was a very strong-willed man. If he snapped, it wouldn't be pretty.

They drove on in silence for a while. They were right out in the bush now, the deserted road snaking ahead of them like a ribbon, the occasional crooked tree flashing by. A small troop of kangaroos appeared from the bushes ahead and bounded across the road in their path, their eyes glowing bright in the glare of the Mean Machine's dazzling lights. Ben touched the brake to avoid them, and sped on.

'There's something else Sammy told me, too,' he said, breaking the silence at last. He'd been debating for the last few minutes whether to mention it at all, until he knew more. 'And I have to say I don't understand this either, not yet.'

'Why am I not surprised?'

'He talked about something that needed protecting,' Ben said.

'What?'

'He didn't say what. The secret, maybe. But also more than that. He seemed to be referring to an actual thing, like an object or a place. Something that someone wants but mustn't get.'

'More fucking riddles,' Jeff grunted. 'If this Sammy guy knows something, why doesn't he just come right out and say it? I'll tell you why. Because he knows sweet eff-all. None of this makes the least bit of sense. It's all bollocks.'

'But right now it's all we have, Jeff. If the rest comes clear later, so much the better. And then we might find out where Kip went.' Ben paused. He was about to go out on a limb here. He added, 'Or where he was taken.'

Jeff twisted around in his seat to stare at him. 'Taken? How'd you mean, taken?'

'You wanted to know what's on my mind,' Ben replied. 'There it is. I don't like it, and I wasn't going to mention it before. But I can't see it any other way.'

'He had a car crash—' Jeff protested.

'I'm not saying his car didn't crash. I'm just saying I don't believe he was in it when it happened. I think someone else was involved. Someone who hasn't been careful enough to hide their tracks.'

'You're basing this theory on a few spots of baccy juice?'

'Kip's pretty damned fastidious about his vehicles,' Ben said. 'The way he's maintained this one we're driving in perfect condition even when he's stopped using it only proves that more. If it had belonged to almost anyone else we'd have found it with a half-dead battery, soft tyres and barely any fuel in the tank, with a family of mice nesting in the engine compartment. Look at the inside of his garage, the way he has all his tools arranged. That says a lot about who he is. Even if he didn't have a specific aversion to tobacco, there's no way a guy like that would leave the cab of his expensive Land Cruiser looking like a spittoon.'

'Okay,' Jeff said. 'I'm listening.'

'What that tells me is that he wasn't the last person who drove it. And my guess would be that that person didn't drive it any short distance. It takes time to chew a quid of tobacco up into tiny pieces. I think whoever was at the wheel drove for quite a few miles to the crash site. So who was this person? A friend of Kip's? Why would Kip let him make such a mess? He wouldn't. That's why I think the tobacco-chewing guy was alone in the car. Or at any rate, Kip wasn't there. The question is, why?'

Jeff said nothing.

'Then there's the matter of the Bundaberg rum,' Ben went on. 'Now, one could suppose that maybe the tobacco-chewing guy was also knocking back the booze as he drove, sitting there with the bottle between his knees the way Sergeant Wenzel described Kip doing. Maybe he got so drunk, he lost control and that's why the vehicle crashed. But what if there's another explanation? If you wanted to set things up to look like a simple car accident, splashing a load of booze around the inside and leaving the bottle there for the police to find would be the perfect cover-up, making it look like the driver was drunk. That's the conclusion the cops would jump to instantly, and they did. Except it doesn't reckon on the fact that Kip religiously avoids touching spirits.'

'All right,' Jeff said. 'So you're saying this was a setup?'

'I'm saying it may very well have been,' Ben replied. 'It's the only way any of this makes sense to me. It explains why there's no trace of Kip in the area of the crash site, even after an air search. Because he was either taken somewhere else, or he was never there at all.'

'But set up by who?'

'Perhaps by the person who's after the thing that needs protecting,' Ben said. 'Or most likely more than one person, because it would take a team of people to pull something like that off. Someone had to be taking care of Kip, if he was no longer in the car at that point. That implies a second vehicle, which you'd also need to get the tobacco-chewing guy away from the scene of the crash. So you're looking at three people, at least. One to drive the Land Cruiser, one to drive the follow-up vehicle, one to guard the prisoner. Three's probably also the minimum number of guys needed to intercept and overpower a man like Kip in the first place. It could be more. Could be there were four or five of them, as an extra caution.'

'Assuming any of this is right.'

'Yes.'

'So let's say it is,' Jeff said. 'They get to the crash site, they spill the booze all over the inside of the Land Cruiser to make it appear like Kip had been drinking at the wheel, and then they deliberately smash it into the rocks?'

'Or just roll it off the road with nobody inside, and let gravity do the rest.'

'And somehow this Sammy Mudrooroo guy has the inside track on all this?'

'Maybe he does,' Ben said. 'Maybe he knows what's behind the whole thing. Maybe Kip knew it too, and that's why he'd been eaten up with stress recently, more than just the grief over losing his uncle. Maybe that's why he refused to tell your mother what was on his mind. Maybe that's why he lied about where he was going that day. Which is one thing we do know reasonably for sure, because someone there would likely have seen him.'

'This is all adding up to a lot of maybes, Ben,' Jeff said dubiously.

'That's what I'm hoping this trip to Mad Mick's place will help to clear up.'

'And if it doesn't? What then?'

'Plan B?' Ben said. 'Keep looking for Sammy Mudrooroo, wherever he's disappeared to. I'd also want to talk to Terry Napier. Which I intend to do anyway, when I can get him alone for another private chat.'

'Napier? Why?'

'Because I think he knows something about all this too,' Ben replied. 'He got all evasive when I quizzed him about a few things last night. One minute telling me he knew Kip better than anyone, then the next acting as though he barely knew him at all. It was as if he was trying to fit into the narrative that someone else made up for him. He's afraid of something. Or someone. Then when I mentioned the silver serpent, he became even more spooked and defensive. I was about to press him for more, but then Finn Mulkey turned up.'

After these last revelations Jeff was suddenly looking a little less dubious, but even more thoroughly baffled. 'So what's going on?'

'If I'm wrong,' Ben said, 'then I have no idea.'

'But if you're right?'

'If I'm right, then what's going on is that someone has made a big, big mistake.'

Chapter 11

Three hours after setting off from Hobart's Creek and true to Ben's map navigation, they found the narrow, twisting and almost imperceptible track that eventually led through a pair of weathered gateposts to Mad Mick's homestead. The house looked like what it was: the former abode of an eccentric old man fallen on hard times and grown too aged or despondent to bother with maintenance, now sadly empty and forlorn. Rust patches spotted its tin roof and the woodwork was warped and peeling. The disused outbuildings clustered around the edges of the beaten-earth yard only added to the general atmosphere of desolation.

Ben and Jeff stepped down from the Mean Machine and gazed around them. The sun was already well up in the sky, bringing the promise of another uncomfortably hot day. The air was stifling, and there was nothing refreshing about the stiff breeze that gusted eddies of loose, dusty soil about the weed-strewn ground like little tornadoes, and sent loose bales of tumbleweed rolling across the yard. The wind was already erasing the Mean Machine's knobbly tyre tracks. If anyone else had been here recently, there wouldn't have been much to show for it.

'So here we are,' Jeff said. 'What are we looking for?'

'I don't know yet,' Ben replied. 'But I'll know it when I see it.'

As a hunter of missing people, he had often found himself in similar situations if not quite such surroundings, searching for random clues with no prior idea of what form they might take. He'd learned to detach his thinking mind in order to let impressions wash over him, taking in everything in a kind of wide-angle scan. Standing by the vehicle he slowly turned a circle, casting his eye over the buildings, the house. Nothing was jumping out at him, but that wasn't cause for concern. Not yet. He was acutely conscious of Jeff's impatient eye watching him, and the risk he'd taken by bringing them out here, so far from the primary search zone. But the little voice in his mind telling him he was right wouldn't go away, even if Jeff didn't share his optimism.

Ben started walking towards the house. He hadn't gone two steps before something on the ground, lying close to the front wheel of the Mean Machine, sparkled in the sunlight and caught his eye. Out of curiosity he squatted down to examine it, and saw it was a fragment of thick glass, vehicle headlight glass. It hadn't come from any of their lamps, which were all intact. He turned it pensively over in his fingers and then dropped it back down into the dirt.

Straightening up again, he suddenly found himself looking directly at more broken glass, this time in the form of a smashed windowpane of the house. Nothing unusual about a half-derelict house having broken windows, but there was something distinctive about this one.

'Jeff, have a look at this.'

They walked over to inspect it. Both men had seen a lot of broken windows in their time, in various war zones around the world, enough to recognise that this one hadn't been smashed in the usual domestic kind of accident, a falling ladder or such. The clean, neat hole punched right through the centre of the pane had been made by a high-velocity bullet of medium calibre. Its passing through had created a circular web of fissures with four main cracks radiating from the centre in an X shape. One quadrant of the X, the shape of a pie slice, had fallen inside the house. Ben peered through the quarter-circular hole and saw that the room within was a small, dingy bathroom.

'Looks like a 5.56 NATO round,' Jeff said, examining the bullet hole. 'Maybe a .243 Winchester. Probably more common in these parts.'

Ben walked over to the front door and found it open. The empty house felt deathly still inside. The only sound was the low buzz of flies. The furnishings were bare and basic, and covered in dust. Orientating himself towards the little bathroom with the broken window he made his way up a narrow, peeling passage past various closed rooms. The bathroom door opened with a creak and he stepped inside. The room smelled of stale water and mildew. The sink was old and discoloured, and some tiles had dropped off the walls over time and never been replaced. The cistern was one of those old-fashioned types mounted high above the toilet, with a pull-chain and a worn wooden handle. The bullet had come through the window at a slight upward angle, hit the cistern dead centre and split it in half, causing a large piece to fall away, covering the floor with fragments of white china along with the glass splinters, and flooding the place with water. A dark stain showed where it had been dripping until the supply tank dried up. Those fortunate enough to have access to water at all out in these remote parts would be on their own spring or rain butts.

Ben yanked away the last piece of cistern still attached to the wall, and found where the bullet had deflected under impact, gone through the plaster and embedded itself not too deeply in a piece of wooden wall batten. He used his small pocket knife to pry it out: a typical conical rifle projectile, full metal jacket, all deformed and crumpled. The splintered wood was still quite fresh.

He met Jeff in the house doorway and showed him the bullet. 'It's not been there long.'

'But does it mean anything?' Jeff said. 'Could just be local hooligans off on a jaunt with nothing better to do, having a bit of fun driving out here and shooting up the crazy guy's house. The way we used to break the jam jars on old Mrs Crawford's strawberry patch with our airguns, when we were nippers.'

'Maybe,' Ben said. 'Long way to drive for a bit of entertaining vandalism, though, don't you think?' Stepping from the front door he looked back at the window and did a rough estimate of the bullet's trajectory. The angle told him it could have been fired from across the yard, over by the outbuildings. He started walking in that direction. He was still just a couple of yards from the front door when he felt something underfoot, and looked down to see it was a spent shell casing. Another one was lying in the dirt just a few inches away.

He bent and picked them both up. Murmured, 'Hello.'

The cases were identical, shiny yellow brass, with very little tarnishing, not long since fired. He could identify their type even before he saw the .30-06 stamping on the case heads. Thirty-aught-six was a fine old rifle chambering, heavier and more powerful and a completely different kettle of fish from the round that had penetrated the bathroom window.

But ballistics aside, that meant that at least three shots had been fired here quite recently, involving two different weapons. The positioning of the .30-06 shooter suggested that he'd been firing away from the house, in the opposite direction of the other shooter.

Two men, firing at each other. That amounted to what was technically known in the trade as a gunfight.

Ben wanted to tell Jeff what he'd found, but by now Jeff had disappeared inside the house. Spurred by his curiosity, Ben continued towards the outbuildings, following the approximate trajectory of the shot that had taken out the bathroom window. His initial thought was that it might have come from the doorway of one of the buildings, but he was wrong; and the proof of that realisation was the discovery of a third cartridge case, which he found among the withered dusty weeds by the corner of the building. Like the first two, it was quite new and shiny and hadn't been here long enough to tarnish its gleaming brass. Unlike the first two, its head-stamping read .243 WIN. Win, short for Winchester.

Above where the cartridge case was lying, a fist-sized chunk of brickwork had been knocked out of the corner of the outbuilding wall at around chest height to a man. Ben found some stone fragments littered around the ground that matched in colour. They were still fresh and powdery. No doubt that they'd been dislodged by a shot from the heavy-hitting .30-06.

What had happened here? Ben leaned against the wall, lit a Gauloise and got to work picturing the scene.

The weapons were both pretty standard hunting rifles of the kind that a lot of people would own in rural Australia, just like the one on the Mean Machine's onboard gun rack. Most likely bolt-action; scoped or open-sighted, didn't matter. The shooters were fairly evenly matched in terms of firepower. Ben decided to call the .30-06 shooter Shooter One, and the .243 shooter Shooter Two. From the position of his ejected shell casing and the damaged masonry, it was clear that the latter had been shooting from behind the corner of the wall. Meanwhile his opponent, Shooter One, hadn't been firing from the cover of the house but had been standing out in the open near the front door. The angle made sense: a rushed snap shot from Shooter Two aimed towards the house could very easily have gone a little wide of its target and struck the bathroom window. There was no telling whether that had been the first shot of the exchange – but hypothetically, if it had been, then Shooter One might have returned fire, missing Shooter Two and nicking the outbuilding wall. Shooter Two would have ducked back behind the corner, working his bolt to chamber a second round, but he apparently hadn't fired it. Whereas Shooter

One had let off two shots, the other possibly aimed at a vehicle parked in the yard, smashing one of its headlights and thereby accounting for the piece of glass Ben had found.

After that brief exchange of gunfire, the confrontation seemed to have come to a halt – more a skirmish than a full-on gun battle. If Ben's reading of the signs was correct, it looked as though none of the bullets had hit anyone. But that in itself didn't mean this wasn't a serious fight, and one that could have ended badly for someone. What had been the outcome? What had it been over? Who was involved?

He was pondering those questions when he heard a yell from the house. He tossed away his cigarette and ran back over.

Chapter 12

Jeff was in Mad Mick's living room. Kip's uncle hadn't been big on comforts. There was a single sofa by one window, its chintzy covering worn thin and faded by the sunlight that filtered through the dusty pane. Opposite stood an ancient TV with an aerial fashioned out of a wire coat-hanger. A pine dresser was covered in junk; a stuffed and mounted wild boar's head surveyed the room with bared tusks.

But Jeff hadn't called him over for an appraisal of the old man's taste in home decor. What was immediately obvious to Ben from the doorway was that a struggle had taken place here: a chair was overturned, another was broken, and the rug had been all rumpled. A length of slim twine rope lay twisted like a dead snake near the overturned chair.

Jeff was standing in the middle of the room, holding something that he'd found and examining it closely with a deeply perplexed expression. The object he was looking at was yellowish in colour, tapered and about four inches long. He was so fixated on it that he didn't glance over as Ben hurried into the room.

'What is it?'

101

'It was lying there on the floor,' Jeff said, pointing. He held the object out for Ben to see. It was a great curved conical tooth, set in silver with a loop, or bail, to hang it from as a necklace. There was only one kind of animal in Australia that such a monster tooth could have belonged to, and that was a large saltwater crocodile. A leather thong was attached to the silver mounting. The thong had been snapped and hung limp from Jeff's fingers.

'It's Kip's,' Jeff said.

'Are you sure?'

Jeff nodded, absolute certainty in his eyes. 'He told me the story of where it came from. This tooth belonged to the first croc he ever owned, three-legged Charlie, who sired a hundred more little baby crocs and helped Kip build up his stock. He calls it his good luck charm. Wears it around his neck all the time and never takes it off.'

'He didn't just take it off,' Ben said, holding up one end of the broken thong. 'It was ripped from his neck.'

Jeff sighed and looked utterly drained. 'Shit, Ben, I think you must have been right. I'm sorry I doubted it.'

'You've nothing to be sorry for,' Ben replied. As he spoke, the pieces of the puzzle were beginning to slot together in his mind. So now they knew that Kip had been here. The fact that he'd obviously met with trouble suggested that whatever had happened at Mad Mick's homestead had happened on the day he'd disappeared. His hypothesis of the set-up car crash suddenly seemed much closer to the mark.

'Yes I do,' Jeff muttered, shaking his head in a disgusted rage.

'I found something too.' Ben showed him the spent brass. 'Two different weapons, firing in opposite directions. I don't think we're dealing with a bunch of local vandals shooting the place up for fun.'

Jeff stared at the three slim, shiny bottle-shaped cartridge cases on Ben's outstretched palm. 'Then that tells us all we need to know. The bastards shot him.'

'Maybe,' Ben said. 'But if he's been shot, I don't think it happened here.' He quickly laid out how he saw things developing. 'I think that for whatever reason Kip chose to come to his uncle's place without telling anyone, he was inside the house when they turned up. How many of them, that's anyone's guess, but I'm going to stick with my estimate of at least four or five men, for the sake of argument. They might have known in advance they'd find him here, or they might not, but either way they'd come armed. They parked their vehicle out there in the yard, close to where we've parked ours. Kip's Land Cruiser was probably there too.'

'I'm with you so far,' Jeff said. 'Go on.'

'Kip spots them from the window as they roll up, and he can see they mean business. Did he know who they were? Possibly. Had he come here expecting trouble himself? Who knows? If he was, then he could have been carrying his own rifle, the .30-06.'

'He's got a few rifles. I don't know if any of them is an aught-six.'

'Or else, maybe the weapon was one that Mad Mick had stashed in the house. I'm guessing Kip would have known where to find it. So with the bad guys getting out of their truck outside and him inside, he's trapped. He can't get

103

to his vehicle, isn't about to make a run for it, doesn't have a lot of options. One option might have been to hunker down inside the house, but he doesn't do that. Instead he walks right out the front door with the rifle in his hand to confront them.'

'Kip being Kip,' Jeff muttered. 'Lying low isn't his style.'

'Which these guys presumably knew about him already,' Ben said. 'Seeing his truck parked outside the house, the instant they get out of theirs they're already splitting up and taking cover. At least one of them is probably crouched behind their vehicle. Meanwhile at least one other runs over to those outbuildings to find a safe vantage point in case the shooting starts.'

'Filthy cowards.'

'As for exactly how it went down after that, your guess is as good as mine,' Ben said. 'I'm sure Kip had words with them. Warning them to get off his property, or else. But after that first shot was fired, the time for talking was over. Kip fired twice. Once towards the buildings, once at the truck. Both shots were misses.'

'He's a pretty damn good shot.'

'And this was a close-range fight. Which tells me he was shooting to scare them off, not to kill.'

Jeff nodded. 'Then what?'

'Then something happened to finish the fight quickly.' Ben pointed at the crocodile tooth, then at the overturned chair and the other signs of a struggle having taken place in the living room. 'What began outside then moved indoors. My guess is that before the confrontation happened, one of them might have managed to sneak around the back of the house unnoticed. While Kip's attention was focused on the men out front, this one could have crept up on him from behind and overpowered him, whacked him on the back of the head or pulled a gun on him. Then they dragged him back inside the house. They brought him here into this room. He didn't come quietly. Which again points at several men, because I don't imagine Kip would be too easy to handle, even if he was hurt.'

'You got that right,' Jeff said, nodding. 'He's been in some wild bar fights in his time, so the story goes. I'd say we're looking at a crew of more like five men than four. Maybe even half a dozen.'

'That's how the leather thong around his neck got broken. It would take a lot of force to snap it clean away like that. One of them was probably grappling him by the collar while another was trying to pin his arms behind his back. He pulled back sharply, or maybe kicked out at the guy in front, and the necklace came away in the guy's hand. But then they managed to get the better of him, forced him into that chair and tied him with that piece of rope.'

Ben picked up the length of cord and jerked it tight between his fists. It was slender, but strong. The kind of twine that a handy, rural kind of guy would maybe use for roping cattle. 'Once he was tied, they must've roughed him up. Maybe they roughed him up quite a bit. But they didn't kill him. I'm sure of that.'

'Who *are* these scumbags?' Jeff said, flushed with rage. 'What did they want with him?'

'I think they were searching for something,' Ben said. 'Something in particular that's somehow connected to this place, or to Mad Mick himself. Maybe that's what brought them all together here. Maybe Kip was looking for it, too.'

'You think this ties up with what Sammy Mudrooroo told you?'

'Seems that way to me.'

'Then it wasn't riddles and mumbo-jumbo after all,' Jeff said. 'This silver serpent thing. You got any ideas about that yet?'

'None,' Ben replied. 'Except that these people are obviously highly motivated to get their hands on it. But whatever facts or information they were trying to press out of him, I don't think he gave them much. Otherwise, I've a feeling he might have still been inside that Land Cruiser when the police found it. Looks to me as though they gave up trying to beat it out of him, bundled him in their truck and took him off somewhere else for further interrogation. Which also tends to suggest that there's a boss man involved, the brains behind the operation, someone the hired heavies defer to. That's how these things generally work. Meanwhile, to cover their tracks they drove his Land Cruiser miles away from here to the crash site and disposed of it, leaving their trail of clues in such a way as to mislead whoever found it.'

'Meaning that they still have him,' Jeff said. 'Meaning he's still alive.'

'And meaning that whatever he knows that they don't know, it makes him too valuable for them to kill, for the moment at least. With any luck, that buys us some time. As long as Kip holds out.'

'He'll hold out,' Jeff said. A look of fierce purposefulness was growing in his eyes, replacing the anger and disgust from before. It was a look Ben had seen in him many times. Jeff's battle face. And when Jeff was wearing that face, the bad guys needed to start watching their backs.

'As for who they are,' Ben said, 'it's time we went and talked to some people.'

Chapter 13

'I'm going to have to tell Mum about this,' Jeff said reluctantly as they drove back towards home. 'She needs to know. I'm not looking forward to it, though. She's going to freak out completely.'

'You want me to talk to her?' Ben offered.

'She's my mother. It needs to come from me.'

Ben asked, 'What about Wenzel? This is a kidnap case now.'

'Since when did you like to get the cops involved in your cases?

'Since never,' Ben said. 'If it was up to me, the last thing I'd want is the police barging around a delicate situation. But it's your family, Jeff. Your call.'

'I'm of the opinion that we should leave Wenzel out of this,' Jeff said.

'And Lynne? What will she want to do?'

Jeff pulled a dark smile. 'I don't think she holds our dear Sergeant Wenzel in any higher esteem than we do.'

On their return to Hobart's Creek, they found Lynne waiting for them on the veranda, where she'd been pacing up and down looking distressed. From her expression, it was clear that there'd been some new development – and not a good one.

'Mum? What's up?' Jeff asked, running up the veranda steps. Following close behind him, Ben was thinking that perhaps Kip's body had been found after all, and that all his theories had just gone up in smoke.

But what she told them instead was completely unexpected.

'There's been a break-in,' Lynne said, pointing behind her towards the house.

The idea of a burglary happening out here in such a remote environment seemed so unlikely it was almost unthinkable. Jeff exclaimed, 'What? When?'

'This morning, not long after dawn. I'd woken up while it was still dark and heard you two going off, and I couldn't get back to sleep again afterwards so I decided to go for a long walk with the dogs to clear my head. I was gone an hour, maybe an hour and a half. When I came back here, someone had been inside. It's a real mess. Drawers pulled out, shelves emptied. They went through the whole house.'

'The dogs didn't sound the alarm?'

'No, and we don't even know how they got in. I've had the boys going round the whole perimeter looking for a break in the fence, and there's nothing.'

'What did they take?' Jeff asked.

She shook her head, frowning. 'That's the strangest thing. I can't see what's been taken, if anything. There's a cash box on top of the kitchen dresser with over a thousand dollars in it, not even locked. They didn't touch it. And my little jewel case in the bedroom with my grandmother's antique rings and a valuable string of pearls – nothing's missing from that either. Whoever broke in, it wasn't a thief. It looks as if they were ransacking the house in search of something.'

Ben and Jeff exchanged worried glances, both thinking the same thing. If someone was motivated enough to risk breaking into a well-guarded and secure property, and if whatever they were looking for was connected with the mysteries surrounding Kip's disappearance, then it most likely meant that the people holding him hadn't yet managed to find out what he knew and were resorting to more desperate means. When crooks got desperate, it was bad news for the innocent. It meant the countdown to when they might decide to cut their losses was ticking away fast. If it hadn't already happened.

Ben asked gently, 'Lynne, have you any idea what they could have been looking for?'

'No idea at all,' she replied. 'I'm just shocked. First Kip, now this. I feel like I'm going out of my mind. I keep thinking it's all some kind of nightmare I'm going to wake up from, and everything will be normal. But it won't, will it? Nothing will ever be normal again.'

'Did you call the police about this?' Jeff asked.

'The police,' she replied with a sour laugh. 'Fat lot of use they've been to us so far. What would even be the point?'

Jeff fell silent for a moment and looked uncomfortable. 'Mum, we need to talk.'

She looked suddenly flustered, as though the morning's drama had driven their visit to Mad Mick's homestead from her mind, and she was only now remembering it. 'What? What? Did you find something—?'

110

'We should talk inside.'

She shook her head. 'I'm not going back in there until that mess has been cleared up. Tell me here. It's bad news, isn't it? I can see it in your eyes.' She was steeling herself for the worst.

'It's not good,' Jeff said. 'But it could be worse, for what it's worth.'

'Tell me, for God's sake. Put me out of my misery.'

'We found this.' Jeff took out the crocodile tooth. Recognising it instantly, Lynne gasped and covered her mouth with her hands.

As gently as he could, Jeff laid it all out for her. Their theory of the staged car accident, and all the evidence stacked up to support it. Their theoretical reconstruction of the armed standoff at Mad Mick's homestead. Their belief that someone had taken Kip prisoner, and that the reason behind it had to do with something his uncle might have known, or possessed, or confided in his nephew, which – whatever it was – had been eating at Kip for some time, enough to compel him to revisit the farmstead that day without telling anyone where he was going.

By the time Jeff had finished telling her, his mother's cheeks had paled to the colour of chalk and she was so overwhelmed with confusion that she appeared numbed by it all.

'Two things we can be pretty sure of at this point,' Ben said. 'One, there's a very good chance that your husband is alive, and that it's in someone's interests to keep him that way, for the moment at least. Two, he's not out there some-where wandering alone and lost through the wilderness.

Which gives us a far better chance of finding him than we had before. This isn't all bad news, Lynne.'

'Who? Who would do this to him?' was all she could say at first, her voice a shaky whisper.

'We don't know,' Jeff replied. 'But you can be damn sure we're going to find out.'

'And why didn't he tell me, if he knew something was up? We have no secrets from each other.'

'I think he didn't want to worry you,' Jeff said. 'Whatever was bothering him, he wanted to fix it himself.' He paused, frowning, then took a breath and added, 'Mum, there's something else I haven't told you yet.'

Her look of consternation deepened. As though this situation could get any more troubling. Almost too afraid to ask, she said, 'What?'

'We think Terry Napier knows more than he's letting on.'

At those words, the change that came over Lynne was instant and dramatic. The agonised worry drained from her expression and her eyes sharpened like a field of spears. Ben could suddenly see where Jeff had inherited his battle face from, because now his mother was wearing it, too.

'Oh, he does, does he?' she said in a very different tone of voice from before. 'In that case I vote we go and talk to Terry Napier.'

Chapter 14

Lynne Malloy led the way down the veranda steps and off down the dusty track from the house. Before she'd been bowed and round-shouldered with strain, but now she marched as straight as a flagpole and there was a determined spring to her step as Ben and Jeff escorted her, one on each side, towards the working heart of the farm.

The first person they found there was a young guy Ben hadn't seen before, at work outside a tin shed where he was busily disinfecting and hosing down the plastic crates in which the raw crocodile feed was stored. The apron he was wearing was spattered with pink bloodstains and he was so intently focused on his duty that he didn't notice them approaching. Turning suddenly, still clutching the spouting hosepipe, he smiled and said, 'Oh, g'day, Mrs Malloy.'

'Carl, I'm looking for Terry. Do you know where he is?'

The terseness in her tone and the hard look in her eye made the smile drop from his face. He hesitated, then turned off the hose tap. Ben and Jeff were watching him like two hawks ready to swoop down on a mouse.

Carl pondered carefully for a moment, chewing his lip,

then shook his head. 'He was around early this morning,' he replied. 'Haven't seen him since. But wait, now I come to think of it, I remember him asking Finn Mulkey to take over the feeding later 'cause he was going off somewhere.'

'Going off somewhere,' Lynne repeated with a raised eyebrow. 'Did he say where to?'

'Can't say that he did, Mrs Malloy. At least, I don't remember. Think he might've needed to go home for something. He was talking to Sue on the phone. That's Terry's wife.'

'I know who Sue is,' Lynne said testily. 'And did he happen to mention when he'd be back?'

'Can't tell you that either. Sorry.' Carl shook his head ruefully.

'All right then. Thanks, Carl. Carry on.'

'If Napier was around earlier this morning,' Jeff said as they left Carl to his work, 'maybe it was him who ransacked the house.'

'But why would he do that?' Lynne asked. 'It makes no sense.'

'Maybe it will make sense,' Ben said. 'When we talk to him. But first we need to find him. I thought all the hands lived here on the farm?'

'Some do stay here full-time,' Lynne said. 'But Terry and Sue have a house in a small town called McCarthy, not too far away from here, and he goes back there two or three times a week. I don't think they get on well.'

Taking out a mobile, Lynne walked them a hundred yards to a spot where she could get some reception, and then tried calling Napier on his own mobile. She seemed unsurprised when there was no reply. 'He never has his phone switched

114

on,' she explained. 'Kip's always having to talk to him about it. What's the point of having these bloody things if you keep them turned off all the time? I'll try the house number.'

Again, no reply. Lynne sighed. 'I'll text him.' She spent a few moments prodding keys. 'There you go. That should do it.'

'What've you said?' Jeff asked.

'That I've been trying to get hold of him because we've got a problem with the backup generator in the incubator room, and I need to know what we're going to do about it. That way he won't get suspicious.'

'Smart thinking, Mum,' Jeff said, smiling.

'Now all we can do is hope he gets the message and wait for him to call back,' she said.

'Alternatively, we could go and pay him a surprise visit at home,' Jeff suggested. 'Might be a quicker solution.'

'What if he's not there? Carl wasn't all that sure where he'd gone.'

'Then we'll wait for him there,' Jeff said. 'Or talk to his wife. She'll know where he is.'

Lynne nodded. 'McCarthy's about sixty-five kilometres, but it's a good road to get there. We could go in my car. I could do with a change of scenery anyway, to be honest. Before I go completely stir crazy hanging around this place waiting for something to happen.'

'Sounds like a plan, then,' Jeff said.

Ben said, 'I'll come too,' but Jeff shook his head. 'No, mate, I've got this. I think I can handle Terry Napier on my own. When we find him I'll bring him back here and we can find out what he knows. We shouldn't be more than a few hours. Meantime, how about you go and see if you can dig up Sammy Mudrooroo?'

Ben hesitated to reply. Jeff was right to suggest that by splitting their resources they were doubling their efficacy. So why did the idea make Ben feel uneasy? After a moment's internal debate he held back his objection, deciding that to insist on coming along would seem unreasonable, even untrusting. He turned to Lynne and said, 'That's something I meant to ask you about. It seems that Sammy's cabin on the farm doesn't get used much. Do you know where else he goes? Does he have family somewhere locally?'

'I couldn't really tell you,' she replied. 'Like I said before, Sammy's pretty much a law unto himself. I recall Kip telling me that he had some people at Ngukurr.' She pronounced it like 'Nooker'. 'It's a little Indigenous township, some way inland. But I think that's going back a few years. I'm not sure they'd still be there.'

It didn't seem too promising, but Ben nodded. 'All right. You go and get Napier. I'll see if I can find Sammy.'

They organised themselves, intent on wasting no time. Jeff rolled Lynne's little bright yellow hatchback out of its lean-to garage, checked the oil and tyres, loaded bottles of water in the back, and then they were off with Jeff at the wheel. Ben couldn't help but notice the surreptitious way that Lynne checked and re-checked her handbag before leaving to make sure she had her pills.

When they were gone, he took a stroll back to Sammy Mudrooroo's cabin on the off-chance that he might have slipped back there unnoticed – but he wasn't surprised to find the place just as empty and unused as before.

Kip's ordnance survey map was in the cubby box between the seats of the Mean Machine. Ben spread it out over the dusty bonnet and soon found the location of Ngukurr. It was quite some way off, but he expected Jeff and Lynne to be gone for a few hours, and he decided that he had time to make the trip.

'Right then,' he said out loud. He fired up a Gauloise, clambered into the Mean Machine's cab, and hit the road with a roar and a cloud of dust.

Chapter 15

The rusty corrugated steel barn was the sole remaining building of the two-hundred-acre sheep farm left standing, and nobody had lived here since the W.F. Cooper & Co. Development Corporation had muscled out its elderly owners in return for a pittance fifteen years ago. Old man Brundle had bitterly regretted taking their money and died within a year of leaving the farm he'd worked for over forty years. His heartbroken wife Aggie was now dementia-stricken and slowly rotting away in a miserable geriatric home. The property development project itself had come to nothing in the end: just another failed investment that the company shrugged off and forgot about, almost as quickly as they'd forgotten the poor unfortunate Brundles. But for the company boss, a man named Wiley Franklin Cooper, owning such remote and desolate tracts of land, even if they didn't pay off financially, had other practical benefits.

A soft breeze was blowing in from the east, whipping up eddies of loose dusty soil and making a loose corrugated sheet on the barn roof creak and rattle. Nothing else was stirring. But change was in the air. Rain was coming, and soon. The parched landscape thirsted for it. The two men who sat in folding chairs under the shade of the tatty awning of their camper van, parked a distance from the solitary barn, could feel it, too. They'd both lived in these parts all their lives and were all too intimately acquainted with the cycles of nature.

The men were called Dave Dorkins and Pete Grubb, and they both worked for Wiley Cooper, an employer they respected and feared in equal measure. Each was dressed in the same rough outdoor clothing they wore every day, each with a well-used leather hat to keep off the sun and rain. Dorkins was surrounded by a cloud of buzzing flies, not unusual for him. He was generally known as Dungfly Dave, because for some unknown reason he seemed to attract them wherever he went.

The pair were in the unhappy position of having been posted on permanent duty out here at the old Brundle place, forced to share the stinking camper van together, painfully far from the nearest pub, with no TV and very little to occupy their limited imaginations. At this moment they were enjoying a cigarette and a cup of coffee brewed on their camping stove, killing time before they got on with their allotted task for the morning.

'So anyhow,' Dorkins was saying, 'according to this doctor fella on the internet I was telling you about, if a bloke's got leprosy, it means he's actually immune from getting tuberculosis. I mean, he can't get it, no matter what. Some half-dead lunger can come right up to him, coughing and spluttering a load of germs all over the place, and he's as safe as houses.'

Grubb considered this amazing gem of knowledge and replied, 'Well, at least that's some consolation to the poor bugger with the leprosy. Got to be a silver lining to every cloud, mate. How unlucky would that be, otherwise?' He shook his head at the horror of it.

'So I'm wondering if that works the other way around too,' said Dorkins, casually swatting at a fly. 'Like, if some poor fella was to catch the old TB, at least he can rest easy knowing he can't ever get all fucked up with his dick turning black and falling off.'

'Let's hope so, anyway,' Grubb said, nodding and gazing down at his feet.

'Good to know, I s'pose. Makes you think, dunnit?'

Grubb yawned. 'That it does, mate. Funny old life.'

'Learn something new every day.'

They pondered these deep truths in solemn silence for a few minutes longer as they finished their cigarettes. Then Dorkins crushed out the end of his stub, ground it into the dirt with his boot heel and let out a long sigh. A new thought occurring to him, he jerked his thumb at the camper van and said, 'Hey, did you order those parts yet?'

The parts in question were much-needed rods and linkages for the vehicle's steering assembly, which was rusted to pieces and falling apart, so that the van often failed to steer straight and occasionally produced a heart-stopping moment by refusing to respond to the steering wheel at all. Looking after the mechanicals was Grubb's responsibility, one he tended to neglect like most things in life. 'I'll get around to it,' he replied casually. 'It's not that bad.'

'Rack off. It's a rolling bloody death trap, is what it is,'

Dorkins muttered. 'Anyhow, I s'pose we'd best get back to work, eh?'

'Yeah, reckon,' said Grubb. They heaved themselves up from their deck chairs and stepped inside the camper van to grab a few items: food, water, a plastic bucket. Carrying those, they trudged across to the barn. The tall, weather-beaten corrugated doors were secured by a rusty old chain and a shiny new padlock. Dorkins dug a ring with a pair of keys from his pocket, undid the lock and let the chain fall away, and they stepped inside the barn.

It was dark in here, just a few chinks of sunlight shining through gaps in the sheeting here and there, too high up to reach. The overall structure of the building was pretty solid. Not that it really mattered either way, because the prisoner was contained within a steel pen of his own and wasn't going anywhere.

Grubb sniffed and pulled a disgusted face as they walked up to the pen. 'Jesus Christ, Malloy,' he complained. 'Smells like something bloody died in here.' Mucking out the prisoner's slop bucket was the worst part of this job. Other parts, he quite enjoyed.

The prisoner made no sound, sitting very still on the makeshift wooden bunk inside his pen, and didn't acknowledge his jailers. He'd said nothing at all for three days, partly out of a refusal to speak to them and also partly because of the pain of his split and swollen lips, which made it difficult even to get down the badly-needed slurps of stale, tepid water from the bottles they brought him. Their treatment of their captive had been anything but gentle. But he was prepared to take whatever the bastards had to dish out. And of course he knew he was about to receive some more punishment from them.

'You've got a special visitor coming to see you today, Malloy,' Dorkins said. 'I hope for your sake that you'll be more cooperative this time. Otherwise you know what'll happen, don't you?'

The prisoner stayed silent.

'I don't think he's listening to us, mate,' Grubb said.

Dorkins said, 'Maybe he'd like another little taste, in case he's forgotten what's coming to him if he acts stubborn.'

'Yeah, I reckon maybe he would,' said Grubb with a grin.

Dorkins used the second key on his ring to open the padlock on the pen door. It had been used for containing bulls before now, and its bars were thick, solid steel. He and Grubb stepped inside and closed the door behind them. The prisoner still didn't respond.

'You want to go first?' Dorkins asked his associate.

'Be only too happy to, mate,' Grubb replied. Planting himself with his feet braced apart in front of the seated prisoner, he spent a moment theatrically rolling up his shirt sleeves. Flexed his fingers and balled them into fists, the knuckles still red and tender from the last beating they'd given him, only yesterday. Then he hammered his hard right fist into the side of Kip Malloy's face with a grunt of effort. He put his back into the blow, using the rotation of his waist and legs to give it more momentum. It struck with a meaty smack.

Kip Malloy went over sideways without a sound.

'That was a good one,' Dorkins commented. 'Do it again. Harder this time. Let's see if we can't make this little bird sing.'

They picked him up and propped him back upright on the bench. This time Grubb hit him with his left fist, to spare his sore knuckles. Same result. What should have been a deeply satisfying experience for the captors was badly let down by the prisoner's frustrating lack of reaction. A cry of pain would have been nice. Even just a grunt. But no matter how hard they hit him, he went down without a peep.

'Now my turn,' Dorkins said, rolling up his own sleeves.

The session went on for a good fifteen minutes. When it was over, Kip Malloy's battered face was freshly bloodied, and so were all four of his jailers' fists. The prisoner still hadn't uttered a word. Grubb and Dorkins locked him back up in the pen and stepped outside the barn.

'This is no good, mate,' Dorkins said, brushing a fly off his cheek and leaving a red smear. 'We carry on like this, we'll end up killing the stubborn git. Then it'll be our bollocks on the line.'

Grubb looked at his watch. 'Boss'll be here soon. I was hoping we might've softened him up a little more by now.'

'He won't be happy.'

'He never is, mate.'

Indeed, it wasn't long before Wiley Cooper arrived at the Brundle place. Dorkins and Grubb spotted the black Audi Q8 cutting across the barren flatness of the landscape from a long way off, trailing a dust plume behind it. They watched in nervous silence as the car rolled up and crunched to a stop. Dust drifted on the wind as the driver stepped out. He was a big, brawny, dangerous man called Steve Rackman, the company foreman, Wiley Cooper's second-in-command. Rackman always wore a large, heavy Bowie knife in a sheath on his belt, and was reputed to be handy at using it on people who disagreed with him. Dorkins and Grubb were almost as terrified of Rackman as they were of their mutual employer.

With no greeting to the pair, Rackman stepped around to the Audi's passenger side and opened the door for old Wiley. All eyes were now on the boss. Eighty-one years of age, as gnarly and tough as a boab tree, he was a short, slender man but after well over half a century as the unquestioned, unchallenged ruler of all he surveyed he exuded such an air of authority that he seemed twice as tall. Few people in living memory had ever seen the man crack a smile, still less heard him laugh. Renowned for being the most humourless, most cantankerous and hard-arsed son of a bitch in all of Australia, he'd amassed his fortune a long time ago and no force on earth was about make him lose his iron grip on it. Today, his habitual look of angry authority was even darker than usual. Grubb was sweating profusely. Dorkins swallowed.

'Anything?' Rackman asked them. His underlings shook their heads ruefully.

With Rackman at his heel, Wiley Cooper sailed past the men and they stepped deferentially aside to let him into the barn. Rackman remained just inside the doorway as the boss approached the prisoner alone.

'G'day, Kip,' Wiley said. His voice was harsh and throaty. 'Thought I'd drop by and see how you were getting on.'

Kip had picked himself up off the floor and was sitting back on the bench. He slowly turned to look at Wiley. And now he spoke at last, his words slurry and indistinct.

'Could've saved yourself the bother. I don't have a lot to say.'

'So I gather,' Wiley replied. 'That's very disappointing. You know what I want. All you have to do is let me have it. It's not like I'm offering nothing in return, now is it?'

Kip knew, all right. He'd known this was coming from the moment Mad Mick died. Ignoring the pain in his tattered lips he answered, 'Cooper, I wouldn't let you get your filthy mitts on my uncle's land for all the money in the world.'

Wiley stepped closer to the steel bars of the bull pen and looked at Kip with something almost like pity in his eyes, if it had been real. 'Come on. Be reasonable for once in your life. You know I don't want all of the land. Who the fuck would? I'm only interested in that one area, the one that's marked on the map I happen to know that crazy loon gave you. The rest, you can keep. As for the money part, my very generous offer still stands. All you have to do is sign on the dotted line.' He reached into his jacket, unfolded the three-page contract and flipped to the back page with the blank signature line. He waggled the paper in front of the bars, like a temptation. 'Just one quick scribble, I get my man over there to witness it, and it's legal. All this will be over and can go home to your lovely wife.'

Kip didn't believe that for a moment. Nor did he need to look closely at the document to understand exactly what it was: a statement of his written consent to allow the bull-dozers and diggers of Cooper's little business empire to come rolling freely onto his uncle's land and rip its heart out.

'You can stick your generous offer up your arsehole,

Cooper. And you can roll that paper up and poke it up there too. I wouldn't sign it with a gun to my head.'

'We haven't tried that yet,' Wiley replied. 'Maybe we should.'

'Go for it, Cooper. Point a gun anywhere near me and you'll see what happens next.'

Chapter 16

Wiley stepped away from the pen, folded up the contract and replaced it in his pocket. Without another word he turned around and left the barn. 'Lock it,' he commanded the men.

'What do we do now?' Rackman asked his boss as they returned to the car. 'We've been at this for days. You know he's not going to budge.'

Wiley made no reply. He sat quietly fuming while Rackman drove away from the Brundle place. After a long time on the empty road, he checked his phone and saw he was getting reception. Mobiles were a hit and miss affair out here, and you had to strike while the iron was hot.

'You calling Napier?' Rackman said.

'We still have other options,' Wiley replied.

'Let's hope the stupid bastard's got his phone switched on.'

'He'd better, if he knows what's good for him.'

As it happened, the stupid bastard did. Wiley put the call on speaker, so that Rackman could hear. 'Well?' he demanded.

'Sorry, boss,' came the reply on the faint crackly line.

'Couldn't find it anywhere inside the house. He's got to have hidden it somewhere else.'

'It's just a fucking map, for Christ's sake,' Wiley exploded. 'A simple sheet of paper. You know what it looks like. You've seen it before.'

'It was only for a moment.'

'Don't answer back. You saw it. It exists. And if it exists, I fucking want it. Understood? Jesus fucking Christ, how hard can this be?'

'I'm sorry, boss,' Terry Napier repeated. 'I turned the whole place upside down looking for it.'

Wiley fell into a brooding silence as those other options he'd talked about now crumbled into pieces. He'd been holding out for that damn map being somewhere in the house. With Malloy proving a harder nut to crack than anticipated, he'd been willing to take the risk of sending his inside man Napier to locate its hiding place. It had been Napier who'd initially seen Malloy sneaking it back from his uncle's place, after all, and he knew the house well. The situation had grown more complicated with the arrival of Lynne Malloy's son and his friend. Napier had had to wait for them to be out of the way before he could make his move.

'So much for Plan B,' Rackman muttered.

And there was no Plan C to fall back on. All that remained to them now was to continue working on Malloy, racking up the pressure to make him spill the beans. But how to do that, without killing him? For the moment at least, Malloy must be kept alive, at all costs. Because if he died, then the secret that Wiley was so desperate to find out would die with him. There had to be another way. Had to be.

And then it dawned on Wiley just how simple that way was. It was just a matter of incentives. Of applying the right kind of leverage.

Terry Napier was still on the line. Wiley said to him, 'Okay, here's what we're going to do. If Malloy won't budge to save his own skin, then maybe he will for someone else's. Like his lovely wife.'

'What about her?' Napier replied after a beat's silence.

'What do you mean, what about her? We're going to grab the bitch, that's what. You're the inside man, Napier. That makes it your job to get her out of there and bring her to me. Then we'll see if dear hubby will talk to us, when she's got a knife to her throat.'

Rackman shot his boss a dubious look, as if to say, 'Are you sure you can trust that galah with a task like that?' Rackman had headed up the crew who'd abducted Malloy from Mad Mick's farmstead. Kidnapping wasn't something Napier had ever done before.

'That's gonna be tricky, boss,' Napier said hesitantly, sounding aghast at being given such a responsibility. 'I mean, what with that Jeff Dekker bloke and his mate hanging around. Those two are a real problem for us. Especially the other one, Hope.'

'Since when was some Pommie outsider ever a problem for us?' Wiley snapped. 'Who the fuck is he, anyway?'

'Ex-Special Forces,' Napier replied. 'Best part of fifteen years.'

'Bollocks,' Wiley snorted. 'How the hell would you know that?'

'Because that's what he told me, boss. And you can believe it, looking at the bloke. Got a quiet way about him, doesn't

129

say too much, but you can tell he's trouble. Been poking around and asking questions, like he knows something. Those Special Forces blokes, they're trained to do that stuff. They're like intelligence agents.'

'He doesn't know anything,' Wiley insisted.

'I wouldn't be too sure, boss,' said Napier. 'The two of them went off in a hurry this morning. Crack of dawn, in that big offroad ute of Malloy's. Looked like a couple of blokes on a mission, if you know what I mean.'

'Are they back yet?'

'Dunno, boss. Soon after that, Missus Malloy went for one of her walks. That's when I saw my chance, went in and turned the place over. Then I made myself scarce, so nobody would put two and two together. Told Finn Mulkey to take care of the feeding time for me.'

'You're an idiot,' Wiley said. 'Making yourself scarce just draws more attention to you. Where are you now?'

'At the Kookaburra Roadhouse.'

'What the fuck's the matter with you? I don't pay you to sit in some bar all day drinking beer!'

'Yes, boss. Sorry, boss.'

Wiley thought for a minute. 'So maybe Hope and Dekker have gone off somewhere. That might be our chance to grab her.'

'I'd have to call Finn Mulkey and find out if they're back yet.'

'So call him,' Wiley said. 'Then call me right back, understand?'

They drove on in silence, Wiley fuming and calculating, Rackman frowning over his misgivings about the wisdom of charging Napier, a third-rate zookeeper, with such an onerous job. On top of that was his concern that maybe, just maybe, they were getting in too deep with all this. He didn't dare openly challenge Wiley about it, however.

Six minutes later, the fragile mobile connection still holding, Napier called back.

Wiley asked, 'Did you talk to Mulkey?'

'Yep, boss. He says she's not there.'

'Where is she?'

'Dunno, boss. Finn says he saw her car going off, just a few minutes ago.'

It was Wiley's nature to interrogate every detail of what he was told. 'Is he sure it was her car?'

'Sure as sure, boss. One of them little Honda hatchbacks. It's as yellow as a banana. Can't miss it. He said her son was driving, with her in the passenger seat.'

'So Dekker and Hope are back at the farm, damn it,' Wiley said. 'If Dekker's with her, then where's Hope?'

'Says he saw him going over to Sammy Mudrooroo's cabin,' Napier said. 'Then he got in Kip's ute and went off too, in the opposite direction. But boss, there's something else you need to know. I got a text message from Lynne Malloy. Only just seen it now.'

'What does it say?'

'It says she's been trying to contact me because they've got a problem with the backup incubator room genny and she needs me to help fix it.'

'So what's that got to do with anything?'

'Thing is, boss, the backup incubator room genny's not at the farm. It's been back at the dealership for servicing the last two weeks or more. So how could she have found a problem with it?'

Wiley's eyes narrowed suspiciously. 'She wouldn't know that, would she?'

'No, she doesn't deal with the general running of the farm, as a rule.'

'Then she's lying,' Wiley said. 'They're probably onto you. Clumsy great galah that you are. You must've let something on.'

'No, I didn't, boss. I swear.'

'Shut your fucking pie hole and listen to me,' Wiley growled at him. 'If they're onto you, then my guess is that she and her son are probably heading over to your place to have it out with you. Which means we might be able to intercept them en route, as long as we move quickly. If this man Hope's as dangerous as you say he is, then with him out of the way this could be our chance to snatch her. Driving a little bright yellow Honda, you say?'

'Hope may be out of the way, but her son's with her,' Napier protested. 'He's another soldier boy.'

'Then we'll make sure we have plenty of muscle to deal with him,' Wiley said. 'It's not like we're short of guns and ammo, or men to use them. Call Murchison at head office on this number.' Wiley rattled it off and made Napier repeat it. 'Tell him to load up with as many of the boys and as much hardware as you think you'll need, then to head for your place pronto and meet you on the road. Tell him that order comes from me.'

'Got it, boss.'

'Call me again when you have the goods. In the meantime,

holding arrangements will be made at the Brundle place, and once those are ready you can deliver them there. Got all that?'

'Absolutely, boss.'

'Now shift your arse, Napier. And do not, I repeat *do not*, fuck this up.'

Chapter 17

Ben made the drive to the township of Ngukurr in a little over two and a half hours, pushing the Mean Machine hard and fast along the rough roads. He'd lost his mobile signal a long way back, and now that he was incommunicado his thoughts began to turn anxiously to how Jeff and Lynne were doing with their search for Terry Napier.

If there was a man more capable than Jeff Dekker of handling whatever adversity came his way, Ben had yet to meet him. And he would have unhesitatingly trusted his friend with his life any day of the week. Yet he couldn't shake off the feeling that he shouldn't have so easily let Jeff talk him into not coming along. He couldn't quite fathom why, but the niggling sense of unease at the back of his mind made him keep checking his phone for a signal. There was none. He drove on faster.

Ben had managed to do a little online research about his destination before setting off. From its mouth not far up the Gulf of Carpentaria coast from Hobart's Creek, the Roper River wound and weaved more than a thousand kilometres inland. What had been the old Roper River Mission lay on

134

its banks up to the north, originally founded by Christian missionaries as a safe haven to protect Aboriginal people from being massacred wholesale by white settlers. The missionaries had succeeded in that goal, while at the same time working hard to re-educate the original inhabitants out of their 'heathen savagery' and prohibiting them from using their own languages or following the traditions of their ancient cultures. Only a few decades ago, the missionaries long since faded into history, had the place been formally turned over to the collective ownership of the Yugul Mangi people and renamed Ngukurr. Pronounced the way Lynne had said it, 'Nooker'.

Ben's route to get there was the Roper Highway, which, despite its name that conveyed images of a smooth, modern metalled road, consisted of rough reddish earth and gravel for the last sixty kilometres. He suspected that in the coming wet season, the road would be all but impassable, perhaps even to an all-terrain beast like the Mean Machine. In such a case he'd have had to reach Ngukurr by air.

That reflection brought a flash of Abbie Logan into his mind. He briefly wondered where she was now: probably ferrying more of her charter clients back and forth somewhere over the outback. Thinking about her was more pleasant than worrying about Jeff and his mother, but the anxiety soon returned.

At last, he passed the weathered Ngukurr town sign and the first homes and buildings came into view, a remote sprawl in the middle of the dusty emptiness. It wasn't a large settlement, with a population of just a thousand or so inhabitants. Even so, he was surprised to find the streets completely empty of people, not a living soul in sight apart from the several feral street dogs he spotted scavenging around for garbage as he drove by.

Where had everyone gone? In the many war zones he'd known back in the day, he'd seen entire villages left abandoned by residents fleeing in terror of advancing guerrilla forces and raiding parties. Ngukurr gave him the same strange feeling of entering a ghost town. Run-down homes, some of them barely more than shacks, stood screened off behind ramshackle mesh fencing. Rusted oil drums littered the kerbsides in service as makeshift bins or braziers. Many of the vehicles parked here and there were wrecks, cannibalised for parts, those without wheels propped up on cement blocks. Even if the streets had been teeming with people, it would have been hard for an observer not to form a sad and depressing impression of this place. Whatever the Northern Territory government authorities thought they were doing to promote happy, healthy, vibrant communities in these parts, it was clearly far from enough.

Just when he was beginning to think he'd find nobody here at all, Ben rounded a corner of the main street and spotted a gang of youths up ahead, walking along the middle of the road towards him. They were a mixture of ages, ranging from gangly teenagers to little kiddies, dressed in shorts and colourful T-shirts, though for all their cheerful attire they didn't look too happy to see him. As he drew level with the crowd and slowed to a halt to greet them and ask directions, one of the teens thumped the door with a hostile scowl and another jumped up on the bonnet and leered at him through the windscreen. The eldest of the group, a young guy of maybe eighteen with a sleeveless top showing long, muscled arms, came up to the driver's window with a confident swagger and told Ben that Ngukurr was a closed community. That was to say, closed to the likes of him.

'I'm sorry,' Ben said. 'I didn't know.'

Ignorance was no excuse, apparently. Unmoved, the elder kid replied, 'Yeah, well, you can't come in here, mate. Best you get turned around and go back.' The rest of the gang crowded around the vehicle, the smaller ones having to stand on tiptoes to see Ben through the windows.

In some countries, the usual way past such a welcome committee would be to offer a bribe, whose generosity would be in proportion to the level of threat on display. At least these kids weren't bristling with automatic weapons and cartridge belts. But Ben opted for another approach. 'I'm a friend of Sammy Mudrooroo,' he explained with a friendly smile. 'Thought I might find him here. I need to talk to him.'

The elder kid pulled a face. Still not impressed. 'Yeah? Why's that?'

'Important business,' Ben said.

'You selling something?'

'No, I'm not.'

'Buying something?'

'Not that either.'

'Then what you want, mate?'

'You might say it was family business,' Ben said.

'You ain't his family.'

'But it concerns them.'

137

Which seemed to strike a chord, because the elder kid's expression seemed to soften a little and he drew back from the window to confer with the others, speaking a language Ben thought might be Kriol. They soon seemed to reach an agreement. The elder kid returned to the window and told Ben that Sammy Mudrooroo's cousin lived in Ngukurr, and if it was important family business, then he could be allowed in to see him.

'What's Sammy's cousin's name?' Ben asked.

'Tyler Roberts,' the kid said. 'He old.'

Ben wasn't surprised by the surname. Many, if not most, Aboriginal family names had been handed down to them courtesy of the European masters their ancestors had once worked for – that was to say, been owned by, being mere slaves. He asked, 'You know where he lives?'

The kid nodded.

'Then how'd you like to hop in and lead the way?' Ben said.

The kid cocked his head and looked at him strangely. 'Yeah? What's it worth, mate?'

Here comes the bribe after all, Ben thought. 'Ten dollars sound about right?'

'Each,' the kid said, pointing at the others.

This could get expensive. But it was the only way Ben was going to get to talk with Sammy's cousin. 'Fifty for the lot of you,' he said. 'Not a penny more.'

The deal struck, the elder kid jumped into the passenger seat while the rest of the gang jumped into the back or onto the load bed, hanging from the roll cage bars for support as Ben took off through the streets. The elder kid was fascinated by the rifle and shotgun on the rack behind the seats. Ben said, 'You want your money, don't touch those.'

'Keep your hair on, mate,' the kid said. 'Just looking.'

'What's your name?'

'Ricky.'

'Tell me, Ricky, how come the streets are so empty?'

'Funeral.'

'Sorry to hear it. Someone you know?'

Ricky gave a shrug. 'Everybody knows everybody. People always dying in Ngukurr.'

'Why's that?'

Another shrug. 'Just how it is, mate. Lot of folks get sick. Doctors don't know why.'

'What kind of sick?'

'Just sick.'

Following Ricky's directions Ben turned this way and that through the dirt streets, past more run-down homes and community buildings. Now he saw where everyone had gone: a large crowd had gathered for the funeral ceremony, which was taking place in a grassy compound ringed by a tall wire mesh fence. Ben halted the vehicle to watch from a respectful distance, because he'd never seen anything like it before. The ceremony was taking the form of a ritual dance, whose performers were if not completely naked then very close to it. Their faces and bodies were daubed with some kind of chalky white pigment that contrasted with their ebony-dark skin to make them look like skeletons. As the dancers went through their motions, some older men sitting around the edge of the compound on blankets laid among the long patchy grass and red dirt were chanting in

139

their Aboriginal language, several of them playing didgeridoos. It was the first time Ben had ever heard the instrument in real life and experienced its strange, haunting, almost hypnotic quality.

He understood he was witnessing something highly privileged, a sacred ritual dating back many thousands of years that very few people from his world would ever lay eyes on. The spectacle of these ancient practices seemed to him to make a strange and saddening contrast with the poverty on display all around them, a direct consequence of the effect of trashy westernisation on their lives. But for all that, there was something indefatigable about these people, as though even the toughest of adversity and centuries of systematic erosion of their culture couldn't sap away their sense of pride.

Feeling he was prying, he moved on. Ricky guided him right across to the far side of the township, and that was where Ben found old Tyler Roberts.

Sammy Mudrooroo's cousin was sitting on the broken-down porch of a tin shanty house that stood in a square of patchy yellowed grass surrounded by more wire fencing. He hadn't been hard to find, because he wasn't going anywhere. His bulky mass was jammed into a wheelchair with no wheels, and his faded Bermuda shorts had been sewn up to cover the amputated stumps of his legs. He seemed much older than Sammy, with long white hair and a straggly white beard that reached down to his lap – though Ben couldn't pin an age on him. His eyes were bleary and hooded in a mass of wrinkles. The missing legs, Ben guessed, were more likely casualties of diabetes than of war.

The old man was awake and seemed reasonably attentive as Ben joined him on the porch and introduced himself as a friend of his cousin Sammy's. To Ben's enquiry as to where Sammy himself might be found, Tyler responded with a wave of his arm, motioning in a direction that could have been anywhere between north and east.

'Do you mind if I stay a while and talk, Mr Roberts? I'd like to ask you a few more questions, if that's okay.'

The old man nodded, seeming not displeased to have the company. He motioned at a rusty deck chair nearby. 'You do what you want, mister. What you say your name was again? Memory ain't so good.'

It wasn't easy speaking to old Tyler because he obviously wasn't quite all there. His focus tended to drift every couple of minutes, and when he spoke, his words, to which Ben had to listen hard to understand at the best of times, would often dwindle to an inaudible murmur or trail off altogether into silence, and he would appear to be falling asleep. Whether it was the effect of senility or some medication he was on, Ben couldn't judge. But with much effort and a lot of gentle prompting to keep the old man on track, he was able to glean at least some information.

What Ben learned was that Sammy did come to visit his cousin sometimes, though he hadn't been here in a while – how long exactly was unclear. Tyler didn't have a contact number to pass on, but when Ben asked him again where Sammy might have gone, this time the old man was more forthcoming. In a spurt of lucidity he talked about the increasing number of his Aboriginal brothers and sisters who, having grown tired of the benefits of so-called civilised culture, were rejecting western ways and choosing instead to go back to living the way their ancestors had. That was where Sammy went from time to time, trekking up into the hills to be with his own people, when he wasn't earning a few bucks working for Kip Malloy.

Kip was one of the decent folks who'd always cared for the old ways and the original Australian people, Tyler said, lapsing into one of his many digressions. His uncle, too. Mick had been a good bloke. The best. 'Not many white folks like him,' he added with a low chuckle. 'No offence, mate.'

'None taken.'

Now that the conversation had moved around to the Malloys, Ben saw his opening to ask Tyler if he could tell him anything about the silver serpent. 'What did Sammy mean by that, Mr Roberts? Is it a real thing? Is it a place? A symbol of something, for indigenous Australian people?'

For just the briefest moment the old man's bleary eyes glittered with a knowing look, and to Ben, watching him closely for a reaction, it was clear that he understood exactly what Sammy had meant by it. But he just shook his head, closed his eyes and said nothing, a tiny enigmatic smile on his lips. It was the same frustrating silence that Ben had got from his cousin.

'Kip Malloy is in trouble, Mr Roberts. I want to help him get out of it, but I need Sammy's help to do that. Because I've a feeling he knows what's going on, who Kip's enemies are. And I urgently need your help too, so I can talk to Sammy. Would you be able to pass a message to him from me? Or put me in touch with someone else who can? Mr Roberts?'

But now the old man seemed to have drifted off to sleep, his chin sunk to his chest and his body so relaxed and still that Ben actually checked his pulse to check he hadn't just slipped away right there in front of him. No; Tyler was still breathing, though Ben doubted he was going to get anything more out of him.

Ben always carried a little notebook. Old-fashioned technology that didn't depend on a power source or a signal. He scribbled a note with his name and number on it, asking Sammy Mudrooroo to call him urgently, tore off the sheet and folded it into the sleeping Tyler's hand. That was the best he could do. He swallowed back his frustration and walked away. He had been here longer than intended, and learned little.

He wondered how Jeff and Lynne had got on meanwhile, whether they'd been able to hook up with Terry Napier yet. Anxious for an update, he checked his phone as he walked quickly back to the vehicle. Still no damn signal. Oh for a proper long-range military radio. He swore, clambered up behind the wheel of the Mean Machine, and took off out of Ngukurr township.

It was a long way back down the road before he got his phone signal back. He quickly pulled over to check for messages and found the voicemail from Jeff that he'd been hoping for, recorded nearly three hours ago. As he went to play the message back he was expecting it to be the news that Jeff, unlike him, had succeeded in his mission and was delivering Terry Napier back to Hobart's Creek. Now they might be getting somewhere at last, Ben thought.

But when he listened to it, his blood froze. Jeff's voice in his ear sounded hard and strained. He hadn't had much time to talk, but what he'd said was plenty enough. The message said, 'We've got a Basra situation here, buddy. Watch your back.'

Ben listened to the recording eight times before the reality sank in. Something had happened to Jeff and Lynne, and Ben knew it wasn't good.

Because he remembered what had happened in Basra.

Chapter 18

Three hours earlier

Jeff and Lynne were heading southwards in the direction of the small outback town of McCarthy, where Terry Napier lived with his wife Sue. Jeff had taken the wheel for his mother's sake, as she was still shaken up from the morning's developments. After living in France for so long it felt strange to him to be driving on the left again. The Honda Jazz was light on luxury but it was quick and nimble, with an air conditioning system that actually worked; and, as Lynne had said, the road was a good one, straight and smooth and almost totally devoid of any other traffic as it cut its way between spectacular outcrops of multicoloured striated rock formations that sometimes loomed up on each side like canyon walls, and other times dropped away to reveal the endless empty vista of parched bushland.

For the first half-hour of the drive they'd talked about the situation with Kip and his uncle and Terry Napier, toying with theories, examining the available facts from every conceivable angle until they'd run out of unanswerable questions, grown tired of endlessly repeating 'I don't know' and of trying to find solace in cautious optimism, and lapsed into silence. Now each was focused on their own thoughts and the task at hand, while the little car went on thrumming efficiently along the empty road, the white line zipping towards them. At this rate they should be reaching McCarthy before too long. What happened next, Jeff was thinking, they'd just have to wait and see. He wondered if Ben was making any progress on his front. With any luck, by the time today was out at least one of them might have something good to show for his efforts. Until then, all any of them could do was hope for the best.

It was in one of the canyon sections of the road that Jeff's thoughts were broken by the sudden appearance of the first other vehicle they'd seen for fifty kilometres. A big utilitarian truck with scuffed bodywork and a faded canvas top, it came lurching out of a junction up ahead that was hidden behind big rocks, and which Jeff hadn't noticed until the truck was suddenly right in front of them.

'Hey, watch it, you cheeky sod,' he muttered, and toed the brake, scrubbing off enough speed to avoid running straight into the back of it.

'Happens quite a bit around here,' Lynne said. 'People in these parts are so used to driving on empty roads, they don't even bother to check their mirrors.'

The truck was wide and heavy and slow and the exhaust belched black diesel smoke as it trundled along at under sixty kilometres an hour with its canvas flaps billowing in the wind. Jeff had no intention of being stuck behind a smelly old crock all the way to McCarthy. He dropped down a gear, flipped on his indicator, put his foot down and went to overtake.

For the first few moments, everything was normal. But as the little Honda was crossed into the right-hand lane and drawing level with the rear wheel of the truck, Jeff was alarmed to see its rear end suddenly veering across the line towards them. He had to brake hard to avoid a collision. The Honda fell sharply back, weaving in the road.

'What the—?'

'Jesus,' Lynne gasped. 'Bloody road hog. What's he think he's doing?'

'Guy's obviously pissed or something,' Jeff said.

Now the truck was filling the right-hand lane in front of them, and it had slowed down even more. Jeff hit the gas hard and swerved back into the left lane to shoot up the truck's inside. An illegal overtake, but who cared? He just wanted to get past this idiot.

The same thing happened. The Honda's nose was pushing past when the truck rocked violently on its worn suspension and came veering sideways to the left. There was no verge for Jeff to run off onto, nothing but a wall of craggy rock that would crumple the passenger side of the Honda like a beer can if he hit it even at this low speed. Again he had no option but to step on the brake and fall back.

And that was the moment when Jeff began to realise that the truck's driver wasn't just some drunken idiot with no respect for the rules of the road. That had been a deliberate blocking manoeuvre. Jeff glanced down at the Honda's speedometer. The needle had dropped to just above fifty kilometres an hour. The truck's brake lights flared and its rear loomed up in his windscreen, and he had to brake yet gain. Now the truck was straddling the white line in the middle of the road, with the driver watching his mirror in readiness to cut off Jeff's escape either side.

'All right, you arsehole,' Jeff muttered under his breath. 'You want to play, let's play.' He feinted left, and the truck followed him; but as it began to move left he swerved hard right to get past. Same result. The gap narrowed, squeezing their escape route tight up against a wall of solid rock.

'Jeff, there's another one behind us,' Lynne said anxiously. Jeff looked in the rear-view mirror and saw what he'd been too distracted to see until that moment. The grille of a big Dodge Ram pickup was almost filling the Honda's rear screen. It seemed to have appeared out of nowhere, but Jeff was certain it had come from the same junction as the truck, quickly catching up with them until it was almost touching bumper to bumper.

Jeff toed the gas to lengthen the gap, but now the big truck in front was slowing even more. He quickly switched his foot from the gas back to the brake so as not to run into the back of it. Behind them, the pickup kept on coming, so close that in his mirror he could see the two guys in the front, neither of them wearing seatbelts. With a solid crunch its massive chromed bumper, looking as big as the cow catcher on a locomotive this close up, connected with the Honda's flimsy rear end. It was just a nudge, but the impact was enough to jolt him and Lynne violently against their seat backs.

'Jeff? What's happening?'

Jeff said nothing. His face was hard, because he knew

exactly what. These bastards were concertedly boxing them in, and they were doing a pretty decent job of it so far.

Jeff was one of the two instructors in defensive driving, along with Ben, on the road circuit and skid pan they'd built back home at Le Val. They taught their trainees never to allow this kind of thing to happen to them. Yet that was the situation that was inexorably unfolding at this moment, and there was precious little he could do about it. The lightweight Honda was being helplessly sandwiched between these two heavy vehicles with no way backwards, forwards or sideways. Another bump from the big Dodge Ram whiplashed Lynne's head against the restraint and she gasped again, staring at her son with alarm.

The truck in front was slowing down even more. Jeff was pressed up too close to the back of it to get past, and he couldn't widen the distance because the one behind wouldn't allow him to. The speedo needle had dropped to below fifty kilometres an hour. If it dropped much more, they'd be moving at walking speed. Then at no speed at all. Then it would be game over.

'Jeff! Talk to me! What's happening?' Lynne was so frightened that her voice came out as a screech.

Jeff had had enough of this crap. He said, 'Hold on tight, Mum.'

'What are you going to do?'

'Give these arseholes a taste of their own medicine, that's what.'

He had no idea if the Honda was going to survive the battering he was about to inflict on it, but he did it anyway. Stamping on the brake as though he were trying to kill it he brought the car to a shrieking halt and they were hurled hard forwards against their seatbelts. Half a second later they were being thrown back with equal force into their seats as the Dodge piled into them from behind with a jarring crash, its driver caught unawares by the unexpected emergency stop.

In that briefest moment of stunned silence that always comes in the immediate aftermath of an accident, Jeff saw the Dodge rolling backwards away from the rear of the Honda. Only by a couple of feet, but enough to widen the gap.

He intended to widen it further. Now he slammed his foot on the gas and the Honda's engine yowled like an angry cat, revs shooting into the red as he accelerated straight ahead for the back of the truck, whose driver had seen what had happened behind him and hit his own brakes.

It was like driving into a brick wall. The little car's front end crumpled with the heavy impact, but its momentum managed to shunt the truck forwards a short way. His view ahead now partly obscured by the twisted bonnet lid, Jeff crunched the Honda into reverse, accelerated hard again and rammed backwards into the front of the Dodge once more. And with a leap of fierce joy he saw his strategy had worked, because now the gap to front and rear was widened just enough for him to scrape his way out from between their assailants. Slamming the Honda into forward gear he twisted the wheel and steered for the opening to his right. The car's battered left front wing caught the corner of the truck's tailgate on its way past, but it didn't matter – they were through, and now surging past the side of the truck with just enough space between it and the rocks to get by.

Lynne let out a whoop of triumph and intense relief. They were out of the trap and getting away.

But then in the next instant, they weren't.

The truck driver had seen the car shooting up his right flank, and he responded fast and aggressively. The truck revved hard with a dieselly rasp and swerved to prevent their escape. Jeff had almost made it through when the truck's front bumper ripped into the car's rear wheel arch, slammed the Honda sideways and drove it into the rocks. The crash tore the right front wheel off the Honda and brought it to a crunching, rending stop. The getaway had failed.

'Mum, are you okay?' She was stunned and in shock, but the seatbelt had saved her from injury. Jeff looked around and saw the Dodge Ram come tearing around the left flank of the truck and skid to a halt to block off the immobilised Honda. The two men in the front of the pickup jumped out, together with three more from the back, carrying shot-guns and bolt-action rifles. Four of them, Jeff had never seen before. But the fifth, one of the men who'd been riding in the back of the pickup, was Terry Napier.

At the same moment the rear flaps of the truck's canvas soft top flew open and six more armed men came spilling out, jumping down to the road, gathering around the car, pointing guns. Someone was yelling, 'Get out of the car! Get out of the bloody car or we'll shoot!'

Jeff knew that if their attackers had stopped them to kill them, they'd have opened fire and riddled the car with bullets by now. This was something else. It was a snatch. The same thing that had happened to Kip was now about to happen to him and Lynne.

151

He couldn't fight them. There were too many. Even if he'd had a gun in the car he wouldn't have touched it, in the sure knowledge that not only he but his mother, too, would be shot to pieces in the ensuing short but bloody firefight. Jeff wasn't afraid to die, but he couldn't go to his death knowing he'd caused her to die too.

The men were crowding closer to the car. Jeff took out his phone and speed-dialled Ben's number. No reply; he was probably out of signal range. Seconds counted. The men were coming closer, all around them, guns aimed right at them. His mother was gasping in fear and shrinking away from the passenger window. Jeff's mind was screaming and his heart was racing, but outwardly he remained calm, as calm as he'd been in a hundred military actions back in the day. With the phone to his ear he waited for the prompt, then left a brief message, one he knew Ben would understand clearly.

'We've got a Basra situation here, buddy. Watch your back.'

Jeff ended the call and laid the phone down on the dash-board. No point in putting it back in his pocket, because in a few moments' time the men would take it off him anyway. He turned to his mother and said, 'Mum, we're about to be taken. I don't think they're going to harm us. Do as they say and don't give them any trouble.'

She was boggling at him, breathing hard, fighting panic. 'What's going to happen to us?'

'Don't you worry,' he replied with a smile. 'We'll get out of this. I promise.'

An instant later, the men had reached the car doors on each side and tore them open. A rifle poked through the driver's door and pointed at Jeff's head. The person holding it was Terry Napier.

'Get out of the fucking car! Out! Out!' Napier's face was flushed and he looked almost as terrified as Lynne. Jeff stepped out of the car. Napier backed away, still pointing the rifle.

Jeff said, 'Take your finger off that trigger, Terry. We don't want anyone getting hurt.'

'On your fuckin' knees! Down! Down!'

Jeff did as he was told, and the men closed around him. On the other side of the car, his mother did the same. 'Go gentle on her,' he warned them as someone jerked his arms painfully behind his back and fastened his wrists with a plastic cable tie. 'Harm a hair on her head, I'll kill you.'

The reply was a vicious blow to the face from a rifle stock. Jeff saw stars and his body went limp. He only vaguely registered his mother's scream of rage at the men to leave her son alone, or the rough hands that grabbed him by the arms and hauled him into the back of the truck while Lynne was being shoved into the pickup, fighting her captors every step of the way.

A voice said, 'Get the tow rope and hook up that bloody Honda. The boss doesn't want any mistakes this time, get it?'

Doors slammed. Engines revved. Lying dazed and bleeding on the hard floor of the truck, Jeff felt the jolting motion as they took off.

And soon the scene of the kidnapping was just an empty stretch of road, with hardly a trace to be seen of what had happened there.

Chapter 19

What had happened in Basra was a joint Special Air Service and Special Boat Service rescue mission to recover two Italian journalists taken hostage by Mahdi militia insurgents, back during the Iraq conflict.

To say things had not gone as planned was to understate the incident quite considerably.

The outcome of military missions, and of behind-the-lines Special Forces missions in particular, could only be as good as the intelligence behind them. In this instance, the information around which the joint SF operation had been designed had been obtained from a potentially corrupt source within the local police and was sadly lacking, both in accuracy and reliability. The senior officers had suspected this from the outset, but with pressure mounting on them from on high to extract the journalists before the militiamen carried out their execution threat, they'd reluctantly greenlit the mission as planned.

At 4.03 a.m. that fateful morning, the crack eight-man British team freshly flown in aboard a C-130 Hercules transport plane entered the house where it was believed the hostages were being held, using their time-honoured explosive methods of speed and surprise. But the real surprise was theirs, when they encountered an enemy force four times stronger than expected, extremely well armed, tipped off and lying in wait for them.

By the time the soldiers realised they'd walked into a trap, it was too late. One trooper (a man Ben had known well) was killed in the battle and four more were taken prisoner, two from SAS and two from SBS. The remaining three narrowly escaped, one of them seriously injured. By dawn the next morning, the captured soldiers were being proudly displayed on Iraqi television, bound and bloodied.

Amid the political fallout and uproar over the debacle, with the senior general at Permanent Joint Headquarters in Northwood, England, initially denying permission for a second rescue operation, it had taken a larger and even riskier mission involving members of the US Delta Force to finally resolve the situation – and even then it had been touch and go as to whether the imprisoned Special Forces soldiers, not to mention the hapless Italians, would ever be seen alive again.

Neither Ben's nor Jeff's units had been involved as they were both deployed elsewhere at the time, but the incident had become one of those dark legends inscribed in the memories of all British Special Forces soldiers, a sobering reminder that even the most highly trained and skilled warriors in the world could end up tethered in a dingy basement with their faces beaten to a pulp by enemy captors. To this day the codeword 'Basra' was used at Le Val in training exercises, to denote a kidnap situation involving captured SF operatives.

In short, by his message Jeff had just told Ben that he and Lynne had been taken.

Still reeling from the news, Ben made the long drive back to Hobart's Creek. What he found there was much what he'd feared. Jeff and Lynne hadn't returned, the Honda Jazz was still gone, and none of the workers he spoke to at the croc farm had seen them. There was no sign of Terry Napier, either. Within moments of hearing Jeff's message, Ben had already decided to keep the cops well out of this turn of events. It was up to him, and him alone, to bring Jeff and Lynne back safe. He was willing to bet Le Val and everything he owned that whoever had taken Kip was responsible for this, too.

Various possibilities churned through his mind. One was that Kip was dead, and this kidnap was a last-ditch desperate attempt on the part of his killers to extract whatever information they needed from Lynne, in the hopes that she might know it, too. But Ben quickly discounted that idea, because then the kidnappers would have snatched Lynne much sooner, or perhaps even opted to take her in the first place, rather than opt for a harder target like her husband. She was often alone at the house. A determined group of men could have grabbed her at any time.

Another option that crossed his mind was that this was all part of some orchestrated vendetta against the Malloys – but that didn't make sense either, given how the events had been unfolding. And yet another was that the sting had been directed not at Lynne, but at Jeff, to take him out of the picture before he and Ben found out too much. That was feasible, and it could explain why Jeff had warned Ben to watch his back, because the enemy would be after him, too. But then they wouldn't have gone to the trouble of taking Jeff alive, and then Jeff wouldn't have identified this as a Basra situation.

No, Ben decided, once the arguments were all weighed up there was only one convincing explanation for what had happened: that Kip was still alive, and continuing to hold out on them. Increasingly desperate to extract whatever it was they wanted from him, and following their presumably failed attempt to find it in their search of the house, their fallback plan was to kidnap his wife to use as leverage. Even the toughest spirit would quickly break when the safety of their loved ones was brought into the equation. Lynne had been the target. Jeff was just collateral damage, the unlucky bystander.

Except the unluckiest players in this were the scum who thought they could get away with it. Because now Ben had just declared all-out war against them.

It was getting late in the afternoon by now. In a few more hours, the day would be ebbing to a close. Terry Napier remained Ben's number one priority. He didn't know Napier's address in the town of McCarthy, or how to get there. But he knew someone else who might. Napier's pal, Finn Mulkey.

Casting his mind back to earlier in the day and Lynne's conversation with the young farmhand called Carl, Ben remembered that Napier had reportedly left instructions for Finn to take over the feeding time that day. That time would be coming soon, when it was cooler and the crocodiles were quieter. Ben waited at the house. Experience, training and some innate natural propensity to inner calm had taught him to still his mind and body, even when life and death were in the balance, even when his friends were in mortal danger, even when the clock was ticking faster than ever. Then, when he thought he'd waited long enough, he left the house and headed down to the water where he expected to find the unsuspecting Finn Mulkey dishing out the nightly helping of dead things to the crocodiles.

His expectations were proven right. Mulkey was in the same spot where Ben had found his buddy Napier the previous evening, with the pickup backed up close to the wire fence and its open load bed piled with the same bloody cargo of chicken carcasses and hacked-off limbs of sheep. He had donned the same slaughterman's apron and heavy gauntlets, and was preparing to start tossing the first tasty morsels over the fence to their recipients, who were well trained to congregate in the same place each day at the same time for their dinner. Like the previous evening, the lakeside was alive with the huge reptiles, and the din of their wild splashing and roaring could be heard from a distance. And like his friend Terry Napier before, Mulkey was too intently concentrated on his potentially risky task to notice Ben coming up behind him.

Mulkey had a dead chicken in each hand and was about to lob them high over the wire when he finally realised he had company, and turned with a surly look that made his rodent features look even more pinched and ugly. 'What do *you* want?'

'Answers,' Ben said, not slackening his stride.

'Go fuck yourself, moron. Can't you see I'm busy?'

Which was definitely not the answer that was going to win the guy any favour. Ben grabbed him by the neck and jammed him hard up against the fence.

'Terry Napier. Where is he?'

Chapter 20

Mulkey struggled in Ben's grip and took a clumsy round-house swipe at him with one of the dead chickens, but Ben blocked the blow and the chicken bounced off the wire mesh. Mulkey yelled angrily, 'Let go of me, you crazy Limey shithead!'

There were two reasons why Ben had wanted to get Mulkey down here alone by the water's edge. Firstly because it was a quiet spot away from the working heart of the farm, where their conversation couldn't be heard by any other than their reptilian audience. The nature of that audience itself was the second reason. Ben let go of Mulkey's neck, and before the guy could try to fight back or get away he quickly bent down, took an iron two-fisted grip of Mulkey's ankles, lifted him clear off his feet and pitched him half over the top of the fence. With a shriek, Mulkey folded over backwards with his body dangling upside-down over the other side of the wire, hooked by the crook of his knees with Ben still tightly gripping both ankles. He squirmed and fought desperately, but he was helplessly pinned there against the wire mesh like a piece of bait.

Which was exactly what the crocs thought, too. Not the brightest of creatures in general, but they weren't slow to recognise that their routine feeding time had suddenly become much more of an interesting proposition. The ones already making their way up the bank on their stubby, clawed legs waddled with a renewed sense of urgency, while those behind came swarming eagerly from the brackish water to join them. There had to be a hundred of the things. At around five hundred kilograms apiece, that equated to some fifty tons of armour plate and massive flesh-ripping teeth, collectively the weight of a main battle tank, steadily advancing towards the sacrificial offering that hung squirming and squealing temptingly from the fence. Their huge dino-saur jaws were opening and snapping in anticipation.

Mulkey's eyes popped from their sockets in horror and his face was turning purple with all the blood going to his head. He wailed, 'Agghh! Please! Don't do this to me, mate!' It was amazing how fast a man's attitude could change when he was being offered up as a starter course to an army of hungry saurians.

'You don't know this about me,' Ben said, 'but I've always been an animal lover. I like to feed my pets the freshest food I can. And it occurs to me that these guys would much prefer the taste of a nice live human, instead of that rotten maggot-infested crap they get ladled out to them every day. Seems to me they feel the same way. Shall we oblige them with a nice juicy treat for a change? Not that you've got a lot of meat on you. I shouldn't imagine they'd take long to finish you off.'

'No! No! Agghh! NOOO!'

'Still, I have to say you're quite a weight for a skinny little rat-arse, Finn,' Ben said. 'My arms are getting tired and I don't know how much longer I can hold you.'

Then out of the seething mass of advancing reptiles came a much larger shape. Trampling over smaller crocs in its path and pressing them into the mud with its huge bulk, shoving others aside in its eagerness to reach the appetising titbit dangling over the wire. Its enormous snout was laced with ancient battle scars. The massive teeth were even longer and more pointed than the one Kip had worn around his neck.

'Look, here comes our friend Flowerpot,' Ben said. 'He's going to pluck you off this fence like an apple off a tree and gobble you up in one swallow, and I'm going to stand here and watch him do it.'

'Please!' Mulkey screamed hoarsely, thrashing in terror, close to madness. 'I'm begging you! It's not human!'

'What's the matter, mate?' Ben asked him. 'Don't you want to get a little kiss from a crocodile?'

'Pull me up! I'll do anything! Anything!'

'Anything? Really?'

The huge croc came closer. Its jaws scissored open and shut with a sickening wet snap, those beady yellow eyes full of intent. Then suddenly it charged the fence, moving with nightmarish speed. Ben yanked Mulkey down from his perch just a split-second before the brute came surging up like an express train with its massive distended maw gaping wide, and crashed against the wire mesh with an impact that almost tore the thick steel fenceposts from their concrete foundations.

Mulkey slithered to the ground, crawled panic-stricken away from the fence, then collapsed and lay there gasping, curled up in a foetal position and shaking from head to foot. His crotch and trouser legs were dark with urine. He seemed to have got the message. On the other side of the fence, the disappointed crocs were roaring and snorting in frustration.

Ben said, 'Ready to start cooperating with me now? Smart decision. So tell me, Finn. What do you know about this?'

'N-nothing!' Mulkey quavered.

'You want to go back over the fence?'

'No! Nononono . . .'

'So talk to me. What's the silver serpent?'

'I don't have a fucking clue, mate! I swear!'

'Your pal Terry does. What's he into? What's he told you? Last chance. Don't lie to me, because you know I won't hesitate.'

'I'm telling the truth. Honestly! You have to believe me!'

Ben looked at Mulkey and saw nothing but terrified sincerity in his eyes. 'All right, Finn. This is the luckiest day of your life, because I've decided I do believe you. But I'm not finished with you yet. One more question. You know where Terry lives? Been there before?'

Mulkey nodded so hard it must have cricked his neck.

'Pleased to hear it,' Ben said. 'I'm intending to pay your friend a visit. And you're going to take me there. Any nonsense from you, I will break both your arms and both your legs and leave you out in the bush for the entertainment of the dingoes. They need a good feed now and then, too. Tell me that you understand exactly what I'm saying.'

'I understand!'

It was too long a distance to drag Mulkey all the way to where the Mean Machine was parked, so Ben stripped him of his apron and gauntlets, frog-marched him to the pickup truck, bundled him harshly into it, told him not to even think about moving, and drove him back over to the house. Then Ben hauled him bodily out of one vehicle and into the other. He used a coil of strong, light rope from Kip's onboard tool chest to bind Mulkey securely into the Mean Machine's passenger seat, with the last loop attaching his neck to the roll cage so he could barely move.

'Sitting comfortably? Then let's go.'

Chapter 21

For what already felt like an eternity, Dave 'Dungfly' Dorkins and his mate Pete Grubb had been getting increasingly bored out of their wits hanging around the Brundle place, with nothing to do but tend to their recalcitrant prisoner. Kip Malloy's stoical way of absorbing any amount of beatings without sound or complaint had taken all the fun out of life. Cabin fever was beginning to set in, too, and the two men were increasingly snappish with one another. Grubb was repulsed by the swarms of large, hairy bluebottles that constantly buzzed around his companion; Dorkins was kept wide awake at night in their shared camper van by Grubb's snoring like a bear. He'd have happily slept outdoors, if not freaked out by the venomous spiders and other crawly nocturnal things that infested the place.

The tension and boredom were alleviated when their new orders arrived, in the shape of a text message from Steve Rackman. Grubb and Dorkins were now to get to work double quick on erecting a wooden building, to serve as a holding cell for a new prisoner. Shortly after they received their instructions, a truckload of timber was delivered to the

Brundle place, surplus materials from one or other of the many construction projects that the boss always had on the go.

Armed with carpentry tools and inspired by the terror of what would happen to them if they failed to get it finished in time, the pair had set busily about their urgent task. The new building was to be sited a hundred yards from the barn. It measured ten feet by ten, with no windows except for a narrow ventilation slot high up near the roof. It was equipped with a primitive metal toilet, bolted to the floor in one corner, a wooden slab for a bunk on the opposite wall, and a small lockable hatch through which necessaries could be passed. It had to be solid, secure and totally inescapable, according to the boss's very clear instructions. And inescapable it would be. The walls were four inches thick, the whole construction tightly bolted down to a heavy wooden floor reinforced with heavy-gauge wire. The door had more locks on it than a bank vault, and a prisoner shut inside would need a chainsaw or a small bomb to get out.

Dorkins and Grubb had barely finished screwing down the last plank when the small convoy of vehicles turned up. Driving the lead pickup was Terry Napier, flushed with victory at his recent captures. He stepped out, issuing orders like an army officer. The men opened up the tailgate of the larger truck, hauled out the male prisoner and dumped him roughly on the ground. Jeff Dekker's face was stained with dried blood from where he'd been hit, and his wrists and ankles were trussed with cable ties. One of the men drew a knife and slashed the bonds on his ankles. Then he was grabbed by the arms and yanked up onto his feet. 'Put him in the barn with Malloy,' Napier said.

166

While that was going on, a couple of the others had opened up the back of the second truck and pulled out Lynne Malloy. Her eyes were wide with fear and rage and her hair was all awry. She was struggling hard, but her hands were tethered behind her back and she was no match for the big, burly men who dragged her away from the truck. Catching a glimpse of her son, she let out a muffled cry from behind her gag. 'Come on, bitch,' said one of the men, and they marched her off across the dusty wasteground to her newly built accommodation. Inside the holding cell, two of them held her tightly while a third removed the gag and wrist tie. Then they shoved her onto the bunk and shut her in. She immediately surged back to her feet and started pounding furiously at the door and yelling to be let out. The men laughed.

'Thump and scream all you like, Sheila. Won't do you any good.'

'And watch one of them spiders doesn't get you,' said another. 'This fuckin' place is alive with huntsmen and redbacks.'

Jeff could hear his mother's cries from a hundred yards away as he was shoved towards the barn. The gag around his mouth was so tight it was cutting into the corners of his lips. His head ached badly from where the rifle butt had whacked him earlier, and he felt dizzy and unsteady on his feet. But it would take more than a mild concussion to stop him. As one of the men holding him got a little too close and let his guard down for an instant, Jeff lashed a savage kick that caught him square in the groin and folded him up with a screech of agony. That earned Jeff another hard clout to the back of the head, but he was smiling as they dragged him into the barn.

His smile vanished when, there in the shadows at the back of the barn, he saw the familiar figure slumped on a bench behind the steel bars of his prison, completely still, apparently dead.

'Kip!'

To Jeff's intense relief Kip stirred and raised his head at the sound of his voice. But even in the semi-darkness he looked frail and weak, his responses slow.

'Kip, it's me, Jeff.'

'Jeff?' Kip's voice was indistinct and slurred. He shifted into a dim beam of light that shone from a crack above, and Jeff saw the mottled bruises and swellings all over his face.

'That's right, you old bugger. Got a housemate to keep you company,' said one of the men, unlocking the door of the pen. It swung heavily open and they shoved Jeff inside. A rifle was pointed at him while someone else cut the tie from his wrists. Then they slammed the barred door shut and walked away, laughing. When they were alone, Jeff checked Kip's pulse and felt his brow. He was worried that Kip was seriously ill.

'I'm all right,' Kip croaked, speaking with difficulty. 'Wish I could say it was good to see you, mate. What are you doing here?'

Jeff had been dreading this moment worse than anything, because he had to tell Kip that Lynne was here, too. There was no easy way to break the news. 'I did all I could to stop it from happening, Kip. There were too many of them. If

168

she hadn't been there, I'd have trashed the bastards. But I was afraid she'd get hurt.'

Kip's face hardened like granite and he said nothing.

Jeff asked him, 'What's this about, Kip? What is it they want from you?'

Kip remained silent for a long moment, his eyes closed. Then he looked at Jeff and replied in his indistinct croak, 'Something they've been after for a long time, mate. Not many people even knew for sure it existed. My uncle Mick was one of the ones who knew. He wouldn't have let them have it. Not for anything.'

'Let them have what, Kip?'

But Kip just shook his head. 'Better you don't know, son. They're going to try to make you talk, as well. The more you know, the more they'll hurt you to get it out of you.'

'I don't talk,' Jeff said. 'It doesn't matter what they do to me.'

'Better hope you mean that, son,' Kip told him. 'Because I reckon we're going to die in this place.'

Chapter 22

Outside under the sultry, clouded sky, Terry Napier leaned against his pickup truck and got out his phone in the hopes of being able to call the boss. Miracle of miracles, one bar of reception, though it could fade out at any moment.

Wiley Cooper snatched up on the first ring. 'Speak.'

'Everything's going to plan, boss,' Napier told him, unable to suppress the note of smug triumph in his voice. 'We're here at the Brundle place now, just like you told us.'

Wiley sounded pleased, or as pleased as man of his severe, vinegarish and joyless nature could allow himself to sound. 'Is everything ready for them? The holding cell is finished and secure?'

'Totally secure, boss. Dorkins and Grubb did a good job. What do you want us to do now? Are you coming over?'

'I've got a fucking business empire to run, Napier. I'm tied up in important meetings for the rest of the day and I can't be running about the bush doing the things I pay morons like you to do for me.'

'Sure, boss. What do you want us to do?'

'Keep the Malloy woman locked up, make sure she's safe

and has what she needs. I don't want her too badly hurt, not while she's still useful to us. Same goes for the son-in-law. Let them stew for a while and think about what's coming to them. By the time I get there they'll be ready to talk to us.'

'Copy that, boss. And what about me? You want me to stay here with Dungfly – I mean, with Dorkins and Grubb?'

'No, you can leave Dorkins and Grubb to look after things there. Your job now is to go and get Hope. You said yourself, he's a bloody liability. And I agree. I can't have anything or anyone standing in my way. So go and get him.'

The flush of pride drained from Napier's face and his mouth fell open. He spluttered involuntarily, 'B-but . . . how'm I supposed to do that?'

'You'll think of something,' Wiley told him. 'Don't worry, Napier. You'll have all the manpower you need. Just carry out my orders. There'll be a handsome extra bonus in it for you if you do. And if you fail, you'll probably be dead anyway, so why worry about what I might do to you? Now get off the fucking phone and go do your fucking job.'

A bemused, sullen Terry Napier repeated the relevant parts of those orders to Dorkins and Grubb. Then he and the rest of the men got back in their vehicles and drove off in a cloud of dust, leaving Dorkins and Grubb there alone again.

Time passed. The pair ambled back to their camper van and sat there for a while, smoking. After three or four cigarettes Grubb remembered what the boss had said about making sure the Malloy woman had everything she needed, and he stumped across to the holding cell to slide a jug of water through the hatch. That only set her off screaming and thumping again, and he hurried back to the safety of the camper van thinking of his ex-wife, who used to beat him on occasion.

With nothing more to do, the boredom soon began to seep back into their bones. Grubb took out his phone, one of the pair of prepaid-for-cash burners they'd been given for this job. You seldom got any reception out here, but with a bit of luck he might be able to browse online for a bit. 'Strewth, I don't believe this. My phone's gone dead,' he moaned.

'Yeah, mine too,' Dorkins said. 'Since yesterday.'

'Where are the chargers?'

That had been Dorkins' department. 'Forgot to bring them,' he replied morosely.

So that was that. They sat there for a while longer, smoking some more cigarettes.

'Fuckin' drag this is, mate,' Dorkins sighed after a while. 'Yeah.'

'I mean, there's got to be something better we can do than sitting on our arses like a couple of dills.'

'We *are* a couple of dills,' Grubb replied philosophically. 'That's what everyone thinks, anyway.'

'That's the whole bloody point, isn't it?' Dorkins said, becoming animated as ideas formed inside his head. He slapped at a fly that was scuttling up his cheek, and it buzzed angrily away. 'That's what everyone thinks about us. That's why they don't trust us with anything better than this to do. But what if we were to prove them wrong?'

'How's that, mate?'

'Well,' Dorkins said with a glimmer of cunning in his

eye. 'What if we were able to do what nobody else has been able to do? What if we could make Kip spill the beans?'

'We've tried that already, remember?' Grubb said. 'Doesn't work.'

'But now we've got the tools to make it work. The woman, I mean. What bloke wouldn't cough up his innermost secrets when a couple of hard bastards poke a bloody hand cannon in his sheila's face?' Dorkins pulled the illegal .44-calibre revolver that was his pride and joy out of his jeans pocket and brandished it with a flourish. The fly was back, and was now crawling up the side of his nose.

'I don't know, mate,' Grubb said, looking dubiously at the gun and thinking again about his ex-wife, whom he'd have happily allowed to be shot dead any day of the week, lacking the courage to do it himself. 'Anyhow, the boss said to let them stew a while, remember? We're not supposed to do anything.'

'I know what the boss said. But imagine if when he turns up, we were able to tell him that we cracked it all on our own? Initiative, see? That's what self-made men like the boss respect, blokes who can take the initiative. Then we wouldn't just be a pair of useless bludgers any more, down at the bottom of the pile with everyone treating us like shit. If we could deliver the goods, we'd be golden boys. Top of the tree, mate. And bollocks to that Steve Rackman who thinks he's cock of the walk. And to fucking Terry Napier, too.'

'You mean, like, winning favour?'

'Exactly. Not to mention, getting a bigger slice of the money that's coming.'

The truth was, neither of them had the slightest notion

of what form that loot might take, or how it might be obtained. What little they knew was gleaned from the loose talk and rumours among some of the men that considerable wealth was headed their way, and soon. But at the sound of the word 'money', Grubb was beginning to warm to the idea, too. 'Hmm. Maybe you're right.'

'Dead right I'm right, mate. And how's this for an even better idea? Maybe we find out where the loot is, then kill all three of the mongrels and go and take the whole lot for ourselves. And screw the boss.'

Better and better. It was a breathtakingly enticing plan, but Grubb was still hovering on the brink. 'So how's this work?'

'It's a piece of piss. We grab the sheila out of there, march her over to the barn, put this here pistol to her head and tell Kip we'll shoot her if he doesn't talk.'

'What if he still won't talk?'

'Then we blow the son-in-law's head off to show him we're serious.'

'And what if he still won't talk after that?'

'Then we blow the sheila's head off too.'

Grubb considered the logic of the plan. 'That's a bit strong, innit?'

Dorkins shrugged. 'Not really. The boss is gonna kill'm all anyway. What do we have to lose? And we've everything to gain. It's a golden opportunity, way I see it.'

'All right then,' Grubb said. 'If you say so.'

Fired up with motivation and already dreaming of how they were going to spend all that lovely money, they strode across to the new holding cell, Grubb rattling keys, Dorkins twirling the revolver around his finger. Grubb unlocked the door. Dorkins said, 'Ready. On three. One . . . two . . .'

They threw open the door. Lynne Malloy instantly threw herself at them with an angry shriek. Dorkins punched her in the face and slung her over his shoulder as she fell. 'See?' he said, grinning. 'Told you this would be a piece of piss, didn't I?'

'Let's go.'

They marched the hundred yards back across the dusty wasteground to the barn, Lynne Malloy hanging limply upside-down over Dorkins' shoulder with her hair over her face. Grubb opened up the barn door. They walked inside. The male prisoners had been talking in low voices. Now they fell abruptly silent and turned in surprise. Kip Malloy struggled to his feet, clutching at the bars for support, and yelled, 'Lynne!'

'Wake up, bitch,' Dorkins said, dumping her back on her feet and slapping and shaking her. 'Come on, wakey wakey.' Lynne swayed woozily on her feet.

'Don't you hurt her,' Jeff warned.

'Shut your fucking mouth,' Dorkins snapped. To Grubb he said, 'Open the pen.'

Grubb hesitated. 'Sure about that?'

'I've got the gun, haven't I?'

Grubb shrugged, rattled his ring of keys and unlocked the pen door.

'Now, you two arseholes,' Dorkins said in a strong voice. 'It's time to start spilling the beans for real this time. Because if you don't, I'm going to blow this silly bitch's brains out right in front of you.' Holding Lynne tightly against him, he pressed the muzzle of the revolver to the base of her skull and thumbed back the hammer.

'Put that gun down,' Jeff said. His tone was completely calm and chillingly cold. His fists were balled at his sides and there was a look in his eyes that Grubb had never seen anything like before. It frightened him, but in this moment he was dominated by Dorkins' confidence.

'I mean it,' Dorkins said loudly. 'You'd better start talking, or she dies. And it'll be on you.'

Kip said, 'All right. Whatever you say. Just please don't harm her!'

Jeff took a step forward. His face was so tight it looked ready to split.

Dorkins took the gun away from his hostage and pointed it at Jeff. 'Whoa, there. You'd better not bloody come any closer if you know what's good for you.'

Jeff took another step.

Kip yelled, 'I'll talk! Get Cooper. I'll sign his damn papers and give him anything he wants. You let her go!'

Grubb said anxiously, 'Dave—'

Dorkins said, 'Shut up, Pete.' And to Jeff, 'You fucking stay back. Not another step.'

Jeff took another step.

'You asked for it!' Dorkins aimed the trembling weapon at Jeff's head.

But it was Dorkins who was asking for it, and he got it. Jeff moved so blindingly fast that the next thing Dorkins knew was also just about the last thing he'd ever know. The gun seemed to magically twist around in his grip, pointed straight back at him; in the same instant Lynne was torn from his grip and launched aside, falling to the floor well out of the field of fire. And then the gun went off with a bright white flash and a detonation like an artillery piece. Dorkins' head blew apart and he went down hard on his back. Grubb screamed, but his scream was cut short by a second blast that caught him in the centre of his chest and flattened him as if he'd been hit by a train.

Then, silence.

Chapter 23

On the long drive to the town of McCarthy, on a stretch of road with high rocky canyon walls to both sides, Ben found the place where he believed Jeff and Lynne had been abducted.

Years spent tracking the whereabouts of vanished kidnapped victims and the people who'd taken them had taught him to spot markers that all but the most practised eye could miss. Beyond that, his ability to put himself into the mind of the abductor, to think the way they thought, gave him a deep intuition for seeing things that weren't even visible to the eye. As he entered that stretch of road something just chimed inside him, and he knew that this was the spot he'd have chosen for the snatch. Its distance from Hobart's Creek made the timing about right, too.

He slowed the Mean Machine to a crawl, scanning the road, then stopped and reversed back a way to scan it again. More and more convinced of what he was seeing, he left Finn Mulkey tethered in the vehicle while he went to investigate more closely on foot, pacing up and down, squatting close to the ground, carefully scrutinising his surroundings in the fading light.

He was right.

The smoothness of the road surface, seemingly a rare thing in these parts, meant that a skidding vehicle would leave telltale tyre marks. Those would quickly be worn away by other traffic or baked off by the hot sun, but the ones he found were still fresh and smelled of rubber, no more than a few hours old. In two separate spots he also found traces of crash damage: some fragments of broken headlamp glass, bits of orange indicator lens and red taillight lens, and a small piece of chrome-effect plastic that looked like part of a car radiator emblem, and could have been the bottom corner of a letter H. H for Honda. Further along, over by the rocky wall that lined the edge of the right-hand lane, were traces of a second collision, suggestive of a vehicle running, or being run, off the road. Among them was a patch of spilled radiator coolant, still moist to the touch. But it was the flakes of bright yellow paint matching the colour of Lynne Malloy's car that left him in no doubt whatsoever about what had happened here.

Ben quickly put the scenario together. It looked as though the Honda had been intercepted by more than one vehicle, most likely fewer than three judging by the different tread patterns of the skidmarks. The little side junction to which he'd retraced his steps was probably where they'd been lying in wait, perhaps using a lookout perched high up among these rocks to spot the distinctive yellow car approaching from a distance. That way they'd been able to coordinate their attack, timing things perfectly to position themselves with one vehicle ahead of the target and one behind. It was a classic sandwich manoeuvre, and the stretch of road had been well chosen for the purpose, as the rocks tight against either verge prevented escape. To get the better of Jeff Dekker, they must have come prepared, numerous and well-armed – but Ben knew his friend wouldn't have wanted to endanger Lynne by putting up a fight. Jeff's hands had been tied. The snatch complete, the kidnappers had towed the damaged Honda away. Covering their tracks, not quite as inefficiently as they'd done when they snatched Kip.

Ben walked back to his vehicle. The shimmering blood-red sun had long since sunk below the ridge of the faraway western hills, and the light was going fast. There was nothing more he could do here, no way to trace where Lynne and Jeff had been taken. His only option was to proceed with his plan and hope Terry Napier would yield the answers he needed.

'I've got to get to a dunny, mate,' Mulkey complained bitterly as Ben got back behind the wheel. 'Busting for a crap, big time.'

'Do it in your pants,' Ben replied.

Darkness had fallen by the time he and his captive passenger reached the outback settlement of McCarthy, a place so small it would barely make the grade as a hamlet in Britain. They drove by the lights of a few scattered bungalow homes and Mulkey said, 'That's Terry's place. The one with the big tree in front.'

Ben slowed as he passed the house, and could see chinks of light shining out of gaps in the curtains. Someone was home. But instead of stopping he continued along the road until they were reaching the opposite end of town. Mulkey said, 'Where're you going?'

Ben said nothing. He drove on until they were out of sight of the last house, then did a tight U-turn and pulled over at the side.

'What're you doing?'

Ben still said nothing. He turned towards Mulkey and knocked him out with a hard fist to the jaw. Then he detached the unconscious prisoner from the passenger seat and used the same length of rope to hogtie him in the rear load bed, gagged with a piece of dirty rag and covered with a tarp.

Once that was taken care of, Ben drove back into McCarthy and parked the Mean Machine outside the bungalow with the lights behind the curtains and the big tree in front. He pulled the pump-action shotgun from the rack, got out and walked across the patchy, desiccated front lawn to the house with the gun in his hand. He knocked loudly on the front porch door and stepped back a step. A dog was barking somewhere in the distance.

A few moments later there was movement inside the house; an inner door creaked open, then the porch door, and the figure of a woman appeared, framed in the soft light from inside. She was wearing a halter top and tight blue jeans. Long black hair, beginning to grey in streaks, though she couldn't be much over forty. Her face had the weary look of a woman who didn't give a crap about much. She folded her arms across her chest, eyed Ben without expression and said, 'Wow, you must be the tall, handsome stranger my mother told me would come knocking at my door one day. What kept you all this time?'

'I'm looking for your husband, Terry,' Ben said.

'He's not here,' she replied. 'He hardly ever is. What's that for?' Looking at the gun.

'Rats,' Ben said. If Napier had answered the door, Ben would have had the business end of the barrel pointed in his face about now.

She seemed unbothered by it, as though men turning up on her doorstep with pump-action shotguns was a fairly routine event for her. She said, 'Well, like I say, he's not here. What do you want with him? Does he owe you money? Is it poker again?'

'Nothing like that,' Ben said, and to show a little more goodwill he set the gun down, propping it on its butt end against the porch. 'My name's Ben. I'm a friend of Kip Malloy. Just wanted to ask your husband something, but maybe you can help.'

She shrugged. 'Yeah, heard about Kip. Shitty thing to happen. You some kind of copper then, are you? Don't sound like you're from around here.'

'You might say I'm conducting a parallel investigation.'

'Then I suppose you might as well come in. You want a cup of tea or anything?'

The bored, lonely housewife invites the tall, handsome stranger inside while hubby is out. It wasn't the first time this had happened to him. He stepped into the porch and left the gun propped inside the door. 'I'm good, thanks.'

'I'm Sue, by the way.'

'It's nice to meet you, Sue.'

He followed her into the house. It was small, unassuming, and smelled of cooking. Some kind of meat stew was simmering in a pot on the kitchen stove. In the living room was a sideboard covered in framed pictures, one of them showing a much younger Terry and Sue, clasped tenderly together and smiling for the camera. Early in their marriage, Ben supposed. She'd looked far happier and been quite attractive back then, before their years together had begun to wear and sour her.

She invited him to sit, and he perched on the edge of an overstuffed sofa while she sat opposite, eyeing him curiously. 'You sure you don't want a cup of tea?'

He declined again with a polite smile, and then asked her who Terry was working for.

'Straight down to business,' she muttered. 'Story of my life.' With a frown she added, 'But you must know who he works for. Or worked for, before what happened. You reckon Kip's alive? Everybody says he must've copped it.'

'I don't mean Kip Malloy,' Ben said, sidestepping her question. 'I mean Terry's working for someone else.'

'If he is, it's the first I've heard of it,' she replied, with no lie in her eyes that Ben could see. 'Then again, he doesn't tell me much.'

'Doesn't tell you anything at all?'

Sue Napier considered for a moment, her head cocked a little to one side, and Ben sensed there was something on her mind. She said, 'Hmm. I mean, Kip's always been a good employer, as far as I know. Always paid a fair wage. We've never wanted for too much. But lately Terry's been talking about money. Big money, coming soon.' She gave a dry smile. 'Suits me. Then he'll have something decent to offer me when I divorce the rotten bastard. I'm not planning on

183

being around much longer, to be treated like his doormat.'

'You've no idea where this big money is supposed to be coming from?'

'I never asked.'

'Do you know where he is now?'

'No idea about that either. As long as he's not around here, I'm happy.'

'All the same,' Ben said, 'I'd like to know.'

'What are you going to do to him?' She narrowed her eyes suspiciously, remembering the gun. 'You're not going to shoot him, are you?'

'Would that bother you so much?'

'Yes, it bloody would,' she retorted. 'If there's money coming my way.'

Ben smiled. 'Would you call Terry for me, Sue? It's really important that I talk to him.'

She shrugged again. 'Why bother? He never answers his phone.'

'Give it a try anyway, will you?'

Sue stood, went over to pick up an old-style cordless phone and prodded out a number with a red fingernail. After a few moments she raised an eyebrow and said, 'Wow. It's actually ringing.'

Ben took the phone from her as Napier answered. 'This is Ben Hope. I'm at your house with your wife, Terry, so I'd advise you not to hang up.'

Chapter 24

There was a long stunned silence on the line, in which Ben could hear Napier breathing hard and fast. Then Napier said. 'Don't you touch her, you hear me?'

Napier's voice sounded strangled and harsh. Ben's was calm and smooth, but underlain with a hardness that left no doubt that he was deadly serious. 'That's up to you, Terry. Depends on how cooperative you're willing to be. Your pal Finn made the right choice. I'm hoping you will, too.'

After an audible gulp and another long pause, Napier said, 'All right, all right. What do you want?'

'Simple. You have my friends. I'd like them back.'

'No, I don't,' Napier burst out defensively.

'But the man you've been working for does.'

'I don't know what you're on about. I work for Kip.'

'Don't lie to me,' Ben said. 'It's not good for your health. The man you work for is the same man who ordered you to ransack the Malloys' house. That was you, wasn't it?'

Napier said nothing.

'That's what I thought. What were you looking for?'

Napier was still silent.

'I suppose, being a pathetic lackey, maybe you're so low down in the pecking order that you don't even know. Or maybe you're just too afraid of what your new boss might do to you if you talk. Then I'll just have to ask him myself. And you're going to meet me and take me to him, so that he and I can sort this whole thing out. I think he'll see sense.'

'I can't do that.'

'Yes, you can, Terry. And you will. Or you're going to face the consequences.'

'He won't see you just like that. I need to make a call.'

'Then make it,' Ben said. 'You have one hour.' He handed the phone back to Sue.

'What consequences?' she asked him, looking anxious now.

Ben said, 'Relax. The worst thing I'm going to do to you is act disappointed if you tell me you've got no coffee in the house.'

'There is.'

'Then perhaps you'd be kind enough to make a cup?'

She nodded mutely and went to the kitchen. While she was busy in there, Ben walked back to the porch and retrieved the shotgun. He laid it behind the armchair in the living room, so as not to alarm her. Presently the aroma of fresh coffee wafted from the kitchen, and a few moments later Sue returned, clutching a pair of mugs. 'How'd you take it?'

'As it comes,' he replied. He sipped the bitter, scalding brew. He'd had worse. He was only interested in the caffeine, because it could be several hours before anything more happened and he'd need to keep his mind sharp.

Sue sat, cradling her mug in her lap. 'Is Terry into something bad?'

Ben nodded. 'I'm afraid he is.'

'How bad?'

'It doesn't get much worse. Unless someone dies. Then it's murder. It might already be.'

'Jesus Christ. Forget I asked. I don't want to know,' she said with an agitated gesture. Then she sucked in a deep breath and let it out slowly. 'I always knew he was no good. He's a bully and a liar and now I find he's a bloody crook as well. I should have got out a long time ago.' She paused, biting her lip. 'Am I in trouble too?'

'You're going to be fine. I can't say the same for him.'

'What about the money? Does this mean there won't be any?'

'I'm afraid it does, Sue.'

'Will Terry go to jail?'

'If he's lucky,' Ben said. 'He's made a big mistake. Now he'll have to pay for that.'

She looked at him. 'Who *are* you?'

'I'm just a guy who has to look out for his friends,' Ben said.

'I could use a friend like that,' she muttered.

They waited. Ben brewed the next coffee, then left Sue alone in the house to step outside and smoke a Gauloise. The night was still and sultry, not a star to be seen in the inky-black sky. It felt as though a storm was slowly gathering, biding its time, waiting for the right moment to break.

Nothing approached on the dark streets of McCarthy. Ben felt calm, that particular kind of calmness he always felt before a battle. It wouldn't come yet. If Napier's mystery boss decided to mount an attack on the house, it would happen deep in the night, no sooner than three or four in the morning, that magic hour when the rest of the world is fast asleep and the body's rhythms are at the lowest point of their daily cycle, when most prospective raid targets were at their most physically and mentally sluggish and vulnerable. Not Ben. He had virtually written the book on night assaults, and he'd be more than ready for them when they came. It was Sue Napier's safety he was worried about, if things got nasty. As he was thinking about the options, she emerged from the house and joined him.

'It's warm,' she said.

'It could get hotter,' he told her. 'Have you somewhere safe you can go?'

She looked at him, understanding his meaning. 'I could go and stay with my friend Molly.'

'Then I think you should do that.'

'Right now? Do I have time to pack some overnight stuff?'

'Be quick,' he said.

Sue went back into the house, and Ben went with her. While she was in the bedroom throwing some items in a bag, he rechecked the shotgun. The magazine carried seven rounds of heavy buckshot, and a shell holder on the butt held another five. It wasn't a lot of firepower to fight off a determined attack with. The hunting rifle was still in the Mean Machine. He was debating whether or not to go and fetch it when Sue emerged from the bedroom with her bag on her shoulder. 'I'm ready,' she announced.

'Then you'd best be on your way,' Ben replied.

But it was already too late, because at that moment a blaze of headlights swept the front of the house. Ben turned off the lights inside, grabbed the shotgun and went to peer through the chink in the curtains.

As he watched, a pickup truck pulled sharply up at the kerbside in front of the house, a few metres behind the Mean Machine. Its driver's door opened, and the interior light came on, showing the solitary occupant.

'It's your husband,' Ben said. 'He's alone.'

'Excuse me if I don't swoon with excitement,' Sue replied. 'So what now?'

'Change of plan. You won't be needing that overnight bag after all.'

'And what are you going to do?'

'What I said I was going to do.'

'You be careful, okay?'

Ben smiled. 'Always. It was nice meeting you, Sue.'

Chapter 25

Terry Napier stepped out of his pickup truck and hovered warily by the kerb, keeping his distance and staring at the house as Ben walked out to meet him carrying the shotgun. Sue stood in the doorway, leaning against the frame with her arms folded and a frown on her brow.

Napier called out to his wife, 'Sue, you okay?'

'Nah, I'm all raped to bits and my throat's been cut,' she fired back at him. 'What does it bloody look like? Not that you'd give a shit, you lousy oaf.' The joys of marital harmony.

Ben stopped a few steps away from Napier. The man didn't appear to be armed, and he looked nervous and edgy. As was to be expected, in his situation. Ben held the gun in a loose grip without pointing it at him, but he could deploy it in an instant and Napier knew that very well.

Ben motioned towards the Mean Machine and said, 'I've got something of yours in the back of the truck. Go on, take a look.'

Napier hesitated, then stepped over to the vehicle and tentatively peeled back a corner of the tarp to reveal the trussed-up shape of his friend Finn Mulkey lying in the load bay. He was conscious and wriggling like a landed fish, eyes open wide at the sight of Napier, his best mate come to rescue him. He tried to speak, his words muffled by the gag.

Ben said, 'Play ball with me and you'll get him back in one piece. If not, then what happens to him is on you.'

Napier gave the captive little more than a cursory glance before he let the corner of the tarp back down over him. 'Yeah. Whatever.' So much for bosom buddies.

Ben said, 'You can step away from the truck now.' Napier retreated back to his own and stood next to it, eyes on the gun in Ben's hand.

'Confession time,' Ben said. 'You going to tell me what this is about?'

'Ask the boss,' Napier replied. 'He's agreed to meet you and he'll tell you the whole story.'

'I'm not interested in stories. I'm interested in the well-being of the three people he's kidnapped. They'd better be okay.'

'Talk to the boss,' Napier repeated flatly.

'Then lead on. I look forward to making his acquaintance. And remember, Terry, no tricks. I know where you live.'

Napier grunted and got back in his pickup. Ben climbed behind the wheel of the Mean Machine and stowed the shotgun in the passenger footwell next to him. They started their engines, turned on their lights, and Ben looked back at the house where Sue Napier was still in the doorway, shielding her eyes from the glare. He gave her a thumbs-up and a reassuring nod. Then her husband was taking off up the street, and Ben spurred the Mean Machine after him.

In a matter of minutes they'd left the tiny town far behind

them and were deep in the bush. The road they were on was heading south, narrower and less well surfaced than the one by which Ben had reached McCarthy. Napier's headlights carved a bright swathe through the night ahead and the flat, featureless terrain all around them. He was driving fast and Ben was right there behind him. The empty road streaked under their wheels. Ben wondered where he was being led, and what was to come of it.

They rolled on into the night for about another ten miles of nothingness before the pickup began to slow. Its brake lights didn't flare red. It looked as if Napier had taken his foot off the gas and let the vehicle coast. Ben peered ahead and could see nothing, no sign of habitation anywhere, just more empty road and wilderness as far as the beams of their headlights could reach. The pickup kept slowing, making him brake. His speedometer needle sagged lower and lower until they'd reduced their speed to walking pace. Now the pickup coasted to a complete halt. Ben pulled up behind, watching. Napier was sitting at the wheel. His engine seemed to have stalled; Ben could see him trying to restart it.

After what looked like a few failed attempts, Napier reached under the dash and Ben heard the faint clunk of the bonnet release. Then the pickup's driver door swung open and Napier got out and walked around the front to raise the bonnet lid, momentarily lit bright by his own headlamps before he disappeared from view behind the lid.

Half a minute went by, during which Napier appeared to be fiddling around with something under the bonnet. Ben considered the various possibilities of what might be happening here. He went on waiting. The road both ahead and behind them was completely still and deserted. Nothing stirred in a great wide circle of open countryside all around them, under the massive inky dome of the sky. He waited a few moments longer, then thought *fuck it*, grabbed a long metal torch from its clip on the dashboard and jumped down from the Mean Machine and started walking towards the pickup to see what was up.

Ben had walked a few steps from his vehicle when he shone his torch through the back window of the pickup and saw that Napier had plucked the key from the ignition. His alarm bells instantly began to jangle loudly in his mind, but there wasn't time to react, because in the next instant Napier suddenly lurched out from behind the raised bonnet lid, broke away from the pickup and bolted like an ungainly, overweight hare for the side of the road, head ducked low, his bandy legs pumping hard.

Ben yelled, 'Napier, stop!'

But Napier didn't stop. Ben shone the strong beam of the torch after him, and saw that he was racing towards a black pool of shadow in the undulating terrain that now, in the torchlight, appeared to be a deep dip fringed with bushes. Ben gave chase. Napier was no athlete, that was for sure. If the guy thought there was even the slightest possibility of his getting away on foot from a fit runner, he was dreaming.

In the bouncing pool of the torch beam Ben saw Napier go wading and scrambling in among the bushes. He ran faster, angry now, intent on catching the idiot and dragging him back up to the road for a good pasting.

That was when the bushes and the hidden dip behind them were suddenly lit up in a blinding glare of white light, and in the next split second came the roaring rasp of a powerful engine. And that was when Ben realised he'd been lured into an ambush.

Like a monster bursting up out of the ground, the offroad truck came surging aggressively up from the dip. Big knobbly tyres ploughing up the loose dirt and crushing the bushes flat. Powerful hunting spotlights that could fry a kangaroo at twenty paces searing Ben's eyeballs. The truck reached the top of the rise and came straight for him. For half a heartbeat, he froze in his tracks. Then he turned and sprinted hard back towards his own vehicle.

But the driver's intention wasn't to run him down. The truck skidded to a halt near the edge of the road. It was quickly joined by another, and the two pulled up side by side at an open angle, illuminating the whole scene like daylight with their dazzling spotlamps.

Ben reached the cover of the Mean Machine and ducked behind it, because he knew what was coming next. Behind the harsh glare of the lights he could make out the flitting figures of running men. How many, it was hard to say, but he guessed if his opponents were numerous enough to fill the crew cabs of two large offroaders, they would be at least ten strong. If the trucks hadn't come roaring right up onto the road to run him down, he supposed that was only because the men had been advised that their lone opponent was armed and dangerous. Now they were digging in for a fight. At least ten men meant at least ten guns. Ben knew the shooting would kick off before too long.

Napier had reached the safety of the trucks, rejoining his cronies. Ben heard him yelling in a voice that was hoarse and almost breathless with mixed relief and glee, 'You should never have stuck your nose into this business, Hope!'

Keeping low, Ben scrambled into the cab of the Mean Machine and grabbed both of Kip's guns from the rack, then flipped the dashboard toggle switch that turned on his own impressive roof-mounted array of spotlamps. If you could fight fire with fire, you could also fight light with light, and the dazzle would help to obscure the enemy's view of him. Then he slipped back down to the ground and took cover squatting down low behind the driver's side wing; the solid metal of the vehicle's engine block and chunky axle and suspension components would help to shield him from incoming gunfire. Peering cautiously out from behind his shelter with his eyes narrowed against the strong lights, he could dimly observe the men spreading out and hunkering down close to the ground near their vehicles and in a scattered line along the roadside bushes. There were more than he'd initially guessed, at least twelve or thirteen.

At times like this, under the kind of pressure that makes most men fold and panic, Ben was at his most focused and composed. He coolly evaluated the tactical strengths and weaknesses of his situation. The former were few, the latter many. Here he was pinned out in the open, spotlit in the full glare of their lights, with no possibility of making a break for it and nowhere to run to if he could. His ammunition was limited to a dozen shotgun shells plus the eight cartridges that his rifle magazine contained. By contrast the enemy probably had hundreds of rounds to fling at him. They had chosen their ambush spot to offer lots of natural cover and a wide field of fire. He was outgunned and outnumbered at least twelve or thirteen to one, plus Terry Napier, who was sure to have been given something to shoot with, too. Theoretically, all things being equal, he was in an unwinnable position.

Except that all things weren't equal. Not by a long chalk.

'Give it up, Hope!' yelled Napier from behind the dazzling glare. 'You haven't got a chance in hell, so come on out and let's talk!'

Which made Ben wonder for a moment whether they were serious about negotiating terms with him. What might those be: to agree to let him walk away from this unscathed if he promised to abandon his friends to their fate and leave Australia on the next flight? Why would they make him an offer like that, given that they had such an overwhelming theoretical advantage over him? More likely, it was a bluff to trick him into throwing down his weapons and walking out, hands raised, into a wall of bullets.

No, his instinct told him that these guys weren't interested in talking. This wasn't about warning him to butt out of their business and go home. They'd come here to kill him and that's what they meant to do.

In the next moment, his instinct was proven right. The first shotgun blast exploded the wing mirror above Ben's head into glassy fragments that sprinkled him like ice. The second punched a colander of buckshot holes into the Mean Machine's aluminium bodywork and rocked the vehicle on its springs. A third obliterated the driver's side window.

The fight had started. Now it was just a question of seeing who would finish it.

Chapter 26

More booming volleys of gunfire rang out from the line of shooters, their muzzle flashes only half visible in the bright dazzle of the lights. Twelve-gauge shotguns, Ben's ears told him. The heavy charges of calibre buckshot slammed one after another into the Mean Machine's body and cab. It was a tough truck, built to absorb a lot of punishment, but even so Ben knew that if this went on too much longer the thing would be riddled with holes and blown to pieces. Assuming he had a chance of getting out of the fight alive and in any state to get away from here, then he was going to need viable transportation – or face being stranded in the wilderness. Not good.

But there was an alternative. Ben raised the shotgun up over the edge of the bonnet, fired off a shell with the sound of a grenade exploding, worked the pump hard and fast and squeezed off a second shot. It was intended purely as a distraction tactic. While the enemy ducked their heads down he grabbed the rifle, jumped out from behind the Mean Machine and, clutching a weapon in each hand, sprinted in a wild zigzag for the cover of Napier's pickup truck. It was just a few metres in front of his own vehicle – but a few metres was a long way to run when you were taking fire.

A few shots sounded as he was dashing across the no-man's land between them. His erratic motion against the glare of his spotlights made it hard for the enemy to get a bead on him. In three seconds he'd reached the pickup and was taking cover behind it. It was a compromise: now he was a little closer to the enemy line, but at least it enabled him to draw their fire away from his own vehicle. Let them use their ammo up on this one, to their hearts' content.

He ducked down tight for a few moments as a renewed storm of gunshots began to hammer the pickup truck. A tyre exploded and the vehicle went down at one corner. A window blew apart. The thumping, percussive blasts told him those were more of the same heavy buckshot rounds; the next one wasn't, as a rifle bullet punched through the front grille and impacted against solid steel with a clang like a hammer smashing into an anvil, followed a split-second later by the loud, barking report of a high-velocity rifle. That was the kind of weapon that concerned Ben the most, because even at longer ranges a bullet from one of those could easily pierce through both sides of a motor vehicle and keep sizzling onwards with enough ballistic energy to blow a man's head off.

Then again, Ben had a weapon just like it to play with, too. And now it was time to start giving back some of what these guys were doling out. Snatching up the rifle and quickly unfolding the legs of its attached bipod he rolled himself prone under the bottom sill of the pickup truck and wriggled deep beneath its belly. The vehicle's raised suspension allowed him to lie flat on his front with his elbows planted on the ground and the weapon resting on its V-shaped metal legs. Once the eight rounds of shiny, pointed .308 full-metal-jacket ammunition in his magazine were gone, they were gone. Better make them count, then, he thought. Bolt back, bolt forward. Loaded and locked.

With his eye to the scope he scanned the enemy line searching for a target, but the glare of the enemy spotlamps was painfully bright in the lens, making him blink and impeding his visibility. He diverted his aim towards one of the bright lights. It was too dazzling to aim at properly, but at this close range it was so large in his reticle that he didn't need to. The trigger broke crisply under his fingertip and the rifle kicked against his shoulder with an ear-splitting crack. Before the sound of his shot had even reached the enemy's ears the spotlight was exploded into a million pieces, instantly dark.

Ben swivelled the weapon to point at another. Bolt back; the tinkle of the ejected cartridge casing hitting the ground, barely audible over the ringing in his ears. Bolt forward; the next round sliding into battery, ready to fire. *Bang.* The second spotlight went dark. For the next shot he lowered his aim to focus his fire on one of the blazing truck head-lamps. Same result.

Three rounds gone, five left in the gun. Thanks to the reduced amount of glare in his eyes, visibility was improved enough to start picking out individual targets in the shadows of the bushes. One of them was dug down in the dirt near to the truck Ben had just fired at, his shape no longer masked by the dazzling lights. Now he filled the scope's field of view, a bulky bearded man in a sleeveless combat jacket, fists clenched around a thick black semi-auto shotgun with a crazed glimmer in his eyes. With no hesitation Ben nailed him dead centre in the crosshairs, pressed the trigger and punched him a third eye, a gaping red one in the middle of his forehead. The man flailed for an instant and collapsed in a limp heap. By then Ben was already working the bolt, smooth and fast, and moving on with calm, implacable predatory efficiency in search of his next target.

He soon found him just a few feet away: the dead man's nearest neighbour in the bushes, filled with panic at the sight of his comrade slumped lifelessly to the ground like a bag of washing, rising half to his feet and scrabbling desperately for deeper cover, and in so doing giving Ben a clean shot, centre of mass. Ben's ears filled again with the crashing thunder of the shot and the rifle's lively recoil thumped against his shoulder. The bullet reached its target before the deafening report ever would, slamming the man down with brutal force. He disappeared into the bushes, from where he wouldn't be coming out again except dragged by the ankles.

Ben worked his bolt slickly back and forward again. The fierce, heady thrill of battle cascading through his veins, all senses in overdrive, mind and body perfectly harmonised, the high-pitched ringing in his ears, the fresh sharp tang of burnt powder from the hot breech of his gun. For the trigger-happy hicks who'd been sent to take him down this was a once-in-a-lifetime experience, one they'd probably rehearsed many times in their macho fantasies, none of which could possibly prepare them for the raw, gut-wrenching, heart-stopping, blood-chilling terror of the real thing. For a man like Ben Hope, who'd done the things he'd done in his life and was still here to tell the tale, this was just another day at the office.

Now the enemy had spotted Ben's bright yellow-white muzzle flash under the truck and began to concentrate their fire in that direction, instead of just randomly blowing holes in the bodywork and shattering windows and headlights. Buckshot and bullets started striking off the road surface just inches away from where he lay, cratering the asphalt and ricocheting dangerously off the truck's underside. It was getting a little close for comfort. He quickly scrambled back on his knees and elbows, dragging the rifle with him by its leather sling, and kept moving until he'd reached the rear of the truck and was able to crawl out from under its back bumper. Staying out of sight, he clambered onto the load bed, reasonably protected from shotgun blasts but by no means impervious to a bullet strike passing through glass and thin sheet metal. The spare steel wheel bolted to the bulkhead behind the cab offered him a little better protection. He settled the gun over it for another shot and directed it at a hunched, running figure that appeared briefly silhouetted against the headlights of the second truck.

Bad idea, moving out into the open like that. In a flash, the man was pinned in the X of Ben's crosshairs and then knocked sideways off his feet before he knew what hit him. The bullet must have passed right through his body, because in the same instant another headlight went dark behind him.

Six rounds gone. Just two left in the rifle.

No sooner had Ben got the shot off, but he was being

driven back again by an intense salvo of shots directed uncomfortably close. The incoming fire was steadily chewing Napier's pickup to pieces. The truck sank on its suspension as a second tyre was shredded, then a third. Every window was blown out, the interior and the load bay covered in pebbled glass fragments, the bodywork perforated by scores of holes. But with three of their men dead the tide had now begun to turn against the enemy, and they surely knew it. These were not men used to battle. They'd most likely come here thinking that taking out one guy on his own would be easy meat. Right now it would be starting to dawn on them that they'd been wrong. Ben knew from a lifetime of war and combat what a demoralising effect that chilling realisation could have on a man's fighting spirit.

Once again, the next few moments proved Ben's instinct right.

Chapter 27

After that brief, explosive crescendo he sensed the enemy's rate of fire slackening, and peered out from cover to see them beginning to fall back. Maybe they were running low on ammunition; or maybe they just wanted to save themselves before what should have been an easy victory for them turned into a rout. Running shapes were abandoning their cover and beating a retreat back to their vehicles. One of them reached his truck, jittery with panic, and went to yank open the driver's door and hurl himself behind the wheel, but he hesitated for just half a second too long in full view and clearly backlit in the glow of one of the remaining spotlamps. Ben's seventh rifle bullet passed through the glass of the open driver's door window and blew the man back from the truck as though he'd been kicked by a horse.

Four men down, one round left in the rifle. If anyone else was thinking of trying to take the guy's place, they were neither brave nor foolish enough to chance it. That vehicle was abandoned as the surviving men all piled into the other truck. Some threw themselves into the crew cab while others leaped up onto the load bed, clinging wildly to the bars of the roll cage or anything else they could latch onto. The truck's engine burst into life and clouds of dust kicked up from its spinning wheels as it slewed violently around in a U-turn, racing back from the road and towards the shadowy dip.

Ben was already tearing out from behind the cover of Napier's bullet-shredded vehicle, slinging the rifle over his shoulder, snatching up the shotgun and pumping round after round into the back of the escaping truck in the hope that he might be able to nick a fuel line or disable something mechanical. A shotgun was an inherently less precise tool than a rifle, and he hit something else instead; there was a howl and one of the men clinging like monkeys to the roll cage came flying off to go tumbling into the dirt. Then the truck was gone, hurtling down into the dip, flooding the shadows with its lights.

Ben's shotgun was empty. He ran towards the edge of the road, plucking cartridges from the holder on the butt and thumbing them into the tube magazine as he went. Moments later, the truck surged back into sight on the far side of the dip, fifty or sixty yards away now, revving like a mad bull, bucking and jolting over the rough ground. The remaining men in the load bay were being tossed around like rag dolls. Ben fired off another blast from the shotgun, but by now the truck was moving fast out of range. Sixty yards, seventy, eighty. He laid that weapon down and unslung the near-empty rifle.

Just one cartridge left. His marksmanship skills may not have been quite on a par with those of master sniper Tuesday Fletcher, back home at Le Val, but they weren't so shabby that he might not still be able to give the enemy something to think about with his eighth and last round.

He lay flat on his belly near the roadside and settled the legs of the bipod in the dirt, giving the rifle a solid rest. All he could see through the scope were the bouncing red dots of the truck's taillights and the bright white beam of its sole remaining spotlight shining ahead. The truck itself was just a small dark blob, jumping about so crazily over the rough terrain that it was hard to get a shot, and getting harder with every passing second.

Ben would rather have kept that last round in the gun than waste it by squeezing off a wild random shot. He was about to give up on the idea when the truck suddenly stopped moving.

What were they doing? As he watched, he saw the spotlight rotate around on its swivel mounting as one of the men deliberately pointed it a hundred and eighty degrees backwards to shine back at him. To the naked eye it looked like a bright star, twinkling alone in the middle of the dark, empty landscape. Seen through the high-magnification scope its glaring light seared Ben's retina, but not so much that he didn't have a clearly illuminated view of the back of the truck. He counted four men there. At this range, which he estimated at something just over seven hundred yards, three of them appeared as little more than tiny matchstick figures silhouetted against the light. But the fourth was standing in the middle of the rear load bed with the beam shining on him in such as way as to show him up in more detail.

Ben realised that man was Terry Napier. Except to say he was standing there didn't quite describe his strange antics.

Napier appeared to be doing a funny little dance, leaping up and down like a lunatic, throwing out his arms and legs in manic gestures as though he were fighting off a swarm of attacking bees. What on earth was the guy up to?

The answer came clear to Ben soon enough. Napier had evidently instructed the driver to stop, and had deliberately turned the spotlight backwards, not on Ben but rather on himself, because he *wanted* to be seen. It was his way of refusing to admit defeat. A show of defiance, a vow that this wasn't over yet. Listening hard, Ben could just about make out the sound of Napier's voice echoing across the wide open ground, screaming insults and curses whose meaning was lost in the wind but whose tone was telling enough. After a series of obscene gestures, Napier turned around, bent over and slapped and waggled his buttocks. *Kiss my arse*, was the clear message.

And there it was. If you couldn't beat your enemy in battle, you could always just retreat to a safe distance to taunt and jeer at him.

Or, at any rate, what you *thought* was a safe distance. Napier clearly believed he was comfortably out of range. Maybe he was right, Ben thought. Or maybe not.

There was only one way to find out.

Ben let his muscles relax and his heart rate and breathing slow. Weapon ready to fire, finger off the trigger, his aim locked on the tiny figure of Terry Napier, still hopping and gyrating about like a man possessed seven hundred yards away. Ben's finger inched forward and gently rested on the smooth curve of the trigger blade. He took in a long breath, let half of it out, then with the crosshairs as perfectly, delicately centred on the minuscule target as he knew how, he touched off the round. The trigger broke cleanly and crisply, with that oh-so-subtle but deeply satisfying instinctive sensation of a shot well fired. By the time the recoil punched his shoulder, the bullet was already on its way, travelling through the darkness at around three thousand feet per second which meant it would take about point-seven of a second to cover the distance, reaching its target ahead of its sound wave so that it would strike in deadly silence before anyone knew what was happening.

Out of range? Not quite.

As he watched, he saw the tiny dancing figure make one last wild leap in the air, spin like a manic ballet dancer and then fold double and slam down hard on the flatbed of the truck. The other tiny figures dived for cover, like ants fleeing a disturbed anthill. Then the truck took off again in a cloud of dust that obscured its lights from view. Next time Ben saw it was the last, bucking over the ruts more than nine hundred yards distant before it finally vanished into the night.

Chapter 28

Ben got to his feet and dusted himself off. Alone again in the stillness of the night, with only dead men for company.

He looked at the two abandoned vehicles. Terry Napier's pickup looked as though it had been used for target practice on a military firing range, chewed all to bits. Ben walked over to the other and examined it. Up close, the first thing he noticed was that the number plates had been removed. Climbing up inside the cab, avoiding the blood spatter on the door frame, he brushed away the mess of broken glass off the driver's seat and sat at the wheel. The keys were still in the ignition. Rummaging around inside the glove box he found some odd automotive fuses, a screwdriver, a pack of Rothmans and a disposable lighter, and nothing to indicate who the vehicle was registered to, if indeed it was registered to anyone.

Next he went to examine the corpses. The effects of a high-velocity rifle on the human body at close range weren't a pretty sight. The first one he'd shot, the bulky bearded guy, had had the top of his head hollowed out like the inside of a canoe, and his face looked like a featureless hunk of raw beef with a beard attached. The blood was seeping into the ground in a wide patch, glistening darkly in the light from the Mean Machine's spotlamps. Ben checked the dead man's pockets and found the usual personal items along with a fat roll of cash that he pocketed as spoils of war, but no wallet, no cards, no ID. Moving on to the others in turn, he got the same result until he scrambled down into the ditch and waded through the bushes and thorny scrub to check the furthest away, who'd fallen off the back of the escaping truck. There he found a slim leather wallet containing a driving licence in the name Kenneth Hardcastle, with a photo that matched the guy's dead, staring face.

Ben pocketed the licence and made his way back to the road. His own vehicle had been hit a few times in the gunfight, but the engine still fired up and it seemed that nothing major had been damaged. The exception to that was Finn Mulkey. In the excitement Ben had all but forgotten about his captive tethered up in the back. Lifting the tarp that covered him he saw it was red with blood. One of those first volleys of gunfire had got him through the heart.

RIP Finn Mulkey. Ben wasn't going to lose any sleep over the guy.

He gazed up and down the road. It was empty and dark as far as the eye could see in both directions. Sooner or later, though, someone was going to turn up at the scene, and next thing Sergeant Wenzel and his cohorts would be all over this place like a bad smell. Ben wanted to get out of here fast, but first he'd need to clear up the mess.

It took a while to drag all the dead men up into the back of their abandoned truck, including Finn Mulkey but leaving out the guy on the far side of the ditch who could stay where he was. The dingoes and other wild creatures would probably dispose of him before he was discovered. Meantime, Ben already had enough work to do. By the time he'd finished, the load bed was heaped with enough corpses to feed the Hobart's Creek crocodiles for a week. He wiped the blood off his hands, got back in the cab, started the engine and circled the truck up behind Napier's destroyed pickup, until they were touching front to back. He got out, released Napier's handbrake and stuck it in neutral, then climbed back behind the wheel and shunted the pickup off the road to the ditch. One last nudge and it went rolling down the steep incline with a ripping and crackling of dry twigs, until it crunched softly against the bottom.

Next it was the other's turn. He let it coast the last few yards to the edge of the ditch and jumped out and watched it disappear into the shadows. Both vehicles were hidden well out of sight of the road, leaving only the debris of broken glass and metal, cartridge casings and other signs that would go unnoticed by most passersby. It wasn't perfect, but it was good enough. Ben returned to the Mean Machine and left the scene.

It was only on the long drive back through the night towards Hobart's Creek that his mind began to settle after the fight, and a dejected heaviness came over him at the knowledge that with the complete failure of his plan, he'd learned nothing of any real value and still had no idea where to find Jeff, Lynne or Kip. If Kip was still alive. If any of them were still alive.

Arriving back at the farm before dawn, he stripped off

his clothes, streaked with dirt and dead men's blood, and stood for a long time under a hot shower letting the water pummel and massage his sore muscles. Feeling suddenly shattered with exhaustion, he fell on his bed and was asleep the instant his head touched the pillow. When he awoke, instantly sharp and alert again, dawn had broken. He put on fresh clothing from his bag and stepped outside as the first of the farm's workers began to appear for their daily duties.

Ben gathered them all together in the yard with an announcement to make. 'Sorry, folks. The business is closed until further notice and you all need to put down whatever you're doing and go home, effective immediately.'

'Where's Terry?' someone asked. 'How come it's some stranger telling us this, and not him?'

'Terry's fired,' Ben said. 'He won't be back.'

'Who's going to look after the crocs?'

'I think the crocs are big enough and ugly enough to look after themselves, don't you?' he replied.

There was a lot of grumbling and some deeply unhappy faces as, one by one, they got in their cars and left. When the last one was gone, he closed and padlocked the gates. Kip and Lynne's thriving little concern now felt desolate and empty, and Ben felt bad for the workers who faced having to find another job. Many of them had worked here for years; some went back all the way to the beginning.

Ben lit a Gauloise and walked slowly back to the farmhouse to prepare for the next round. He felt physically hungry but he had no appetite for food, and made do instead with a mug of strong black coffee. The house was still a mess after the ransacking job. Among the tipped-out contents of a drawer in Lynne and Kip's bedroom he found a fresh box of rifle ammunition and another of twelve-gauge shotgun shells, and topped up both of his weapons. There was every chance that the enemy were going to come for him here at the farm. But that was what he wanted. Because he still had nothing to go on, and no clue about who these people were.

All that was about to change, though Ben didn't know it yet.

With a thousand thoughts on his mind and a cold hollow feeling in the pit of his stomach, he sat in a chair with the loaded shotgun laid across his knee. He was good at waiting; had spent countless hours poised on standby before going into action, or on stakeouts where nothing might happen for days at a stretch, patiently biding his time, ready to move at an instant's notice. But something about this situation was different, and it was eating him. At last his restlessness got the better of him, and on an impulse he left the house and set off across the eerily deserted farmstead to revisit Sammy Mudrooroo's cabin. What that impulse was exactly, or where it had sprung up from, he didn't know. It was almost as though a voice in his head was telling him to go there.

As it turned out, his impulse was wrong. When he climbed the steps to the cabin and pushed open the door, he found the cabin as empty as the other two occasions he'd seen it. But at the same time, it was right. Because someone *had* been there since Ben's last visit.

The small sheet of notepaper had been placed very deliberately and conspicuously in the middle of the otherwise bare table in the cabin's tiny living room. Picking it up, Ben soon realised why. It was a note to him. As letters went, it was short and pithy, but it conveyed a great deal of information in just a few words and numbers. The numbers were instantly recognisable as a set of navigation coordinates. And the words, all six of them, were handwritten in an oversized scrawl that just said:

THE TRUTH IS WAITING FOR YOU

Underneath, the signature was a plain 'S'. S for Sammy. As mysterious as ever. Ben understood this was Sammy's way of inviting him to talk.

He walked quickly back to the house, hunted through the mess of books and periodicals and papers that had been torn down from the kitchen dresser, pulled out the rest of Kip's collection of Northern Territory ordnance survey maps and found the one he needed. He carried it over to the kitchen table, spread it out and got to work pinpointing the coordinates from Sammy Mudrooroo's cryptic note.

As he soon discovered, they denoted a location a long way south of Hobart's Creek, on a latitude parallel with Mad Mick's enormous tract of land, but far to the west. It was right out in the deepest heart of the outback, a long distance from anywhere with a place name or any kind of road or track marked, not even on the highly detailed large-scale map. Closely studying the topographical features of the area, he saw that Sammy's chosen rendezvous point was on high ground, bounded by tall hills and deep valleys and rivers, and almost certainly impossible to reach on four wheels – even for a vehicle as ruggedly capable as the Mean Machine. It appeared that Sammy wanted to speak very privately indeed. Ben had a serious desire to hear what the man had to say. He was going to have to figure out a way to get there, fast.

There were only two types of transportation Ben had ever come across that could carry you across terrain like that. One was a horse – and even a horse had its limits. The other was yet more versatile. And that was just the thing he needed. Something that could take you just about anywhere, set you down in places where there weren't even any places.

And as Abbie Logan's very words came back to him, he knew who he needed to call.

He soon found the number on which he and Jeff had contacted her charter company to book the flight from Darwin to Borroloola. The receptionist told him that Ms Logan was on a job but expected back at base shortly, and he left his number. Thirty minutes later, his phone rang and her bright, cheery voice came on the line.

'Let me guess why you're calling. You and your cobber have finished up your business and you're ready to head back to Darwin?'

The words stung Ben more than he was willing to let show. He replied, 'Not just yet. Still a few loose ends to tie up before we leave.'

'Pleased to hear it, mate. I thought we were going to lose you.'

'Listen, Abbie, the reason I called is that I might have

another little flying gig for you, if you're up for it. How's your schedule for the rest of today?'

'Chocka, mate, but I can make space. Because it's you.'

'It's a helicopter job this time. Might be a bit more challenging than the last.'

She laughed. 'Sounds like just the thing I need to liven up my dull and empty life. Never said no to a challenge yet. Let's give it a whirl. Where to?'

Chapter 29

At seven-thirty that morning, Wiley Cooper was in a portable office unit at one of the eleven industrial development sites currently maintained by W.F. Cooper & Co. Always an early riser, he'd been juggling phone calls and emails for the last forty-five minutes, during which time he'd fired three employees, hired half a dozen more, bullied a new business contact into accepting some tough contractual terms and arranged the purchase of additional plant equipment to the tune of quarter of a million dollars. Anyone secretly hoping that their tyrannical company boss might retire at some point – and there were a lot of them – was in for a disappointment.

At this moment Wiley was bent over a desk reviewing some structural engineering plans with his habitually obsessive attention to detail. Men in yellow vests and hard hats were busily to-ing and fro-ing outside, supply vehicles rumbled in and out of the gated site, and in the background could be heard the constant clatter and grind of heavy machinery. Through the dusty windows of the prefabricated office Wiley had a view of the two large cranes lifting construction parts into place. The plant equipment and materials all came from his company base, a large fenced security compound outside the outback town of Elliott, where the majority of his business took place and most of his employees worked.

He was deep in his plans when his mobile began to burr. He'd been expecting the call, and he snatched up the phone without bothering to look at the caller ID. He was about to snap, 'Turnbull, you'd better be calling to say you got that fucking shipment of concrete you promised me for last Tuesday.' But then he realised that it was his other phone ringing, the phone he used for the less legitimate side of his business affairs.

The caller said, 'Boss, Mr Cooper, sir, it's Kev Souter.'

Souter was one of the lower-down members of the crew that Wiley had entrusted to Terry Napier. He sounded extremely nervous, and the moment Wiley heard his voice he knew he was in for some bad news. Which came as little surprise. He'd been calling Napier's mobile every thirty minutes through the wee small hours for an update on the Hope situation, until he'd finally given up sometime after four. Best-case scenario, the idiot had forgotten to turn his phone on again, in which case there'd be hell to pay. Worst-case? Wiley didn't want to even consider it. But now it seemed his fears were about to be confirmed.

'It . . . ah, um, it didn't quite go the way we planned it, boss.'

Wiley felt the sharp jab of a migraine starting up somewhere behind his eyes. He screwed them tightly shut, pinched the bridge of his nose and let out a deep sigh. 'Go on. What happened?'

'Hope got away,' Souter said, sounding even more nervous. 'And . . . we didn't come off so well.' He gave a brief, stumbling account of the failed mission.

Wiley gripped the phone, feeling the pressure of the white-hot rage surging up through him, from his feet upwards. Then he exploded. 'Stupid useless fucking imbeciles! All those men against one, and you let him make fools out of you. How many does it take to bring this bastard down?'

'He had help,' protested the hapless voice on the line. 'Must've been at least five or six of them, maybe more. The lads reckon he's enlisted a whole bunch of special forces blokes to back him up.'

'Did you see them?'

'N-no, b-but— I mean, he must've.'

'Bullshit!' Wiley yelled down the phone. 'You just haven't got the guts to admit you fucked up. Why am I talking to you, anyway? Put Napier on the line.'

'Can't do that, boss.'

Was this man actually refusing a direct order? Wiley seethed, 'Why not?'

''Cause Hope shot him, that's why.'

'I see. Is he dead? He'd better be. Or else I'll fucking kill him myself.'

'He's not dead, boss.'

'Then what kind of state is he in? Why can't he report to me personally?'

Souter replied, 'What kind of state would any bloke be in, with his bollocks shot off?'

'His bollocks?'

'That's right, boss. I mean, what kind of sick piece of shit would blow a man's bollocks off? And Hope did it from about a thousand bloody yards away, with one shot, in the dark. I'm telling you, the guy's not human. It's going to take a bloody army to stop him.'

Which wasn't at all what Wiley needed to hear. He ended the call, hurled the phone into a wastepaper basket and began pacing up and down, gnashing his teeth in fury. What were they going to do about this Pommie bastard? Wiley could feel his heart thudding and his blood pressure rising. He needed to calm down before he got an apoplexy. He sat down and put his hand on his heart and took ten deep breaths. Things weren't all bad, he reminded himself. He remained in the winning position and he still had his most important ace to play, what with the Malloy woman and her son in his pocket. All it would take was to apply the right kind of pressure.

Feeling a little calmer now, Wiley retrieved his phone from the wastepaper basket and dialled Steve Rackman's number. 'Rackman, where are you?'

'En route to you as we speak, boss.'

'Get as many men together as you can, and bring them with you. There's another job to be taken care of.'

The black Audi rolled up outside the office within the hour, with three more trucks full of men at its tail. Not counting Steve Rackman, Wiley had, or *had* had, over thirty hired guns at his disposal. Most of them were little more than hooligans, loyal and obedient only for the money; and for sure none of them was what anyone would have called sharp-witted, which was why he'd entrusted certain jobs to

Terry Napier, himself no genius but marginally a cut above. In retrospect, Wiley had to admit that hadn't been one of his better ideas.

Rackman stepped into the office. 'What's up, boss?'

'You heard the news?'

'Yeah, Souter called me after he called you.'

'How many men do we have left?'

'We're down four from last night, and from what Souter says, looks like another seven have run for the hills after what happened. That leaves us with just twenty-two. You can forget Napier. The poor bloke's going to be out of action for a while.'

Wiley gave a sour grunt. 'Spare me the fucking eulogy for Terry Napier's late, lamented testicles. We don't need the stupid mongrel anyway. And we don't need those seven cowardly shits either. They'll regret it soon enough, when I catch up with them.' He went on pacing, organising his thoughts. 'But for the moment, twenty-two men is enough, and there's always plenty more where that came from. Rackman, it's time we started kicking arse. I'm putting you in charge of this whole operation, with special priority to getting this Ben Hope character out of our hair once and for all. If you need more men, get them. Raise a whole fucking army if needs be. Whatever it takes, you hear?'

Rackman nodded solemnly. 'Loud and clear, Mr Cooper. Don't you worry about Ben Hope. He's a dead man walking.'

'Make it happen. But first things first. How many men have you brought with you?'

'A dozen.'

'That'll do, for what I have in mind. Take me to the

Brundle place. I think Dekker and the Malloy woman have been kept stewing long enough. It's time we started ramping up the pressure, and I want to oversee it personally.'

Wiley left some necessary instructions with the development site manager, then climbed into the Audi with Rackman at the wheel and the attaché case containing the contract documents for Kip Malloy to sign on his lap. The procession of vehicles swept out of the gates and hit the road.

Chapter 30

The W.F. Cooper & Co. project site was located a hundred and thirty kilometres south of the Brundle farmstead, which was just down the road by Northern Territory standards. Wiley's convoy maintained a high speed for the first half of the journey, then were forced to crawl along unmade roads for the remaining distance with Wiley becoming increasingly impatient and irritated that neither Grubb nor Dorkins was responding to his phone.

'What's the matter with those two fuckwits?'

'You know the mobile reception's touch and go out there,' Rackman said. 'Or maybe they're busy tending to the prisoners.'

'And maybe they're busy shoving their thumbs up their arses,' Wiley growled. He added with meaningful emphasis, 'Or something else.'

Rackman turned to him with a raised eyebrow. 'Poofs? You reckon?'

'No question,' Wiley said. 'I can spot them a mile off.'

'What's the bloody world coming to, eh?' Rackman said, shaking his head in disgust. 'Tell you what, boss, I'd string the lot of them up, if I ran this country.'

'That's nothing compared to what I'll do to those two, if they don't have a damn good excuse for not answering my phone calls.'

At last, the convoy arrived at the old Brundle place, rolling to a halt in a cloud of dust. Rackman did a quick check of his personal phone and found it without reception. Maybe Grubb and Dorkins were innocent. 'So what's the plan, Mr Cooper?'

'It's not fucking rocket science, is it?' Wiley replied. 'If Kip won't listen to reason, then maybe the sound of his wife's screams will make him come to his senses. We'll strip the bitch naked in front of him. Some of the boys can hold him and make him watch. Then you get out that big knife of yours and get to work. Start by slicing one tit off. If he still doesn't feel like talking, then we'll slice off the other. Then cut her eyes out.' He opened the attaché case and lifted out the paperwork. 'I'll be very surprised if we have to go that far, but you never know.'

Rackman nodded. The prospect of carving up a woman didn't unduly bother him. 'What about afterwards? We can't let them go.'

'Not a chance,' Wiley replied. 'The wife and son-in-law will have to be disposed of first. That'll be your job. Burn, bury, chop 'em up and feed 'em to the fucking dogs, I don't care, whatever gets it done. As for Kip, he's staying alive until I'm good and sure of my investment. If it's down there like it's meant to be, then we'll give him a nice quick death. If not . . .' He shrugged. 'He'll have to suffer for it. That'll be your job too.'

'No problem, Mr Cooper.'

Rackman got out of the Audi and walked around to the passenger side to open the door for his boss. The sheathed Bowie knife slapped against his side as he walked, so long that it dangled down his left thigh like a sword. The rest of the crew were getting out of their pickups. Several of them had been involved in last night's events, and they looked tired, moody and ready for revenge.

Wiley stepped out of the cool, air-conditioned Audi into the heat of the morning. The temperature was increasing steadily and the air was thick with humidity, almost unbreathable. He looked around him. There was the barn; there was the new wooden holding cell. But, he suddenly realised, something else about the place was different. It took him a second to figure out what had changed. He stared in cold fury at the empty patch of ground where Grubb and Dorkins' old wreck of a motorhome had been parked before. The area was littered with empty beer cans, cigarette ends and food wrappers. But there was no sign of Grubb and Dorkins themselves.

'Where the bloody hell's their camper van?'

'That's a good question, boss,' said Rackman, who had just noticed its absence as well. 'Looks like they've gone and buggered off.'

Wiley snapped, 'I can see that. Question is, where have the fucking dropkicks buggered off *to*? Forget what happened to Napier. I'll have these morons served their own balls on a plate!'

Rackman had been unhappy about leaving Dorkins and Grubb in charge, and he'd tried to say so on a couple of occasions. But to remind the boss of that now didn't seem quite the thing to do. 'Better check on the prisoners,' he said. 'No telling how long they might have been left unattended, and in this heat.' He pointed at the gang of men and said, 'You, you and you, come with me. You four, run over to the holding cell and check on the sheila.'

'You want us to bring her over to the barn?' asked one of the four, called John Plaster.

'Keep her in place for now,' Rackman told him. 'I reckon the boss wants to talk to Malloy first.'

'Got it.' Plaster and his team set off at a jog towards the holding cell. Still fuming, Wiley had returned to the cool of the Audi to sit waiting for the men to carry out their duties. Rackman and his three men strode over to the barn.

Everything looked in order, from the outside. The padlock was in place, the hasp securely fastened. Rackman took out the spare key and popped the lock. The barn door creaked open, fingers of light creeping in among the shadows. He stepped inside. It was oppressively hot inside the tin building, and utterly still and silent except for the droning buzz of insects. Peering towards the back of the barn at the bull pen, in the semi-darkness he could make out the expected pair of figures within their prison cell, slouched on the crude wooden bench with their backs against the bars and their chins on their chests, sitting there like a couple of drunks propping each other up at a bar. The rays of sunlight from the open doors didn't penetrate deep enough into the barn for him to make them out clearly, but he could see they weren't moving and appeared to be asleep.

'Dekker! Malloy!' Rackman called out. 'Shake a leg, boys. Someone's here to see you.' And aren't you just going to love it, he thought to himself. This was going to be quite a show. And if Kip Malloy hadn't signed on the dotted line by the end of it, then Rackman was a scrub-headed turkey. He fingered the hilt of his knife. Good thing it was nice and sharp for the occasion. Wouldn't want to disappoint the boss.

'Oi! Arseholes, wake up!' he called more loudly to the two immobile figures as he walked closer to the pen.

Still not the slightest stirring of a response. Rackman felt a prickle on the back of his neck that told him all was not well. Maybe they were crook, he thought. Then the worrying thought occurred to him that perhaps they'd been left without water for dangerously long. With the hot sun blazing down all day on the metal roof, the temperature inside the barn could bake a bloke as dry as a dead dingo's donger, and who knew how long it was since Grubb and Dorkins had abandoned their post?

He walked towards the pen, letting his eyes adjust to the dimness. But before he reached it, a sudden shout of alarm and a commotion from outside the barn doorway behind him made him whirl round. He could see two of the men framed in the bright rectangle of light, Nathan Carrick and John Plaster, whom he'd sent over to the holding cell to check on the Malloy woman.

'What is it?' Rackman called out.

'It's the sheila!' yelled Plaster in a panic, holding his arms out wide.

Jesus Christ. Rackman was instantly thinking that his fears were right, that Dorkins and Grubb had deserted their post neglecting to leave the prisoners anything to drink, and that all three of them were in a bad way from water deprivation.

Steve Rackman was a big, tough man and he was afraid of almost nothing in this world. Wiley Cooper was the exception. The boss might be small and old and physically weak; Rackman might be able to easily pick him up with one hand and twist his head off with the other; but he'd never met a man more deeply vicious, more unforgiving, ruthless or cruel, perfectly prepared to use every ounce of his power and every penny of his fortune to enforce his will. If the prisoners died, Wiley wouldn't stop at punishing Dorkins and Grubb. He'd see to it that every last man in the crew was nailed to a cross, even if it meant calling in big hitters from Melbourne or the Gold Coast. Drug boys, professional hardmen who'd go to work on you with pliers and chainsaws just for the hell of it.

Rackman called out, 'Is she okay? Is she alive?'

'I don't know, mate,' Plaster yelled back.

'What d'you mean, you don't *know?*'

'Because she ain't bloody there, is she?' Plaster yelled. 'The cell's empty. The sheila's up and gone!'

Rackman stared at him, confused and speechless for a moment. Wheels spun helplessly in his mind. The missing camper van. The vanished female prisoner. What the hell was going on?

Then a new, terrible thought dawned. He turned back towards the bull pen and ran the last few steps to peer in through the bars. The two slumped figures inside were still completely inert and silent. He still couldn't see their faces. He whipped out his phone, activated its built-in flashlight and shone the thin beam through the bars. Two pairs of open, glazed eyes stared sightlessly back at him from the shadows.

'Strewth,' Rackman said, out loud. 'Oh, shit.'

Because the two men inside the bull pen weren't Kip Malloy and his son-in-law at all. They were Dorkins and Grubb, and they'd been shot dead with some kind of large-calibre weapon that had made a gory mess of each of them.

Rackman ran back outside, shoved past the men and hurried over to the Audi. Wiley was sitting waiting with his eyes closed as though lost in meditation, clutching the precious documents on his lap. Rackman tapped on the passenger window. Wiley's eyes instantly snapped open and blazed at him. 'Yes? Is everything ready for us to begin?'

'Not quite ready, boss. Ah, I hate to have to tell you this, but the prisoners have escaped.'

The reaction was slow to come, delayed as it was by a few instants' stupefied disbelief before the full demonic force of Wiley's rage hit like an ocean squall and nearly bowled Rackman off his feet, while the others watched and cowered a safe distance away. Amid the repeated demands for an explanation all Rackman could say, over and over again, was 'I don't know, boss.'

But one thing was clear enough: somehow, in a total flip-flop of the power balance, Dorkins and Grubb had contrived to allow the prisoners to get the better of them, shoot them dead with their own weapon, strip them of their phones and steal their vehicle. A more perfect storm of incompetence, it seemed impossible to imagine. Either that, or one of the prisoners was some kind of ninja warrior.

Rackman was thinking about Jeff Dekker. They'd been warned about his possible background. They'd failed to heed the warning, and this was the price to be paid for it.

After a few minutes Wiley's volcanic superfury settled down to a point where he was merely extremely angry, and thinking about damage limitation. 'With any luck they won't have been able to get any reception on those phones.' The word 'luck' didn't normally feature in his vocabulary.

Rackman hated to say it, but 'The bodies are cold and stiff, Mr Cooper. They've been dead all night. Which means the prisoners have been gone a long time and they've got a hell of a head start on us. They could be anywhere by now, which means they're bound to have found reception at some point. For all we know, they've already called the cops.'

Wiley stiffened, refusing to contemplate the unthinkable. 'We'll worry about that when it happens,' he replied brusquely. 'For the moment we're going to contain this situation. We have to find them. Split into search parties. We'll scour every inch of the whole fucking Territory if we have to.'

'Yeah, and how're we supposed to do that?' blurted Nathan Carrick. John Plaster shot him an appalled look for daring to openly challenge the boss.

'By doing the job I pay you for,' Wiley replied icily. 'Or else consider yourself fired.' Which Carrick already was, the instant he'd opened his mouth. He'd find out about it later; for now, Wiley needed the manpower.

'I have an idea,' Rackman said. 'Not saying it'll work. But there's a guy. Supposed to be the best tracker in Australia.'

'Tell me about him,' Wiley said.

'Last I heard he was based in Katherine. Uses a light plane to get around and can cover big areas. Homes in on his target like a bloody falcon. And on the ground, nobody can follow a trail like he can. The rozzers've used him to find crooks on the lam.'

'Police?' Wiley said, narrowing his eyes suspiciously.

'No worries, Mr Cooper. He's not one of them. Bloke works freelance. He's basically a bounty hunter, and a right mean bastard at that, if the stories I've heard are true. He'll get the job done, no questions asked, if the price is right.'

'Sounds promising.'

'And the price does have to be right,' Rackman said. 'He'll cost you some big bikkies.'

'Money is no object,' Wiley said. 'I'll spend whatever it takes.'

'He's also an abbo,' Rackman said. 'Hope you don't have a problem with that. Name's Jaice Wullabarra.'

'If he's that good at his job,' Wiley snapped, 'I don't care if he's a fucking Chinaman, part Pygmy, crossed with an Eskimo. Can you contact him?'

'No reception on my phone,' Rackman said.

'Use this.' Wiley reached into his attaché case and handed him the expensive sat phone he carried for when his normal mobile was out of range.

Rackman took the sat phone. 'I know a bloke who might know a bloke.'

'Call him. When you get through to this Jack or Jaice or whatever his name is, tell him he's working for me now. He's to drop whatever he's doing and get on it. Whatever his rate is, I'll double it. I'll write him a blank cheque. I don't care. Just get him for me, pronto.'

As Rackman was making the call, Wiley stood away from the group and shielded his narrowed eyes to scan the flat, sparse, totally empty horizon. He knew that if Kip Malloy talked to the cops, he was finished. The thought made his mouth go dry and his hands shake. He wasn't about to let his underlings see that he was anxious. But Rackman was right, of course. Malloy and the others could be anywhere by now.

Chapter 31

In fact, at that moment the fugitives were barely more than twenty kilometres away from the Brundle place, which by Territory standards was virtually the same as being next door. But that was as far as they'd managed to get before things had taken a catastrophic turn for the worse.

The escape had gone badly right from the start. The moment the second of the two guards had hit the floor stone dead, Jeff had known that something was terribly wrong with his mother. He jammed the warm, smoking revolver into his belt and rushed over to where she was lying sprawled on the barn floor. There was a big red weal across one cheek and a trickle of blood at the corner of her mouth where of the bastards had punched her. But neither that alone, nor the shock from having had a gun put to her head, explained the dead faint she seemed to have fallen into.

Alarmed, Jeff checked her pulse and found it fluttering unnaturally. That was when he remembered those little green and white capsules that she pretended were for dizzy spells when in fact they were medication for some heart complaint she was too proud to admit to. He checked her pockets;

they weren't there. It occurred to him that she might have been carrying them in her handbag. That had been taken during the abduction.

Jeff grasped her shoulders and shook her. 'Mum? Mum!' He could hear the sharp edge of fear in his own voice. His mother's eyes opened a little and she tried to speak, but her voice was too faint to make out the words.

'Lie still, Mum,' he said, fighting to sound calm and reassuring. 'You're going to be okay. I'll get us out of here.'

Lynne spoke again, and this time she managed to mumble, 'Kip? Where's Kip?' She struggled to raise her head, looking around in confusion. Her breathing was short and fast.

'I'm right here, darling,' Kip croaked, but Lynne had already passed out again. He saw her go limp in Jeff's arms and gasped, 'Jesus Christ. Is she—?'

'She's alive,' Jeff said, rechecking her pulse.

'Thank God. Oh, thank God.' Kip tried to come over to her, but his legs folded under him. He fell to his knees, bent double and threw up violently. He tried to force himself upright, but he was so weakened by his captivity and the beatings he'd taken that he couldn't stand. 'She's going to be okay, Kip,' Jeff said. 'Don't you worry. We're getting out of here fast, and we'll get help for both of you, I promise.'

There wasn't a moment to lose, in case more of the enemy returned. Jeff's first priority was to get his mother out of the murderous heat of the barn and into fresh air. He scooped her limp body up in his arms and carried her outside. Things were scarcely any better out here, in the burning sun and the chokingly warm sultry air, barely stirred by the slightest breeze. He laid her gently down in the only bit of shade he could find, the threadbare awning of the old camper van parked across from the barn. 'Jeff,' she murmured weakly, fingers raking at his arm. 'Stay with me. Where's Kip? What's happening?'

'Hold on, Mum. I'll be back before you know it.' He hurried over to the barn, where he found Kip still on his knees, hugging his ribs in obvious great pain but far too proud to admit to any kind of weakness. He made another heroic attempt to clamber to his feet, and this time ended up on his face. Jeff helped him to sit up, told him to remain still and went on talking reassuringly to him as he quickly searched the two dead men. No wallets or identification, and no more useful weapons, but each had a phone, and on one he found the keys to the camper van. Jeff stuffed the phones into his pockets, then left the dead men where they lay and returned to Kip's side. 'Come on, buddy, let's get you out of here.'

'I can walk,' Kip insisted, swatting away Jeff's hand.

'Yeah, I noticed that. I really don't need you to be a stub-born plonker right now, okay?' Jeff grabbed Kip's reluctant arm, wrapped it around his neck, hauled him upright and, in the well-drilled move they used to use to carry the wounded in the field, hefted him over his shoulder. Kip wasn't a small man and he was heavier than he looked. Jeff was still a little weak from his own blow to the head, and his knees sagged under the strain as he carried Kip out of the barn and laid him down under the camper awning next to Lynne. She was starting to become more alert now, and seeing Kip in daylight for the first time she groaned in despair at the bloodied, puffy state of his battered face. Tears welled out of her eyes and she clasped her husband tightly in her arms, rocking him. 'Oh, my poor baby, what have they done to you?'

Jeff hurried inside the camper van. From the absence of any other building apart from the cell block where they'd been keeping his mother, the van must have been home to the two guards. Its interior certainly looked, and smelled, like something that had been lived in by a couple of rough-neck bushies. Among all the discarded dirty clothes, junk food wrappers, empty drink cans and water bottles and cigarette packs were some more useful items, however: a couple of dirty old blankets; a gallon water container, three-quarters full; a few tinned provisions. Jeff guessed that they must have been expecting a resupply soon, because the food stores were running low. He grabbed the gallon container along with a pair of chipped coffee mugs he found in a cupboard, sloshed out a little water and went back outside to attend to Kip and his mother. 'Drink this. Don't gulp it. Small sips. Nice and easy does it. There, now.'

Next Jeff took out the phones, hoping there might be some reception out here. If so, his intention was to call Ben first. He was also hoping one of them could give him a fix on their location. Then, once they were a safe distance away from here, either he or Ben could call for medical assistance.

But even if there'd been any reception, as it quickly turned out, both phones had dead batteries. A quick but thorough search of the van revealed no chargers. Jeff swore, tossed the phones away and turned his attentions to the van itself. It was an ancient petrol-engined model, twenty years old with rust-eaten skirts and a missing headlight, and not surprisingly it lacked any kind of onboard sat nav to tell Jeff their geo position. Which could be anywhere, because Jeff had no idea how long he'd been unconscious in the truck that had brought him here, nor any sense of their route. Until he orientated himself by finding some kind of road sign or marker, unless Kip or his mother were able to get their bearings, he'd be going by pure guesswork.

Jeff didn't like it, but decided he'd worry about that later. He told himself things could be worse: he had half a tank of fuel and two spare jerrycans strapped to the rear load rack. The small kitchen stove worked, connected to a propane bottle housed along with a spare in a compartment near the side hatch. An old but unused first-aid kit under the driver's seat would allow him to touch up Kip's cuts and bruises, once they reached a safe place to stop. There were some nasty but usable saucepans and basic implements for warming up their tinned provisions if needed, and their water supply should last them until they reached civilisation. He inspected the tyres, which were in reasonable enough shape. Most importantly of all, after a bit of gentle coaxing the engine spluttered into life. Jeff did a fist-pump. They were good to go.

He helped Lynne, then Kip, onto the parallel bunks of the rear lounge area, each with a rolled-up blanket under their head as a pillow. He closed the greasy, grubby curtains to help protect them from the vicious sunlight streaming through the windows. Then he wound up the awning and jumped behind the wheel, filled with a triumphant energy that helped to dampen his extreme worry for the two of them, and they took off.

The place where they'd been kept had obviously once

been a farm of some kind, judging by the few stretches of rickety animal fencing they passed as the van bumped and pattered along a rough track that eventually led to a dilapidated gate. An ancient, weathered and barely readable wooden sign hung lopsided from a rotten post and said BRUNDLE FARMSTEAD. Next to it, a newer and larger billboard-sized panel warned: PRIVATE PROPERTY – KEEP OUT. In smaller letters below was the name W.F. COOPER & CO. DEVELOPMENT CORPORATION and some further warnings about prosecution for trespassers. The name meant nothing to Jeff. The development company had obviously abandoned the place a long time ago, leaving it open to be used as a bolthole by the kind of sick scumbags who'd kidnap, imprison and torture innocent people.

The track continued from the gate, but Jeff didn't want to take a route that might be too easily followed, if anyone came after them. So instead he cut across country, bumping and lurching over the undulating landscape, winding between the thicker thorn bushes and rolling through the smaller ones, until eventually they came to another track. There wasn't a signpost to be seen, still nothing to tell him where the hell they were. After a couple more kilometres a fork in the track pointed roughly north and south, going by the position of the sun. Jeff took the north fork. Then a couple more kilometres after that, another fork presented him with the choice of east and west. He took the one to the east. They'd surely end up somewhere, sooner or later. Then, after five more kilometres, the track met with something more like a road. *Now* we're making progress, he thought, and his spirits began to lift a little.

They didn't stay lifted for long. Soon after they hit the open road and were able to go a little faster, Jeff began to realise that something was seriously wrong with the camper van's steering. Special Forces operatives with behind-the-lines experience were used to having to sometimes commandeer, sometimes steal, whatever kind of vehicle they could get their hands on. In some war-torn Third World countries those could be pretty ropey indeed. But this one took the biscuit. Try as he might, he just couldn't get the thing to stay in a straight line: one moment trying to veer off to the left, the next to the right, like a badly-trained dog on a lead yanking its walker this way and that to cock its leg in the bushes. The steering wheel felt loose and unresponsive in his hands, as though it was barely connected to the rest of the vehicle. What the hell is wrong with this piece of junk, he wondered. Had he damaged something when he'd chosen to cut across country?

The problem was compounded by the fact that within just a few short kilometres, their route carried them up into an area of rocky, arid higher ground where the road builders had been forced to blast out an almost impossibly snaky path between the bigger crags. Negotiating one hairpin bend after another, a few heart-stopping near-accidents taught Jeff to slow to a crawl on the approach and gently accelerate through the curve, as gingerly as driving on ice. He was beginning to think he'd got it sussed.

Then a blind left-hander he'd thought he could comfortably take at fifty kilometres an hour, skirting the overhanging crag of a huge red rock with a steeply sloping drop into a rocky valley on the other side, suddenly tightened up dramatically. Jeff twisted the wheel harder, and that extra bit of force suddenly proved too much for the steering to take. He distinctly felt the *crack* as something gave way.

The van lurched uncontrollably leftwards towards the rock. Jeff sawed at the wheel; nothing. He stamped hard on the brake to avoid a collision, and now the van shot wildly off in the opposite direction, heading straight for the drop to their right. He ground his boot with all his strength against the brake pedal, teeth gritted and knuckles white on the wheel as the edge came flashing towards them. If they went over, there was nothing to stop their headlong descent straight down the vertiginous slope to the rocks and a few dead trees a hundred feet below.

They didn't go over. But it was close thing, very close. The van skidded to a halt teetering precariously right on the edge as though suspended in mid-air, with its front wheels jutting right out over the edge and its weight lifting the rear wheels off the ground. One tiny shift of balance could spell disaster.

'Oh, shit,' Jeff muttered to himself. This wasn't good.

Very carefully, he eased out of the driver's seat. Even just that small movement made the teetering van creak and groan ominously. He froze, afraid even to breathe. Waited for the heart-stopping creaking to subside, then edged his way backwards between the cab seats towards the rear lounge where Kip and Lynne were still curled up on the bunks, unaware of their situation.

With his weight transferred from front to back, Jeff was reasonably confident the thing wouldn't tip over just yet. But only reasonably. He urgently shook Kip and Lynne awake, told them they had to get out *now*, and as they rose blinking and confused from their bunks he helped them hurriedly to the side hatch. Lynne got off first. She was the lightest of them by far, and her weight made little difference. But as Kip managed to hobble out, the balance began to shift alarmingly and the counterweight of the engine was suddenly dragging the vehicle's nose downwards. Jeff felt the tilt under his feet, heard the rasping grind of the rocky edge against the van's underbelly as it began to slide, and launched himself out of the hatchway with less than a second to go before it tipped right over and went careening nose-first down the slope.

They watched it go bouncing and crashing to the bottom. By some miracle it didn't overturn, flip or roll, but stayed on its wheels all the way, until it slammed with a crunch into the rocks, taking two dead trees with it, snapped clean off at the base.

Well, that's that, Jeff thought, gazing down at the drifting dust. At least nobody had been any more hurt than they were already. But now he was going to have to figure out a way of getting the hell out of here. At his last check of the tachometer they'd covered only about twenty-two kilometres from their starting point. Sooner or later the men would return to the barn, discover the guards dead and the place deserted, and all hell would break loose. They'd be certain to send out search teams to hunt for the missing prisoners. Their chances of finding them would depend on how many men they had at their disposal, and how successfully Jeff had managed to weave a route that was hard to follow. He wished he could be more confident on both scores.

But rather than stand here worrying, he needed to make sure his mother and Kip were safe for the moment. A couple of hundred metres back down the road he found a sheltered nook among the rocks that would offer them some shade from the hot sun, as well as hiding them from view should the wrong people come looking for them. It wasn't much, but it was something.

Once he'd got them safely installed in the shelter, Jeff returned to the slope and made his way down to the wrecked camper van. He didn't have to be an expert mechanic to know that the vehicle definitely wasn't going anywhere again – not without the necessary tools, spare parts and a powerful winch to drag it back up to the road.

The situation was dire. There was no possibility of moving his mother or Kip for any distance, in their condition. If it had been just a single person, he'd have been willing to carry them on his back. To carry them both was plain impossible. Which meant he'd have to leave them here if he was to set off on foot in search of a busier road, or a farm – better still, a small town where there might be a doctor – and Jeff absolutely refused to leave Kip and his mother alone out here, sick, hurt, vulnerable and far too close for comfort to the scene of their escape. His best option was to simply wait it out and hope someone might come by who could offer help and transport. It was leaving things to chance, which Jeff hated doing. But what other choice did he have?

He gathered together from the van the most essential things they'd need short-term: a couple of tins of food, water, a jar of instant coffee, cooking utensils, first-aid kit, two thick branches of the dead trees the van had smashed down, a cigarette lighter he'd found in the glove box. He rolled his supplies up in the blankets, tied the package with a length of bungee cord, and made the tricky climb up to the road carrying the bundle on his shoulder. Back at the rock shelter he broke the branches into smaller pieces and used the lighter to kindle a small campfire, over which he heated a tin of beans and sausages in a saucepan. It might not have been haute cuisine, but the nourishment would keep them alive. The walls of their shelter sloped inwards in a roughly triangular shape, forming a narrow gap a few feet overhead that allowed campfire smoke to escape. As long as the rain stayed off, Jeff couldn't have picked a better temporary refuge for them, though he knew they couldn't stay long.

After he'd managed to get some food down him, Kip fell back into a deep, semi-comatose sleep. 'Is he going to die, Jeff?' Lynne whispered as Jeff covered him with a blanket.

'Nobody's going to die, Mum.' *No, just the people that did this*, Jeff thought.

Nobody came. Kip slept on and on. After a while, Lynne curled up next to him and fell asleep too. Evening fell, and with the darkness the temperature dropped quickly. Jeff spent his evening hacking up and down to the camper to bring up the rest of the provisions and more firewood. Their meagre stash of tinned fare wouldn't keep three people fed for very long.

Jeff sat pondering by the light of the flames until the fire eventually died and their little nook fell into darkness. It was going to be a long night. And what tomorrow might bring, he could only wait and see.

Chapter 32

Of all the countless hours Ben had spent in the air during his time with the SAS, the majority had been aboard short-range choppers rather than conventional aircraft. For the kind of operations that had generally required his expert services and those of his comrades, the helicopter was prized for its ability to insert troops – and even more importantly to extract them again – virtually anywhere, fast and efficiently without even the need to touch the ground, in areas of the most rugged and inhospitable terrain, places where the only way to land an aeroplane would be to crash it.

For that reason it was ideal that Abbie Logan's charter company should include a helicopter among its small air fleet, and that she was qualified to fly it. From what Ben could tell by the ordnance survey map, it seemed highly doubtful that their destination offered even the most primitive form of runway. The option of a chopper also meant that, in the interests of speed and time, they were free to choose a rendezvous point independent of Borroloola or any of the other local airstrips scattered around the Northern Territory. Abbie had suggested a meeting place that was about a third of the distance between his base at Hobart's Creek and the GPS location Sammy Mudrooroo had given him, still accessible on four wheels before he quite literally ran out of road.

Early that morning, Ben closed the farm gates behind him and set off. He didn't like to venture away from his base unarmed but, the presence of a loaded shotgun and rifle being a little hard to explain to his pilot, he'd had no choice but to leave his weapons behind. Warm sultry air blasted in his open windows as he drove fast to make his RV in time. With each passing day the temperature seemed to grow more oppressive and the sky grew greyer and cloudier. Bad weather was coming, and when the threatened storm finally broke it was going to be a big one.

Hours passed. Endless kilometre after kilometre of near-empty road streaming towards him, speeding through a landscape whose immeasurable savage beauty he barely registered. He felt sickened by his frustration at not knowing where his friends were. Everything, *everything*, depended on what Sammy could tell him – and yet Ben was afraid of depending too heavily on it, because if that lead turned out to lead nowhere either, he'd be left with zero, lost in the dark. But right now he had no choice but to latch on tightly to the one little scrap of hope that he could.

After what seemed like forever, the Mean Machine surged over the crest of a rise, a broad flat dusty plateau opening up below him, surrounded on three sides by a halo of distant red-tinged mountains, and he spotted the landed helicopter sitting at the centre of a windswept circle of flattened scrub grass a way from the road with a tiny figure sitting on the ground beside it that he instantly recognised as Abbie Logan. She must have beaten him to the RV point by just a matter of minutes; the chopper's rotors were still lazily turning and the dust cloud they'd whipped up was still floating like a mist in the hot air.

Abbie was wearing her dark glasses and sun-faded baseball cap with her tousled blonde hair tied up under it. She jumped up and dusted her jeans as he pulled off the side of the road and went bumping over to park by the chopper. There was a broad smile on her face and a cheery spring to her step. Ben felt good to see her, but his face was too grimly set to allow his lips to return her smile.

He'd done a double-take at the helicopter the instant he first saw it. His half-formed expectation had been of the generic type of light chopper that was ubiquitous across the world, something like a Bell Jet Ranger or a little Robinson R22 workhorse, brightly coloured and sleekly attractive with the charter company logo emblazoned on its sides. To his amazement, Abbie's mode of transport was an old military model of Huey UH-IH Iroquois, still sporting its original matt olive-green paintwork and military insignia, scuffed and weathered from some half a century of hard use. Ben had flown in many near-identical machines, piloted a few of them himself, and seeing it brought back a flood of memories.

He jumped down from the Mean Machine to meet her. 'G'day, mate,' she said brightly, taking off her shades to reveal those startlingly blue eyes. 'Had a feeling I'd see you again.'

'Hello, Abbie. I appreciate you coming. Sorry it was so last-minute.'

She smiled wider. 'Hey, no worries. I like your ute. Very butch.'

'It belongs to a friend.'

'All alone this time, then?' she asked him, nodding towards the empty passenger seat.

'Jeff's a little tied up at the moment.'

'Looks like I've got you all to myself then,' she laughed. 'So remind me where we're going? Got to say, mate, I don't normally take on a job where the client won't give me the destination.'

That was true, because Ben had been deliberately vague, not wanting to give away too much on the phone and telling her only the approximate flight distance they'd have to cover and what direction the LZ lay in.

'The place we're going doesn't have a name,' he replied. 'At least, not one that's marked on this map.' He turned back to the vehicle to pull out the map to show her, and she stood close to his shoulder as he spread it out on the Mean Machine's bonnet and pointed out the location. He'd written Sammy's GPS coordinates in the margin.

Abbie made a low whistle. 'Crikey. This is way out in the hinterlands. You couldn't have picked a more remote destination. I've covered pretty much every inch of the Territory but that's one place I've not been to before.'

'Because it's so hard to get to?' he asked.

'That's one reason. The other is that this is a sacred Aboriginal site area. It's protected land. I'm not sure I'm even allowed to touch down there. It could be forbidden by the tribal authorities.'

Ben thought about Sammy Mudrooroo's message. It

hadn't said much, but as far as it went it was a clear invitation for him to go there in person. 'I take full responsibility, if we do anything we shouldn't do. But I don't think anyone's going to complain.'

She shrugged. 'Okay. On your head be it.'

'Besides, you did say you'd fly anywhere,' he said.

'And I meant what I said. If there's a sky over it, I can get to it. As long as I'm in fuel range. Which we are, just about. I've landed in some tight spots in my time, believe me.'

Ben pointed at the Huey. 'In that?'

Abbie laughed. 'Not what you expected, eh?'

'You're full of surprises, Ms Logan.'

'She may be an old girl, but she's still got what it takes. They don't build 'em like this any more. The Yanks brought in the Blackhawk to replace this model. Piece of crap.'

They walked over to the chopper, and Ben ran his eye along the familiar lines of its fuselage. The last one he'd flown in had been equipped with rocket launchers and rotary machine cannons, which it didn't surprise him to see were absent from this example. But other, more subtle, traces of the aircraft's military past were still visible. He pressed his fingertip into an old bullet hole whose edges had been repainted over. 'Looks like she's been in the wars, once upon a time,' he said. 'Vietnam?'

Abbie nodded, and affectionately patted the helicopter's side the way a person might pat a horse. 'Oh, she's got a few tales to tell, I'll bet. She was built in 'seventy-three and did more than five hundred combat hours as an assault gunship with the US 101st Airborne Division before she got shot down over Laos. Dad bought her cheap as a basket case from some backstreet dealer guy when I was still just a kid, brought her over by ship as a container full of broken-up parts and spent two years putting her together again and restoring her to flying condition.'

'Fascinating,' Ben said. It wasn't an unfamiliar story to him. He'd crossed paths with a few individuals, including his old acquaintance Chimp Chalmers, who after leaving the forces (honourably or otherwise, as the case might be) had plunged into the shady waters of arms dealing and become specialised in being able to sell you any kind of military hardware you wanted, for the right price. Chimp had once sold Ben and Jeff an ex-Soviet seaplane, when they were dealing with a situation off the coast of Africa.

'Looks like she's not the only one to have been through it, though, mate,' Abbie said. She'd noticed the somewhat fresher bullet holes that peppered the bodywork of the Mean Machine.

'Trust me to go and park it in the wrong place,' Ben replied nonchalantly. 'Right in the way of someone's target practice.'

She looked at him curiously for a moment, as though not quite believing his story. 'Yeah, well, shit happens. You can't be too careful around these parts. Now, we've got a bit of a way to go, so hop on and we'll get going.'

The utilitarian Iroquois had never been made to be civilian-friendly. Ben slung his bag aboard and hauled himself in after it with practised agility. That didn't escape Abbie's notice, either. She donned her headset and mic, and Ben did the same. As she was flipping switches going through her pre-flight routine she observed wryly, 'You look pretty well at home in this thing. Anyone'd think you must have flown in one before.' The turbine motor started up with a low whine that mounted in pitch as the rotors cranked into life and slowly began to turn.

'No, this is all completely new to me,' he replied, with the same air of innocence.

'Uh-huh. What did you say you do again?'

'I told you, I'm in education.'

'Yeah. I remember you said that. Thought about it afterwards. Hang on, here we go.'

The two-bladed rotors had reached their full speed, rippling a wide circle of grass all around them and making that classic 'Huey thump' that generations of combat soldiers had come to know so well. Ben felt the old familiar sensation of his body going heavy as the helicopter's skids parted company with the ground and they started to rise into the air. The helicopter's nose dipped, the tail rose up, and then the forward thrust pressed him back into his seat and they were off. Abbie was grinning as though she delighted in every moment of it. She said nothing for a few moments, but there was a meaningful look on her face and he sensed she hadn't finished making her point.

'So my dad, he was in education, too,' said her voice through his earphones.

'Was he?'

'Yeah, he was an SOC drill instructor.' She gave Ben a sideways glance as she said it, as though watching his reaction. His expression was blank. Abbie said, 'You don't need me to spell out what SOC stands for, do you?'

Ben knew perfectly well what it stood for. SOC was the Special Operations Command of the Australia Defence

Force. It comprised the Australian SAS, the counter-terrorist Tactical Assault Group or TAG, and various other high-level units, some of which Ben had trained and operated with back in the day.

'I'm afraid I've no idea,' he said.

That sceptical look again. 'Hmmm.'

He said, 'What?'

'Nothing.' But her meaningful expression hadn't gone away, and the dark glasses did nothing to hide it.

'Is your dad retired now?' he asked, diverting the subject.

'You could say that. He died four years back.'

'Sorry to hear it.'

'So was I, mate. Shit happens. Problem is, it always seems to happen to the wrong people, doesn't it?'

Ben had to agree with that.

Now the chopper was flying at full thrust with 110 knots showing on the gauge and the limitless vista of open country skimming by far below them. Ben lit a Gauloise, to which Abbie didn't object, and relaxed back into his seat. The pulsing, thudding vibration, the clattering roar, the Spartan green-painted bare metal interior of the cabin with its original military dials and switchgear, even the smells, all added up to give him that heady feeling of going into combat again.

Maybe he was, he thought. He didn't know what awaited him at his destination. But one thing he knew for sure: there would be more battles to fight, and bigger ones, before this thing was over. And he knew that whatever happened, one way or another, the people who'd started it would be made to pay for their actions.

Abbie seemed content to fly in silence, and that suited

Ben fine. He felt as comfortable in her company as if he'd known her for years. In her aviator shades and with the baseball cap pulled low over her eyes she looked even more in her element than she had flying the plane down from Darwin. There was a calmness to her, a sense of officer-like composure and confidence born out of discipline and self-belief, that he admired very much and had seldom seen in a civilian. In another life she could have been a soldier, or an air force commander; probably a very good one, too. He hadn't been surprised to learn that she came from a military family. Part of him would have liked to be able to talk more about that side of things with her, but according to his nature he was reluctant to reveal too much about himself.

On, and on. And then on some more. It was a big country, all right. Ben worked his way through his pack of cigarettes and watched the terrain slowly morph from wide open flat yellowed bushland resembling African savanna to the dense tree cover of a rainforest, the sun-parched greenery intercut here and there with meandering blue rivers and tall tree-dotted hilltops above which the Huey thudded, the aircraft's faint black shadow flitting over the craggy red rocks directly below them now that the sun was at its peak in the sultry sky. He saw no settlements, no roads, no sign that other humans existed anywhere on this strange, remote planetary system called the Northern Territory. A landscape utterly unspoilt and unchanged since the times when dinosaurs had roamed its surface. It had been ancient even then.

'Coming up on our LZ pretty soon,' Abbie's voice said in his headset some time later, jolting him from his thoughts. Then a few minutes after that, 'Here we go. This is it.'

Chapter 33

They were overflying much higher ground now, a sprawling ochre-coloured escarpment whose plunging valleys either side were screened from the air by dense green forest. Ben hadn't spotted so much as a dirt track for the last hour or more, still less any sign that anybody might be out here waiting for him to show up. But some instinct told him that Sammy Mudrooroo would be true to his word.

'I don't have anywhere to set down among those rocks,' Abbie said. 'Too steep for a landing. But that might just about do it.' She pointed towards a deep cleft far below, where her sharp pilot's eyes had picked out a natural clearing among the trees. 'It's a bit of a squeeze, but I reckon we can drop her down there.'

'Looks good to me,' Ben said.

'Roger that. Then hold onto your knickers, mate. This is going to be a fun one.'

And down she went. The clattering roar of the Huey slapping back at them off the sheer red rock faces as they plunged in altitude towards the trees. One mistake, the smallest error of judgement, and a rotor blade could foul the cliff and shatter into a million pieces, and it would be over. Ben found himself gripping the metal frame of his seat. Now the green canopy came racing up to meet them, as though they were going to crash straight down through it and be dashed to pieces in the treetops. But Abbie knew what she was doing, and judged it perfectly. Without so much as clipping a twig or a leaf, she brought the chopper squarely down to land on a patch of even ground in the middle of the clearing. 'How's that?' she asked with a triumphant smile.

'Not too bad,' Ben said.

She punched his arm. 'Not too bad, my arse. I reckon you owe me a pint, mate.'

'It's a date.'

'I'll hold you to that.'

'Well, thanks for the lift. I'll give you a call when I'm done here,' he said, pulling off his headset and grabbing his bag.

Abbie said something that he couldn't hear over the noise of the helicopter. She made a stabbing motion of her finger towards her ear to tell him to put the headset back on. Her voice in his phones said, 'How the hell are you planning on doing that?'

'I'll find a way.' He plucked off the headset a second time and was about to jump out of his hatch when he saw she was flipping switches to shut down the turbine motor. The clattering din of the rotors immediately began to fall in pitch and settle into a diminishing *whap-whap-whap*.

'What are you doing?' he yelled over the racket.

'What does it look like?' she yelled back.

'I thought you were dropping me off and flying back to base.'

Abbie shook her head and tapped a gauge. 'She's running a little hot. Like to let her cool down a bit. I'm not in a hurry. Besides, have to say I'm curious.'

Before Ben could reply, she'd yanked off her headset and jumped out of her hatch. Cursing, he jumped out of his side and walked around the chopper, ducking low out of the wind blast, to rejoin her a distance away, further from the dying noise where they could talk more easily.

'Curious about what?' he asked her.

'Curious about what a bloke like you is doing coming out here into the middle of nowhere, acting all secretive about where he's going and why. I'm intrigued. So I decided to stick around and find out.'

'What do you mean, a bloke like me?'

'You're not fooling anyone,' she replied with a sly smile. 'I spent my childhood and teens hanging out with guys exactly like you. They all had the same look, the same ways about them.'

'Got me all figured out, have you?'

'Damn right. You're a soldier. Practically got it tattooed on your forehead.'

'*Was* a soldier,' he said. 'Not any more.'

'Ha. Knew it. What unit?'

'I spent some time in Special Forces,' he admitted, regretting his candour the moment it came out. Abbie had a way of winkling out the truth, even from a very private personality like his.

'Ha,' she snorted. 'Knew that, too.'

'You're always right, aren't you?'

'I'm also a nosey bitch,' she said. 'And I can tell something's up. You've got trouble.'

He said, 'Then all the more reason why you should fly back to base and let me handle my own affairs, Abbie.'

She shrugged. 'Yeah, but I don't want to. Maybe I'm a sucker for living dangerously. Or maybe I just don't have anything better to do. Life's pretty boring for a single girl around here.'

'Maybe I'm not safe to be around,' he said. 'Maybe I'm a ruthless criminal, meeting my dodgy associates out here to do a drug deal.'

She shook her head again. 'No, you're not. You're a decent bloke who's mixed up in something he doesn't want to talk about, but he can't hide the fact that he's desperately worried. Is it your mate Jeff? You said he was tied up at the moment. Sounded innocent enough. But the look on your face was telling me something more.'

Ben said nothing.

'Seriously. You can trust me. I'm a good listener. You never know, I might even be able to help, in some way.'

The complete sincerity in her manner, the imploring look in her eyes, were impossible for him to resist. There was only so long he could go on bottling everything up inside. He sighed heavily and said, 'All right. Some friends of mine are in danger. I'm here to meet with someone I'm hoping will help me to fix it.'

'That's why you didn't want to tell me too much before.'

'I'm a careful guy,' Ben said. 'It's the reason I'm still around.'

'What kind of danger are we talking about?'

'Kidnap. Or worse.'

'What's worse?'

'Torture and death,' Ben said. 'As bad as it gets.'

Abbie's tanned face had turned a shade paler. 'Who did this to them?'

'That's what I need to find out.'

Her shocked expression hardened into a look of resolve. After a beat's hesitation she said, 'I'm coming with you.'

'Abbie—'

'It's what my dad would have wanted me to do,' she said. 'He brought me up to be strong like he was, like the men he served with and trained. Gave me a moral standard to live up to. And the kind of people who've done this to your friends, he hated more than anything. Please, let me help.'

'I can't be responsible for you,' Ben said.

'I don't expect you to be. I'm responsible for myself.'

'You've got a busy work schedule.'

'I just gave myself a few days' break.'

'Just like that?'

'It's my charter company,' she said. 'I'm the boss, now Dad's gone. I can do whatever I want.'

He hadn't known that. He said nothing.

'You need me,' she said. 'I know this country. I can get you from place to place better and faster than you ever could on your own. I can be an extra pair of hands. I can look after myself. I won't hold you back or slow you down. Believe me, I'm actually quite a useful person to have around.'

He was silent.

'Besides,' she said with a smirk. 'You try getting rid of me, mate.'

He looked at her. 'Then what are you waiting for?' he said. 'Let's go.'

While they'd been talking, the Huey's turbine whine had died away and the rotors had slowed to a stop. Ben shouldered his bag and checked the map once more while Abbie radioed her base to arrange for a colleague to cover her for a few days. It sounded as though they had a lot of schedule rearranging to do to make up for her absence, and she was apologetic. He could hear her saying over and over, 'It's okay, I'm fine, nothing to worry about.' When she got off the radio she grabbed a small backpack from behind the pilot's seat, and her water canteen. He hoped it was a good decision, letting her come along with him like this.

His next objective was to get to higher ground, where he could get his bearings and take a look around. He led the way from the chopper towards the far side of the forested valley, where the red rock escarpment rose up like a cliff. The trees grew thickly beyond the edge of the clearing, and after just a short distance the helicopter's olive-green shape was screened completely from view. In places it was as thick as a jungle, and Ben stopped every few paces to check Abbie was coping. 'Stop fussing,' she told him. 'I can keep up.'

He pressed on, moving fast and silently, the way only a trained man can move through dense cover. Abbie kept pace behind him. At last the ground began to incline; soon afterwards the thick foliage thinned out and they could see the sheer rock face looming up in front of them. Ben approached its foot and looked up. There were lots of craggy foot and hand holds, forming a natural stairway up the escarpment to a prominent ledge about eighty feet up. As Abbie caught up with him, he pointed and said, 'I'm going up there to take a look around. You stay down here.'

'Not on your life,' she replied.

The climb was hot and dusty. They paused midway for a drink of water. Already they were above the valley's tree-tops, and the helicopter was completely invisible from up here. Reaching the higher vantage point of the ledge, Ben took a pair of binoculars from his bag and made a wide, slow sweep of the landscape, a two-hundred-degree arc from west to east covering thousands of square kilometres. At first he could see nothing, and was gripped by the anxious thought that there was nobody out here. Nobody, except a fool who'd involved a too-willing companion in a wild goose chase.

But then he spotted something move through the trees across the valley. It was just a tiny shiver of leaves, but it caught his eye and he swept his field of vision back towards it, trying to focus more tightly. Was it an animal?

Then he saw it again, emerging from the cover of the trees. Not an animal. A man. But a man like few others Ben had ever seen before. He reminded Ben of the ritual dancers he'd seen at the funeral in Ngukurr, almost completely naked with white pigment body markings contrasting against his skin. There for only a brief moment, he looked up at the escarpment and raised a hand to wave; then he was gone again, vanished as suddenly as he'd appeared.

Ben lowered the binocs.

Abbie said, 'See anything?'

'I need to get down there.'

It was another hot trek as they made their way back down the rocks and cut across the valley in the direction of where Ben had seen the man. By the time they reached the spot, the figure had long since been swallowed up by the forest as though he'd never been anything more than an apparition.

'Are you sure he was there?' Abbie asked, wiping perspiration from her brow. 'I didn't see anything, and I've got pretty good eyes, mate.'

'I saw him,' Ben insisted. 'And he saw me, too. He waved.'

'If you say so,' she replied. 'But if he was here, now he isn't. What do you want to do, go searching for him? He could be anywhere now.'

Ben shook his head. 'No. If they know we're here, they'll come to us. We wait.'

And they waited. Sitting in the relative cool of the shade of the trees, surrounded by the cackle of birds overhead in the treetops and the hum of the insects that swarmed all around them in the humid air. Nothing happened for the next two hours. The sun's trajectory followed its slow arc overhead, gradually dipping below the escarpment to the west. Ben fell into that trancelike state in which he could sit immobile for days on end, and often had, on military operations and since. Outwardly completely still, he was fully keyed into his environment, aware of the tiniest sound, every subtle shift in the wind; and through it all, he couldn't shake off the strange sense that he was being watched, even though there was nobody there – as if the forest had eyes of its own.

'Nobody's coming, Ben,' Abbie said after three hours had gone by. 'Sorry to say it, but I think you've been stood up.'

Ben didn't want to accept that. He was about to reply when he saw Abbie's eyes suddenly open wide and she shot to her feet. She was staring his way, but not at him – past him, at a point right behind his shoulder.

Ben turned. Three dark figures of men were standing there, having apparently materialised out of nowhere. He hadn't heard the tiniest sound of their approach. The one on the left he recognised as the man who'd appeared and waved to him earlier. The one on the right might have been his brother, stocky and muscular with a shock of black hair. But Ben's attention was on the man in the middle, because he was someone he'd met before.

'Hello, Sammy,' he said.

Chapter 34

Sammy Mudrooroo it was, though a very different-looking Sammy Mudrooroo to the one Ben had last spoken to by the water's edge at Hobart's Creek. Like his two companions he wore nothing but a loincloth. The markings of chalky pigment daubed on his barrel-chested body were the colour of his mass of white hair. In one hand he carried a long knobbly staff, a foot taller than he was. His bloodshot, bleary eyes peered intensely at Ben from under bushy white brows.

'I'm getting used to you sneaking up on me like this,' Ben said.

'Knew you'd come,' Sammy replied with a smile.

'A lot has happened since we last met,' Ben said. 'My friends are in danger.'

'I know that too, mate.'

'You seem to know a lot of things, Sammy. That's why I'm here.'

Sammy just smiled once more, then beckoned with a gnarly finger for Ben to follow. Without a word or a glance between them the three men turned and slipped away into the trees, suddenly gone again. Ben snatched up his bag and chased after them, with Abbie hurrying along in his wake.

Ben had tracked the most elusive of men through the hardest kind of terrain and prided himself on being pretty damn good at it – but Sammy and his brethren seemed to have the ability to melt in and out of the background like ghosts, and he was worried about losing them. For a moment he thought he had, glancing around him and seeing nothing but foliage in all directions; but then a half-seen darting dark shape among the bushes ahead told him where to follow. They seemed to be moving slowly but somehow were able to cover a lot of ground with amazing speed. Ben could tune into his environment, but these people were *part* of theirs.

They walked for almost an hour, taking a winding rocky trail that skirted the foot of the vast escarpment and then took a gradual rising path upwards into a deep canyon with sheer sides that looked as though they'd been formed by some prehistoric seismic event. The canyon walls loomed high above them on both sides as they climbed up, up, up. Every so often one of the three dark figures ahead paused, turned and waved for them to keep following. The sun was dipping lower by now, with just a couple of hours to go before it set, and the shadows in the canyon were lengthening. On and on they went, and Ben had the strangest intuitive feeling that he and Abbie were being led to a special place to which very few, perhaps none, of their white race had ever been invited. Only Sammy and his people came here, his intuition told him. It was their land, and to be brought here as a guest was a deep honour.

They'd climbed several hundred feet by now, the canyon walls gradually subsiding as they neared the summit of the tall escarpment. Just when Ben was beginning to wonder how much further they would have to walk, the three figures ahead stopped and turned to wait for their guests to join them. Ben and Abbie now found themselves at the end of the trail, in a wide natural circular hollow that could have been a meteorite crater from ten million years ago, fringed with scrubby bushes and a few gnarled, ancient trees.

At first Ben thought they were alone up here, but even as he thought it he saw more figures appearing from between the rocks and gathering at the edges of the hollow. The men were naked and painted like Sammy and his two companions. The women were mostly clad in colourful long dresses, to which the children clutched as they peered out at the strangers with huge wondering eyes from behind the safety of their mothers. Abbie smiled and waved at the kids. One or two tentatively waved back. Others, like some of the elders, didn't seem convinced. But it was clear that Sammy was a person of high authority among them, and that it was understood generally that the guests were to be welcomed into the community's domain.

Ben sensed that these people were among the last of their kind who had chosen to go on living in their true natural habitat rather than submit to the semi-westernised urban lifestyle that had brought such degeneration and unhappiness, addiction, poverty and disease. He knew that if he'd been born here as one of them, he'd have wanted to do the same. It was a magical place, imbued with a haunting kind of spirituality. They might have been living here undisturbed for a thousand generations. How many more the future held for them as the outside world went on changing and shrinking in these unstable modern times, was anybody's guess.

Looking around him, through a tall inverted V-shaped cleft in the rocks, like a natural archway, Ben could see a circle of standing stones, and behind it a huge natural rock overhang formed an open-mouthed shelter or cave. Close at his side Abbie whispered, 'Looks like they've brought us to a religious place. This must be an important meeting or we'd never be allowed here.'

But before any kind of meeting could begin, Ben and Abbie's hosts offered food and water, for both of which they were grateful after their long journey. As the womenfolk carefully prepared the meal over a wood fire whose smoke drifted high over the escarpment, some of the men gathered at the foot of an old dead tree that seemed to have some significance for them, and played music. This second time Ben heard the sound of a didgeridoo was even more haunting and evocative than the first, while two of the musicians tapped out a hypnotic rhythm using hollow sticks, as intricate as any jazz percussionist he had ever heard and quite beyond his ability to follow. This went on for a while, then the food was ready.

As befitted the occasion, Abbie noted, the hand-painted bowls of mashed cereals, ground nuts and fruit and meat with which they were presented weren't just your regular bush tucker. The meat could have been lizard, or maybe snake. Ben had eaten python in Africa, and it tasted like pork. This was similar, only better. Everybody shared in the food, some forty or fifty tribespeople seated on rocks and log benches or cross-legged on the ground. Gradually the novelty of the two strangers' presence seemed to wear off, and there was a good deal of animated talk while the younger children ran about and amused themselves in the background. The sun kept dipping lower and lower throughout, and while the vast dome of the western sky began to turn a million magnificent shades of crimson and amethyst, shot through with streaks of shimmering gold, Ben had to hide his pressing impatience to learn the reason why Sammy Mudrooroo had brought him here.

Finally, as the sun finally dipped below the horizon and the meal was over, Sammy laid down his empty dish, patted his round belly, got up from his rock seat and motioned for Ben to accompany him through the cleft into the stone circle. Abbie said in a low voice, 'I think he means for you to go alone. Some types of ceremonial spaces are forbidden to women. Others, to men. It's okay. You go.'

Sammy led the way through the V-shaped arch, and for the first time Ben noticed that he was carrying a small leather pouch on a strap around his neck. He wondered what he was carrying inside. Such modern trappings as money, credit cards, keys and mobile phone seemed unlikely. A fishing line, maybe, or a flint striker for lighting fires. Ben followed him, ducking his head under the arch being some eight inches taller. Sammy padded carefully around the stone circle's outer edge, and Ben did the same so as not to tread anywhere he shouldn't.

'This way,' Sammy said, pointing at the cave. Ben followed him up a path to its mouth that had been worn smooth by a million feet belonging to Sammy's tribal ancestors as they came here to shelter from the elements or perform their religious ceremonies. In the fading light Ben could see the paintings that adorned the back wall, depictions of people and animals and other more abstract designs done in colourful pigments.

'Now we can talk,' Sammy said. The depths of the cave made his voice echo. He squatted in the shadows and invited Ben to do likewise.

'You told me that the truth was waiting for me here, Sammy,' Ben said. 'Is that what you're going to tell me now?'

Sammy smiled.

Then, in his own way, in his own time, Sammy told Ben everything.

Chapter 35

Ben had a feeling he was in for a long, unhurried one-to-one. Because that was the way Sammy seemed to do things.

Ben was right.

Sammy made a slow, sweeping motion of his arm and said, 'Look around you, mate. What do you see?'

They were sitting in the deepening darkness at the back of a cave and, truthfully, Ben couldn't see very much at all. But he understood the deeper meaning of the question, and he replied, 'I see the mountains and the forests, the bush and the rivers, and the whole land all around. More land than I've ever seen before. It seems to go on for ever and ever. It's beautiful. It makes sense to me why it's so sacred to you. It would be to me, too.'

Sammy looked at Ben with an approving glitter in his eye. He nodded sagely. 'Yes, mate. But some other white men, they're not like you. When they look around them, that's not what they see. They only see the money they can make from hurting the land. All they want to do is tear out its heart. They don't understand that the land and the people are all one, belong to one another.' Sammy meshed the fingers of both hands together. 'Like this, see?' Then he pulled them abruptly apart in a violent ripping motion. 'And when you tear out the heart of the land, you tear out the heart of the man, too. These people, they don't care. Because they already dead inside.'

It was a surprisingly loquacious and impassioned flow from someone Ben had regarded until now as a man of relatively few words. But there was more to come, much more, and not wanting to interrupt his stream, Ben listened in silence as Sammy began to describe the long and painful history of the exploitation of ancient Aboriginal lands, first by the white settlers and later by the big corporations that had inevitably sprung up in their wake.

Ever since the white man first landed on these shores, the native Australian inhabitants had been made to suffer one way or another. When they weren't being abused, robbed, raped, enslaved and massacred, they'd simply looked on in bemusement as the white men inflicted just as much pain and suffering on their fellows, those unfortunates transported to Australia by the thousand aboard the prison ships and subjected to a living hell ashore. But an even more insidious evil from the Aboriginal viewpoint, the violation of the land itself, didn't begin until the middle of the nineteenth century with the discovery of gold in Western Australia. The gold rushes of the 1850s quickly spread all over the continent as prospectors hungrily rushed in from across the world, tripping over each other to set up huge mining camps and get digging. Vast fortunes were made, the population skyrocketed, and the new moneyed classes turned Melbourne into a prosperous, modern capital city.

However, gold fever had been only the beginning of the story, as the new Australians began to realise the diversity and sheer enormous scale of their land's mineral wealth. Sammy had all the facts and figures at his command and was able to trot them out effortlessly, while Ben was struck by his own ignorance of the matter. Today, Sammy explained, the Australian continent was the world's largest producer of iron ore, and number one also for lithium; it was the largest exporter of coal; the second biggest producer of lead, cobalt and aluminium. Uranium additionally featured high on the list, mining operations having begun in the early twentieth century. Then in the fifties, uranium had been found within the Northern Territory at a place called Jabiluka, which Sammy explained to Ben was home to many ancient Aboriginal sacred sites. Needless to say, the protestations of neither the native Australians nor the rights protection groups who'd tried to intervene on their behalf had halted the devastation of these sites and many other areas of hitherto virgin landscape. No protection at all was offered by government authorities, and the ravages of uranium mining in the Territory had continued unabated for half a century. Australia was now Number Three globally for uranium production.

Meanwhile, Sammy went on, Australia was also the world's fifth largest producer of nickel, the sixth for copper, the eighth for silver. While all that was going on, the gold supply opened up in the nineteenth century showed no signs of diminishing, with Australia's international position in that market currently second only to that of China. Then when it came to precious stones, Australia was the world's top producer of opals and one of the largest for diamonds, rubies, sapphires and jade. On, and on.

'I had no idea,' Ben said.

Sammy could probably have continued rattling off the apparently endless list, but the point was made. While more than ten million hectares of land had been irreparably destroyed in total, it was the ancient sacred sites of the Aboriginal tribes that seemed to have come off worst of all. He described to Ben how the mining companies had razed ancient Aboriginal caves in the Pilbara Desert. Elsewhere they had dug out a huge iron ore mine on land containing sacred native rock shelters – just like the one they were sitting in now – that Sammy's ancestors were using fifteen thousand years ago. Once more, the hallowed relics of the old culture were obliterated without a trace or a blink of remorse. The value of the destruction? A cool $3.2 billion into the pockets of the mining company bosses. More recently, further devastation of ancient rock shelters had taken place at a location called Juukan Gorge. The same story, yet again.

The evening was growing colder, and at that point Sammy paused his narrative to light a fire, using a bag of dry sticks that had been left at the back of the cave. Ben felt like offering his Zippo lighter to speed things along, but Sammy might be offended. He took his time, head bowed, fully concentrated on rubbing two sticks together until the heat of the friction produced tiny embers that he carefully dropped onto a small pile of tinder and blew on to encourage the flame to grow, adding more sticks to build it up. It was the oldest way of making fire known to man, and Sammy was as expert at it as any hard-core survivalist Ben had ever known. No new-fangled fire steels or flint strikers for him, that was for sure.

Despite his impatient anxiety for his host to cut to the chase, Ben understood that Sammy felt it necessary to lay the groundwork for what was to follow, and wasn't a man to be rushed. Ben asked, 'Why are they allowed to go on doing these things?' As soon as he'd said it, he was aware of how naive the question sounded.

Sammy chuckled, his face half-lit in the flickering orange firelight. 'Who going to stop them, mate? The government?' He explained that when yet another large and powerful mining corporation had wantonly blasted into smithereens Aboriginal sacred sites dating back more than 45,000 years, it was done with the formal approval of the government's own Minister for Indigenous Australians.

'Looks like we can't trust the politicians, then,' Ben said.

No chance, Sammy agreed. Forget any appeal to democracy, let alone the ballot box. The men in suits were all bought and sold by the powerful corporations. Under pressure they'd squirm and waffle in their oily way and go on about protecting indigenous land rights and culture, but it was all talk. Now and then a company caught more flagrantly in the act than usual might be fined or made to apologise for their acts of vandalism. But compensations were endlessly stalled in the courts, and orders to rebuild demolished sacred sites were treated as a matter of minimum priority. The various legal acts passed had done virtually nothing more than pay lip service to Aboriginal property rights. When a dispute arose between the interests of the corporations, their puppet politicians and the various lobby groups gamely trying to fight for the indigenous people, the law always came down on the side of big industry. The Aboriginal heritage laws themselves had been drafted back in the early seventies, balanced heavily in favour of the proponents of mining. You couldn't win, literally.

Meanwhile, to nobody's great surprise, government approvals for further destruction of Aboriginal heritage sites kept on coming, year after year. Sammy told Ben that at present there were over 1,700 such approvals on the slate, waiting to be put into effect. It was even less surprising, when you considered the economics. The mining industry in the Northern Territory alone was worth over $3.5 billion and a lot of greedy people were intent on getting their slice of the cake.

'What do you expect, mate?' Sammy said, resignedly shrugging his shoulders. 'Nobody care about us. We ain't got no money. We ain't got no power. And soon we won't be here at all.' The impacts of these continued assaults, he said, would eventually push Aboriginal culture past the brink of extinction. It was a form of genocide. And it was a deliberate agenda.

'White man wanted us gone from the beginning,' Sammy said. 'No offence, mate.'

'None taken,' Ben said.

The modern form of genocide by attrition was just a more subtle development of the more overt methods that had been used in the past, Sammy explained. Back when the British Empire had first colonised Australia in the late eighteenth century, their tactic had been just to round them up and massacre them. Sammy could list over three hundred documented such atrocities spanning over a hundred and fifty years, carried out at the hands of the British army and various regional police forces under their control. In addition, with the advent of clever agricultural chemicals in the nineteenth century, there had been many deliberate mass poisonings of his people. Thousands had been murdered. Not a single conviction had ever been recorded.

Warming to his theme, Sammy dwelled for a moment on the ways those centuries of systematic undermining of their culture had affected his people. Alcoholism had become the scourge of Aboriginal communities across Australia. He was appalled and heartbroken by the degenerate behaviour and drug-taking of the younger generation. 'They're even sniffing petrol, mate. This is what we've been brought to.' There was no anger in Sammy's voice, just a philosophical kind of acceptance of the sad reality.

'I hear you,' Ben said. 'And I wish we could turn back the clock and undo all of those things, and a lot more besides. But explain to me why you're telling me all this. And what it has to do with Kip Malloy.'

By way of a reply, Sammy reached into the leather pouch that hung around his neck, and came out with something clenched in his fist. Now Ben was about to find out what he'd been carrying in there.

Sammy extended his arm and opened his fingers to show Ben what he had. On his broad palm was an object the size of a large egg, wrapped in a piece of rag. 'Go on,' Sammy said, offering it to him.

Ben reached out and took it. The object felt hard and

heavy, denser than rock or iron, lighter than lead. With a puzzled glance at Sammy he delicately unwrapped the piece of rag. As the cloth fell away, the object glittered by the glow of the fire. Its surfaces were rough-hewn but shinier than steel.

It took Ben a few moments to realise that what he was holding in his hand was a large lump of pure, unpolished silver. And a few moments longer for him to make the connection in his mind. Then, suddenly, it became clear why Sammy had been telling him all this.

'The silver serpent,' Ben said.

Chapter 36

Sammy Mudrooroo nodded wisely, and his eyes gleamed as brightly as the silver nugget in Ben's hand.

'Where did this come from?' Ben asked him.

'Came from the earth,' Sammy said, pointing downwards at the ground under him, with a smile of sympathy for anyone who could be so stupid as not to know that. 'Been there a long, long time. Since always.'

And now, before Ben could fire off any more of the questions that were crowding his thoughts, Sammy launched into telling a story. It was part of the ancient history that formed the foundation of the core beliefs of Australian Aboriginal people. 'So don't interrupt, mate.'

Way back at the beginning of all things, the legends told, there was the Dreamtime. That was when the Spirits created the world. They made the rivers and the hills, the rocks and the trees. They made the people and the animals. They declared the laws of nature, taught the tribes their rituals of initiation and the proper ceremonies to allow the souls of the dead to travel peacefully to their spirit-place. In their wisdom the Spirits also provided people with their own tract of land and the tools and skills to live and hunt. So were born the great hunters, of which one of the greatest of all was Woomera, the spear thrower.

Around the same time, Sammy recounted, the Spirits created a giant magical serpent that roamed these lands more than 65,000 years ago. The serpent was a hundred miles long and glittered like moonlight on the water. But the serpent also had the ability to make men mad and turn them against each other, and on learning this the great hunter Woomera decided to go in pursuit of him. Woomera's reputation was so fearsome that the serpent fled from him and hid underground. Woomera knew that if he were ever to re-emerge he would soon go back to his old nefarious ways, so he ordered him to remain there for all eternity. The serpent obeyed him, and over time he became part of the land, buried deep under the ground.

Ben turned the lump of silver over in his hands, examining it. He was no expert on these things, but he was pretty sure a chunk this size and weight had to be worth a lot of money. 'It's a wonderful story, Sammy. But this is no legend. This is something real. Where did you find it?'

'Kip gave it me,' Sammy replied simply.

'Kip Malloy?'

Sammy nodded. 'Wanted it to be put in safe hands. Said it was part of the land, my people's land, and nobody else should have the right to take it.'

So there had been more to this all along, Ben thought. Things Kip had never told Lynne. And money was involved. When was money ever *not* involved, somehow? 'And where did Kip get it?' he asked.

'At Mick's,' Sammy replied.

'Kip's uncle, Mad Mick?'

'Mick weren't mad,' Sammy said, shaking his head with a frown.

'I'm sorry. You knew him well, didn't you?' Ben remembered Lynne saying so.

'Me and Mick were brothers,' Sammy replied. 'He was like one of us.' In his unhurried way, Sammy talked for a while about Mick and his land, and the Horseshoe Ridge where he'd met the taipan that ended his life. Ben could sense how close they'd been, and how deeply saddened Sammy was by his passing. He listened politely, but then it was time to bring Sammy back on track.

'And so Mick told you he'd given the silver nugget to Kip?'

'No, mate. Mick was dead by then. Kip found it when he was going through his stuff.'

'And he brought it back to Hobart's Creek, then he gave it to you for safekeeping.'

'Yeah. Keep it secret from folks.'

Ben asked, 'And do you know where Mick got it?'

'Found it.'

'Found it under the ground?' Ben held up the heavy lump. 'Is there more where this came from?'

'Oh yes, mate. Lot more,' Sammy said. He raised his arm in another sweeping gesture, as though he were drawing a line right along the horizon.

Ben looked at him earnestly and asked, 'Sammy, are you telling me there's a giant seam of silver underneath Kip's uncle's land, a hundred miles long? Is that what this is all about?'

'Folks in the Territory been talking about it for years,' Sammy said. 'But nobody believed it.'

'Except for the Aboriginal people,' Ben said.

'Mick too,' Sammy replied. 'Mick always believed in the old stories. Reckon he knew just where it was, too.'

'And he knew what would happen if word got out. Next thing there'd be a dozen mining companies looking to tear the place apart.'

'Wanted to protect the land,' Sammy said. 'He understood what it means.'

'And so did Kip.'

Sammy nodded. 'Kip's a good bloke. Secret should have been safe with him, I reckon.'

'But someone else knew about it, too,' Ben said.

'Bad men,' Sammy said. 'Lots of bad men around. Always was, always will be.'

'We need to know which ones,' Ben said. 'I get the feeling you do.'

Sammy paused to toss another piece of gnarly dry wood on the fire and embers flew up like a swarm of fireflies. Then he said, 'I heard'm talking on the phone. He didn't know I was there. But I was listening. Knew he was a bad fella. Never liked him.'

'What did you hear, Sammy?'

Sammy said, 'It was that Terry Napier.'

Ben cocked his head. 'Napier? Had Kip told him what he'd found?'

'Nah, mate. Kip wouldn't have told him. Napier saw Kip bring it back from Mick's place. Kip was looking for a place to hide it.'

'Before he decided to entrust it to you,' Ben said.

'The map, too,' Sammy said.

'Map?'

Sammy nodded. 'Mick drew it. Kip found it.'

'Did Kip give you the map to look after?'

'No, mate. Hid it at the farm.'

So it was Napier who'd broken into the house later on, searching for the map. And now Ben also understood what the big money prospect had been that Napier had excitedly told his wife about. But too many things were still unclear. 'If we knew who Napier was talking to on the phone that day—'

'Talking to his boss,' Sammy said. 'Not Kip. His other boss. Man he works for. Cooper.'

'Cooper?'

'What he called him. Yes, Cooper. No, Cooper.'

'Telling him about the silver?'

'Yeah. All about it. And about Mick's land.'

It was all slowly starting to make sense to Ben now. 'You say people have been talking for years about the legend of what was under the ground, and that most people thought it was just an old tale that only the Aboriginal peoples believed. But what if there were some others who believed it, too?'

'And now they know it's true,' Sammy said, 'they gonna try to get it any way they can. Now Cooper's got Kip and his missus, and your mate, gonna make Kip sign the land rights over to him so he can rip its heart out.'

Ben asked, 'Who's Cooper?'

'Name's Wiley Cooper,' Sammy replied. 'He's the boss.'

Chapter 37

They were coming to it now. Ben felt a surge of relief mixed with fresh anger and resolve as the truth he'd come here to discover now finally revealed itself. His grip tightened on the lump of silver and he said, 'Cooper's the boss of what? A big mining company?'

It was hard to believe. He was perfectly aware of all the kinds of double-dealing and corrupt skulduggery that went on in the world of big business. Greasing palms in government, a bit of gentle extortion, was one thing. But was it possible that a major corporation, with so much to lose if they got caught, would take the risk of stooping to actual kidnapping, or worse?

'You mean big like Rio Tinto and BHP?' Sammy replied with a dark chuckle. 'I wouldn't say that, mate.'

Sammy explained. In an era of increased media attention and public awareness when scandals like RTZ's blowing up of the 46,000-year-old sacred site at Juukan Gorge were splashed all over the internet and sparked angry demonstrations in the streets, the powerful multinationals who'd been feasting for so long on Australia's vast resources were nowadays forced to tread just a little more lightly. The big company bosses and their lawyers lived under the constant threat that the badly outdated Aboriginal heritage legislation could be redrafted at any time, the legal loopholes they'd exploited for decades might be sewn up tight and their practices subjected to a far tighter rein and increased scrutiny. If that happened, the party might not actually be over, but it would be a lot less fun than it used to be. Enter the smaller-scale outfits, independent local operators whose names were still to achieve the same degree of public notoriety as their larger multinational competitors. They were thus less hampered by the need to play by the big boys' rules, and could move in under the radar to enrich themselves by hook or by crook while the going was still good.

Ben asked, 'And this Wiley Cooper is one of those?'

Absolutely, Sammy told him. The W.F. Cooper & Co. Development Corporation, to give it its official title, ranked somewhere near the bottom of the list of mining companies in terms of its size and turnover, which was somewhere in the $75 million range annually. 'Looked it up on the internet,' Sammy said. Sitting there in a smokily firelit cave in the remoteness of the outback, Sammy looked pretty much like the last person on earth who'd ever be found researching company profiles on Google. But he knew his subject, and he'd gathered a good deal of information on Wiley Cooper, both the man himself and the company he'd founded over half a century ago.

W. Franklin Cooper had been born in 1941, to a poor and humble family who earned a frugal living from their little hardware store in the dusty outback settlement of Kurrawarra – a name that Ben remembered from the map Lynne had given him. After nearly dying in the polio epidemic of the early fifties young Wiley's health had never been solid, but from an early age he'd showed a remarkable toughness of spirit, leaving school at fifteen to start his first business. Before long he knew exactly where he was going. It was a boom time for the mining industry, and companies across Australia were quick to engage local contractors to help set up their infrastructure and build camps for their workers. That was how Wiley got his start, swiftly rising up the ladder and making his first million before the age of twenty-six. Just three years later, he'd founded the industrial development company that he still presided over to this day.

W.F. Cooper & Co. currently operated just eleven sites across the Northern Territory and employed fewer than five hundred people. It might be the smallest fish in its particular pond, but it punched far above its weight in terms of the environmental damage it had wreaked on the virgin land-scape over the years. Wiley's big breakthrough mining venture had been manganese, used in the production of stainless steels. Within a year of starting operations his mines had been responsible for the desecration of four Aboriginal sites and the total destruction of two more. The company had been lightly rapped on the knuckles in Darwin Magistrates' Court and ordered to fork out a few thousand dollars' compensation to the owners of the land, which Sammy knew for a fact had never been paid, because he knew some of the people involved.

Undeterred, the Cooper company went on wantonly

ravaging areas of special importance to local Aboriginal people. Another of their crimes was the blasting of a sacred rock formation 170 kilometres north of Tennant Creek. The rock was known locally as the Horse's Head, but to the Aboriginal residents of the area the site related to a Dreaming story about a marsupial rat and a bandicoot that had fought violently over food. The animals' blood had leaked over the rocks, turning them the dark red colour that was now known to signal the presence of manganese. And that had been their downfall, when Wiley had his way.

'He's a right proper bastard, he is,' Sammy said, letting his philosophical composure slip for a moment.

But not all of Sammy's knowledge about Wiley Cooper stemmed from internet research. As he explained, it was well known in certain circles, especially among the Aboriginal peoples of the Territory who had good cause to mistrust and dislike the man intensely, that aside from his regular company workforce he also employed local muscle whose job it was to intimidate rivals, coerce folks into doing deals, stifle anyone's objections about the company's often shady business practices, and protect the boss from the many people who'd have liked to get even with him.

'I think I might have run into a few of those guys already,' Ben said.

'Yeah, heard about that,' Sammy replied.

Ben smiled. 'Is there anything you don't know about what goes on around here, Sammy?'

'Not much, mate. Problem is, he's got plenty more where that came from. Bloke like Wiley Cooper, he thinks he can do whatever he wants. He got all the money and all the guns.

283

Anyone goes up against him gonna have big trouble.'

'It's no more than I'd expect of a crook like Cooper.'

'He's a crook, all right,' Sammy agreed, shaking his head sadly. 'Always was rotten. Mick always said it. Bad blood between him and Wiley, going way back.'

'So there was history between them?'

'Lot of history, mate. Mick, he told me the whole story.'

'Tell it to me,' Ben said.

As Sammy recounted, Mick had grown up as a farm kid and never attended the school in Kurrawarra, the nearest town. But now and then the local boys would all get together, sometimes with a few girls, too. Someone's elder brother would always have access to a ute; Mick had a BSA dirt bike, and they'd congregate in the bush to mess around, smoke, drink, indulge in some innocent target practice, and all the things that rural kids used to get up to back in those days. Mick was a year older than Wiley and had known him since they were nine and ten respectively, but he'd never liked him much. Mick was a proud boy who had been brought up to live true to his principles. He was incapable of telling a lie even if it earned him a whipping from his father, and his generous and open-hearted nature made him popular with other boys, and even more so with the girls. By contrast, young Wiley Cooper was known for being somewhat two-faced and conniving. The girls disliked him for his smarminess toward them. In sports and games, if he couldn't win by his own merit he'd always try to cheat. And if there was something he coveted but couldn't have, he'd either attempt to steal it or fly into one of his furious tantrums.

The trouble between Mick and Wiley had started during

the long, hot summer of 1956, when Mick was sixteen and Wiley fifteen. Sammy related the story the way Mick had told it to him.

As usual, a gang of local kids had got together in the bush that day, and as usual it wasn't long before they turned to messing around taking pot shots at empty pop bottles balanced on a fencepost. Back then many of the teenage boys went around with guns and knives, but they were taught to be responsible with them and nobody ever got hurt. It was all perfectly legal and regarded as just a normal part of growing up. On this occasion Mick had brought along his new prized possession, a well-used Colt Bisley revolver that his granddad had left him, and which his father had given permission to use, on the strictest conditions. The old Colt shot straight and true, and after an epic target practice session Mick carefully stowed it away safe in his haversack, along with what was left of the ammo. But when it came time to go home, he discovered that someone had been into the bag, and that the revolver and ammunition were was missing.

Mick immediately confronted the others, because it was obvious that one of them must have taken it. Not one of them owned up. But while the other kids were visibly shocked at the theft, one was acting all shifty and red-faced, edging away and saying nothing: Wiley Cooper. His guilty behaviour wasn't lost on Mick, who challenged him to admit he'd taken it. Only losers tell lies, he'd said. Is that what you are? Whereupon, Wiley produced the revolver from where he'd hidden it. He'd put the bullets back in, and now he pointed it at Mick, screaming that it wasn't fair he had a gun like that all of his own, and that Wiley should have it, and that if Mick didn't let him have it he'd shoot him.

'What did Mick do?' Ben asked.

'He let him have it, all right,' Sammy replied. 'With his fists. Mick grabbed that gun off'm and beat the crap out of'm. Wiley went off howling like a baby, swearing that he'd get his own back one day.'

'And that was the bad blood between them?'

'Nah, then it got worse,' Sammy said. 'Later, when June came along.'

June Sinclair had moved from Alice Springs to Kurrawarra with her family in the spring of 1965, when her father became headmaster at the school. She was nineteen years old and the most gorgeous thing that Mick Malloy had ever laid eyes on. Twenty-five, a handsome young bachelor recently come into his inheritance, he was smitten and showered her with attention until she finally relented and they started going out together. After two years of courtship they were engaged in September 1967, and to her father's disapproval she left home to move in with Mick.

But it soon became clear to June that Mick had no intention of following in his family's glorious footsteps and building up the farm. On the contrary, he was already doing everything he could to dismantle what generations of Malloys had set up, virtually giving away the large cattle herd he'd inherited and happily squandering the family fortune on, as he put it, rewilding the land. Even in his mid-twenties he was getting a name for being, well, colourful. A little too colourful for June, who became disenchanted and broke off the engagement just two weeks before they were due to marry.

Mick was heartbroken, but more trouble was in store. Not long after June left him, he heard the devastating news that she had married. Not just married, but to none other than Wiley Cooper.

Wiley had left school the same year as their famous fight; some speculated it was because he was so ashamed of the way he'd got beaten up in front of the other kids. Whatever the case, he'd been busy these last few years and was now a rich young entrepreneur, on his way to making his first million. The local gossip mill reported that he'd used his newfound wealth to seduce June into marrying him. And it worked, because in 1968 she became the first (though she wouldn't be the last, Sammy said) Mrs Cooper.

Ben, who had been listening quietly to all this, said, 'You think perhaps Mick knew about the silver under his land even then? Maybe June told Wiley about it.'

'Dunno, mate,' Sammy said. 'But they weren't married long, anyhow. Only lasted a year before she buggered off to Darwin. Folks said when she left him, she told him he wasn't half the man Mick was.' He grinned. 'Bet that hurt. Made Wiley hate Mick even more.'

While Mick was broken-hearted and alone at the farmstead where he'd remain for the rest of his life, Ben thought. He asked, 'Did he ever marry?'

'Never, mate. Never stopped loving June, I reckon. Believed that Wiley took her away from him on purpose. She'd have come back to him, otherwise.'

Ben wondered if this whole thing came down to the lifelong enmity between two bitter old men. Wiley had never had the courage to face his enemy face to face. But as much as he must have despised Mick Malloy, if he was half the cunning prospector Sammy made him out to be, his lust for the fabled mother lode of silver beneath Mick's land burned with an even stronger passion. All these years, he could have done nothing about it, and couldn't have been sure it really existed – not until his lackey Terry Napier had seen Kip with the hunk of raw silver and the map he'd found among his late uncle's things. Had Wiley deliberately cultivated Napier as a spy in the enemy camp? Knowing what he knew about the man's devious ways, Ben wouldn't have been surprised.

Then at last, with old Mad Mick finally out of the picture, maybe Wiley had seen his opportunity to move in. Just one obstacle stood in his path: Kip Malloy. And Wiley Cooper was clearly a man who couldn't tolerate anything stopping him from getting what he wanted. Which meant that Wiley had a big problem. Because Ben Hope couldn't tolerate people like him, who thought they could use force and intimidation to impose their will.

Ben's thought stream was broken when he realised that Sammy was watching him intently, the firelight flickering in his eyes. 'So now I told you all there is to tell, mate. There ain't nothing left to say. And there ain't anything us folks can do. We can't stand up against bad men like these. Old Wiley, he got all the money and all the guns. Can't fight against that. Not on our own.'

Sammy paused for a long moment. Then, speaking in a different tone, he said, 'I knew you was the one. First time I seen you. Sammy knows things, see.' He tapped his head. 'That's why I brought you here. Things you needed to know.'

'I was the one? The one to do what?'

'To protect the land,' Sammy said. 'And put things right. It's what you was chosen for.'

'I wasn't chosen. I'm not some kind of Messiah. I just came to help a friend.'

'Nah, mate, you was chosen. And you got to stop them. Before it's too late.'

Chapter 38

Jeff had been right about their first night in the wilds being a long one. Kip and Lynne had slept fitfully, huddled together under one of the blankets, Jeff propped nearby against the rocky wall of the shelter, on sentry duty with the revolver cradled in his lap until he'd drifted off to sleep himself around four.

As the next day dawned, Jeff emerged outside into a world bathed the colour of blood, still and silent apart from the yammering flock of parakeets that had come to roost in a nearby tree. Above the little nook loomed a large, tall rock from whose top he could peer down through the narrow fissure of the shelter's chimney. But his purpose for coming up here was to scan the long, winding road in all directions as far as the eye could see.

Nothing stirred anywhere in that vast bowl of empty landscape, as huge as the dome of the sky over it. Which was a good thing, Jeff reflected, in that it meant the enemy hadn't come looking for them – they might not even know about the escape yet. But it was a bad thing, in that if help didn't come sometime soon, he worried that Kip's condition might deteriorate to dangerous levels. At around three that morning he'd heard Kip raving feverishly in his sleep. Jeff had done all he could for him. He needed a doctor.

Breakfast consisted of the last two tins of beans and sausages, with mugs of hot black coffee. Kip was awake and feeling strong enough to sit up and get a little more food down, but any attempt to get to his feet and he'd be overcome by nausea. Lynne was faring slightly better, though without her medication she was taking a long time to recover from what she still insisted on calling 'just another of those little dizzy spells'. Neither of them was in a fit state to walk more than a few steps. Jeff had never been one for religion, but now he repeated his prayer that help would come today.

No sign of its coming throughout the long, hot morning, and none during the longer, hotter afternoon that followed. When their gallon water container ran dry, Jeff returned down the rocky slope to drain whatever was in the camper van's fresh-water tank into the empty receptacle, with a couple of purification tabs he found in a drawer. The food supply was all but gone now, too.

Ten, fifteen, times throughout the day – he soon lost count – Jeff went compulsively scrambling up to the top of his watchtower rock, as he'd dubbed it, to scan the horizon for any glimpse of a distant dust cloud that would signal an approaching vehicle, either friend or foe. The possibility of the latter was constantly on his mind. By his calculation, a circle with a radius of twenty-two kilometres had an area of over 1,500 square kilometres. Which was a pretty large stretch of terrain over which to search for three missing fugitives who might by now in any case have managed to travel much,

much further, widening the circle far more. All the same, you never knew that the enemy might not get lucky.

If they came, after what had happened to the two guards they would be numerous and well armed. Jeff was ready for that. On his last trip down to the camper van he'd found a small firewood-splitting hatchet in a stow box, now added to his meagre arsenal of weapons. There were just four rounds left in the revolver. Very powerful and potent rounds, but nothing like enough firepower to hold out against a concerted attack if their pursuers found them here. He knew it would be a suicide mission for him to even try, because of the three of them he was by far the most expendable from the enemy's point of view. Though he'd try, all right, and he'd go down fighting if that was the best he could do to protect his mother and Kip.

But nobody came. Nobody at all. This was the road that time forgot, or so it seemed to Jeff. The long, long, uneventful day dragged into evening, and then into night. With their food supply now completely used up, Jeff stuck the revolver in one side of his belt and the hatchet in the other, and went looking for more.

On the far side of the rocky slope where the van was, the land continued sloping more gently downwards until it levelled out into a plain of sparse bushland. He walked for a couple of kilometres through the darkness, treading lightly around thorn bushes, pausing now and then to listen hard for the slightest sound. This was when all the creepy-crawlies came out, and Jeff had learned that Australia had an awful lot of those. The bushes seemed alive with tiny pattering feet. At one point, what he'd first thought to be a strangely low-flying and slow-moving swarm of tiny bright fireflies, shining in the darkness, turned out to be the countless beady eyes of a whole cluster of large predatory spiders out on the prowl. At last, hearing the crackling and snuffling from a patch of bushes that was definitely being made by something more relatable than an arachnid – the damned things made his flesh crawl – he drew the gun silently from his belt and stalked carefully towards the sound.

The young wild boar was too busy foraging in the under-growth to notice him until he was just fifteen paces away. Now it emerged from the bushes and stepped into a patch of moonlight, stopped and gazed at him. Now or never, Jeff thought. He raised the gun, cocked the hammer and squared the sights on the animal's flank just behind the shoulder where the heart was. The gun kicked hard in his hands and the echo of its report rolled all around the horizon, probably audible for a great distance. But the job was done. The boar buckled at the legs, went down, sprang up again and gamely tried to bolt but made it only a few bounds before it crashed into the dirt, this time for good.

Hunting for meat was never a pretty business. It was something all Special Forces operatives were trained in, and often had to rely on, though Jeff had always felt a pang of regret killing an innocent wild animal. He stripped off to his boxer shorts to avoid getting his clothes all bloody, then used the hatchet to skin, gut and quarter the carcass. He bundled up his kill in a bag, dressed and headed back to camp, where some time later the hunks of roasted pork were sizzling over the fire.

The fresh meat seemed to give both Lynne and Kip an

293

injection of much-needed energy and vigour. 'Been a long bloody time since I last ate bush tucker like this,' Kip said, in an attempt at levity that ended in a fit of coughing. Lynne patted and fussed him until he was over it.

Jeff was happy to see the two them showing signs of rallying round. 'If you're up to it, Kip, perhaps it's time we talked. Mum and I need to understand what this is all about.'

'It's about money,' Kip grunted. 'What else, mate?'

'Whose money, your uncle's?'

'Worked that much out, ain't you?'

'Then tell us the rest of it.'

'I'd better start from the beginning.'

'We're listening.'

'Mick had a secret,' Kip said. 'Then when he died, it became mine.' Leaning against the wall of the firelit nook, speaking softly and now and then having to pause to catch his breath, he told them the whole story, dating all the way back to his youth, when his uncle used to regale him with magical tales about the land and its hidden wonders. Most of all, about the old, old legend of the silver serpent, almost unknown outside of Aboriginal communities.

'Just stories,' Kip said. 'Never really reckoned any of it was true. Then after the old bloke passed, I went there to sort through his things. And that's where I found it.' He told them about his discovery of the silver nugget, along with the map.

'So it was real,' Lynne murmured, entranced.

'It's real all right. That one nugget's just a spit in the ocean. The seam of silver under that land could be a hundred miles long. And after all them years looking, Mick bloody went and found it. When he did, I don't know. But I reckon it was just months before he died. The nugget still had dirt on it and the map hadn't been drawn long ago.'

'So if Mick had lived,' Jeff said, 'was he going to dig for the silver?'

Kip shook his head. 'You don't understand, mate. Far as he was concerned, the land's every bit as sacred as the people say. Why else do you think he spent nigh on sixty years letting his spread go back to nature? He wasn't going to dig it up. He wanted to keep it safe.'

'Safe from who?' Lynne asked.

'From the same bunch of bastards he knew couldn't wait to roll onto the land and tear it apart,' Kip said. 'That can't happen. Not ever.'

Jeff suddenly remembered the sign he'd seen as they were leaving the Brundle farmstead. He hadn't twigged it before, but now the connection was dawning on him. As well as the sheer brazenness of these people. 'The W.F. Cooper Development Corporation?'

Kip nodded. 'Old Wiley. Wiley by name, wily by nature, I reckon. The worst, lowest, meanest, dirtiest independent mining operator this country's ever had the misfortune to spawn. Bet your arse he's been aching to get his filthy mitts on the silver for God knows how long. He's lived in the Territory all his life, always looking out for the main chance, always with an ear to the ground. He must've known the stories were true, just couldn't prove it. I still don't understand how he found out.'

'Your man Terry Napier,' Jeff said. 'He's one of them. Go figure out the rest.'

'That mongrel,' Kip muttered. 'I'll murder him.'

You might not have to, Jeff thought, if Ben's already caught up with him. Out loud he asked, 'And so Cooper's plan was to force you to let him dig up your uncle's land? Or should I say your land, now Mick's gone?'

'Bastard's got all the paperwork ready to go. Thought he could press me to sign it. Anyhow.' Kip gave a dark smile. 'What Cooper doesn't know is it ain't going to be my land for much longer.'

'I don't understand,' Lynne said. 'You're selling it to someone else?'

'No, love. Not selling it. See, when Mick passed I got a letter from his lawyer, bloke by the name of Muldoon, telling me the news, and how everything his client owned was mine now, seeing as I was his only kin. But there was more to it. Turns out, according to Mick's wishes before he died, Muldoon was drafting up a contract to have to have the whole half million acres transferred to the ownership of the Aboriginal people, lock, stock and barrel without a single penny changing hands. The two of them had been working on the deal for months, ironing out the details, making sure it was all watertight and copper-bottomed. But now Mick was gone, Muldoon said it was up to me whether I wanted to keep the land, or sell it, or press ahead with the transfer contract.'

Jeff asked, 'Does Muldoon know about the silver mine?'

'Not a clue,' Kip said. 'No more than I had meself, then. He'd have mentioned it otherwise. So there I was, wondering what the hell to do. Hated the idea of selling up, but then what was I supposed to do with all that spread? Couldn't make me mind up either way, and it was driving me bananas. But then it all came clear to me, when I found what Mick had hidden away and I realised what he'd been thinking. I soon worked out in me mind what I had to do. Called Muldoon and told him to go ahead with the deal.'

'He's still working on it?'

'He was almost done when I last spoke to him. That was the day before I got nabbed. Reckon he'll have polished it off by now. Then all it takes is me signature in front of a witness, and it's all legal and Wiley can go and screw himself. He so much as steps on that land in a dream, Muldoon will throw the book at him for trespassing. Muldoon's a pretty sharp bloke, not like them government lawyers who let the mining companies act like they own the bloody place. He'll keep a tight rein, make no mistake.'

'And the mother lode will stay under the ground where it belongs,' Jeff said, nodding. 'The Aboriginal folk get to preserve their land, and everybody's happy. Everyone except for Cooper and his cronies. What about the silver nugget and the map? Do you still have them?'

'Gave the silver piece to Sammy Mudrooroo. Reckoned he could keep it safer than I ever could. As for the map, that's still back at the farm, where nobody'd ever find it. It's just a bit of paper. You can hardly even make it out.'

'I'll bet that's what Napier was looking for, when he turned the house over,' Jeff said. 'You were refusing to talk and they were getting desperate. But you had it too well hidden. That's why they had to move up to the next level, by snatching us.'

'Napier,' Kip growled. 'He must've been spying on me

the whole time. Probably got a good eyeful of the map before I'd the chance to hide it.'

'And reported it back to his lord and master Cooper,' Jeff said. 'But we've got them over a barrel now, with any luck. Your uncle was a genius, to come up with an idea like that. I just can't believe he didn't tell you what he was planning.'

Kip shrugged. 'Mick was a shrewd sort of fella. Liked to keep his cards close to his chest and you never quite knew what he was thinking.'

Lynne had been mostly listening, but now she looked reproachfully at her husband and said, 'Just like you never mentioned a single word to me about any of this, either. What's the matter, don't you trust me?'

'I'm sorry, love. I truly am. It ripped me guts out to hide it from you. I thought I was doing the right thing, honest I did. But now I can see I was wrong.'

'You *lied* to me, Kip. All that bullshit about going to see a man about a horse. I deserved to be told the truth. It hurts, you know?'

Kip hung his head and looked penitent. 'I know.'

'Why'd you even go back to Mick's that day, if you'd already decided to let go of the place?'

'I wish I could tell you, babe. Think I just wanted to say goodbye. It was part of me life for so long. And I didn't want to worry you with all me problems. You've got enough stress of your own to deal with. You know what I'm talking about,' Kip added with a significant look.

She blanched, and put her hand to her chest. 'What are you – do you mean my heart?'

'That's just what I mean, love,' Kip said.

'Just how serious is it, Mum?' Jeff asked, concerned.

This was the touchy subject. 'It's nothing,' she shot back at him, unwilling to discuss it at all. 'It's perfectly under control. Oh, Kip, you don't always have to carry everything on your own shoulders. There are people around you who care and want to help. But you had to play the strong silent type and look where it's got us. You put us all in danger.'

'Yeah, I can see that now,' Kip replied ruefully. 'What more can I say, except I'm sorry? It wasn't supposed to happen that way. Please forgive me.'

'Of course I do, you . . . you . . . oh, come here.' She held him tight. The rawness of their emotions was hard to watch, and Jeff diverted his gaze towards the fire.

Some moments passed. 'What next, Jeff?' Lynne asked.

Jeff shrugged. 'Well, we can't stay here, that's for sure. Nobody's coming to help us, and it's not safe.'

'But what are we supposed to do? Kip can't walk, in his state.'

'No, and I wouldn't let either of you even try,' Jeff told her.

'I bloody can,' Kip protested. 'That bit of tucker's done me the power of good. And I'll carry you on my back, too. You just watch me.' He tried to get up, but he was very wobbly and soon sank back down again. 'Bugger it. Maybe I can't.'

'If only we knew where we were,' Lynne said. 'We can't be that far from a main road, or the nearest farmstead, or even a small town.'

'This is the outback, sweetheart,' Kip muttered. 'You know as well as I do we could be days and days' walk from anywhere.'

'He's right,' Jeff said. 'But that wouldn't stop me going off to get help. If I had to crawl on hands and knees to get there. There's just one problem. I can't leave you two behind.'

'Then what are we to do?' Lynne repeated. 'If we can't stay here either? It's an impossible situation. Jeff? Jeff?'

'Shh.' Jeff held up a finger, suddenly distracted by something outside.

'What?'

'Hear that?'

'I don't hear anything,' Lynne said.

Jeff leaped to his feet and stepped out of the shelter. No, he hadn't imagined it. A faint droning sound in the distance, so tiny it was almost inaudible, but growing steadily in volume.

Lynne joined him at the mouth of the shelter, now able to hear it, too. 'What is that?'

'It's not a car,' he said.

Chapter 39

'Wait here.' Jeff urged his mother back into the shelter, then quickly scaled the watchtower rock. He knew the way so well by now that he could spring up to the top like a mountain goat in the darkness. From its vantage point he scanned the night sky and, with a thrill, soon spotted the source of the faint sound: far off in the distance, the green starboard wingtip and white tail position lights of a small plane were tracing a blinking line from west to east among the stars. The drone of the aircraft was growing steadily louder all the time. The unmistakable note of a single-engined light plane, almost identical to the sound of Jeff's own Cessna Skyhawk back home.

Help at last! Jeff had been starting to feel as if he, Kip and Lynne would never see another living soul again. If he could only catch the pilot's attention with some kind of distress signal, he might be able to get him to land, or at the very least radio the authorities for help. But as he watched, he could see with a sinking heart that the plane was on a course that would curve away from them. Already he could see the faint glimmer of the red port wing light as

301

it banked gently off towards the north. In a few minutes it would be gone again.

How to attract the pilot's notice? Jeff looked down through the rock fissure at the glow of the dying fire inside the shelter below him. If he could grab some burning embers and quickly rebuild a brighter blaze at the mouth of the nook, it might be visible from a distance. But even as he thought it, he knew that the pilot would be likely to think of it simply as what it was: a camp fire. Hardly sufficient reason to divert course and come and check it out.

But something else might work.

Jeff scrambled back down the watchtower rock, barking both shins and skinning an elbow in the process. He hit the ground running and hurried away from the shelter without a word to Kip or Lynne, sprinting down the road to where the steep rubbly path led down to the wreck of the camper van. With little regard for his own neck he plunged down the slope and went slithering over the loose rocks. The rumbling drone of the plane was still clearly audible, and looking up he could make out the flashing pinpricks of bright light scudding across the night sky. As he'd predicted, it was slipping away to the north. But there was still time.

Jeff was only going to get one shot at this. Working feverishly fast, he wrenched open the compartment that housed the van's two onboard propane gas cylinders. He'd already checked them and knew that the spare was full. He ripped the other one loose from its regulator house, grabbed one in each hand and dragged them around to the rear of the van where the fuel filler was. Next he leaped inside the camper and tore down one of the grimy little curtains from

302

the rear lounge window. Back outside, moving so fast he hardly had time to breathe, he opened the fuel filler cap and stuffed the piece of rag down into the neck of the tank so that its length trailed down the side. He yanked the pair of green metal jerrycans from the rack on the back. Opened them up and sloshed out fuel, making sure to soak the dangling length of rag but avoiding getting it all over himself. The night air was suddenly heady with the sharp tang of the gasoline.

The aircraft's sound was starting to grow fainter. He glanced skywards and saw the lights slowly, steadily curving away from their position. Seconds counted. Jeff's fingers were a blur as he opened the valves of the two propane bottles. The hissing escape of gas merged with the petrol fumes in the air.

'Party time,' he muttered to himself, pulling out the cigarette lighter from his pocket. He touched its flame to the dangling end of the curtain material. It quickly burst alight, burning greedily up its length towards the mouth of the filler neck. The bright flames licked up the side of the van, scorching the paintwork. Pieces of blazing curtain material fell to the ground and ignited the pool of spilled petrol from the jerrycans in a fiery lake that spread over the ground and surrounded the hissing propane bottles.

Jeff felt the heat on his face. Things would soon get much hotter. He kicked over the jerrycans, spilling the last of their contents, and then beat a hasty retreat to safety, leaping and bounding back up the slope towards the road.

He'd almost reached the top when the fast-spreading fire touched off the propane bottles. One went off slightly ahead of the other in a ragged double explosion that ripped the night like a bomb blast and ruptured the van's fuel tank, igniting its volatile load all at once. The vehicle was lifted off its wheels and hurled up and over by the huge force of the detonation. A gigantic fireball came rolling and mushrooming up high in a spectacular great towering column of light that illuminated the dark sky, a blazing beacon that could be seen for a vast distance. The searing heat of it scorched Jeff's back even from this distance, but he barely glanced around – his eyes were intently focused on the blinking lights of the aeroplane. For a few breathless moments it seemed to be continuing on the same tack, away from them. But then Jeff saw the angle of its port and starboard wingtip lights change, and he knew his plan had worked.

Now the plane was banking hard to starboard, veering south towards the blazing beacon of flames. Closer and closer. The rumbling drone growing louder with every passing second. The pilot dropped two hundred feet and did a low pass over the scene, then banked sharply and came looping around for another, turning on his bright white landing lights to use as spotlamps.

There was no possible doubt that he had seen it. The question only remained what he intended to do about it. These little planes could put down just about anywhere, as Jeff knew from experience – but if instead the pilot chose just to radio the authorities to report a burning vehicle and possible casualties on the ground, it could still be hours before anyone came to help. Which wouldn't be a terrible thing to have to endure, but during that time Jeff was acutely aware that his beacon could also draw other, more unwanted attention.

It was essential to get the urgency of the situation across to the pilot. Standing in the middle of the road to make himself as visible as possible from the air, Jeff jumped up and down and frantically waved his arms, yelling at the top of his voice 'Over here! We need help!' even though there was no chance of being heard. The plane did a third looping pass and its dazzling white landing lights washed over him as it roared by. Jeff went on waving his arms as the pilot banked around once again, dropping more altitude.

Yes! He was coming in to land! The pilot had lowered his landing gear and was now circling the scene in search of a good spot to put down. He picked out a straighter section of road, about four hundred metres to the far side of the rock shelter, to use as his landing strip. He handled the aircraft skilfully, descending in a smooth curve and touching down neatly with a yelp of tyres. The plane taxied up the road, an almost surreal and infinitely welcome sight, weaving in and out of view now as it navigated all the hairpin bends on the approach to the rock shelter and the stretch of road where the camper van had lost control.

Jeff ran to meet it, wanting to shake the guy's hand and give him all the thanks in the world for landing. He was still seventy yards or so away when it reappeared around the last turn before the mouth of the shelter, one wing tip almost scraping the rocks to one side of the road. Shielding his eyes with hand against the dazzle of its landing lights as he ran, Jeff saw it stop. He grinned.

And then the grin dropped from his face as the plane's

side hatch swung open and a lone silhouetted figure of a man stepped out behind the glare of the lights, carrying something Jeff's trained eyes instantly recognised as the dark outline of a Heckler & Koch automatic battle rifle.

Jeff skidded to a halt in the road. His heart froze as the man with the rifle started purposefully striding in his direction. But Jeff's stupefied disbelief lasted only the split second it took for the thought to form in his mind: *this guy hasn't come to help – he's one of them* before he bolted towards the edge of the road and threw himself down behind the cover of a clump of prickly bushes. There was hardly time to think. Just to act.

Jeff tore the revolver from his belt. It was pure luck that he hadn't left the weapon lying idly by the campfire. He automatically checked the cylinder: only three rounds left. He clicked the action closed and peered over the top of the bushes. He could clearly see the man with the rifle. He was black, which here in Australia meant he was probably Aboriginal. But he didn't look like he'd taken arms to protect his ravaged homeland. This guy had found another way to make sense of the modern world around him. He was a killer for hire.

Working for who? *Take a wild guess,* Jeff thought.

Jeff didn't know if the man had seen him disappear into the bushes. It looked like he hadn't, in which case Jeff thought his best option was to wait for him to get a little closer before he made his move. He could have done with a long-arm of his own, something like the assault rifle his opponent was carrying, all decked out with Picatinny rails and optical sight and tactical light. Jeff was expert at most martial disciplines, but he was no pistol champion, especially not with an old-school sixgun. What constituted effective pistol range was really down to the skill of the user. He'd seen Ben take out the hearts and diamonds of playing cards at fifty metres offhand with a big-bore hand cannon like this one. Jeff wished, now more than ever, that he was in that league.

The man walked closer. He was just sixty metres away now, nearer than Jeff was to the mouth of the rock shelter by about a third of that distance. Jeff knew he had to take the guy out before he got there. *Just a bit closer,* he urged him. *Just a few more steps . . .*

But then the worst thing happened. Because at that moment, Lynne emerged from the shelter and stepped out into plain view of the man with the rifle, almost directly in his path. She'd seen him, but with the dazzle of the aircraft's lights full in her face she couldn't see the gun. 'We're over here,' she called out as loudly as she could manage, waving excitedly at their saviour. 'Please! We're over here! My husband's hurt and sick and needs help! Jeff? Jeff! Where's Jeff?'

Where Jeff was, was in the worst place imaginable. He wanted to scream at her, '*Mum, no! Get back inside!*' But he couldn't do that without giving away his position, and it could do little good anyhow. The man with the gun had redoubled his stride and was marching straight towards her. Now he broke into a run, and as he loomed closer Lynne saw the rifle in his hands and went rigid and jumped back in alarm, ducking back towards the shelter.

But too late. The man was almost there. As she retreated

from him he snapped the rifle up to his shoulder, activated his tactical light, and a strobing white flash and a rattle of gunfire erupted from its muzzle, bullets splatting off the rock where Lynne's head had been just a fraction of a second ago. In that moment Jeff realised that the man had come not just to capture, but to hunt down and kill anyone his bosses didn't strictly need alive. And that suddenly it wasn't just Jeff himself who was expendable – his mother was too.

Jeff no longer cared about giving away his position, about anything at all except protecting her. He surged up out of the bushes with an angry roar and the revolver raised in a two-handed grip and squeezed off two shots as fast as the weapon's heavy recoil would let him. The first bullet sparked off the rock wall a foot from the killer's shoulder and the second, rushed too quickly in his wake, passed over his head.

Without a flinch or a moment's hesitation the killer swung the rifle towards Jeff, shining the tactical light in his eyes, and returned fire. He had far more of it to return. The rattling stream of high-velocity bullets raked the bushes and clipped leaves and spat up little explosions of dirt all around Jeff as he hurled himself back under cover. Jeff hit the ground and went crawling for all he was worth to get out of the deadly firestorm.

Then as suddenly as it had started, the shooting fell silent. Jeff froze for a heartbeat, thinking that this was a ruse to get him to break his cover again, and this time to nail him dead. But Jeff broke it anyway, leaping from the bushes with the gun in his hand, one round left in the cylinder and murder in his heart.

And saw that the man was gone. He had disappeared into the rock shelter after Lynne.

Gripped by total horror, Jeff ran towards the shelter. At any instant he expected to hear gunfire from in there, but he could hear nothing. He knew that if he went bursting in after them, he was a dead man. Instead he reached the watchtower rock at a bounding sprint and went leaping and clambering up it like a lunatic, too terrified to breathe as he spreadeagled himself flat against the hard rock at the jagged edge of the fissure, angling his body to try to peer down to see what was happening below him.

He had a clear view, lit by the dying glow of the fire and the bright white light shining from the killer's rifle on his targets. The man had pressed Kip and Lynne right up against the far wall of the nook at gunpoint. Kip was on his feet, wobbly and swaying but standing strong with his wife clasped tightly in his arms and shielding her body with his own. 'You're going to have to shoot us both, you scumbag!'

Jeff needed to make that last round in his gun count. He took aim through the fissure, thumb-cocked the hammer and squared his sights on the top of the man's head, ready to blow out his brains. His finger curled around the trigger. But just then, alerted by some sixth sense, the hunter-killer seemed to detect the presence above him, and whirled round and brought the rifle up and fired.

Both shots sounded almost simultaneously, stunningly loud within the confined space. The rifle bullet ricocheted off the edge of the fissure and hit Jeff in the shoulder with a massive jarring impact that told him his left collar bone was broken. In the same instant he saw his enemy stagger and drop his rifle, a red spray bursting from the side of his neck catching the light. The falling rifle hit against the rocks and the light went out.

But then Jeff felt himself falling too, as his grip on the edge of the fissure failed him and he went sliding downwards through the crack. The empty revolver dropped from his hand. His fingertips raked against rough stone, but nothing could stop his fall. For the briefest moment he was tumbling into the shadows through empty space; then he landed on top of the killer with a grunting impact that knocked the breath out of him and brought the two men crashing to the floor, instantly locked together in a savage hand-to-hand fight.

They rolled together through the remnants of the fire, scattering the embers across the floor and plunging the inside of the shelter into almost total darkness. In the confusion of pain and chaos Jeff heard his mother scream. He tried to shout at her to stay back, but then strong fingers were locking around his throat and the shout was choked off. Pinned to the floor, Jeff battled to loosen the grip on his neck. The killer was badly hurt, perhaps mortally hurt, but he was fighting like a wounded tiger that will use up all its very last reserves of energy to survive.

In the struggle Jeff felt something hard and angular jammed under his back and realised it was the fallen assault rifle. Managing to twist himself slightly free of the stranglehold for an instant, he reached under him with a shocking jolt of pain from his damaged shoulder and grabbed the weapon. He couldn't bring it to bear as a gun so he used it as a club, driving the hard polymer stock forend viciously up into his enemy's face. He felt the cheekbone give and the fingers lost their grip around his throat. Jeff battered him again, then again. The guy seemed to be made of wood, capable of absorbing any amount of punishment without so much as a grunt of pain. Next thing Jeff knew, two powerful fists were latching onto the rifle, trying to rip it out of his hands. But Jeff wasn't letting go.

They rolled over and over with the rifle locked between them, each trying to rip it free or smash it into the other's face. Suddenly Jeff felt it tear loose of the man's grip, and for an instant it seemed he was winning the fight. Too late, he realised the ruse. The man had let go on purpose, so that he could draw the concealed knife from his boot. The steel of the blade flashed in what was left of the firelight, lancing towards his belly. Jeff twisted out of the way of the stab. The jerking movement made him dizzy with pain from his broken collarbone, but at least the cold steel didn't punch into his guts. The rifle clattered back down to the ground. Jeff rolled, trying to clamber to his feet, hitting his head against an unseen rock and seeing stars.

The knife came at him again. Jeff was trapped against the shelter wall and could no longer roll out of the way. He thrust out his right hand to try to deflect the strike and trap his enemy's wrist. But in the darkness, half-stunned from the blow to the head, he misjudged his move and felt a piercing, icy-cold shock of agony as the knife went through the palm of his hand.

Jeff swallowed back the scream that wanted to come

bubbling up out of his lips. He tried to wrench away his injured hand but it was pinned like a butterfly, the thick blade locked tight between bones and tendons. Then the killer was rolling over on top of him, straddling him like a horse, twisting the knife so that Jeff's hand angled back towards him, the sharp, bloody tip of the blade just inches from his neck. Jeff struggled to deflect it aside and tried to use his other hand to push back, but the pain of his broken collar bone was too much and he had no strength. There was little he could do to resist the weight bearing down on him, or the knife sinking down inch by inch towards the soft flesh of his throat.

Both men were hurt badly now. Jeff could hear the man's laboured breath rasping in his ear. Taste the blood from his own hand as it dripped into his face, and feel the slippery warmth of it pouring from the gaping gunshot wound in his enemy's neck. It was just a question of who could hold out the longest. And Jeff could feel his energy ebbing fast. The tip of the knife sank lower towards him. It felt as if there was a hydraulic press bearing it inexorably down on him.

He couldn't stop it.

He was going to die. He felt suddenly very cold. His mother's scream sounded infinitely far away.

So did the scrape of something metallic against the rocky floor of the shelter, and the movement that Jeff sensed from somewhere in the shadows. Then, suddenly much closer, a familiar voice rasped, 'Suck on this, you piece of shit.'

The whoosh of something heavy cleaving the air; and Jeff

felt, as much as heard, the meaty impact and the solid *thunk* of a honed wedge of carbon steel burying itself deeply into a wooden chopping block.

Except it wasn't a wooden chopping block. It was a man's skull being split down the middle by a massive downward hatchet strike. Something hot and wet splattered Jeff's face. In the same instant the terrible, irresistible pressure that had been bearing the knife towards his throat suddenly slackened away to nothing. Coming as if out of a dream, Jeff struggled from under it and the weight of the dead man fell off him.

The darkness was all-enveloping. He thought he was fainting. Lynne's voice in his ear, calling his name, and her arms wrapping tight around him as he tried to get up, not yet fully understanding what had just happened.

'Oh, Jeff!'

'Mum?'

'You're hurt. Oh my God, Kip, he's so hurt!'

'I'm fine,' Jeff tried to protest. But his hand was still impaled on the knife and every movement was excruciating agony. Then the darkness was suddenly lit bright, and Jeff looked up to see the figure of Kip Malloy standing as tall as a giant over him. He was holding the rifle and shining the tactical light down on the collapsed lifeless heap that had been their attacker. The shaft of the wood-splitting hatchet protruded from the back of the dead man's head.

'Not as hurt as this bastard is,' Kip grated. 'That's for bloody sure.' He looked as if he wanted to pump the rest of the rifle's magazine into the body.

'Owe you one,' Kip, Jeff gasped. His hand was on fire.

Blood was pouring out of it like a tap, dripping from the blade, slicking his shirt sleeve to the elbow.

'You don't owe me a thing, son. I'm only sorry I couldn't have given this rat-arsed mongrel the chop a few seconds sooner. Now you'd better let me take a look at that hand.' Kip leaned the gun against at an angle so that the light shone on them. He examined the wound and the knife and said, 'I'm no surgeon, mate, but seems to me you can either leave that bloody thing stuck in there, or you can take it out. I know what I'd do.'

Jeff nodded. 'Take it out.'

'This is going to hurt a little.'

'Go for it.' Jeff gritted his teeth. Kip grasped Jeff's wrist in one hand and the wet, sticky hilt of the knife with the other, took a good firm grip, counted to three and yanked it out in one clean tug. The grinding scrape of steel against bone was indescribable. Kip wiped the knife blade clean against his trouser leg, then used it to slice a long strip of denim material from his own shirt. Lynne knelt at Jeff's side and wound the makeshift bandage round and round his hand. The blood soaked through almost immediately and dripped to the ground in large red splashes. Kip helped him to ease his other arm out of its sleeve, and took off his belt to use as a sling to lessen the strain on the broken collar bone.

'Been in the wars, aintcha, mate.'

'I've had worse,' Jeff muttered, blinking away the pain and forcing himself to focus. 'I'm fine.'

'No you're not,' Lynne sobbed. 'You're cut to pieces.'

'And we're getting out of here.'

314

Lynne stared at him and said, 'In what?'

Jeff nodded beyond the mouth of the shelter, towards where the killer's plane was parked out on the road. 'In that,' he said.

'But how?'

'I'm a pilot too,' Jeff said. 'Remember?'

'Not with no hands and arms, you're not,' Kip said.

'You just try and stop me.'

Chapter 40

It was late into the night by the time Ben returned to the communal area. The remains of the feast long since cleared away, the tribespeople had built up their fire and were sitting around it in a wide circle, forty or fifty voices all talking animatedly, some laughing, others more pensive, their faces bathed in the soft glow of the flames. Most of the children were asleep by now, curled up on rugs or in their mothers' arms. Ben spotted Abbie among the circle, sitting on a log bench next to a sturdy woman in a flowery dress. They were deep in conversation and Abbie was cradling a small infant girl on her lap as they spoke, holding her as tenderly as if she were her own child.

Abbie turned to him with a warm smile as he stepped towards the circle of light. 'Hey, Ben. This is my new friend Jeddah.'

'It's a pleasure to meet you, Jeddah.'

'And this little poppet here is Maali. Isn't she adorable?' But then, seeing the look on Ben's face, her own expression became more serious and she passed Maali back to her mother. They stepped away from the fire, where they could talk discreetly. 'Did you find out what you needed?' Abbie asked.

Ben nodded. 'I know who has them, Abbie. And I have to move fast if there's any chance of saving them.'

'Then what are we waiting for? Let's go.'

Things happened quickly. Sammy offered guides to escort them back down the escarpment and across the valley to their helicopter. Ben asked him if he was coming too, and Sammy shook his head. 'Then I'll be seeing you around, Sammy. You take care, now, won't you?'

'You too, mate,' Sammy said, and clasped Ben's hand in his strong, dry grip. Ben had a feeling they'd be meeting again before too long. Remembering that he still had the silver nugget, he went to give it back, but Sammy shook his head. 'You hang onto it, mate. Might need it.'

'Might I?' Ben asked, but Sammy just gave him a twinkling, knowing look. Then as they parted, Sammy pressed a slip of paper into his palm, and to his surprise Ben saw it had a mobile number written on it.

'Gotta keep pace with the modern world sometimes,' Sammy said with a shrug. 'You need me, you call.'

'I'll do that.'

On the long trek back to the chopper, Ben filled Abbie in on everything he'd learned. 'Of course I've heard of the Cooper Development Company,' she said, shocked by the things he was telling her. 'Flown over their sites many a time. They seem to be everywhere these days.'

'Not for much longer,' Ben said tersely.

'What are you going to do?'

'Now I know who started this, I'm going to finish it. And Wiley Cooper's going to regret he ever messed with my friends.'

'Don't forget this friend,' she said. 'I'm with you, Ben. Come this far, and I mean to see it through.'

'Don't start this again. It's not safe for you.'

'Hey, I fly planes and helicopters for a living,' she replied. 'Nerves of steel, that's me. Takes more than a little bit of risk and danger to frighten Abbie Logan. Besides, I told you I was good in a scrape. You haven't seen me in action yet.'

'The action I have in mind—' he began.

'Is no place for a sheila?'

'You didn't hear me say that.'

'But you were thinking it.'

'People are going to get hurt, Abbie. You can't be part of that. It would be wrong of me to let you.'

'Seems to me like people already are getting hurt,' she shot back. 'The innocent ones who don't have it coming. So we'd be doing a good thing, putting a stop to it.'

'What if something happened to you? I can't have that on my conscience.'

'We've been through this already, Ben. It's my choice. I'm a big girl.' She shook her head. 'I just wish Dad was here. He'd have been only too happy to have a bash at these scumbags.'

'What about the law?' he asked.

'What about it?'

'It'll be smashed into a thousand pieces by the time we're done here. That doesn't concern you?'

'Why the hell should it? If the law did its job instead of letting a bunch of dirty crooks run around harming decent folks, then these things wouldn't be left to the likes of us to take care of,' she said. 'That's how I see things.'

'You're an unusual kind of lady, that's for sure.'

'Dad had a saying. I used to hear it all the time, growing up. DTRT.'

'DTRT?'

'Do the right thing,' she said. 'That's how I try to live my life. And I know it's how you live yours too. So I'm in on this, no matter what happens. Because the right thing has to be done. Besides, where would you be without me?'

Ben said nothing more until they'd reached the Iroquois. When he turned around to say goodbye to their escorts, he found they'd already disappeared, slipped away into the night like spirits of the forest.

They climbed aboard the aircraft, donned their headsets and Abbie spent a few moments going through all her pre-flight procedures, flipping switches and checking dials and gauges. Soon the rotors were winding up to full speed and the howling blast of the turbine was filling the cockpit. The whole raucous din was a symphony orchestra to Abbie's ears and she couldn't repress the infectious dimpled grin of a person totally at home. 'Let's go, sport,' her voice said cheerily in his headset. He turned to her and saw the glitter of excitement in her eyes. He was glad to be with her. Where would he have been without her, indeed.

With the same skilful precision by which she'd dropped them down through the impossible gap in the treetops, she lifted them up, brought the Huey's nose around, and they streaked off in the direction they'd come. 'So where to from here?' she asked.

There could be only one answer to that. Ben wanted to strike directly at the heart of the enemy. A shock raid on Cooper himself was the best way to do that. 'I need to know where Wiley Cooper lives.'

'Doubt you'd be able to find that out too easily,' Abbie replied. 'But I know where his main offices are. The company's based outside a town called Elliott. It's in the Barkly Region, on the Stuart Highway, about halfway between Darwin to the north and Alice Springs to the south.'

Ben asked, 'How big a place is it?'

'Pretty small, population of around three hundred-odd. Used to be an army camp, back in the war. The people call it Kulumindini.'

Such a tiny population made it unlikely there'd be much in way of a police presence for some distance. Ben nodded and said, 'Sounds good to me.'

'But his offices will be shut this time of the evening.'

'So much the better. Then we'll just have to open them.'

'You got a plan?'

'Only to draw Cooper's attention by causing as much noise as I can, then grabbing him and making him talk. He wants to go on breathing, he'll have to take me to where he's holding them.'

'That's a plan.'

Abbie set her course for Elliott and told him it would be more than an hour's flight to get there. Ben leaned back in his seat and closed his eyes, trying to let his heart rate sink and his tense muscles relax. He'd been sitting that way for forty minutes when the sensation of his phone vibrating against his hip bone brought him back to the present. He opened his eyes and fished the phone out of his pocket to find that they'd re-entered a reception zone and a text message had landed in his inbox.

He stared at the text, too stunned for a few instants to register what he was seeing.

'It's from Jeff.'

Chapter 41

Abbie turned from the controls with wide eyes and her incredulous voice said in his headset, 'What's the message?'

'They're free. They got away.'

She burst out, 'That's bonzer!'

'But they're hurt,' Ben said, reading on.

Abbie's face fell. 'How hurt? What happened?

'He doesn't say. Change of plan, Abbie. Can you get me to Tennant Creek hospital? That's where they are.'

She nodded, deadly serious and already replotting her course. 'Yup. I know it. Tennant Creek's not far. There's a helipad the Careflight air ambulance uses all the time. I can radio in ahead to let them know we're coming.'

'Do it,' Ben said.

Abbie banked the chopper off full throttle on its new bearing. Ben sat anxiously silent, re-reading the text over and over, wondering how on earth they'd managed to get away and how badly hurt any of them were.

He'd soon find out. Within the hour, just before two in the morning, the lights of the Stuart Highway and Tennant Creek, the Northern Territory's seventh largest town, came into view below. Soon afterwards, Abbie was coming in to land on a small concrete square adjacent to the twenty-bed hospital facility. Ben was tearing off his headset and swinging out of his hatch before the skids had even touched the ground. 'Go,' she yelled after him. 'I'll see you inside.'

Ben sprinted head low away from the hurricane blast of the rotors and ran towards the main reception building. At the main desk he urgently presented himself as a friend of the newly admitted patients and was redirected to a deserted waiting area, where he was pacing up and down when a breathless Abbie joined him a few minutes later. 'Well?'

'Nobody's told me anything yet.'

It was an anxious half-hour's wait before the welcome appearance of a female doctor, blonde-haired and startlingly young, who introduced herself as Dr Monroe. She was wearing a blue surgical smock, and looked drained and badly in need of sleep at this late hour. 'I'm sorry to say your friends have been involved in some kind of incident,' she told them. 'The police are on their way.'

'How are they?'

'Mr and Mrs Malloy are doing fine. He's got multiple facial contusions and some concussion, nothing too serious. Mrs Malloy has suffered from some complications relating to an existing heart condition. Again, she's stable and doing all right. But they're both going to need lots of rest and recuperation.'

'What about Jeff Dekker?' Ben asked.

Was that a tiny smile that flickered on Dr Monroe's lips for an instant at the mention of Jeff's name? 'Mr Dekker. Quite a character, isn't he?'

'I can attest to that,' Ben said, not able to hide the impatience in his voice. 'But it's his medical condition I'm more interested in.'

'Your friend is going to be okay. He's being treated for some acute injuries, one being a broken collar bone. He's going to be out of action for a while with that.' She frowned. 'The other injury—'

'What?'

The doctor frowned. 'Mr Hope, how much do you know about the situation your friends have been in?'

'I don't know anything,' Ben said, unwilling to reveal even what little he did know. 'Just that they've been hurt. What have they told you?'

'Nothing much either, and the details are more than a little hazy. Mr Dekker has received what I can only describe as a knife wound. He's clearly been in a fight, or been attacked, and there's some significant damage to his right hand. But it's obviously connected to Mr Malloy's injuries, and the police are going to want to know more.'

'How significant?'

'We've done all we could for the moment. I'd say he'll recover full use of it, in time. But a lot depends on how well the tendons heal. The knife went all the way through.'

Ben had experienced stab wounds in his time, and their cold, sharp memory jumped into his mind like a tangible sensation at her words. No man ever born, not even an elite warrior for whom fighting and death were their bread and butter and who could stand their ground against heavy enemy gunfire, was immune to that visceral, primal fear of getting cut. He shuddered inwardly and said, 'Can I see him?'

The doctor looked at her watch. 'He came out of surgery twenty minutes ago and he's sedated. You might be able to see him in a few hours, though only for a short time.'

'Then I'll wait,' Ben said.

'Me too,' Abbie chimed in.

Dr Monroe went back to her duties and Ben and Abbie to their seats in the empty waiting area. The chances of getting comfortable in the flimsy plastic chairs under the stark neon lights were fairly poor, but Abbie managed to doze off after a while, pressed against him with her head resting on his shoulder for a couple of hours, a pleasant respite from all the thoughts and emotions and questions that kept Ben awake through the night.

Not long after dawn, a Northern Territory police patrol car rolled by the waiting area window. *Here we go*, Ben thought with an inward groan. But before the cops could make their appearance, Dr Monroe arrived, now looking a little fresher and wearing her white coat and a stethoscope draped around her neck like a fashion accessory, to say that Jeff was awake. 'He's still quite heavily sedated for the pain, but knows you're here and wants to talk to you. Fifteen minutes max, okay?'

'Thanks, doctor.'

'I'll wait,' Abbie said. Ben touched her hand and said, 'Sure?'

'He's your mate.'

'One more thing,' Dr Monroe said as she led Ben off at a brisk, clicking pace through the hospital corridors. 'The police are here. A Sergeant Wenzel wants to interview the three of them. He was very insistent. But I thought I'd let you have a few moments with your friend first.'

'I appreciate that,' Ben said, his heart sinking.

'Speak of the devil,' the doctor muttered under her breath, whether or not she intended Ben to hear. They'd rounded a corner and there stood Wenzel, accompanied by the same skinny sidekick constable Ben had met on his first day in Australia. It was impossible to avoid having to pause and talk to them. Wenzel folded his thick arms over the slab of his belly and eyed Ben with an officious, cold glare. 'It's you. Mr, ah, Hope, isn't it?'

'Nice of you to make an appearance, officers,' Ben said. 'Only took you all night to get here.' For which he was secretly grateful; but in the mood he was in, he had to get a dig in somehow.

Wenzel glowered at him. 'Be assured that we're taking the matter very seriously indeed. I'm heading up the inquiry. We'll get to the bottom of this.'

'I'm sure you will,' Ben said. 'Just like you did last time. At least now we know Kip didn't get drunk at the wheel and go wandering off alone into the boonies. Maybe you should start by offering an apology to his wife.'

The young constable hung his head and shifted on his feet. Dr Monroe said nothing and looked uncomfortable. 'I'm here to gather facts,' Wenzel said. 'And I'd like to speak with you, too.'

'I'll be glad to help in whatever way I can, Sergeant. Bearing in mind, I know as little about this as you do.'

Wenzel grunted. 'Yes, well, I think we'd like to start by speaking with Mr Malloy.'

'Nurse Baxter will take you in,' the doctor said, pointing in the direction of a door and waving over the nurse in question. 'Now, Sergeant,' she added in a more authoritative tone, 'may I remind you that the patients are not to be subjected to any unnecessary stress. They've been through a lot already. So please keep it brief as you can for now, all right?'

Ben thought he heard her discreetly mutter something to herself as they walked on. It could have been a soft cough, but it sounded remarkably like 'Jerk.' He was prepared to like this Dr Monroe. Moments later, they'd arrived at the door of the small private room where Jeff was sitting up in his metal-framed bed with his upper torso all bound up, his neck in a brace and his injured hand suspended from a support in front of him, heavily bandaged with only the tips of his fingers showing. A machine blinked and beeped on the stand beside the bed, and a drip was connected to his arm. He looked pale and drawn with dark rings around his eyes, but he broke into a gaunt grin at the sight of Ben walking into the room.

'Hey there, buddy.'

Chapter 42

Ben was filled with emotion to see Jeff again, alive and more or less in one piece. But men don't gush, so he just said, 'You okay?'

'Feel great. So would you, if you'd had half the drugs they've pumped into me.'

'Fifteen minutes,' Dr Monroe repeated firmly with her hand on the door handle.

'Thanks, Marilyn,' Jeff said.

When the door was closed, Ben looked at his friend with a raised eyebrow. 'Marilyn? Seriously?'

'Better believe it,' Jeff said. 'That really is her name.'

'Imaginative parents she must have had. Get her phone number as well?'

'Working on it.'

'Bit young, isn't she? Can't be more than a year or two out of medical school.'

'So what? And don't look at me like that. You're not above dating lady doctors yourself.'

That was true. The last time Jeff had been banged up in hospital, back home in France on that occasion, Ben had ended up having a romance with his surgeon, Dr Sandrine Lacombe.

'I'm just happy to see you making a speedy recovery,' Ben said.

Jeff glanced at his bandaged hand. 'Well, you know. There goes my glittering future career as a concert pianist. Apart from that, never been better in my life.'

'You have an official visitor,' Ben told him, jerking his thumb back at the door. 'Our old pal Sergeant Wenzel is here. Saw him lurking in the corridor just now.'

'Fuck. I might've guessed,' Jeff sighed, rolling his eyes. 'Well, anyway, don't worry about Kip and Mum. They won't say a word to the cops.'

'I'm not worried about that,' Ben said. 'But I won't lie that I wasn't worried about you.'

With a few more minutes to talk, Jeff filled Ben in on the details of the escape: the demise of their two guards, the ropey old camper van, the accident, the hired killer sent out to hunt them down, and the way that Kip had saved his life.

'I'm sorry for what happened,' Ben said. 'I should have been there.'

'Not your fault, buddy. I'm only sorry that Mum had to witness that.'

'How did you get here?' Ben asked.

'A certain dead scumbag kindly left us the use of his plane. I don't think he'll be needing it any more.'

Ben felt a surge of admiration. Only Jeff Dekker could fly a plane with one arm out of action and the other hand half sliced off. He asked, 'Where is it now?'

Unable to move his head more than a degree or two with

the neck brace on, Jeff rolled his eyes sideways towards the shuttered window to his right. 'Couldn't exactly land in the bloody hospital car park, could I? Wasn't much traffic on the highway that time of night, thank Christ, so I set down a couple of miles up the road. We started walking, but I was pretty knackered up and Mum and Kip were at the end of their tether too. Then as luck would have it, a truck came by and the bloke stopped to give us a lift. He couldn't do enough for us. Practically carried Mum in the emergency room door. Name's Ken Lipton. I owe him a couple of beers when I get out of this place.'

In typical fashion Jeff was playing it down, but Ben could see the strain behind his eyes and was all too aware of what they'd all been through. And all because of the greed and ruthlessness of one man. 'Our friend Cooper has a lot to answer for.'

Anger flashed across Jeff's face, his easy-going front slipping for an instant. 'You'd better believe it. And I want to be there when he does.'

'I think you need to let me take care of things from here on,' Ben said.

'No way. You must be nuts if you think I'm sitting this one out.'

'You're in no fit state, Jeff. Your eyes look like two burnt holes in a blanket.'

'Piss off. I got us here, didn't I?'

'You did great. But you won't be doing much else for a while. Doctor's orders.' Ben smiled. 'And I get the feeling you'd better obey them, or else.'

There was a knock at the door. Dr Monroe said, 'Your

fifteen minutes are up, fellas,' though she'd allowed them more than twenty. 'And Sergeant Wenzel is here for Mr Dekker.'

Ben and Jeff exchanged glances. Jeff winked. 'Good morning, Sergeant,' he said pleasantly as Wenzel came striding into the room with his constable in tow.

'I'm sorry to disturb you,' Wenzel said without much sincerity, planting himself at the foot of the bed while the constable hovered in the background, 'but the doctor says you're able to have a word.'

'No problem. Don't think I'll be able to help much, though.'

'All the same, any information you can give me will help with our inquiry. Seems a lot's gone on since we last met. Care to tell me your version of events?'

'There isn't a lot to tell, Sergeant. I've no idea who did this to us, or why. All I know is that I was driving in the car with Mum – that's Mrs Malloy—'

'I know that,' Wenzel said testily.

'—when all of a sudden these guys appeared out of nowhere, hijacked the car and kidnapped us,' Jeff went on.

Wenzel pursed his lips thoughtfully. 'Which, as it turns out, is also what appears to have happened to Mr Malloy a few days earlier.'

'Seems that way, doesn't it?'

'The Northern Territory hasn't seen a kidnapping case in over ten years. Now we've had three within a matter of days. And you say you've no idea why this happened?'

'None, officer.'

'Tell me more about these kidnappers,' Wenzel said.

'What's there to tell? They were driving a big truck. They bundled us into it and another car, and took us away.'

'Could you identify either of those vehicles?' Wenzel asked.

'It all happened so fast,' Jeff said.

'What about where you were taken?'

'Don't know.'

'Not even a rough idea?'

Jeff considered. 'It was right out in the middle of nowhere. We were being held in this rundown old building. There was a lot of open, flat ground around us, as far as the eye could see. And a few bushes, and the odd tree here and there, and some rocks.'

'That could be almost anywhere in the Territory,' Wenzel grumped.

'It's the best description I can give you, Sergeant. Sorry I can't be of any more help.'

'That's what your mother says too. And her husband, who's apparently been held by these same mysterious kidnappers since he disappeared, but again has no idea why.'

'It's a mystery all right,' Jeff said.

'You're telling me,' Mr Dekker, Wenzel agreed exasperatedly. 'So far nothing is making any sense. May I ask how you were able to escape?'

'They let us go,' Jeff told him matter-of-factly.

Wenzel balked. 'Why would they do that?'

'I really can't say. Perhaps they realised they'd got the wrong people.'

'A case of mistaken identity?'

'There's a theory for you, Sergeant. But you'd really have

to ask the kidnappers. Maybe Kip or Mum had some thoughts?'

'None,' Wenzel said, looking more perplexed by the second. 'None at all.' Flailing to come up with more questions, he managed to ask, 'How did you get here?'

'Shanks's pony,' Jeff said, sticking to that much of the truth. 'For a way. Then we hitched a lift with this guy in a pickup truck.'

Wenzel brightened for a second, thinking he might have a lead here. 'Didn't get the driver's name, did you? They might be able to give us an idea where you were.'

'Sorry,' Jeff said, dashing the sergeant's hopes. 'I never asked.'

'But you must have had some idea how far you travelled in this man's truck. That could help us.'

'I was asleep most of the way,' Jeff said. 'Completely out of it, what with being injured and all that. Could have been two hours, could have been six.'

'Ask'm about the plane, Sarge,' the constable piped up laconically from behind. Wenzel's flustered memory was jolted back into focus and he said, 'I was just coming to that. A light aircraft was found abandoned last night, just a few kilometres from here. It's a Cessna 172, registered to a Mr Jaice Wullabarra from Katherine, but there doesn't seem to be any trace of his whereabouts. Don't suppose you would know anything about that, either, would you?'

Jeff would have shrugged, if he'd had the mobility in his neck and shoulder. 'What's it to do with me? Can I help it if silly rich people leave their aeroplanes sitting abandoned about the place? Maybe it ran out of fuel and the owner went to get a can of petrol.'

'You can't refill a plane with a can of petrol,' the constable said.

'Goes to show what little I know,' Jeff replied.

Wenzel had managed to think of another question. 'The doctor said you have a knife injury to your hand. How'd that happen?'

'Cutting firewood,' Jeff said. 'This country of yours gets awful cold at night. The knife slipped and I gashed myself like a silly twit.'

'Where'd you get the knife from?'

'Found it.'

'So how'd you break your collar bone?' the constable asked.

'Fell,' Jeff said. 'What can I say? I'm just clumsy.'

'I can testify to that,' Ben chipped in. 'He's always hurting himself, breaking this and that, slicing bits off.'

'And what about getting kidnapped for no apparent reason and then released again?' Wenzel snapped. 'Make a habit of doing that too, do you?'

'No, this was a first for me,' Jeff replied.

Ben asked, 'Are you done with all these questions, officers? The patient's getting tired.' That much was true. Jeff was gradually sinking deeper into his pillow and looking increasingly pale as his pain meds began to wear off.

Wenzel didn't seem to have noticed. 'Not giving me much to go on, are you, gents,' he complained. 'I mean, we're not miracle workers. Without some kind of information to base my inquiry on, where do I even start?'

'It's a tough one,' Ben said. 'Guess we'll just have to leave this in your capable hands, Sergeant.'

Wenzel left soon afterwards, scratching his head in puzzlement and saying he'd be in touch and to give the police a call if they happened to remember anything important.

'You can count on it, Sergeant.'

Alone again, Ben spent a few more moments with Jeff, telling him to rest easy and not worry about a thing. Then Dr Monroe returned with Nurse Baxter to check on the patient, do whatever they had to do and shoo Ben away. He lingered outside in the corridor, waiting for the doctor to come out so that he could thank her for her good care of Jeff.

'Still no idea what happened to them?' she asked in a low voice.

'Not really,' he replied. 'But they're safe now, that's the main thing.'

'I don't know what kind of madness has come over the world these days,' she went on sotto voce with a mournful shake of her head. 'So much more weird violence happening all the time. Like, only just last night this poor man was brought in here with his testicles shot off.'

'That's terrible,' Ben said. 'Were you able to save them at all?'

'I'm afraid there was nothing we could do. It was a total gonadal ablation, as clean as a surgical orchidectomy. Nobody has any idea how it happened, either, and the man wouldn't say a word. Looked like someone blew them off with a rifle or something.' She shook her head. 'Can you imagine someone doing that to another person?'

335

'Sounds like another crime mystery for the redoubtable Sergeant Wenzel.'

'There you go. Sign of the times, I suppose,' she replied philosophically. 'But like you say, at least Jeff and his family are safe now.'

Ben thanked her again, then headed back to the waiting area by way of the reception desk, where he left his contact number in case of any developments. Abbie had been sitting patiently waiting for him, and stood up with an anxious smile as he appeared. 'Well?'

'Let's get some air,' he said, and they went outside. The air wasn't much fresher there, thick and hot and sultry with dark storm clouds gradually gathering in the far western sky. 'Looks like some heavy weather coming in,' Abbie commented, scanning the horizon with her pilot's eye. 'Been threatening on and off for days. I reckon we're in for a right gully raker. So how is he?'

'He's tough,' Ben said. 'But he's been through the mill a bit. So have Kip and Lynne.'

He lit a Gauloise and leaned against a railing as he recounted to a silent, dark-faced Abbie all the things that Jeff had told him about their treatment at the hands of their captors and the events that had followed.

'Jaice Wullabarra,' Abbie said, narrowing her eyes at the mention of the name. 'I've heard of him through the grape-vine. They call him the flying bounty hunter. Scary character, by all accounts.'

'He won't be troubling anyone again,' Ben said. 'Jeff took care of that.'

'Took care of?' she repeated, looking at him.

'I told you this was going to get serious, Abbie. And that people were going to get hurt. Still time for you to duck out and go back to the normal, happy life you knew before I came along.'

'Uh-uh. No chance, mate. DTRT, remember?'

He nodded. 'DTRT.'

'So now it's just you and me,' she said. 'You got another plan?'

'It's simple enough,' Ben replied. 'Wiley Cooper goes down. It's open war now. Time to hit back, and hard.'

'Funny, I thought you were going to say that. I've been thinking about it. How hard is hard?'

'Hard,' Ben said. 'So he never gets up again.'

She smiled. 'I have an idea to run by you. But let's get some breakfast first. You ready for another hop in the old girl?'

Chapter 43

They walked slowly back towards the helicopter. Ben said, 'Breakfast sounds good, Abbie. But please don't tell me you're going to land this crate outside some local café and frighten the customers half to death.'

'That'd be fun. No, I was thinking we could go somewhere more private.'

'So you can run this idea of yours by me?'

'That, and I also want to show you something.'

'Show me what?'

'You'll see.'

'I hate surprises,' he said.

'Don't be a grinch.'

Minutes later they were back in the air, this time thumping north away from Tennant Creek and leaving civilisation far behind them as they overflew more endless expanses of empty bushland, the landscape marked here and there by a gorge or a river, or by the occasional solitary road or remote farmstead. After forty-five minutes Abbie descended low over the ground, pointed and said cheerily, 'Here we are.'

Ben looked down and saw a lonely winding track leading through some trees to an old, long, single-storey white-painted wooden house with a red tin roof, an attached barn and assorted outbuildings dotted around. A rickety fence around the property disappeared off into the distance. 'Your place?' he asked.

'Dad's,' she replied. 'He lived on his own here for years after Mum walked out on us. It's only fifty acres, just a hobby farm. I use it as a weekend hideaway, come to chill out for a few days now and then, or to party with mates or do a bit of maintenance on the old place. Keep thinking I might move out here full-time one day.'

With the skill and confidence that Ben was getting used to by now, she brought the helicopter down to land in a scrubby pasture near the house, the downdraught of the two-bladed rotors flattening the sparse grass and bushes. The howl dwindled, the thump of the blades became a diminishing *whip-whip-whip* and the wind pulled at their hair and clothes as they disembarked and headed towards a gate in the rickety fence. Beyond the gate was a young apple orchard. Abbie explained to Ben that that had been her father's dream, though he hadn't lived long enough to see the trees he'd planted come to maturity. Crossing the orchard they came through another gate and over to the house. Abbie clearly took good care of the place, woodwork freshly repainted, weeds kept down.

'I like it,' Ben said.

'I've kept it the way Dad wanted it, simple and basic. Call it rustic charm. No TV, no internet, pretty much off grid. He was old-fashioned in his ways, didn't trust any of the newfangled tech. Believed we're all being spied on inside our homes.'

'He might have been right.'

She chuckled. 'Well, good luck to anyone who wants to spy on us out here. I doubt many people even know the place exists.'

The inside of the house was as simple and functional as the outside. Abbie led him to a small utilitarian kitchen and sat him down at the Formica table while she busily set about making breakfast, banging cupboard doors and rattling pots and pans. Eggs and bacon sizzled in a huge cast-iron skillet and produced a mouth-watering aroma while a pot of coffee that could have catered for a regiment bubbled and hissed on the stove. 'How'd you like your coffee?'

'As it comes, black, no sugar.'

She set a heaped plate and a steaming mug in front of him, stood back proudly with her hands on her hips and said, 'Right, get that down your neck, mate, and I'll brew up another pot of coffee afterwards.'

'You were going to tell me your idea.'

'After,' she insisted. 'You need your energy.'

'Is this you looking after me?'

'It's a rotten job but someone has to do it,' she said with a smile.

'Thanks.'

'You always put everyone else first, Ben. It's okay to take care of your own needs once in a while, you know? So shut up and eat.'

'Yes, skipper.' He dug into his food.

'Good?'

'Delicious.'

'Plenty more where that came from.'

'I'm not used to being looked after,' he said.

'Then she's doing a crappy job.'

With a forkful of egg and bacon halfway to his mouth he paused and said, 'Who is?

'Whoever you've got waiting for you back home.'

'I don't,' he said.

'Nobody?'

He was silent for a moment as he ate. 'There have been, on and off. Nothing long-lasting.'

Abbie laid a modest couple of bacon rashers and a fried egg on a plate for herself, and sat down opposite him, looking at him keenly and enjoying watching him eat. 'Never been married?' she asked.

'Once,' he said. He didn't like talking about it.

'But not any more?'

'She died,' Ben said. Which was the reason he didn't like talking about it.

'Oh. I'm so sorry.'

'What about you?' he asked.

'Married? Same story as yours.'

'He died?'

'No, he didn't die. The marriage carked it, though. After a couple of years we'd just run out of reasons to stay together. So I went back to being Miss Abbie Logan and got on with my life. I kind of like being on my own. Who knows,' she added, looking at him with a one-sided smile. 'Maybe someday.'

'Yeah. Maybe someday.'

They fell silent as they finished their breakfast. Ben pushed away his empty plate and she topped up his coffee mug. 'Now tell me your idea,' he said.

And so she did.

Chapter 44

'Wiley Cooper's not just one man,' Abbie said. 'He's a general in charge of a whole army. And now your cobber's out of action, you're all on your own. Or you would be,' she added, 'if you didn't have me tagging along.'

'As you keep reminding me.'

'Now, armies need to fight,' Abbie said. 'Right?'

'They've been known to engage one another in battle, now and then,' Ben said.

'And to fight they need firepower. Cooper has a lot of it. We don't. We're outnumbered and outgunned. Now it's become open war, we wouldn't have a snowball's chance in hell of even getting close to the leader. He's as cunning as a dunny rat, this one.'

'They're not going to make it easy,' Ben agreed. 'That's for sure. What came before was just a taste of what's in store. They'll be twice as ready for us this time.'

'So we need an equaliser,' Abbie said. 'Something that'll make the sons of bitches sit up and take notice. I mean *really* take notice.'

'And you have that?'

Abbie sipped coffee, set her mug down and nodded. 'Remember I told you about the time when Dad bought the Iroquois?'

'You said he got it from a shady dealer who shipped it over from Vietnam as a crate of broken-down parts.'

'Right. But I didn't tell you everything. And Dad didn't tell people everything either. Fact is, when he opened up the crate and started rebolting all those parts together, he found there were some extra bits and pieces in there that probably shouldn't have been, if you get my meaning. How they got past the import inspectors is anybody's guess.'

Ben thought maybe he did get her meaning. 'I see,' was all he said.

'You'd be the first except for him and me who did see them,' she replied. 'Dad rebuilt them, reconditioned them, got them up and running again, but afterwards he kept them stored away and deadly secret.'

'And these items you're talking about, you know where they are?'

She nodded. 'I know exactly where they are. I was the only person Dad trusted with the knowledge.'

'And now you're trusting me?'

'Because I know I can.'

'I'm flattered. And I can guess what we're talking about here.'

'I'll bet you can't guess it all. But don't even try. Why spoil the surprise?'

He said, 'Is this the part where you have something to show me?'

Abbie nodded. 'Uh-huh. If you've had enough breakfast,

how about you come outside with me and take a peek at what's in the barn?'

'It's here?'

'Of course. What better place than a secret hideaway to keep something you don't want anyone to know about?'

'Lead on.'

He followed her outside under the cloudy sky. The adjacent barn was painted red and taller than the house, with two huge doors big enough to drive a combine harvester through, fastened together with a heavy chain and two strong padlocks. Abbie reached down the front of her blouse and came out with a ring of keys that she wore around her neck on a string. She used it to unfasten the padlocks and the chain swung loose. She grabbed the big metal handle of the left-side door, and Ben grabbed the one on the right, and together they heaved the barn open.

As he stepped inside the shadows and Abbie turned on the lights, Ben was reminded of the storage shed where Kip Malloy had kept his Mean Machine – except Abbie's father had converted his outbuilding into some kind of expert hobby engineer's workshop, neatly lined with big tool chests, bench-mounted lathes, milling machines, pillar drills and presses and jigs and other equipment whose purpose Ben could only guess at.

Abbie's father had been hard at work restoring a couple of classic British motorcycles when death had interrupted him. Their sleek lines and polished chrome gleamed softly from the shadows, occupying the large central space where the Bell Iroquois had once stood as it was being rebuilt. But as beautiful and elegant as they were, it wasn't the bikes that commanded Ben's attention. It was the stack of large wooden crates right at the back of the building, standing raised on wooden runners to protect from damp, painted drab olive green with white stencilled lettering. Next to those was an oblong wooden box covered with a thick layer of sackcloth.

'This is it,' Abbie said, pointing at the crates. 'Dad's little secret.'

'Show me,' Ben said.

'This one first.' Abbie led him to the sackcloth-covered oblong box and pulled the covering away to reveal more olive-green wood marked with white stencilled letters. With another key from her ring she undid the padlock fastening the box's lid, then stood away and said, 'Be my guest.'

Ben raised the lid. He already had a pretty good idea of what he was going to see, but the contents of the box still made him whistle. Because, nestled inside within a cosy bed of oiled cotton and plastic wrap, lay an identical pair of items that were most definitely prohibited for civilians under Australia's fairly stringent laws, not to mention those of most countries worldwide.

The M60 belt-fed general purpose machine gun had been a mainstay of US military forces since 1957. Helicopter gunships in Vietnam had generally carried a mounted pair, one on each side. Ground troops had nicknamed it 'the pig' for its brute ugliness, bulky weight and greedy appetite for ammunition. But for over half a century there'd been little doubt about its efficacy as a tool of war. The combination of its blitzing rate of fire and powerful 7.62mm cartridge enabled it to deliver a storm of devastation that could level a small forest and lay waste to buildings, vehicles and their unfortunate flesh and blood occupants.

And old man Logan had had two of the damn things. The original armament that had come as part of the highly illicit package of goods when he'd bought the dismantled Bell Iroquois.

'I come and check on them once every year or so,' Abbie said. 'Not because I thought they'd ever be used again. Just because Dad spent so much time on them. I keep them oiled and clean, the way he'd have done. When I was little he taught me how to strip them and put them back together. It keeps me close to his memory to do that.'

'You really are an unusual kind of lady,' Ben said.

She flashed him a grin. 'You ain't seen nothing yet, mate. Check out this one.' She nudged another, slightly larger, crate with her foot. Ben could tell she was enjoying this, taking charge of the revealing of her father's secret like a parent guiding her child to open their Christmas presents in a particular order, saving the best for last.

He lifted the lid. This time he didn't whistle, instead murmuring 'Jesus.' Because the second crate contained the rest of the weaponry that would restore Abbie's chopper almost fully back to its former capability as a helicopter gunship. 'Seventy-millimetre rocket pods.'

'Dad was a bit disappointed that she didn't come with TOW missile launchers or a couple of mini-guns,' Abbie said. 'But you can't have everything.'

Ben tore his eyes away from the gleaming black monsters in the crate and asked, 'Are you saying your father actually got these things up and running?'

'He only test-fired them for his own technical interest, in the old quarry out back. Anything he restored, he had to be satisfied that it worked like it was meant to. That was his way. The ammo's in the rest of the boxes. They're too heavy for me to shift. Give me a hand if you want to look inside.'

They heaved down the top crate from the stack, and once again Abbie popped the padlock and Ben stared in amazement at its contents. By the time they'd opened every ammo box, he was surrounded with enough ordnance to restart the Vietnam conflict. The M60s were catered for by a selection of standard ball, tracer, and explosive-incendiary ammunition all in neatly coiled belts. There were enough 70mm rockets to load each six-barrelled pod twice over.

Ben could still hardly believe what he was seeing. Abbie was smiling at his dazed expression. 'Told you it'd be a surprise. You said you wanted to hit Cooper hard. I'd say this gives us enough firepower to redress the balance. I'll fly the chopper, you work the guns. The bastards won't know what hit them. What do you think?'

He was silent for a minute. Then shook his head slowly and replied, 'I think you're even crazier than I am.'

Her smile spread into a grin. 'I'll take that as a compliment. Now, those last couple of boxes in the corner, they contain all the mounting gear you need to rig the stuff up to the Iroquois. Some bits were missing, so Dad made them himself. Said all it needed was to bolt everything on, reconnect the electricals that activate the rocket firing system, and you'd be in business. The workshop's got all the right tools for the job. Reckon it shouldn't take more than a few hours for two of us, working together. I'm pretty used to tinkering about with aircraft.' She looked at him. 'So what do you say, Ben? Shall I go and fetch the chopper? We get started now, should have her all ready to rock'n'roll by late arvo.'

A renewed plan was already starting to form in Ben's mind. 'Yes, I think that sounds like a pretty good idea.'

Abbie grinned even more widely. 'Beauty. Let's get to work.'

The rest of the morning and most of the afternoon were a busy time. Ben lugged all the crates outside and began sorting through the weapons mounting gear while Abbie was fetching the helicopter over from the paddock and landing it in the yard in front of the barn, a tight squeeze through the trees that she pulled off with her usual aplomb. The rotor blast rattled the windows of the house and threatened to blow half the tiles off the roof, but soon the helicopter was in position for them to start turning it back into a gunship.

With mugs of coffee and tools and equipment scattered all around the ground, they set about fixing the weaponry into place. First went on the mounting brackets, which were a perfect fit, professionally drilled and tapped to bolt neatly into place above the runners by the chopper's side hatches, one to port and one to starboard. Once those were securely mounted, the heavy six-barrelled rocket pods had to be carried across and fixed to the solid lugs that Abbie's father had made. Already the Iroquois was beginning to take on a whole new, far more purposeful, aspect. If machines could talk, this one would be laughing with pleasure at being brought back into combat service after all these years. Abbie produced a set of diagrams her father had drawn up, showing how the rocket firing mechanisms should be wired up, and Ben got to work fixing the connectors into place. By then it was mid-afternoon and the brooding sky was growing heavier and darker. The heat was oppressive. Abbie kept looking up and frowning. 'Gonna be a corker of a storm when it breaks,' she muttered to herself. 'Just our bloody luck if we get grounded for the next two days.'

But so far, the weather seemed to be holding. Next it was the M60s' turn to be mounted in place, each one pointing menacingly from its side port, able to swivel towards the front and rear to cover a wide area of ground below. Ben fitted the starboard gun with a belt of explosive-incendiary ammo, the kind with the yellow tip that was able to spectacularly blow to pieces and reduce to a blazing wreck anything it hit. For the port-side gun he loaded a belt of standard ammo, mixed with orange-tipped tracer rounds whose brightly-illuminated trail was useful for helping to direct automatic fire accurately at night. The belts trailed through the cargo cab to two large boxes each containing about a thousand rounds. Which seemed like a lot of bullets, but Ben knew from experience that the old 'pigs' would chew through them pretty quickly. The ammunition was dated, but it appeared to have been well stored, and could last almost indefinitely in the right conditions. He'd soon be able to put them to the test himself.

At last, late in the afternoon, the job was done and the Iroquois was now restored to its intended purpose as an airborne assault vehicle. Ben and Abbie stepped back to admire their handiwork.

'Pretty ace, eh?' she said.

'Not bad at all.'

Until this moment Ben's attention had been too taken up with the mechanical complexities of the job to share the plan that had been coming together in his head. Now he told her what he wanted to do.

'That'll work.' Abbie looked at her watch. 'Take us a while to get there, but we don't have to leave until after dark. Leaves us a few hours to kill in the meantime. What do you want to do, catch up on some lost kip?'

'I'm not that tired,' he said.

'Neither am I.'

'You could show me around your dad's hobby farm.'

'Some other time,' she said with a glimmer in her eye. 'I have a better idea.'

'Tell me.'

The glimmer had taken on a more serious look. She took him by the hand. 'How about you come inside the house, and I'll show you.'

'I told you I hate surprises,' he said.

'Not this one, you won't.'

Chapter 45

They bided their time, in one way and another, until after midnight before setting off on that night's mission. Its success or failure depended on whether the rolling dark clouds that obscured the moon and stars would open up and deliver the threatened rainstorm, which could make flying conditions impossible and force them to abort the whole operation.

In the event, the rain held off. They made their final preparations, closed up the house and barn and climbed aboard the helicopter.

'Ready?' he said.

'Are you kidding? I can't wait to give this twisted little mongrel the pasting he deserves.'

'Then let's get it done.'

Ben had worked out his plan down to the last detail, and he was convinced it was a good one. As much as he wanted to see Wiley Cooper go down in flames personally, to use the newly recommissioned gunship to launch a direct attack on human targets would be an act of premeditated murder on a scale that couldn't fail to bring every cop in Australia down on their heads. Instead, Ben had settled on a slightly more subtle means of drawing Cooper out.

'We're going to give him a message he can't ignore,' he'd said to Abbie as he laid out his plan earlier. 'Once we have his undivided attention, we'll dictate the terms.'

'The terms of what?' she'd asked.

'Of the deal we're going to offer him. It'll be his choice what happens next.'

There was a tenderness and a rapport between them that hadn't been there before that evening, but even so they spoke little on the flight. He sensed she was nervous; as for himself, he'd long ago learned to accept that pre-battle jitters were just a normal sign that his mind and body were primed for action. As the moment approached, the thumping of his heart would settle into a state of Zen-like inner peace and the fluttering butterflies in his stomach would line up like a well-ordered squadron.

It was just after two in the morning when they arrived at their destination. The headquarters of the W.F. Cooper & Co. Development Corporation lay within a fenced compound three kilometres to the west of the tiny town of Elliott. The compound was well out of sight of the town at the end of its own private road. Abbie approached from the east so that their presence might be unseen, if unavoidably heard, by the town's residents. As the compound came into view below, lit by floodlights on masts all around the tall wire mesh perimeter marked with the company billboard and big red KEEP OUT signs, she brought the chopper down low and hovered over it in a slow clockwise circle, banked over to the right, so that Ben could observe the facility carefully through binoculars.

The high security gates were locked and chained from the outside, which confirmed to him that the place was empty of personnel, apart from a pair of night watchmen who emerged from a security hut and craned their necks up at the overflying helicopter, squinting at its lights. One of them was getting on a radio, probably alerting Cooper or one of his minions to the presence of their unexpected visitor. Ben wasn't worried about them. He and Abbie had painted over the chopper's registration markings to make it unidentifiable from the ground. In any case, the security guards would quickly make themselves scarce once the show kicked off.

The compound covered an area of maybe three acres. One section was a cluster of prefabricated offices, another was a builder's yard with a depot for construction materials, and there were various steel buildings for storing vehicles and other equipment. A couple of large articulated lorries were standing outside the storage buildings, one fitted with a crane arm and the other with a long trailer on which three big mechanical diggers were loaded. Ben wondered what area of special sacred heritage they were due to go off and destroy in the morning.

Or *had* been going off to.

Not any more.

Ben turned to Abbie and asked her 'Ready?' through his mic, having to yell over the din of the rotors and the blast of the wind through the open hatches on both sides. She gave him a thumbs-up and a grin. The anxiety had left her face, replaced with a glow of excitement. He clapped her on the shoulder, then slipped out of the co-pilot's seat and moved nimbly back towards the open midsection of the chopper, the floor sloping like the roof of a house under his feet, nothing between him and the open air, the powerful wind ripping at his hair and clothes. As Abbie went on circling the compound's perimeter in a long, slow clockwise turn he settled himself behind the starboard machine gun, angled downwards to point over its target. The weapon's action was cocked and ready, bolt back, charging handle forward, the first of a long belt of incendiary-explosive rounds nestled in the chamber. He gripped its pistol grip and peered through the sights. The nerves were gone. The jittery butterflies had fallen into formation, and all that remained was his intense desire to strike back against Wiley Cooper. He thought, *okay, here we go*. Flipped off the safety and squeezed the trigger.

His next thought was obliterated by the ear-splitting percussive rattle of the M60 that all but drowned out the roar and thud of the helicopter. The bullets raked the compound in a long sweeping line, instantly exploding on impact and lighting the place up in a hellfire display of pyrotechnics. For unsuspecting civilians on the ground, nothing in the world was more terrifying than a sudden air attack. Out of the corner of his eye Ben saw the two night watchmen fleeing in panic and jumping into a van parked outside their guard hut. They'd surely head straight for the nearby town, calling the police as they went. It would be hours before the law showed up.

When they did, they'd be greeted with a scene of devastation such as they'd never seen before. He maintained his squeeze on the M60's trigger and the beast went on jumping and vibrating in his arms like a pneumatic road drill. Spent cartridge cases spewed from its ejector in a steady stream and links from the disintegrating belt showered the floor of the chopper. Down below, Ben saw the raking line of gunfire score a direct hit on the articulated crane lorry and its cab violently blow apart, flames erupting from its windows, wreckage flying. He went on firing, letting the path of the chopper dictate where the relentless stream of bullets went. He had no particular target; the whole three-acre compound was his target. Now the destruction slashed and burned through the office buildings, which were instantly pulverised one after another in a series of ripping explosions. Another vehicle leaped blazing into the air, turning a somersault and landing on its roof belching flame.

In just a few seconds of sustained fire Ben had eaten through much of his ammo belt. He stopped firing, and at that prearranged signal Abbie brought the chopper tight around and banked to port, circling the compound anti-clockwise now while he clambered across the tilting, wind-blown cargo bay to the other gun. At the squeeze of the trigger the wild deafening hammering clattering fury of the machine gun resumed, eating the noise out of the chopper's turbine and rotors and shuddering in his hands like a living thing. This time the tracer rounds lit up the trajectory of the bullets as he pummelled the burning facility with more shattering gunfire, reducing everything that passed through his sights into a shredded mess. One of the steel buildings collapsed at one corner and then twisted and buckled to the ground in a heap. A stack of fuel drums burst apart and caught the flames from the burning truck, and suddenly a huge lake of fire was spreading all across the ground, engulfing everything in its path like the flow of lava from an erupting volcano.

Ben gritted his teeth and kept firing. Nothing was safe down there as his gunfire punched unstoppably through steel and brick, tearing apart target after target, debris flying in all directions. His shooting hand was getting numb from the vibration. Then the M60 had run itself empty, the barrel too hot to touch. The smoke from the breech was whipped away by the wind. He was squatting in a sea of spent brass and bits of belt link.

But he was far from finished yet. He left the gun and scrambled back towards the front, careful not to slip on all the rolling shell casings. Plunging into the co-pilot seat next to Abbie he grabbed the control box to activate the rocket pods. Back in the day, the Huey's support role as a gunship would have been to spray a withering cover fire into the enemy-infested Vietnam jungle while the accompanying slicks touched down one after another at their LZ to land ground troops. The gunship's 70mm rocket pods were about the most potent weapon a helicopter could carry. The electric firing system control box had been mostly built from scratch by Abbie's father, along with the sighting device fixed to the aircraft's nose. Now both would be put to the test, for real.

Abbie stopped circling the perimeter, banked up and then came thudding back down in a direct swoop over what was left of Wiley Cooper's base. At just the right instant Ben let go of the first rocket, then the second, then the third. They whooshed down to the ground and impacted against the already shattered buildings with total destructive energy, each earth-rocking explosion flattening a wide circle around it into the ground. Then she banked around again and came back for another longer pass, and this time Ben emptied the rest of the starboard rocket pod into the steel storage sheds that were still standing, laying them level as if a force nine earthquake had ripped the ground out from under them.

After two more passes, there was nothing left to destroy down there. Not a single building was still standing, and there were barely any patches of ground that weren't on fire. Secondary explosions were still popping off here and there as gas bottles detonated in the heat and the fuel tanks of burning vehicles ruptured. Thick black smoke poured from the fires and was dispersed by the rotor blast. It had taken them less than four minutes to reduce the entire place to rubble, wreckage and utter ruin. Even some of the hottest little battle zones Ben had seen in his SAS days had been less comprehensively flattened. If this exercise had been a punitive mission, at least in part, then he was satisfied that Wiley Cooper's establishment had suffered just about all the punishment he could give it.

He nudged Abbie's shoulder and pointed downwards. She nodded, understanding the signal. Swooping low over the wrecked fence she brought the chopper into a hover twenty yards from the compound perimeter and four feet off the ground, whipping up dust and stones and tearing at the bushes, just long enough for Ben to jump out, run back to the fence and leave his message.

Ben reckoned that the message would be clear enough. The simple handwritten note consisted of just four words: WILEY

COOPER – CALL ME, with his mobile number below. He pinned it to the smoke-blackened wire mesh with a clothes peg from Abbie's washing line, then ran back to the waiting chopper, leaped aboard and they took off, leaving the blazing, razed compound behind them. Within minutes the scene was far behind them in the darkness, just a faint red glow on the horizon.

'What about the police?' Abbie had asked him with a frown when he'd described his plan to her earlier that day. She'd had no problem with destroying Cooper's place, but she was dubious about the wisdom of leaving a calling card. 'What if Cooper's got a whole bunch of cops listening in when he phones your number? You'd be laying yourself wide open to a trap.'

'Except that Cooper's already in a trap himself,' Ben had replied. 'He knows we have him by the balls for kidnap, attempted murder and enough other charges to finish him for ever. The last thing he needs is to involve the law. So when the emergency services have finished poring over the place trying to figure out what the hell happened there, even though he'll know damn well who did this to him he won't be inclined to point the finger at me. He'll want to settle this his own way, and get rid of me quickly and quietly without anyone else knowing. Meanwhile, the chopper won't be easily identifiable in the dark and with the registration marks painted out. Even the shell casings on the ground were from unregistered weapons. So the police won't have any evidence to link us to the attack.'

'The note itself could be evidence. If they find it before Cooper does, won't they try calling the number on it?'

'And risk letting the perpetrator know they're onto him?' Ben had said. 'No, what they'll do is try to trace that number. Let them. They won't get very far.'

Now, after the event, any trepidation Abbie had felt was washed away in a flood of excitement. She talked nonstop for the whole journey back, so pumped full of adrenaline that she couldn't stop grinning. 'Oh, my God, did you see that? Did you *see* that?'

'Now it's just a matter of waiting for Cooper to take the bait,' Ben said.

Chapter 46

In the meantime, the pair of them would be kept busy enough. The moment they landed back at the secret sanctuary of old man Logan's place, the armaments had to be dismantled from the helicopter, stripped, cleaned, reassembled and put away safe. No trace could be allowed to remain of the temporary modifications they'd made to the Huey. Once the weapons and their mountings had been removed, Ben tidied out the inside of the cabin, carefully disposing of every last shell casing that might have rolled under a seat or into some nook or cranny, along with every small piece of belt linkage that the M60s had liberally spat all over the floor. In the end he had a heavy bagful of scrap steel and brass that he buried deep in a hole at the far end of the apple orchard.

By the time dawn cast its bloody light through the mist of morning, he'd finished cleaning down the outside of the aircraft, washing off the smoke stains and fired weapons residue from the dull olive-green paintwork. He kept looking up at the sky, watching the turbulent dark clouds scudding overhead and thinking that if the impending storm chose this moment to break, a deluge of rain would clean the helicopter a damn sight better than he ever could. The threat had been waxing and waning for what felt like forever – but it was close now, very close. He could feel it building by the hour, teasing the parched earth with its promise. There was a smell in the air like static electricity. *We're in for a right gully raker,* Abbie had said; nobody knew the Northern Territory weather better than a keen-eyed aviator born and raised in this land, and he wouldn't have taken a million-dollar bet that she was wrong.

After a rushed breakfast eaten on the hoof, the chopper was brought inside the barn on a moving dolly so that they could repaint the registration markings on the sides of the fuselage.

'I still can't believe we did it,' Abbie chuckled as they worked. 'Cooper must've blown his gasket by now.' They'd had the workshop radio tuned to a local station all morning, but so far there'd been no mention of anything unusual having taken place in the Barkly Region overnight. There was no question in Ben's mind that the company boss would have been roused from his bed in the early hours of that morning and been among the first at the scene of the carnage. The note clipped to the wire would soon have been discovered, and while it would lead the cops nowhere, it would mean plenty to old Wiley.

'You did a great job,' he told her.

'So did this baby,' Abbie said, fondly stroking the helicopter's side. The veteran warrior had made its brief comeback and acquitted itself perfectly. 'Now she's a civvie again, I reckon the old girl's earned herself a long, happy retirement. We've got an empty hangar at the airfield. She can live there, and maybe I'll take her out for a spin now and then. She can't just be a museum piece. Dad would have hated that.'

'Before you hang up her spurs,' Ben said, 'there's one more little mission for her to complete. I need you to fly me back to my car.'

Abbie looked at him, crestfallen. 'Don't tell me you're leaving?'

He smiled. 'You won't be rid of me just yet.'

And Ben was right, because there was plenty more work to be done in readiness for Cooper's next move, a lot of detailed planning to figure out, some long-distance driving to do, and some people to contact. The flight out to where he'd left the Mean Machine and the drive back to her place took several hours, and it was mid-afternoon when he returned to what was now their base of operations. He'd called the Tennant Creek Hospital from the road, to check on Jeff, Kip and Lynne. Dr Monroe sounded pleased with their recovery, especially Jeff's, who was healing well, and said she'd be happy to discharge them all in a few more days.

Ben was glad to hear it, partly out of relief that they were doing fine and also because a few more days' confinement in the safety of the hospital would keep them out of harm's way while he finished what he'd started. Not even the long arm of Wiley Cooper could reach them there. Ben expected things to start happening soon, possibly within a matter of hours.

It didn't happen. The rest of the day went by, a blur of activity spent making more phone calls and travelling more miles to and fro in preparation for the next phase of his plan, and by the end of it there had still been no contact from Wiley Cooper.

'You know what, maybe we scared him so badly he won't call at all,' Abbie reflected late that evening, as the two of them sat close together relaxing on the comfortable sofa in the darkened living room, her head resting on his shoulder, his arm around hers. She was wearing a velvety dressing gown and her damp hair smelled pleasantly of fresh apples. 'Maybe he's scarpered off to Tasmania or New Zealand and he'll never be seen in these parts again.'

Ben had considered that possibility, but his instinctive understanding of his enemy told him different. 'I doubt that.'

'Or maybe he didn't even get the message,' she said, raising her head from his shoulder at the thought, her eyes gleaming anxiously in the semi-darkness. 'Is that possible?'

'He'll call,' Ben said. 'He's just considering his options. Wondering what's next, trying to second-guess us and making his plans, like we are. His mother didn't name him Wiley for nothing.'

'I don't know, Ben,' Abbie said uncertainly. 'I just hope this is going to work.'

They went off to bed, and Wiley didn't call. Long after Abbie had gone to sleep cuddled up beside him, Ben lay awake staring at the darkness and listening for the phone, but all he heard for the rest of that night were the distant calls of the nocturnal creatures through the window and the gentle, slow, steady sound of Abbie's breathing close by, like the soft whisper of the tide that made him think of his old stretch of pebbly beach in Galway and all the many hours he'd sat there on the flat rock gazing out to sea. Those had been sadder, emptier times in his life, but simpler times; some innermost part of him yearned to be there again. Sometimes he felt so lost that he didn't know what he wanted at all.

The phone remained silent as another red dawn crept through the bedroom window, and as Ben slipped out of the bed, careful not to wake her, to go for an early-morning run. It lay on the kitchen table between them as they sat eating breakfast a couple of hours later; and it was still resolutely mute that mid-morning as he was making some final adjustments to things in the workshop. All through that time, he never doubted for an instant that Wiley would call sooner or later. Abbie's optimism, by contrast, was ebbing fast and the sense of anticlimax was wearing her down, making her sullen and depressed.

And then, as midday approached and those dark thunderclouds were gathering ever more ominously, blanketing the whole sky and blotting out the sunlight so that even the squawking flocks of galahs in the trees abandoned their chorus and went off to seek shelter from the coming storm, Ben's confidence was proved to have been well founded.

He let the phone ring five times before he picked up. The caller ID was anonymous, but the moment he heard the raspy, harsh voice on the line he knew who it was.

'That you, Hope?' growled the voice.

'Hello, Wiley. What's been keeping you so long?'

'Some piece of shit blew up my fucking place of business last night, that's what's been keeping me. And I've a feeling it was you.'

'I have no idea what you're talking about.'

'Yeah, yeah, right. Well, you got my attention. So what the fucking hell do you want, Hope?'

'To have the pleasure of meeting you face to face, so we can discuss the situation we find ourselves in,' Ben said. 'Something tells me you'd like that too, wouldn't you?'

'What's there to discuss? You fucked me over, now I'm going to fuck you over back, a thousand times harder. This isn't finished.'

'I know that,' Ben said. 'Which is why I have a proposition for you. One that settles this thing for ever.'

A thoughtful silence on the line. Then Wiley rasped, 'All right, Hope. I'll meet you. Name the place.'

'It's somewhere I think you know,' Ben said, and told him where it was. 'Come alone. Five hours from now. That gives you plenty of time to get your act together.' It also gave Ben time to finish making his own final arrangements.

'Oh, don't you worry, Hope. I'll fucking be there.'

Chapter 47

Five hours later

Nothing stirred out here in the remote middle of nowhere. Nothing, except for the small gecko lizard that scuttled indignantly away among the bushes, disturbed by the approach of the strange and much larger predator that had appeared from behind the nearby mound of rocky boulders.

That predator was the toe of Ben's dusty boot. He walked a few steps from where he'd left the four-by-four. Then he paused to light a Gauloise, glanced up at the heavy dark clouds and took a long, careful scan of the horizon, or as much as he could see of it with the towering striated red-rock monument of the Horseshoe Ridge behind him to the west, in whose shadow he would have been standing if there had been any visible sunlight on that darkening afternoon.

The ancient rock formation was well named, rising up to an inverted U-shaped plateau that stood the height of a twelve-storey building and curved for several hundred yards from its southern to its northern tips. It was mostly bare, just a few straggly bits of vegetation struggling to make a living among the barren crags. Here and there over the course of eons landslides had torn rubble-strewn paths down the concave slope of the rock face; Ben imagined it was up one of those steep, winding paths that old Mick Malloy had taken his last walkabout before he'd met his lonely end up there on the crest of the scarp.

The great reddish boulders, each one taller than a man, had once been part of the long, curving cliff face before some earthquake or landslip, maybe millions of years ago, had detached them to form the craggy mound behind which Ben had parked his vehicle. It was the same Mitsubishi Shogun, borrowed earlier that day from Hobart's Creek, in which he and Jeff had driven to Minyerri to collect the crashed Land Cruiser. Just days ago, but it seemed like a long time had passed since then, with all that had happened.

Ben surveyed the ridge from one tip to the other. Seeing no movement of any kind up there he turned to gaze again at the apparently infinite vista of bushland north to south. In the far-off distance, more than three kilometres away to the south-east, he could just about make out the abandoned buildings of Mick's farmstead. It was a desolate location, as empty and remote as anywhere in the Territory. And as private.

It was perfect for Ben's needs.

He checked his watch. If Wiley Cooper meant to keep his rendezvous he would be rolling up any time now. Ben was fairly certain that he would. He was equally certain that Cooper wouldn't come alone, as he'd been told to. The general couldn't go anywhere without his army. And Ben expected a bigger army than the one he'd faced the night he shot Terry Napier.

Minutes passed. Ben finished his cigarette and crushed the stub into the dust, thought about lighting another but then thought better of it. The black clouds scudded slowly overhead, their unbroken canopy hanging so low in the sky that he imagined he could almost reach up and poke a hole in them with his finger. The atmosphere felt as thick and stifling as steam, the electric burning smell stronger than ever in the air. The wind had dropped to zero, and an utter silence blanketed the land from one end of the empty horizon to the other.

And then they came.

The moving white plume of dust cloud was in the east, the direction in which Ben had expected it. Still a great way off, but approaching fast, heading due west straight towards him. As it drew gradually closer he raised his binoculars and was able to make out the line of vehicles: ten of them, no, eleven of them, mostly pickup trucks and boxy off-roaders, with a black Audi at the head of the column.

He laid down the binoculars, stepped further away from the boulder mound and stood there in the open to make himself more visible, with his arms by his sides and his hands in plain view to show he wasn't armed. When the convoy got within a hundred yards of him, they broke their line and spread out wide. The black Audi at the centre, five vehicles to each side of it, spaced evenly ten yards apart like a battle formation. They rolled closer, dirt and stone crunching under their tyres, dust drifting up in eleven separate clouds in their wake.

Thirty yards from where Ben stood waiting perfectly still, they came to a halt. Their line was a rough semicircle a hundred yards long, mirroring the curve of the ridge's rock face opposite. Ben was trapped right there in the middle of the circle, with nowhere to run. But then, he wasn't planning on running anywhere.

The dust drifted slowly in the still air. Doors opened. Men got out. Men with guns. Four to a car. Forty men. Forty guns. Against one unarmed opponent.

The black Audi's doors opened last. Only two men had been riding in it. One man was big and bulky and somewhere around middle age, though his features were hard to make out through the floating dust and with the broad-brimmed leather hat shading his face. He wore jeans and boots and a check shirt, an enormous knife strapped to the left side of his belt and a holstered pistol to the right. The other man was small and shrivelled and old, with sparse white hair and a long thin face framed by elephantine ears. In a black suit and tie, he might have passed for an elderly funeral director, except that the expression on his wizened, wrinkle-etched face was anything but sympathetic.

So this was the general, Ben thought. Wiley Cooper appeared to be unarmed, though appearances could be deceptive. He took a step closer. The old man advanced a few yards, while his burly companion and the rest of the gunmen stayed where they were. All eyes were fixed on Ben. Some expressions were detached and impassive, others were hostile. The guns weren't pointing at him yet, but they could be deployed at an instant's notice.

'I'm so glad you could make it, Wiley,' Ben said. 'Welcome to Mad Mick's land.'

'I know where I am,' the old man grated savagely with a

reptilian coldness on his face. 'Think I'm a fucking idiot? And where'd you get off calling me Wiley? It's Mr Cooper to you.'

'Sorry, Wiley. It's just that after hearing all those stories, I feel I know you.'

'Yeah, well, I stopped believing in stories when I was six years old,' Cooper growled. 'Anyway, you got me here, Hope. You got something to say, let's hear it, and make it snappy because I don't have all fucking day to stand here listening to a piece of shit like you. What do you want?'

Ben held up his right hand and then moved it to his jacket pocket, very slowly and deliberately to show he wasn't about to whip out a hidden weapon. Instead he produced the silver nugget that Sammy had let him keep, in case he needed it. Once again, the man had shown his uncanny ability to foretell the future.

'It's not about what I want, Wiley,' he said. 'It's about what *you* want.' He held it up for Cooper to see. With perfect timing, a ragged tear appeared in the dark storm clouds overhead and a momentary ray of sunlight shone down to make the silver nugget sparkle like a cut diamond in Ben's hand. Then with his other hand he slipped a creased piece of paper from his back pocket and held that up, too.

Cooper's eyes were bulging with lustful greed at the sight of the items Ben was showing him, and he was suddenly too choked up to utter a word.

'You know what these are, don't you, Wiley?' Ben said. 'You've been itching to get your mitts on them. The proof of the biggest mother lode of pure silver in Australia. The thing you've been dreaming of all these years, and it's right here on

Mad Mick's land, just like the old legend says. People didn't believe it, but Mick knew it was true, and so did you. And here's his map showing exactly where it is, just waiting for you and your boys to move in and dig it all out. You'll be the richest man in the whole history of the Northern Territory.'

It had been Kip, given permission by Dr Monroe to talk for a few minutes on the phone from his hospital bed, who'd told Ben exactly where at Hobart's Creek he'd hidden his uncle's map. Not in the house where Terry Napier had been searching, but in the outbuilding where the Mean Machine was stored, concealed under a greasy, dirty pile of auto parts where nobody would have thought to look for it. When Ben had sped back to Hobart's Creek with Abbie to pick up the Mitsubishi, it had taken him seconds to find the map just where Kip had described. It wasn't quite what he might have expected: hardly the kind of curly old treasure map he'd pictured from reading those stirring tales of piracy and adventure as a boy. Instead, what he found was a barely intelligible scrawl written on the back of a creased, grubby and probably unanswered tax demand letter. But it did have all the right features: some crudely-drawn topographical details, along with geo coordinates and the essential X marking the spot. And if it was what it purported to be, then as far as Wiley Cooper was concerned, this dog-eared, grimy sheet of paper was as precious and irreplaceable as the original manuscript of Magna Carta.

Cooper licked his lips like a starving dingo offered a hunk of raw beefsteak. Finding his voice he said, 'So what the fuck's this about, Hope? I don't get it. First you destroy my place of business, now you've come here to negotiate?'

Ben nodded. 'That's exactly what I had in mind.'

'So you've had a change of heart, have you?' Cooper said, with a satisfied leer. 'Your kind always do. You're pathetic, Hope.' He reached out a gnarly hand and snapped his fingers. 'Come on, then. Let's have them. The map first, so I know you're not just blowing smoke. Then we'll talk terms. And I'll still need Malloy's signature on that land contract, so he'd fucking better be in on this too.'

Ben smiled and shook his head, drawing the map far back out of Cooper's reach. 'Jumping the gun a bit there, Wiley. I'm afraid it doesn't work that way. Enjoy the moment, because this, right here, right now, is the closest you'll ever get to your precious silver mine.'

'Eh?' Cooper blurted, not understanding, still holding out his grasping hand. Then before he could say any more, Ben had taken out his Zippo lighter, flicked it open with a soft metallic clang, thumbed the flint wheel and bathed one corner of the paper in its little orange tongue of flame. The map was as parched and dry as the sun-baked tract of land it depicted. It caught fire as if it had been soaked in petrol. Cooper yelled 'NO!' and rushed forward to rescue it from being destroyed, before Ben's dangerous look and a raised palm checked him in his stride.

It was already too late, anyhow. Ben let go of the burning paper as it singed his fingertips, and the blackened twist fell smoking to the ground. Cooper stared at it as though witnessing a death, his face turned pale.

Behind him, all the guns were suddenly pointing straight at Ben. Cooper held up his hand and shouted 'Hold your fire!'

'That's right, Wiley,' Ben said. 'Might not be too clever to let your goons shoot me just yet. Not now that I'm the only person left alive, apart from Kip Malloy, who knows exactly where the silver serpent is buried. Kill me and you'd just be guessing. It could be right here under our feet. Or it could be anywhere inside half a million acres all around us.'

He held up the silver nugget again. 'As for this, you're welcome to it. But if you want it you'll have to come crawling for it on your hands and knees like the festering little maggot that you are.' He dropped the nugget in the dirt between his feet.

Cooper's face had gone from deathly pale to livid purple. A vein was throbbing in his temple and he could barely speak coherently for rage. 'You've got some fucking balls, talking to me like that. Who'd you think *you* are?'

'You know who I am,' Ben replied calmly, standing there in the sights of forty guns ready to blast him at the first signal from their master. 'You've already had just a small taste of what I'll do to you. I'm the guy you should never, ever, have messed around with, not even in your dreams. I'm the guy who takes you down completely and for ever. That is, unless you agree to my deal.'

'Go screw yourself.' Cooper jabbed a thumb against his thin chest. '*I'm* the one who makes deals! Me! *I'm* the one who tells people what to do. You hear me?'

'Not any more,' Ben said. 'You're dealing with me now. Now, here are the terms, so listen very carefully because I'll say this just once. Listening?'

Cooper said nothing and stood there quivering with fury.

Ben went on: 'You have a straight and very simple choice between two options. Option one, you walk away from this negotiation with the promise that you will disband your operation, leave the Northern Territory immediately and never show your ugly face around these parts again. Option two is even simpler, because it means that you'll stay here forever. Either way, I absolutely assure you that you'll never get your hands on a single atom of Mad Mick's silver.'

Cooper had recovered some of his composure and his rage had subsided a little as he considered Ben's deal terms. He pulled a face. 'That's ridiculous. Those are my choices?'

'You heard me.'

'So what's stopping me from deciding to take option two and staying here for ever? That's what I'm planning on doing anyway.'

'Don't make any rash decisions, Wiley. You need to think carefully about what it means.'

Cooper's eyes narrowed as he chewed it over. 'Ah. I see.'

'I'm glad we understand each other,' Ben said. 'Because I mean what I say. And I intend to enforce those terms, whichever you choose.'

Cooper snorted. 'Oh really? You and whose army?'

Ben replied, 'This one.'

Chapter 48

Without turning around, Ben raised a hand in a signal that was easily visible to the watching eyes behind him. An instant later, the Mean Machine came into view at the top of the ridge, dead centre of the curving horseshoe-shaped rock face. It rolled slowly towards the edge, then tipped sharply downwards and descended one of the landslide paths, bucking and jolting over the rocks in a speeding, near-vertical descent before the slope levelled out and the vehicle came bouncing to a rest in a cloud of drifting dust thirty yards behind where Ben stood.

Abbie Logan got out from behind the wheel and clambered nimbly over the back of the seat and the roll cage to take up position between the twin machine guns that had been mounted to where the roof light bar used to be. A protective rectangle of thick steel plate was welded to the roll cage between them. She hunkered down behind it with a pistol grip in each hand, training the guns over the top of the windscreen towards Cooper and his men. Twin belts of incendiary-explosive ammunition coiled from the guns like pythons. Every last round that hadn't been used up in the air attack was packed into two crates in the back of the vehicle. All that was missing were the rocket pods.

Cooper was speechless for a moment, but only a moment. He threw back his head and roared with laughter, a harsh guttural grunting sound that made Ben think of the crocodiles' feeding time at Hobart's Creek. He couldn't have known it, but that was the first time in living memory that anyone had heard the man laugh.

Still grinning in amusement, Cooper made a sweeping motion towards the assembled troops at his rear. 'You might not have noticed, Hope, but it just so happens that we have one or two more guns than you,' he chuckled. 'You seriously expect me to bow down and surrender to one man and some little blondie sheila?'

'I'm not finished yet,' Ben replied. And he keyed the radio throat mic that had been concealed under his jacket collar and said into it, 'Unit Two, move into position.'

The smirk of amusement dropped from Cooper's lips. He stared at Ben; then his stare was diverted back upwards towards the top of the ridge. Not just the middle of the ridge, like before.

The whole ridge.

Of the various phone calls Ben had made during the last twenty-hour hours, the most productive had been to the mobile number Sammy Mudrooroo had given him. Sammy had listened gravely to Ben's plan and pledged his support and that of his people in whatever way they could help. And he had delivered on that promise.

All along the crest of Horseshoe Ridge, from one end to the other, figures appeared and gathered in a wide curving line, silhouetted against the sky. Hundreds of them. More precisely, a number Ben knew exactly, three hundred and eleven of them. They represented every able-bodied volunteer militiaman, ranging from skinny youths to frail elderly men still full of spirit, to the main body of strong warriors in-between, that Sammy Mudrooroo had been able to muster from among his people, and other tribes where he had connections. They'd gathered from all over the Northern Territory in a ragtag convoy of whatever old vehicles they could get hold of, including a school bus. Some had come on foot, hiking through the night to join their comrades. All of them with one thing in common: each and every man and boy present had witnessed first-hand, or at least heard vivid accounts of from others who had, the ravages committed against their sacred heritage by the worst scourge of humanity they could imagine, the mining companies. Now at last they had their chance to strike back at their enemy and prevent yet more irreparable damage being done to the land.

The people hadn't risen up in anger like this for many, many years, not within living memory. But they were here now, and they were ready to fight, to the death if needed, to protect their land. Sammy was there, at the centre of his massed militia, standing proud in his war paint and looking as severe and menacing as it was possible for a pot-bellied, white-bearded man of five foot four to appear. A large number of his people had come prepared to face death naked, or very near to it; others, many of the youngsters, had opted for the less traditional garb of jeans and T-shirts. But they weren't any the less committed to battle for it. Sammy's little army had equipped itself with whatever weapons they could gather together, with a bit of help from Sammy's old friend Kip, who'd happily agreed to donate his collection of hunting rifles and shotguns for the occasion. There were some bows and arrows in the battle line, a crossbow or two, and a variety of bladed weapons, cleavers, machetes and axes. Some of the fighters had armed themselves with the long spears they used for fishing. A few of the older men, raised in the bush, were adept hunters with a slingshot and could knock out a bird in flight.

Cooper's mouth fell open. He'd been about to say something dismissive about bringing a bunch of savages with knives and spears to a gunfight. But all he could do was stammer and gulp. Perhaps the general didn't too much relish the idea of being skewered on the end of a lance. Still gaping up at the assembled fighters on the ridge he retreated back a step towards the protection of his own men.

'I'd say that evens things out a little, wouldn't you, Wiley?' Ben said. Now it's decision time. What's it to be?'

Cooper said nothing. His face looked pale and gaunt and suddenly much older. His henchman in the hat and check shirt drew a big Smith & Wesson automatic from his holster and came up and stood defensively by his boss's side, glowering at Ben. The rest of the forty guns were mostly still pointed straight at Ben, too, though now a few of the men were aiming up at the ridge and the makeshift armoured car behind him.

Cooper still said nothing. The opposing battle lines stood off against one another in absolute silence, every man waiting for the signal to fight. The tension hung as heavily in the air as the brewing storm. Something had to give. The breathless moment of climax was right on them. It was just a question of what would happen in the next few moments.

And that was when the sky opened at last and the black clouds threw down a torrent of warm rain that fell over the landscape with shocking force and suddenness, like a tropical monsoon. The lashing deluge instantly soaked them through. Those who were wearing clothes had them stuck to their skin. Water cascaded down the rock face, hammered off the roofs and bonnets of the vehicles and ran in rivulets along the ground. You could almost hear the grateful sigh of the earth, refreshed after the long dry season.

Still nobody moved. Cooper's army stood poised, guns steady. Water pouring from the brims of hats, dripping from wet hair and beards. The curtain of rain was hammering down even harder now. Lightning rippled violently among the clouds, followed almost instantly by a crash of thunder that rolled all around the vast bowl of the wilderness.

Then Wiley Cooper, drenched and slick in his black suit and his sparse white hair plastered across his brow, raised a pointing finger at Ben and screamed, 'Fuck you, Hope! You and your fucking sheila and all your abbo friends. Fuck the lot of you! Open fire, boys.'

And then the battle of Horseshoe Ridge had begun.

Chapter 49

The opening shots came in a scattered tirade from Cooper's line of guns. Most of it was directed at Ben, and bullets cracked off the red rock boulders as he darted behind them for cover. He ran to the Mitsubishi, grabbed the pump-action shotgun he'd left propped out of sight against it and wedged the weapon through a narrow gap in the rocks to return fire. It was hard to get a good aim through the sheeting downpour. He fired once, saw the windscreen of one of the enemy trucks disintegrate and the man next to it jump for cover. Fired again and the man stumbled and fell behind his vehicle. Then more of their gunfire was fiercely peppering the rocks and Ben ducked down.

If Cooper's gunmen thought they were off to a pretty good start, their optimism was about to be short-lived. Because now Abbie opened up with the twin machine guns. Their overwhelming blast drowned out the enemy fire, drowned out the rumbling thunder, seemed to suck the oxygen out of the air. Suddenly Cooper's men were scattering like rabbits. Hurling themselves down to the wet ground, splashing through the mud in their desperation to escape the swathe of devastation coming their way. The heavy machine-gun fire cut a scything arc through the row of trucks, blowing anything and everything in its path into blazing wreckage. A car exploded. Then another. The figure of a man on fire ran screaming through the rain, then was cut down. Wiley Cooper and his burly henchman had thrown themselves flat to the ground and were trying to crawl towards their Audi, which so far had escaped destruction. Ben had his sights on the big man, but then a cloud of black smoke billowed over them and shielded them from view.

Meanwhile, letting out a collective yowling unearthly war cry, the three hundred warriors came leaping and bounding down the landslide paths in the face of Horseshoe Ridge. Spears were raised, machetes brandished with murderous intent. Those with more modern weapons paused here and there in their stride to kneel and squeeze off a potshot at the enemy before they resumed their charge, yelling wildly, some of the older men falling behind, some of the younger fitter ones helping them along while the most aggressive fighters raced to be the first to meet the enemy head-on. For a few moments the whole rock face seemed covered with running figures, like ants swarming from an anthill. Then they reached the foot of the ridge and kept coming, sprinting full pelt across the level ground, bounding over rocks and bushes and keeping up their yowling battle cry. As they reached Abbie's position the crowd split into two surging bodies that flowed past the Mean Machine and kept pressing on towards the enemy, and now Abbie's machine guns fell silent for fear of hitting them with friendly fire. The massive damage she'd inflicted had already softened Cooper's men up quite considerably. Now Sammy's infantry charge would mop up the remnants that weren't lying on the ground or bolting for their lives.

Even as the enemy fire was still rattling off the rocks all around him, Ben had broken cover and was at the front of the charge. Sammy Mudrooroo was right there at his side, running as fast as his stumpy legs would carry him, wielding a massive bush knife and fully prepared to chop it into the first opponent who came within his reach. It wasn't a battle any longer; it had quickly become a rout. Cooper's men were falling back in total disarray and there was hardly a shot coming from them any longer, the occasional weapon fired off in an inaccurate panic before its owner dropped it and ran. Some of the braver ones were still putting up some spirited resistance, using empty weapons as clubs or fighting with their bare hands. The rain was sheeting down more intensely than ever. Six hundred running feet trampled the earth into a sea of mud. The fires of the blazing vehicles were being dampened and doused by the downpour, belching out so much thick, black smoke that it was almost impossible to see.

Ben reached the spot where he'd last seen Wiley Cooper, crawling away towards his car with his henchman. But Wiley wasn't there any longer. Ben scanned left and right, searching for him, seeing nothing but the press of running figure all around, the yells of the fighters loud in his ears. A heavyset man with teeth gritted in his shaggy beard came lurching at him out of the smoke; Ben pummelled him down with the butt of his shotgun before the guy had a chance to raise his own and trampled over him, kicking him brutally half unconscious as he went.

Then just by chance the billows of smoke parted for a moment, and through the lashing rain Ben caught a glimpse of Cooper and his henchman. They'd somehow managed to beat a retreat unscathed to their Audi, which was damaged by shrapnel with nearly all the windows gone, but apparently still serviceable. Ben saw the henchman pile his boss into the back and then dive behind the wheel and fire up the engine. The Audi's spinning wheels dug down hard into the dirt and sent up a wet spray, and then it was taking off in a hurry, bouncing over the rocks, skidding wildly, engine roaring. A shotgun blast blew out its back window and a hurled spear stuck for a moment into its side and then fell away. Ben spotted Sammy Mudrooroo in the thick of the fight, pointed at the escaping Audi and yelled, 'Cooper's mine!' Sammy nodded.

Ben tore back to the boulder mound and leaped into the Mitsubishi. As he gunned the engine he keyed his throat mic and said, 'Abbie, all good?'

Her voice came crackling back an instant later, 'Roger that, mate.'

'I'm going after Cooper. Stay put.'

'Watch yourself, Ben,' she replied, but Ben barely heard her as the Mitsubishi tore out from behind the boulder mound and he slewed it hard around to point in the direction the Audi had gone off in.

Racing away from the fiery, smoke-strewn battlefield he soon caught sight of the black car speeding off due east through the rain, the way it had come. It was a far faster and more powerful vehicle than his, and there was a serious chance it could get away from him. But not if he could help it. He spurred the Mitsubishi on faster, wipers working at full blast to bat away the rain that washed like waves over the windscreen, his right foot hard to the floor, forcing the vehicle to go bucking violently over rocks and crashing through ruts and hoping that the tired suspension would take the abuse. He didn't care if the thing came to pieces, as long as he caught up with Wiley Cooper first.

And now his reckless pursuit was paying off, because he was gaining a little ground over the Audi. Through the sheeting downpour and his quarry's shattered rear windscreen he could see the Cooper's burly henchman bent over the wheel, driving for all he was worth. The slight, black figure of the old man was in the back, leaning between the seats as though he was barking orders at his man, telling him, 'Faster! Go faster!'

Ben gritted his teeth, willed the Mitsubishi not to fall apart just yet, and saw that he was still gaining. By now the column of black smoke slanting up from the scene of the battle was far away behind them, and as the Audi curved slightly off to the right of its due east course, it was clear that they were heading towards Mad Mick's homestead. The buildings were just about visible through the rain, less than a kilometre away now as the two vehicles sped wildly over the open ground.

Still gaining. Ben had the shotgun propped against the passenger seat next to him, ready to hand. He'd lost count of exactly how many rounds were left in its magazine: maybe three or four. Cooper might not be armed, but if the big man had held onto that Smith & Wesson auto, then there would be a gunfight at the end of this chase.

It happened sooner than that. Up ahead, just forty yards in front of him and closing fast, Ben saw the Audi hit a deep ditch filled with rainwater, surge upwards in an explosion of spray and then veer around sideways. For an instant he thought its driver had lost control and was about to go into a roll. Instead the Audi slithered to a stop in the torn, muddy bushes, rocking on its springs.

Ben sped towards them. The Audi's driver door flew open and the big man leaned out through the gap, clutching not the pistol Ben had expected but another shotgun with a stubby black barrel that he levelled at the approaching Mitsubishi. There was a muffled boom and Ben's windscreen dissolved into a tissue of white cracks. Then a second boom, and a third, and a fourth, and he felt the thump and rattle as his front right tyre went. The guy was evidently shooting to kill but he was pumping out the rounds so fast from his hard-recoiling weapon that his fire was hitting all over the place. Crude and clumsy, but effective. Ben stamped on the brakes and was about to try to swerve out of the field of fire when he felt the vehicle go into a skid. He turned a complete three-sixty, hit the ditch sideways and barely had time to brace for impact as the vehicle flipped. Its momentum carried it over onto its roof with a crashing impact and then half over again, so that it came to a rest on its side with its rear end still in the ditch and the front sticking up at an angle.

Ben hadn't been wearing his seatbelt, and the roll had thrown him about enough to stun him momentarily. He was lying wedged against the passenger door, which was now underneath him and the driver's door above him, its window glass gone. Coming to his wits he struggled to his feet, ignored the sharp jolt of pain in his ribs and arm, shook the fragments of broken glass off himself, grabbed the shotgun and clambered up out of the wrecked vehicle through the driver's window and jumped down to the muddy ground. The rain spattered his face and trickled through his hair. He looked around him.

No sign of his enemies. They could have finished him off inside the overturned car, but instead they'd cut and run. The Audi was gone.

No, it wasn't. Blinking water out of his eyes he saw its distant brake lights flare red through the murk as it slowed on the approach to the homestead. Rather than stand and fight here out in the open, it looked as though they were trying to take cover among the buildings, or lie in wait there knowing he'd keep coming after them. They weren't wrong about that.

The distance was about eight hundred yards. Ben checked his weapon. Three rounds left. Not too great, but better than none. He slicked his wet hair out of his eyes and started running.

Chapter 50

When he reached the homestead, he spotted the Audi parked at an angle in the middle of the yard in front of the house. It was empty and both front doors were hanging open. The rain was rattling down on its bodywork with a sound like marbles landing on a tin roof. Water sheeted from the eaves of the house and buildings and flowed in rivers over the ground.

The place looked deserted, but Cooper and the big man were here somewhere. Ben could feel them. He tried to imagine where they would have gone to lie in wait for him. They might have split up, the old man hiding somewhere while his companion lurked among the buildings to ambush their pursuer. Or perhaps more likely, Cooper would have insisted on his bodyguard staying close by for protection.

At the same time as he was evaluating the situation, Ben was trying to remember how many shots the big man had fired at him. Four, his memory told him, though in all the excitement he couldn't be sure. A repeating shotgun's capacity was more or less dictated by its length. And a gun that short probably couldn't hold more than five. Then again, the big man could be walking around with his pockets stuffed full of extra cartridges.

Either way, Ben had a feeling they'd make their presence felt any time now. And his feeling was soon proved right.

The gunshot came from the broken window of the house that he and Jeff had investigated on their visit here that day. Ben felt the ripple of buckshot pellets cutting through the water-laden air half a foot from his head. He instantly snapped his weapon to his shoulder, returned fire and the broken window shattered completely apart. He thought he heard a shout from inside. He ran towards the front door of the house. Bolted from the inside. He jammed the muzzle of his weapon against the door and fired again, blasting the bolt away in a shower of splinters, and booted the door open with a crash and stepped inside the house.

Silence within. The front hallway was empty. He stood there very still for a long moment, listening hard but hearing nothing but the drip, drip, drip of water from his soaked clothes pattering on the floor. Slowly, he began to move. The passage beyond the hallway was murky, little light filtering through its one window. He remembered the layout of the place from before. The shot had come from the bathroom at the far end of the house, but it wasn't a large home and it would have taken them just moments to move to any other room. He stalked down the passage with closed doors either side of him, easing them open as he went. Kitchen: empty. Storage cupboard, the same. There was just one round left in his gun; there would be no room for mistakes.

The next door he came to was the living room door, to his right. It was locked, too. Or jammed shut from inside.

389

Living rooms didn't have locks, as a rule, and he didn't recall having noticed one there, when he and Jeff had found Kip's croc tooth pendant. He jammed his shoulder against the door and pushed hard, but it felt solid. He didn't dare risk his last round blasting it open. Was someone inside? Or was this a feint to make him think there was?

Just then he tensed, certain he'd heard a noise from further down the passage. The soft thud of someone moving about. Had he imagined it? No, there it was again.

He moved away from the living room door. Stepped a couple of paces down the passage.

Straight into the trap.

At the same instant as he heard the thumping noise a third time, louder now, the living-room door behind him tore open and the big man surged out into the passage. There was blood on his face and on his shirt from where Ben had winged him through the window. He had no gun. He'd fired off his last shotgun round and he must have lost his pistol back at Horseshoe Ridge. But the huge broad-bladed hunting knife was drawn from its sheath and clenched in his fist as the big man hurled himself at Ben in a berserk rage of fury, bellowing at the top of his lungs. And in the same moment, there was Cooper appearing at the bottom of the passage, like a drowned rat in his black suit, screaming, 'Kill him, Steve!'

There was no such thing as absolute stopping power. Not in the real world, not even from a close-quarters-battle tool as devastatingly lethal as a twelve-gauge shotgun. Unless you were armed with a howitzer or something that could just vaporise him on impact, if the enemy was determined enough, if he was coming at you with sufficient energy and momentum, then it was practically impossible to guarantee halting him in his tracks and putting him straight down on the floor. Ben knew that. And he knew that sometimes even the guy with the superior firepower doesn't walk away unscathed, or walk away at all.

That was potentially the case in this moment. The big man moved so fast and launched himself into the attack with such crazed violence that Ben was aware that even if he managed to get the gun turned around quickly enough in the narrow passage and blasted the last round into his opponent at point-blank range, the vicious diagonal chopping lunge of the blade would still have found its mark and slashed his head half off his shoulders.

So Ben let go of the gun and fell back on the most deeply instilled part of his training. The knife flashed towards him so fast that it was just a dully gleaming blur in the dim light. But in his perception it was as slow-moving as a bird's feather spiralling gently to the ground on a sunny, windless afternoon, so you could just reach out and pluck it delicately from the air. Which was what Ben did. Stepping slightly to the side of the blow's arc he trapped the big man's knife hand at the wrist, twisted the knife out of it and kept twisting, feeling the wrist bones reach their maximum point of leverage and then snapping with a horrible brittle popping sound. The big man screamed.

Ben could have killed him then, so, so easily. But he didn't think the big man deserved to die; not like this, in cold blood. So instead he just broke his arm. And then the other arm. And then both his legs, and left him lying there in a

391

disjointed mess on the floor as he turned around to face Wiley Cooper.

Cooper backed away, but there was nowhere to escape to. His eyes were wide and his cheeks were as pallid as death. Ben walked up to him, and stood there looking at him. He felt no real rage against the man, and certainly no hate. Only the sense of revulsion and disgust that he would have felt towards any other vile piece of garbage that needed to be expunged from this world.

He said, 'I told you I'd only explain the deal terms once. But I'll repeat them, just in case you need reminding. Option one, you leave the Territory immediately, today, and never come back. Option two, you stay here forever. Which is it to be, Wiley?'

Cooper stared back at him blankly. Then his expression wrinkled into a snarl of loathing and in a shrill screech he shouted, 'You think you can get rid of me? This is the place I was born, and this is where I stay! You'll never make me leave! I'm here forever! You fucking hear me? FOREVER!'

'Your choice,' Ben said. And he reached out and snapped his scrawny neck.

Chapter 51

By the time Ben rolled through the smoke of the smouldering vehicles, the storm had rained itself out and scraps of sunlight and blue sky twinkled through the dissipating clouds. The battle of Horseshoe Ridge had long since been over. Climbing out of the Audi he was greeted by a hundred happy smiling faces, a lot of elated laughter and cheering, and a crushing handshake of gratitude from Sammy Mudrooroo. Sammy's little fighting force had suffered only three casualties, none of them serious. Cooper's men had fared less well. There were six dead men on the ground and three times that many had been badly knocked about before they'd managed to flee, mostly on foot. They and their comrades would be scattered all over the wilderness by now, and those who made it home would soon be looking for alternative employment.

'Cooper?' Sammy asked.

'He decided to stay with us,' Ben said, opening the back of the Audi. Sammy peered dispassionately at the crumpled little corpse. 'Well, that bloody sod won't be giving us no more trouble, that's for sure.'

Ben pointed at the much larger form slumped unconscious in the back of the car. 'This other one needs a hospital. Got someone who can drive him to Tennant Creek or wherever's nearest, and dump him in the street outside without being seen?'

'No problem, mate. Leave it with us.'

Just then Ben heard a familiar cry behind him and turned around to see Abbie pushing through the crowd to fling herself into his arms, her eyes filled with tears of happiness and relief as she hugged him tight and kissed him over and over again. 'I was so worried about you.'

'You don't need to worry about him, Miss,' Sammy chuckled, watching them benevolently. 'Not this one. He's a pretty special bloke, I reckon.'

'Yeah, I reckon that myself,' she replied with a beaming smile.

Things got busy after that. Cooper was removed from the Audi and laid unceremoniously on the ground with the other dead, while a couple of volunteers drove off in the Audi to deliver his broken henchman into the hands of someone who might care enough about his welfare to patch him up, which, it was generally agreed, was more than he deserved.

The rain had softened the iron-hard ground, and it didn't take long for many willing hands to dig out the deep hole at the foot of Horseshoe Ridge where Wiley Cooper and his six men would spend the rest of eternity communing with nature. The old man had had his wish. He wasn't going anywhere.

Then it was time to clear up all the mess of destroyed vehicles. From Sammy's point of view it wouldn't have done to leave them there, a polluting eyesore on the sacred land. From Ben's, it was preferable that all traces of evidence of what had happened here be carefully erased. Fortunately, these considerations had already been taken into account. One of Sammy's more distant cousins, from somewhere near Minyerri, worked for another indigenous Australian who operated a junkyard with a car crusher, and also owned a large trailer truck he used for collecting wrecks. Ben had found those kinds of establishments to work very well for him in the past – and according to Sammy, his cousin's boss was known for his healthy disrespect of the law. He also had a particular dislike of mining company executives, and would be more than happy to help them clear things up.

And so, after a few hours' waiting, by which time night had fallen and the burnt-out vehicles had cooled off, Sammy's cousin came bumping over the uneven ground in the huge truck. With an enthusiastic three-hundred-strong workforce and a powerful electric winch they made short work of loading the ten wrecks aboard the trailer.

Then their task was finished, and as the Milky Way shone incandescent above them in an incredibly sharp and clear night sky, it was time to part ways again. Sammy gripped Ben's hand again and thanked him once more for what he'd done for them. 'I knew you would be the one, mate,' he said with a twinkle as bright as the billions of stars overhead. 'Always said that, didn't I?'

'It's not quite over yet, Sammy,' Ben told him. 'We still need your help one last time.'

Chapter 52

Five days later on a bright afternoon in Alice Springs, Ben and Jeff accompanied Kip and Lynne Malloy to the law offices of Rex Muldoon, along with Sammy Mudrooroo and three other senior Elders of the tribal council. There, in Muldoon's crowded little office with two of his law partners present and with Ben acting as a formal witness, Kip officially signed his five hundred thousand inherited acres and everything they contained over to the Aboriginal people of the Northern Territory. Kip had never been much of a writer but he penned his name on the line with a flourish, before shaking hands with Sammy and the elders and then, to the astonishment of Lynne and Jeff, lighting up a Havana cigar the size of a carrot.

A highly meticulous lawyer as well as a man of scruple and compassion, Muldoon had gone through every line of the legal documentation with them to explain how the land would be protected by statute, with a specific condition that no form of mining or excavation could ever take place within the life of the contract, which was effectively for all time. The legendary silver serpent, if it really existed – 'Oh, it exists all right,' Kip interjected at this point in Muldoon's long spiel – along with whatever else might lie below the soil of his former client's property, would remain exactly where it had always been, untouched and inviolable. Muldoon and his law partners gave their solemn assurance that they would be watching like eagles to make sure it stayed that way.

'Then that's that,' Jeff said as they stepped back outside into the warm sunlight. Lynne was hanging on Kip's arm, both of them wearing enormous smiles, Sammy was bubbling with high spirits, the elders were chatting away like school-boys and all was good with the world once again. 'What time is it?'

'That's the seventh time you've asked me this afternoon,' Ben said irritably, pulling up his sleeve so Jeff could peer at the dial of his Omega.

'Well? How am I supposed to know what time it is, when I can't wear a watch for this bloody great cast on my arm?' Jeff retorted. He still hadn't quite forgiven Ben for leaving him malingering in a hospital room while he went off and had all the fun.

Ben asked, 'What's the hurry, anyway? It's not like we have a plane to catch. Not for two more days.'

'Hmm? Oh. Got a date,' Jeff replied casually. 'Meeting her in about an hour's time, and then later we've got a table booked at the best restaurant in Alice Springs. Or so I'm told.'

'Meeting who?' This was the first Ben had heard of it.

'Why, Marilyn, of course.' As though it were supposed to be obvious. 'She's taken the day off work and she's driving up from Tennant Creek.'

Ben stared at his friend. 'Dr Monroe?'

'Yeah. What's the big deal? And stop looking at me like that.'

'So what's this, the big romance? Am I going home without you?'

'Don't be daft,' Jeff snapped back. 'This is just another sordid conquest.'

'With a neck brace and a plaster cast?' Ben shook his head in amazement. He was really something, that Jeff Dekker.

They were staying the extra couple of days in Australia because that was the soonest Ruth's Steiner Industries jet would be available to come and pick them up at Darwin. Ben wasn't complaining. He spent nearly all his time out at Abbie's father's place, exploring the land by day; food and wine, lazy mornings and late nights in front of an open fire, savouring every moment of their last bit of time together: two days as golden as her hair, under a sky as blue as her eyes and sunsets as vivid crimson as her lips . . .

Oh shut up, you damn fool, enough of that silly nonsense. You didn't come to Australia to go falling in love like an idiot. Did you?

And yet, he hadn't felt this relaxed and contented in years, and his only regret was that it would all have to end soon.

As for Jeff, when he wasn't dallying with the lovely Marilyn he was recuperating at Hobart's Creek, being fussed over by his mother and spending late evenings on the veranda with Kip. None of them paid much attention to the news reports. The Northern Territory police were still trying to work out what had happened to the business premises of W.F. Cooper & Co., as well as pursue their latest investigation into the apparent disappearance of the man himself. It was all a bit

398

of a mystery, though nobody seemed particularly upset over it, and in the nature of these things it would probably all blow over soon enough when the police investigation came to its inevitable dead end. They put the whole thing behind them and concentrated on getting the best out of the last two days in each other's company.

Two days that flew by much too quickly, as they'd known they would. Soon it was time for Jeff to say goodbye to his family and join Ben on the long trip north to Darwin. Ben's emotional goodbyes would come just a little later, because it was Abbie who flew them back across country in the same Beechcraft Baron as before.

She and Ben spoke little on the journey. He kept looking at her, his heart full of things he wanted to say, but she seemed more concerned with just flying the plane. Had he mistaken her feelings for him? Or was she just hardening herself to the pain of their parting? Perhaps it was better this way, to say nothing. They were two grown-ups. It had been a fun time. Let that be an end to it.

Chapter 53

The Beechcraft Baron landed at Darwin some hours later. Ben and Jeff disembarked, and for a minute it looked as though Abbie was going to stay in her pilot's seat and fly off again without a word. Ben turned away and walked across the tarmac, feeling terrible. The big, sleek Steiner Bombardier Global was there at the private terminal, waiting for them, right on schedule. It made the little Beechcraft look like a toy by comparison. Pierre, the pilot, was standing by the gleaming jet ready to greet his passengers.

'Ben!'

He turned. She'd jumped out of her cockpit and was running towards him. His heart filled. This was crazy.

'You wouldn't just leave me like this, would you?' she said. Tears were in her eyes.

'I don't want to leave you at all,' he replied.

'I'm going to miss you so much, Ben Hope.'

'I'm going to miss you too, Abbie Logan.'

'You're a complete piece of shit, you know that?'

'Am I?'

She nodded. 'Yes, you are. You can't just walk into a

girl's life like this, and then just walk out again, and think it's okay.'

'I don't think it is okay,' he replied. 'That's not how I feel about it.'

She was blinking tears. 'I can't bear to see you go. Don't let this be it forever. Just . . . just don't.'

'I promise,' he said.

'I don't believe you.'

'I'm sorry, Abbie.'

Jeff had reached the Steiner jet and was talking to Pierre. Ben was aware of the two of them turning to look at him and Abbie, but he ignored them .

She sniffed and wiped her eyes. 'Christ. Look at me. It's pathetic. I thought I was well past this kind of thing. God, I hate goodbyes.' Then, putting a braver face on her emotion she gazed admiringly at the sleek white Steiner Industries Bombardier Global. 'Wow, eh? She's a beauty.'

'I suppose she is,' Ben said, without looking at it. Big magnificent multi-million-euro luxury private jets meant very, very little to him except as practical modes of transportation.

'Believe it or not, I've never been in one of those things.'

'It's just like jumping on a bus,' Ben said. 'You can come and go wherever you please. You don't even need a passport when you've got the right connections.'

'How the other half live, eh?' Abbie laughed. 'Does that mean you'll pop back and see me now and then, Mister Big Shot Fancy Pants?'

'I'd love that,' he said.

'That'll be the day. At least call me from France, won't you?'

'The moment I get there.'

'I've never been to France either,' she said. 'But then you knew that already. I'm just gabbling, aren't I? I always gabble when I'm nervous.'

'I don't suppose you have been there,' he replied, a little distractedly because a fresh thought had just come to him. A thought so obvious that it hit him like a pistol shot between the eyes and he couldn't imagine why it hadn't occurred to him until this very moment. He looked at her. Then looked over at Pierre, who was standing there smiling at them, motioning for Ben to come on. Jeff had already disappeared inside the plane.

'Would you like to?' he asked her.

'Would I like to what?' she replied, looking blank.

'Ride on a corporate jet. See France. Spend some time there, let me show you around. It's a little different from the Northern Territory.'

Her mouth fell open. 'I . . . I . . .'

'Because if you would like it, I would too.'

Abbie was almost speechless. 'Oh my God. I can't believe this is happening. Is this an invitation, Ben Hope?'

'It's an awful big plane to have only two passengers,' he said. 'Seems like a waste of space.'

'Are you serious?'

'I'm serious about you, Abbie. I wouldn't ask you if I wasn't.'

'Sorry to speed you along, folks,' Pierre said, coming over, 'but we need to get moving.'

Ben held up a hand to him, like saying, 'Hold on a minute.'

She'd gone quiet, her cheeks reddening.

'Well, Abbie?'

Flustered, she replied, 'I suppose I could make a quick call, get one of the guys to take the Beechcraft back to base. It wouldn't be such a big deal, really.'

'Is that a yes?'

Abbie said nothing more for a few moments. Then tears came flooding back into those brilliant blue eyes and spilled down her dimpled cheeks as she nodded, too emotional to speak. Ben turned to the pilot and said, 'Pierre, do you think we can make room for one more?'